PRAISE FOR *THE DISASTER GAY DETECTIVE AGENCY*

"Can important work also be wildly entertaining? Is it possible to balance issues of identity and acceptance with madcap hijinks? What about deliciously sexy on one page and scream-out-loud scary on the next? Lev A.C. Rosen answers with a string of thrilling yeses in this delightfully queer mystery. I ate it up!"

—Rob Osler, award-winning author of *Cirque du Slay*

"Madcap and criminally good. Lev Rosen has served up a sharp mystery with verve and heart. Think *Only Murders in the Building* but with queer twentysomething besties at brunch. *The Disaster Gay Detective Agency* reads like the BFF group thread of your dreams solving a murder. Brandon, Ollie, Nicole, and Ian are perfect…unlucky at love, tremendously unqualified to sleuth, and utterly unforgettable. (I'd do anything to hire them.) Not a cozy but not noir, Rosen has minted a new genre: edgy and campy crime. The smart and feel-good murder mystery we've been waiting for!"

—Margot Douaihy, bestselling and award-winning author of *Scorched Grace*

"There is no cast I'd rather solve mysteries with than these clever, fierce, hilarious, and endearing disasters, characters bursting with heart and laugh-out-loud wit. While these detectives might be messes (complimentary), Rosen is at the top of his game, crafting not only a brilliant mystery but an ensemble that radiates queer joy and freedom. A balm for the soul and a knockout suspense."

—Ashley Winstead,
USA Today bestselling
author of *This Book Will Bury Me*

"Twisty, heartfelt, sly, and sharp, *The Disaster Gay Detective Agency* is exactly what would happen if me and my messy friends got in way over our heads. It's a total blast."

—John Fram,
USA Today bestselling
author of *The Midnight Knock*

"A murder, a missing hottie, and one extremely active group chat? Sign me up! *The Disaster Gay Detective Agency* is hilarious, surprising, and fast-paced, with the most loveable and chaotic friend group I've read in a long time. A winner in every way!"

—Tom Ryan, award-winning
and bestselling author of
The Treasure Hunters Club

PRAISE FOR LEV ROSEN

"Movingly explores the strain of trying to pass as straight at a time when living an authentic life could be deadly."

— *New York Times Book Review*

"Rosen's smart, bittersweet tale plays with the oldest truth of all: the price we pay for our identity in America."

—Walter Mosley

"A new take on a Golden Age crime novel…richly cinematic."

— *Washington Post*

"With a mid-century mystery as sprawling as its titular mansion, the velvet knives in this one are sharp as hell"

–P. J. Vernon, bestselling author of *Bath Haus*

"*Lavender House* is unlike any crime novel I've ever read"

–Rachel Howzell Hall, bestselling author of *These Toxic Things*

"[A] well-built procedural with fascinating tidbits of queer history… The real magic, though, is in Rosen's depiction of the struggles and triumphs of mid-century queer life: He highlights pockets of LGBTQ+ resilience, including Evander's San Francisco community and emergent gay subcultures in L.A., without painting the past in too rosy a light. This series deserves a long life."

—*Publishers Weekly*, Starred Review

"As with earlier series entries, character development and world-building take center stage. Should appeal to fans of Cat Sebastian and KJ Charles and those who enjoy a gritty noir detective story with an appealing protagonist."

—*Library Journal*

"If you are in the mood for a throwback to mystery writers like Dashiell Hammett, take a look at Rosen's 1950s noir series… *Mirage City* is a fascinating and sobering read, giving historical context for attitudes and ideas that have yet to be fully consigned to the dustbin of history."

—*BookPage*

"A mystery that cuts uncomfortably close to the bone."

—*Kirkus Reviews*

"Rosen is a master at tightening the screws."

—*Lavender Magazine*

"Gripping… Readers will be ready for the next Mills adventure as soon as this one ends."

—*Publishers Weekly*

"Rosen is a star. Standing ovation!"

—Hank Phillippi Ryan, *USA Today* bestselling author of *All This Could Be Yours*

ALSO BY LEV AC ROSEN

All Men of Genius

Depth

EVANDER MILLS SERIES

Lavender House

The Bell in the Fog

Rough Pages

Mirage City

FOR YOUNG READERS

The Memory Wall

Woundabout

AS L.C. ROSEN

Jack of Hearts (and Other Parts)

Camp

Emmett

You've Goth My Heart

Lion's Legacy

King's Legacy

THE DISASTER GAY DETECTIVE AGENCY

LEV AC ROSEN

Cover design by Erin Fitzsimmons/Sourcebooks
Cover and internal art © Eleanor Laleu
Internal design by Laura Boren/Sourcebooks
Internal images © NatalyaBurova/Getty Images

Published by Poisoned Pen Press, an imprint of Sourcebooks
1935 Brookdale RD, Naperville, IL 60563-2773
(630) 961-3900
sourcebooks.com

Cataloging-in-Publication Data is on file with the Library of Congress.

Printed and bound in Canada.
MBP 10 9 8 7 6 5 4 3 2 1

For Les, Des and Theo –
None of you are disasters,
but our group chat sometimes is.

1.
Brandon

A BEAUTIFUL MAN WALKS IN.

He's so gorgeous, Brandon almost blushes, feeling like he's been caught staring. Then he remembers he's a concierge and he's allowed to stare, as long as it's expectantly, with a smile.

So he smiles.

The man looks around, and Brandon follows his eyes—the lobby is small, tasteful, and without any personality, the way a boutique hotel in Lower Manhattan should be. It reveals nothing and implies whatever the guests want it to: black marble floor, wood walls, mirrors everywhere reflecting the man back in flattering low light. There are empty armchairs and a table in one corner, for people to wait at, but no one is doing that now, just after midnight. Brandon watches the man's eyes take all this in, looking pleased, then come back around to the desk, where he sees Brandon, still smiling, and so he smiles in return.

He walks beautifully, too, his hips swaying slightly, shoulders back, like a dancer. He's tall, maybe six three, in his thirties, Brandon thinks. White, with short dark hair and a beard, wearing a plain cream Henley and jeans that seem tight only because of how he fills them. Just one evening bag slung over his shoulder, a few bangles on his wrists. No jacket, even with how cold it is outside.

Brandon lets himself imagine a life with the man for a moment; he does that with beautiful men he sees. Pictures their job—his would be environmental lawyer—their home together—a cozy loft in the West Village—their life—intimate, quiet, he cooks, Brandon would have to go vegetarian but wouldn't mind, they'd have two dogs, travel all over the world.

The man is at the desk now, and he pauses, looking deep into Brandon's eyes. Brandon knows he's not like this man. He's at best an awkward twink, white, with dark curls and brown eyes. Another nebbishy-looking twentysomething New York Jew—a dime a dozen here. Not the type to inspire fantasies of a life together. But still, the man looks deep into Brandon's eyes for a moment, searching, like they're connecting, maybe—like there's chemistry.

"Hi," the man says after a moment. "I'm checking in. Sorry, I know it's late."

He was waiting for Brandon to say hi first, Brandon realizes.

"That's no problem," Brandon says in his best, non-salivating-over-this-hot-guy work voice. "What's the name?"

"Jon Engle," the man says.

Brandon smiles, looking it up on the computer. "Like Lady Bunny."

"What?" Jon asks.

Brandon feels himself blushing again. "Sorry, just…the name."

"Like Lady Bunny's real name," Jon says. "I know. Just most people don't. But it's with an *e*, not an *i*."

Brandon locks eyes with Jon, who knows who Lady Bunny

is. Not a drag queen you would know in passing, probably. Not if you were straight. Jon smiles, and Brandon thinks for a moment maybe he was right, maybe there was a moment between them before they spoke.

Jon leans forward on the counter. “Not many people know drag queens’ real names.”

Brandon smiles, looking at Jon, forgetting about the computer, the counter, the hotel. “My friends and I do a game night sometimes, and that’s one of the trivia categories.”

“Yeah?” he asks. “That sounds fun.” Jon’s hand lifts up to support his chin, bringing his face a little closer. He looks at Brandon, not blinking. He licks his lips. Brandon isn’t sure, but he thinks this might be flirting. If it is, should he flirt back? Yes. But also no; he’s a guest. And, honestly, Brandon isn’t sure he knows how to flirt.

“It is fun,” he says, staring back at Jon, trying to not blink like Jon is, in case that’s part of the flirting. “There are other categories, too, of course.” *Keep the conversation going.* That’s flirting, he’s almost positive.

“Like?”

“Um…” Brandon’s eyes feel dry from not blinking. “Porn stars who are couples in real life, rumored gay celebrities.”

Jon’s teeth are perfect and white as he smiles, leans a little closer. “That sounds amazing. Your boyfriend part of that?”

Brandon shakes his head. This is definitely a moment, right? “Don’t have one.”

“Really? A cute guy like you? I guess what they say about the New York dating scene being rough is true.”

“Yeah,” Brandon sighs. “Not for you, I’ll bet.” He blushes, realizing what he’s said. “I mean, where you’re from. Where are you from? Someplace with lots of hot people, probably." He swallows. Did he just say that? What does that even mean?

Jon's smile holds, and his eyes narrow a little, pleased with something. "Oh, all over. Seattle originally. Dating's okay there." He pauses, and they stare at each other too long. Brandon swallows. "So…my room?"

Brandon feels heat on his face again, and it grows warmer as he thinks of how many times he's blushed since Jon walked in. He looks down, checks the computer, presses the buttons, and inserts the blank card to turn it into a key.

"Yes, we have you in room 310 for four nights," he tells Jon, then hands him the key in one of the little envelopes, writing the number down. "Just one key?"

"Just one," Jon says, taking it. Their fingers touch as he does, and Brandon swears there's a jolt, not electric but something deeper. "Thanks. I've had a long day, need a shower." He turns and starts to walk toward the elevators in the back but then stops and looks back at Brandon. "What's your name, anyway?"

"Brandon," he says, swallowing it, trying not to think of Jon in the shower.

Jon nods and heads to the elevator. When the doors open, he turns around, and Brandon keeps looking at him. Jon stares back in a way that feels like it means something, but Brandon isn't sure what. He stares back, unblinking. The doors close. Brandon's eyes immediately have one of those little seizures of blinking like they always do after he works hard not to blink for a while.

Brandon takes a deep breath like he's been underwater and tries to think of things that will make the bulge developing in his briefs go away: his grandmother, that time he vomited in front of that hot guy at a club, that other time he vomited in front of a different hot guy at a different club, that time his friends all told him he should consider drinking less… He takes another deep breath. His skin prickles with sweat from the encounter. He takes one of the water bottles meant for guests from under the desk and cracks it open, takes a long drink, then takes out his phone.

BRANDON

I'm in love

IAN

No you're not

BRANDON

The most beautiful man just came in

IAN

A guest? No you're not

OLLIE

He could be! Love at first sight could happen.

IAN

It happens every day with Brandon. You're not in love, and if Nicole didn't have her phone on silent, she'd agree.

NICOLE

You're not in love

IAN

See?

OLLIE

Nicole! Are you actually out of work? Before 2am? Early!

NICOLE

No, I'm just in the bathroom.

OLLIE

Crying again?

NICOLE

No

IAN

Yes you are

NICOLE

Shut up

IAN

I'm on in ten, gotta check my wig. Don't do anything stupid with a guest, Brandon.

BRANDON

But he's so beautiful

NICOLE

Is he? Or is he just a tall guy with a beard?

BRANDON

He can be both.

NICOLE

I'm going back to work

BRANDON

I think he was flirting

OLLIE

That's awesome!

BRANDON

What should I do next?

OLLIE

I have no idea. Maybe go to his room? But also, I just took this new gummy, the guy said it was like a head high, but I am feeling it in my body for sure. Things are pretty cool. So maybe my judgment isn't the best right now. Y'know?

My feet are like butterflies

BRANDON

Ok

OLLIE

I might be sleepy

BRANDON

Do you need me to call someone to watch you?

OLLIE

No, I'm just going to put on one of my podcasts and fall asleep

BRANDON

You can sleep to those?

OLLIE

Oh yeah. Nothing chills me out like an unsolved murder. Night man

BRANDON

Night

Brandon sighs and puts his phone away. Amber emerges from the back room as he does, but he's become good at pocketing his phone before anyone sees it. It's not like anyone cares if he's texting, especially not on the night shift, but Amber always makes a face when he takes it out. Like she's offended, because she thinks it means he finds her boring. Which she's not wrong about. But he didn't invest in a degree in hotel management to take the night shift either. The least he can do is talk to his real friends.

"A guy checked in," Brandon says.

"Late," Amber says, pulling her hair back into a ponytail.

"Yeah." He thinks about pulling his phone back out, but then the hotel phone rings. Brandon picks it up. "Bergamot Hotel, front desk."

"Brandon?" The voice is deep, soft, and it takes Brandon a moment to realize it's Jon, who just checked in.

"Yes," he says, realizing he waited a beat too long. "Can I help you?"

"It's Jon, room 310."

"I know. I recognized your voice."

Next to him, Amber raises an eyebrow.

Brandon turns away from her. "Because you just checked in, I mean."

Jon laughs, low and throaty. "Yeah. I was calling because I need a fresh towel. I just got out of the shower, and there are no towels."

"Oh, I'm so sorry about that," Brandon says, feeling his pants tighten slightly again. "I will send someone right up."

"Why don't you come yourself? It could take a while otherwise."

Brandon licks his lips. Ollie said to go to his room. Ian said not to do anything stupid with a guest. "Sure, I'll be right up."

"Thanks." The line goes dead with a sigh.

"You'll be right up?" Amber asks, narrowing her eyes.

"Towel missing. The guy who just checked in said he was just out of the shower. Wants it fast. I was going to take my break soon anyway, maybe get some air on the roof, since the alley smells so bad. Mind the desk?" The lie tumbles out of his mouth, feeling obvious, jumbled, like he's vomiting alarms.

She pauses for a moment, then shrugs. "Sure."

He nods and walks away as slowly as he can, adjusting his underwear out of her sight. He goes into the back office and, from there, through the warren of tunnels that are for the people who work at the hotel but never stay there. Here the lights are bright and buzz slightly, the floors are linoleum, and the walls are drab and dirty white. He goes down to the laundry room and nods at the maid there, Hanna, washing the whites.

"Clean towels?" he asks. She nods at a pile, and he takes one. "Guest wants it now; I said I'd do it so you can keep on this."

"Okay," she says, barely looking up.

He takes the towel and folds it as he walks, quickly now, excited. He knows what's going to happen. He knows it's a bad idea. But he can't stop. It's intoxicating, inevitable. Who cares if it could get him fired? That's barely registering in his mind. He feels pulled toward Jon, dripping, naked in his hotel room. His smile, his body. He could be *the one*, that's what this pull could be—destiny. They could fall in love, get married, go vegan and travel the world, just like he'd imagined. All that is easily worth a job, especially one this crappy.

The elevator and halls are empty. It's past midnight on a Thursday. People are already in for the night or will be out for another hour. The halls have navy carpets patterned with yellow half stripes, like the lines next to a spaceship when it zooms on TV. They make Brandon feel like he has to run, but he doesn't. He walks fast though, and it's enough.

He knocks on the door of 310 and hears the lock click. It opens just a sliver.

"Hello?" Brandon asks. There's no one behind it. It opens wider, and Brandon steps inside. He feels someone behind him as he does. He's been an idiot, he realizes. Going into the dark room of a man he doesn't know. That's how people get murdered. He turns quickly, almost tripping over his own feet, swaying a little as the door shuts.

Only a few lamps are on, so the light is dim, but it's enough to catch every nook of Jon's naked body. He was waiting behind the door.

"Hi," Jon says. He's wet but not dripping. He takes the towel from Brandon with one hand while the other arm wraps around Brandon's waist. "Is this okay?" he asks.

Brandon nods but then instinctively pulls away as Jon rests his hand softly on his chin. "Sorry."

"Don't apologize. We don't have to—"

Brandon kisses him. He tastes beautiful, too, like mint and gin. Jon pulls him closer, wrapping both arms around Brandon and lifting him in the air, mouths still together, hungry. Brandon drops the towel. Jon throws Brandon on the bed. Brandon starts to undo the buttons on his vest, his hands shaking.

"Here," Jon says, undoing the buttons slowly.

"I have to be careful with the uniform," Brandon says. His voice comes out in a whisper. "And my break isn't long."

"I won't need long."

The sex is a mix of exhilarating and awkward, unsure where their bodies go, asking each other what they want, or assuming it without asking. Brandon doesn't especially like having his nipples bitten but flinches through it, not wanting to ruin the moment. He keeps staring at Jon instead. He's gorgeous. Six-pack, sculpted shoulders, beautiful eyes, amazing ass, and best of all: he wants Brandon. He kisses Brandon, nibbles at his neck, fucks him, with passion, with desire. Brandon's not sure he's ever felt this desired. Ever felt like a hungry man's first meal. He loves it. He loves the way Jon keeps pulling him closer, their bodies inseparable, their mouths barely able to breathe. This want, this heat, it must mean something. Maybe Ollie was right—maybe love at first sight is real and this is what it feels like.

When it's over eight minutes later, Brandon takes a breath in and feels strangely calm. Confident.

"Thanks for that," Jon says. "That was great."

"Yeah," Brandon says, eyes closed, panting on his back. "It was. Best mistake."

"Mistake?"

Brandon turns onto his side, opening his eyes to look at Jon, who is staring at the ceiling. He's still wearing his bracelets, and Brandon runs a finger down Jon's arm to them, fingering a chunky blue rubber bangle. "Rule breaking. I'm not supposed to sleep with guests."

"I won't tell." Jon pulls his hand away and rolls to face Brandon. They look into each other's eyes, and it feels quiet and meaningful.

Then Jon pecks him on the lips, then rests his head in the crook of Brandon's neck. "You smell good."

"So do you," Brandon says, wrapping his arm around Jon's shoulder. He laughs. "I can't believe you did the 'I need a towel' thing."

Jon laughs too. "I feel like I've seen it in some porno. I was going to just open the door naked, but then I was worried someone else might be there, so..." He laughs again, high and a little unashamed, like he's giddy with love. "I can't believe it worked."

"You didn't think it would work?"

He's quiet. "I mean, I felt like we had a moment down there."

"Me too."

They're silent in the dim light, Jon's hand tracing down Brandon's torso, to the tattoo just over his right hip.

"Is this from *Die Spitzel der Liebe, oder Wenn die Liebe der Spion ist*?" he asks.

Brandon's eyes go wide. No one knows DSLWLS. It's an obscure German comic from the mid-2000s that he got into while trying to impress this broad-shouldered art major in college who'd been especially into weird comics. He'd been taking German classes because his grandmother spoke some and he needed it to fulfill a requirement, and after some googling of unknown comics so he'd have a conversation starter, he found DSLWLS, the story of two spies in the 1980s, one in East Berlin, one in West, who fall in love while also working opposing missions. It's a beautiful story about fate bringing two people meant for each other together.

The art major wasn't impressed. Brandon was so sure they'd had a moment, but then he made out with Brandon's freshman-year roommate. But Brandon kept up with the German, eventually minoring in it. And he's read DSLWLS over a hundred times now. It's the perfect love story. He can't get anyone else into it though. They never translated it, and no one, not even Ollie, seems to want to have it read aloud to them by Brandon.

"I'm impressed," Jon says, finger circling the tattoo—the cipher disc Ingrid used to translate Rolf's messages with their key cipher word, and his last message to her, on it—*Heimweh*, the longing for home, or a person who is home. The person Brandon hopes he'll find someday. The person who might be touching his tattoo right now. "No one knows DSLWLS."

"I know," Brandon says, sitting up. "And it's so good!"

"So good," Jon agrees, bringing Brandon in for another kiss. Brandon is so excited by this connection—this obvious sign—that he almost wants to keep kissing, have sex again, but he remembers he can't be gone long, so he sits up, looking for his briefs. "I'm sorry, I can't stay. I'd like...to talk more."

"Go for round two?"

Brandon smiles, slipping his clothes on. "If I had time."

"I get it." Jon nods, looking only a little disappointed.

"Maybe if you give me your number?" Brandon can't believe his own boldness—but Jon said it, right? They had a moment. "We can go out, grab some food sometime, talk more DSLWLS, maybe go back to my place, or somewhere I won't get fired."

"Your place?" Jon smiles broadly, like he doesn't believe the invitation.

"It's not as nice as here, I'll admit." Brandon sits back on the bed to put his shoes on.

Jon sits up behind him and kisses his neck in a way that makes the hairs there stand on end. "Sure. Give me your phone."

Brandon takes it out of his pocket and hands it over as he

checks himself in the mirror next to the bed, making sure his hair isn't too tousled, his uniform not too wrinkled.

Jon hands him his phone back. "Text me."

"I will." Brandon leans forward and gives him another kiss, long and deep, tasting him, inhaling him. *Is this Heimweh?* Then he pulls back. "Gotta go." He almost sighs it. "Sorry. I want to stay."

"It's fine. I'm about to fall asleep anyway." Jon smiles, his eyes half closed, then lies back on the bed.

Brandon leaves quietly. The hall is empty. It's been only twenty minutes. He should be okay.

In the elevator down, his heart starts to pound. What did he just do? It was amazing, right? It was worth it? It feels like it was worth it.

He takes out his phone and opens the group chat.

BRANDON

I am definitely in love

No response. He checks his contacts for Jon's number. Nothing under *Jon Engle*. His body goes hot at that, some fake trick to make him think he was getting Jon's number, but not really. Was Brandon bad in bed? Was it just some quick pump and dump? Why not say that? Why talk after?

Then he sees it under new contacts: *L. Bunny*. He smiles. Funny.

He texts Jon right there, in the elevator.

BRANDON

Let me know when you're up. We can do something fun. Again, I mean.

He hits Send as the elevator doors open on the lobby. It's still quiet, and he walks back over to the desk and takes his place behind it.

"Did he open the door naked?" Amber asks. She's doodling penises on the notepad in front of her. She did several pages of them in the time Brandon was gone.

Brandon swallows. "What?"

"Since he needed a towel. Like in a porno. I've heard of it happening, but not to me. At least not yet. Did you beat me to it?" She pauses to leer at him.

"Oh." Brandon shakes his head quickly. "No. He was wearing one of the robes. Dripping though."

"Too bad." She goes back to her doodles.

They stand in silence, Brandon feeling his phone heavy in his pocket, willing it to buzz with a message back, knowing it won't because Jon is asleep, like he said he would be. Nothing to worry about. They'll talk tomorrow. Plan a date.

Jon doesn't text back the next morning, but Brandon's friends do.

IAN

No you're not

OLLIE

That's so sweet, congrats!

IAN

Stop encouraging him. It's fine to fantasize about the guests but they're guests!

BRANDON

We did kind of end up in bed together

IAN

You could get fired

BRANDON

No one knows. He gave me his number so we could hang out when I'm not working. We talked. He's funny.

NICOLE

Is he, or is he just a tall guy with a beard who had sex with you?

OLLIE

Are you crying again?

NICOLE

I am waiting in line getting coffee

IAN

Isn't that an assistant job?

NICOLE

Every junior associate is an assistant to the senior associates. It was my turn.

BRANDON

No one wants to hear about my new guy? His name is Jon. He knows DSLWLS!

IAN

He's not your guy. He's a guy you very stupidly fucked at your workplace

BRANDON

You fuck people from work all the time

IAN

I'm a drag queen, it's different, and not all the time. You made a bad decision. And he's not going to text you

OLLIE

He might!

BRANDON

He will!

You're just bitter because you're still not over Victor.

IAN

I am not bitter, I am justifiably angry

NICOLE

It's been over a year, honey

IAN

Stop deflecting, this is about Brandon's bad choices

BRANDON

I got home before you last night—where were you anyway?

IAN

I was closing up the bar. I helped put away chairs

NICOLE

No you didn't

IAN

Why are we picking on me now?

NICOLE

Did you do that thing where you tracked down Victor's car and keyed it again?

IAN

It was parked in front of his boyfriend's place like it always is

NICOLE

Ian

BRANDON

Ian

OLLIE

I hope it helped you let go a little

IAN

Okay, so let's go over this—I keyed my ex's car again, Brandon slept with a guest, Ollie you still have no place to live, and Nicole remains a lonely workaholic who got home after 2 a.m. again, I'm guessing

OLLIE

I'm house-sitting

NICOLE

It's a hard job

IAN

I love you broken bitches

BRANDON

I want you guys to meet Jon, maybe have a party?

IAN

Absolutely not.

Brandon laughs aloud in bed at that. It's a small two-bedroom in Bed-Stuy that he shares with Ian, where one of the bedrooms used to be part of the living room but the landlord threw up a thin wall so he could say it was a two-bedroom. Which it technically is, even if Brandon has to let Ian know if he's bringing anyone home, because even the softest moan can be heard clearly in the living room—which has no windows. The floors are scuffed, the shower has a window that looks directly into their neighbor's place, and the fridge is older than Brandon, but the water pressure is good, and Ian is a fine roommate. Especially for a drag queen. Brandon was worried the apartment would be all dresses and wigs everywhere, sequins raining from the sky, but Ian is organized. Everything's in boxes. They're meticulously tidy, a compulsive cleaner, and they even cook. Brandon knows how lucky he is.

He slips out of bed and puts on some pajamas before opening his door and walking out into the living room. There's a TV here and a coffee table that doubles as a dining table. To the right is the kitchen, a narrow little strip that juts off the rest of the apartment, barely big enough for one person. Ian is already in there, frying bacon in a long floral dressing gown and plaid boxers. They're hot—the kind of person Jon would absolutely be texting back already. Korean American, with a thin, muscular body, even a six-pack, and close-cropped black hair. They keep cooking without looking over at Brandon.

"We are not having a party for your one-night stand," Ian says.

"He might be more than that." Brandon flops down on the futon, legs curled up on one side.

"You've gotta stop going home with every guy who flirts with you and then assuming you're in love." Ian holds the pan up and lets it sizzle. "It's giving me anxiety."

"I'm gonna tell Ollie you don't believe in love anymore, and then he's going to pester you all day about how *love is real*." Brandon sings the last three words, clutching his hands under his chin.

"Oh gods, please don't. I'm making you breakfast."

Brandon drops his hands. "Fine, but then stop telling me not to like guys."

Ian looks over at Brandon and smiles a little. "I just don't want you getting hurt. You always get hurt."

Brandon shrugs, looking down, thinking of how many nights he's cried because a guy he went home with didn't text him back. "I guess." It won't be like that with Jon though, right? It feels too much like something more. Their connection.

"And do not expect me to say sleeping with a guest at work was a good idea. That was stupid."

"Okay, yes, it was," Brandon admits. "But he was so hot." He closes his eyes, and his head rolls back as he remembers Jon's body and how, unbelievably, he was invited to touch it.

"You get photos?" Ian looks over, raising an eyebrow.

"No, but if we do a party and you meet him…"

"No." Ian turns back to the stove.

"I told him about the trivia we do; he thought it sounded fun."

Ian sighs and opens the oven before slipping on a mitt and taking out a tray of biscuits. They take out plates, load them with bacon and biscuits, then pull a pan out of the oven, filled with baked eggs and kimchi, which they ladle next to the biscuits. They hand a plate to Brandon. "Here, just like Umma used to make."

"Thanks," Brandon says, taking the plate and going back to the living room, where he sits on their approximation of a sofa: a futon that lists to one side.

Ian comes and sits beside him, eating their own breakfast.

"Tell you what," Ian says between bites. "If he texts you back, bring him to my show tonight. If he seems cool, maybe we can throw a party on Sunday night or something. Low-key. If you want to. I don't know why you would though. Go, like, have lots of sex and keep him private. Why bother introducing us to him?"

Brandon cuts into the eggs. They run a little and taste delicious. "He feels special. And I guess I just thought you would, like, impress him."

Ian leans back on the futon. "Honey. If you want to impress him, trust me, we are not the way to do it."

"I mean, he's staying at the hotel, so he must have money, right? And he was in his thirties, I think, so older. Why did he even bring me up there last night?" He thinks of his phone, still on his nightstand. Maybe Jon texted while he ate. He puts his plate down and rushes to grab it. No messages from Jon, just one in the group chat.

OLLIE

I love a party!

"Nothing?" Ian asks.

Brandon shakes his head, a little embarrassed. "Maybe you're right. Maybe it was just—"

Ian throws their arms in the air. "I could be wrong! I'm fucking nuts." Their arms drop, and they speak quietly as they break apart a biscuit. "Last night I keyed Victor's car again. We all make bad decisions. Cheating asshole." They drop the biscuit, looking up. "Did you know his new boyfriend is a top only? For years Victor said he was top only, even when I wanted to switch it up a little, and now he's some butch guy's li'l bottom bitch?"

"You gotta block him on Instagram," Brandon says.

"I did. I saw this on one of my other accounts."

"Is it an account specifically for stalking him?"

"It's not stalking." They point at Brandon with their biscuit. "It's gathering intelligence. For vengeance."

"What about that guy you hooked up with last month? Tim or something?"

"Tom. What about him?"

"Didn't he, like, ask you out?"

"Yeah, but I'm not ready to date again." They say it quickly, clearly wanting the conversation to be over.

"Nicole would say you're obsessing."

"Nicole is a workaholic with no social life who falls asleep trying to masturbate most nights."

Brandon snorts a laugh, trying to keep a bite of food in his mouth. "She told you that?" he asks after swallowing.

"Yeah. Poor thing. Woke up with the vibrator still half inside her. She's never going to land a girlfriend that way. But she's 'choosing work' for now. That's her call. Just like I'm choosing vengeance. And you're choosing—"

"Love," Brandon says, at the same time that Ian says, "Bad decisions."

Brandon laughs. "Oh no, what if Ollie is the only one making good choices?"

"The couch-surfing dog walker?" Ian asks, getting up. "I don't think so." They reach out for Brandon's plate, which Brandon hands over, empty now, and takes both dishes back to the kitchen. "Can you hit the grocery today? I have a list on the fridge. I'll Venmo you, but Kate asked me to pick up an extra shift at the bookstore today, and I need the money."

"Sure," Brandon calls back. He picks up his phone. Nothing new. "My shift isn't till six. When is your show tonight?"

"Midnight, last slot," Ian says with a frown. "I keep saying they gotta move me up, but…"

"You'll get there," Brandon says.

"Fuck yeah, I will. Maybe not at the Wreck Room, but somewhere." They stretch out for a moment, shoulders rolling. "Now I'm gonna shower. See you tonight. And stop staring at your phone."

Ian goes into the bathroom, robe flying out behind them, and shuts the door. Brandon picks up his phone. Nothing. So he texts Jon again.

BRANDON

Sleep well?

2.
Ollie

OLLIE WAKES UP IN A huge white bed and blinks for a moment, trying to remember where he is. He lifts his head and examines the room: white everything, except for some stray black dog hair, which reminds him—the Strongs'. He usually just walks their dog, Pete, a cute black Chug with an extensive sweater collection. But they were going to Capri for a few weeks, and not wanting to send Pete to a doggie day camp where "he wouldn't get the attention that he needs" and not wanting to bring him along "because the restaurants there aren't as cool as they should be about having dogs, even super well-behaved ones like our li'l Petey," they asked Ollie to house-sit for a few weeks.

He was happy for the gig, since his last house-sitting stint for the Blakes had ended a few days before and he didn't want to crash on Brandon and Ian's tilting futon again or ask Nicole about her home office with the pull-out bed (that always made her look sad, like she just remembered she even had an apartment outside the office). So it was perfect timing when the Strongs asked. It usually was.

Ollie knows he's lucky, the way these opportunities keep falling in his lap, and he knows part of it is because his mom knows a lot of rich people, and those rich people tell other rich people, and now he's Park Slope's number one house sitter and dog walker. But it's not nepotism, right? Maybe. He should think about it, try to figure out if taking these jobs is the right thing to do. But later.

For now, he throws off the fluffy white comforter and looks for Pete, who is curled up on the bed in the master bedroom (Ollie is staying in the guest room "because you can make it your space, and that'll be so much more comfortable"). Pete's head lifts nervously when Ollie stands in the doorway, but he quickly recognizes Ollie and trots over, looking at him expectantly.

"Breakfast time?" Ollie asks. Pete keeps staring. "Okay."

Ollie goes downstairs, Pete following, his short legs not quite long enough to reach the steps in front of him, so he practically tumbles past Ollie to the kitchen, a wide-open space with white tile, a white island, and white dog bowls, which Ollie fills up. Pete happily dives headfirst into the bowl of deeply expensive organic dog food, and Ollie takes out some cereal. The house has a smart-home system, complete with HomePods, which the Strongs let him connect his phone to, and as he eats, he tells Siri to resume his podcast, and it goes on, the sound seemingly coming from everywhere. This is a good one. An unsolved murder of two college girls in Colorado. Ollie couldn't say exactly why he loves true-crime podcasts so much. Or, more worryingly, why he finds them so soothing. Maybe it's the voices, the hosts always speaking in low, serious near whispers, but more likely it's the knowledge that these things happen far away from him. They're real, and he can try to solve the case, ask questions that no one can hear, watch a whole life and death play out, feeling like he can help—even if he never does. But it still feels like he helps. Listening to it helps somehow, right? He'll have to think about that later, too.

Pete finishes breakfast before Ollie and then sits by the table with his favorite toy, a blue rubber teething ring. Apparently it's the same kind he had when he was a puppy, and the Strongs have since bought a new one for him each month, instead of letting it get worn out from all that biting. Ollie found a stack of them in a closet. This one seems fresh though, gleaming. Ollie goes to pet his head, and Pete leans into his hand, staring at Ollie, waiting. He hasn't given up his dog-walking route for these two weeks, so he should get going soon.

He heads upstairs and takes a quick shower in the guest bathroom, rubs some T gel into his shoulders, and waits for it to dry. Then he takes some of the Strongs' fancy hand cream from the bathroom and layers it on, to cover the astringent smell with sea fennel and oud, and because the T gel dries his skin so much. He puts on a T-shirt, jeans, beanie, flannel. The whole time, the podcast keeps playing—how the body of the second girl was discovered, how there were no signs of sexual trauma, how she had oxycodone in her system.

"Maybe it was the mom," Ollie says aloud to Pete as he dresses. "She had the prescription because of that car accident." Pete looks at Ollie, confused. Ollie shrugs and goes to his stash, a little Tupperware of edibles he bought from around the city. Not the ones from last night though; those were too strong. He plucks out a small mint, pops it in his mouth. It's a mellow one, so he'll barely notice. Then he scoops up Pete and hugs him to his chest, bringing him downstairs.

He takes his phone out of the smart-home attachment and

pops in the earbuds, continuing the podcast: "But as Kaylee would soon discover, the music of life can sometimes end in a deafening crash and an unbearable silence. The kind you don't hear coming..." He picks out a sweater for Pete—pink tweed—and puts it and the leash on him. Then they go outside.

It's still early. Park Slope is filled with parents bringing their kids to school, all of them in little fall coats that look like brightly colored bells ringing in the cool weather. Ollie starts the walk around the neighborhood to pick up his puppies. That's how he thinks of them, though many of them are older, and none of them are really his. But they're his puppies for a few hours a day, once in the morning, once in the afternoon. Mostly the dogs are left home alone all day, and Ollie has keys to get into the houses and apartments to go grab them. Sometimes a housekeeper or live-in nanny brings him the dog. In one building, the doorman does. There are seven puppies in total, six not counting Pete: a Pomchi named Samba, a Weimaraner named Zoey, a shihpoo named Harpo, an Afghan named Pepper, a Frenchie named Linus, and a standard black poodle named, unfortunately, Malkia, because, as her white owners had told Ollie, it meant *queen* in an African language. He doesn't hold any of the owners' awfulness against the puppies though. They're all good dogs who create a lovely fan pattern, pulling him along like a kite as he walks them on the sidewalk, attracting smiles from the kids walking to school and sometimes photos from other pedestrians.

Ollie likes to take them to different dog parks every day, and today he chooses the Washington Park Dog Run, which is new and unpretentious, with good turf that the dogs love running up and down, sniffing each other. Ollie sits and watches them all, listening to his podcast, feeling the mint start to kick in and make his body feel slower, in a good way, a sort of walking-through-jelly way.

The group chat dings as Brandon and Ian wake up. Nicole has undoubtedly been awake for hours but keeps her phone on Do Not Disturb until late. She can't be distracted from work. Sometimes Ollie thinks it's sad, how focused on it she is. She can't see anything else. Other times he feels jealous that she knows what she wants and is willing to give up so much for it. Ollie doesn't have a clue what his life should look like. He knows he'll figure it out though. Later.

OLLIE

I love a party

NICOLE

Won't a guy you just met think it's weird if you throw him a party?

No one responds to that, which means Ian and Brandon are probably talking over breakfast. Ollie feels kind of left out when they do that, wonders what they're saying in those silences. He should talk to them about that. Think of how to phrase it. Later.

A party would be fun though. Aside from going to Ian's shows at the bar when he can (and where it's so loud, Ollie can barely hear the conversation), and their weekly Saturday brunches (Ian works a Sunday drag brunch, so they do theirs a day early), Ollie feels like he barely sees them anymore. When they were all in college four years ago, they met in the common area of their dorm every day. They had classes together. They saw each other even when they didn't want to. Now it's just...brunch. That's not enough time to get through everything. The group chat shows only slices and always ends up being everyone teasing each other. Ollie likes the quiet moments best. Walking together outside, talking about ideas. Things. TV. Podcasts. What they want to do with their lives. It used to be that they'd share the boring parts of their days. Now they have time only for the big, exciting moments. Ollie doesn't have any of those.

He worries, a little, that maybe they've noticed that. That maybe he's getting too boring for them. Too quiet too. Maybe that's what Ian and Brandon talk about in their apartment, far from Ollie.

"Oh yes, you're a good puppy," he says, throwing the ball back for Linus, who chases it, thrilled. The mint is strong now, and all his thoughts seem to have slipped away. Just him and the dogs. He had some stuff he was thinking about, he knows, and some stuff he was supposed to think about. Oh well. He'll remember it later.

After about forty minutes, he gathers the dogs up again and walks them back to their respective homes, making sure each of them has done their business along the way. Back at the white house he's staying in, he has eggs, spinach, and some of his father's homemade pique. *All you need to eat for a week, mija. Ah,* mijo. *Lo siento. Still getting used to it.* He never quite got it right, but he always apologized. He died last year in a hit-and-run in Flatbush. There were jars and jars of his pique in the basement. Mom doesn't use it. *Too spicy for my white taste buds, honey.* Still, she keeps it for Ollie, even after she moved out to New Jersey, to a little retirement community she's technically a year too young for.

Ollie closes the fridge. He doesn't need to go shopping. He had some things he wanted to think about though. Maybe figure out what comes next. In two weeks, when the Strongs get back, he has to find a new place to live. Or maybe figure out if he should find a real job, one that doesn't rely on his mom telling all her friends to tell their kids to hire him to walk their dogs. Maybe something... He looks down at Pete, who is holding his teething ring in his mouth and looking up at him with an expression of *what next?*

"I dunno, bud." Ollie hits Play on the podcast, and it echoes through the house. "I don't think it was the mom though. It was definitely the sister."

3.

Nicole

NICOLE IS AT WORK.

Nicole is always at work. She knows this. It's the price to pay for what she wants. She's a Black Lesbian Trying To Make It in Corporate America, and that is not easy. She has to be the first one in the office, the last one to leave. She has to do everything better than everyone else. Sure, she whizzed through law school a year early—Penn, too, a good one—and was top of her class. But that doesn't mean she got any of the judicial clerkships she applied for. Those go to people with real contacts, not the daughter of a sculptor and a senior engineer.

So she took a job at a law firm—that was hard enough to secure. There are too many lawyers now, carpeting the streets the way bees cover honeycomb, dense buzzing layers of them. Or at least they carpet the halls of this building. There are seventy-seven other junior associates. Everyone knows only around forty will make it to midlevel without being fired or burning out, and probably half that will make it to senior associate. That's seven years, if she's good. Once she reaches that level, then she'll be able to take some bigger cases, earn a reputation, and after four or five years, maybe she can find a job as in-house counsel for a big movie studio. That's the ultimate legal job; the agents and producers do most of the work, so you're just there to put the official seal on everything. Normal work hours, lots of money, and the chance to schmooze with Hollywood stars. Maybe she'll even achieve something akin to work-life balance. That's her dream: queen bee.

But that's a while off. So, for now, she lives on coffee. She sleeps four hours a night, five if she's lucky, and six on weekends. She has a nice apartment in Midtown but since moving in has forgotten about it just as often as she remembers, her feet taking her on autopilot back to her parents' place after work. She's stopped outside the door more than once and just turned around, not wanting to wake them. She has no social life aside from brunch, the one thing her friends made her swear never to give up. And they're the only friends she has left. Three of them.

"That research done for the Jones case, Nikki?"

She hates the nickname but instinctively plasters on a smile and turns to Don, one of the senior associates who has stopped next to her desk in the junior associates' bullpen. She's near the edge, which means it's easier for her to escape, but also for the folks walking by to pop in. Unfortunately it also meant learning to tune out the traffic of people walking by, which means every time one of them stops, it's jarring. She wonders if they know that. She wonders if they enjoy it.

"I already emailed it over to you," she says to Don, smile still on. "You want a hard copy?"

He takes out his phone and checks it. "Huh, not sure how I missed that."

Nicole shrugs, making a face she hopes conveys that she's as shocked and confused as he is that he missed it in the two hours since she emailed it to him. But she's not. He was out to breakfast with one of the partners—his godmother. They have one-on-ones every Friday, and they both come back smelling like expensive wine. Today they found time for breakfast, too—they'll practically spend the whole day together. How nice for him.

"Well, let me look this over, see what you missed."

"Let me know," Nicole says with a smile she hopes doesn't appear as fake as it feels. She didn't miss a fucking thing. She never does.

"Oh, and Barbara would like a coffee, if you don't mind running down to the place," he says, walking away, eyes still on his phone.

"Her assistant can't manage it?" Nicole ventures.

"Making copies."

"Sure," Nicole says, standing. It'll be good to stretch, get some fresh air, maybe make some eye contact with the partner, Barbara, so she knows Nicole's face, at least. She stands up from her cubicle in the pen, then grabs her coat and purse.

"Can you get me one, too?" Don asks, eyes still on his phone. "The usual."

"Of course," she says.

"You're the best."

She is. But not for this. She heads to the elevator. One of the partners, Ellen Kang, suddenly appears beside her, and they wait together in silence. She's in a beautifully fitted black suit with red trim, but from what Nicole knows about Ellen Kang, brownnosing right now would not help her career, so she stays silent, professional, as they get into the elevator.

She really wishes she were alone in the elevator though. Her head itches, and she wants to scratch it, but not in front of a partner. She braided her hair down too tight under a wig getting ready this morning—natural hair won't get her ahead at work, she knows, so she wears a simple, flat black wig every day, in a bun or just hanging to her shoulders. At least it's Friday. Everyone leaves early on Friday, so she can be out of here by eleven, maybe even get a drink, scroll through Bumble looking at pretty girls she'll never have the time to message. When the elevator door opens, Ellen Kang walks out without even a look back. Nicole scratches her head.

Outside, the air hits nice. It feels like she hasn't inhaled fresh air in days, although it's only been three hours since she got in at 6:00 a.m. The bullpen of junior associates doesn't have windows, just the light that comes through the glass-walled offices and conference rooms around it, so the air is recycled and stale, often smelling like sweat, coffee, books, mouthwash. Outside though, in the financial district in Manhattan, it smells like...well, like traffic, tourists, and distantly, the water. But it's still an improvement.

There's a park next to the building their office is in, a threadbare kind of thing, barely a block, mostly paved over in pretty brick but with at least a few dozen trees all lined up. Once it starts to turn cold, they string white Christmas lights all over them, and at night it turns sort of beautiful, like a set for one of those interactive theater experiences. Nicole went to one of those on the last date she had, years ago. She loved looking around, admiring the design, even watching the actors play their scenes, but when one tried grabbing her hand, she pulled it back and noped right out of there, leaving her date behind. That's when she realized she wasn't cut out for dating yet—the fun, the wonder, the adventure other women her age wanted. Experiences. She'd have those when she was older and her world was comfortable. For now, all she wanted was to enjoy an occasional nice dinner and to get laid. But even that would require more time out of her days than she has.

She walks to the coffee place around the corner, not part of a chain, like the one in the office building; that's for people who don't know better. This place is slightly out of the way, but not enough to prevent people from coming by—a lot of them today, making a line out the door. She doesn't mind waiting. She checks her phone, goes over what she has left to do today—research mostly, and her own projects, some ideas she wants to write down for the partners, make sure they know her name.

And her boys (Ian gave her the okay to refer to them as that when it's collectively) are finally awake. Must be nice, sleeping in. She texts them for a minute, smirking at everything—Brandon's hookup, Ian's stalking. Ian isn't wrong exactly, though she'd never describe herself as broken. She's…on hold. Success—then she'll let go a little. It's like there are two clocks going, one for her job and one for everything else, and the everything-else one isn't broken; she's just unplugged it. For a little while.

OLLIE

I love a party!

NICOLE

Won't a guy you just met think it's weird if you throw him a party?

She doesn't even look up until she's at the counter, and it's Sam. She shouldn't know Sam's name. She shouldn't have even looked at the name tag after her third time spotting her; it's weird to know a barista's name. But she's...well, cute. Mid-twenties, with long braids and onyx skin. She's got cheekbones that were made for modeling, high-end stuff, the cover of Italian *Vogue*.

"Hey," Sam says, smiling. "How are you?"

"I'm okay," Nicole says, then swallows. "You?"

"Can't complain. What can I get you?"

Nicole rattles off the orders instinctively. Don, Barbara, hers, and one for Jim, who brought her one yesterday without asking. Sam writes them down, nodding, the tip of her tongue sticking out the side of her mouth, and Nicole taps her company card to pay before moving aside to the pickup area, close to the counter. She can see Sam begin making the coffees, moving from the stack of cups to the espresso machine. Her eyes flick to Nicole and stick.

"So, what do you do, anyway?" Sam asks. "You look too important to be getting coffee."

Nicole smiles, a little taken aback by the compliment. *Important.* She's not sure anyone has ever thought of her as that.

"Junior associate at a law firm," she says. "Bottom of the rankings, so I get coffee for whoever asks."

"That doesn't seem like lawyering," Sam says, pulling down one of the levers on the machine. It makes a loud whooshing sound Nicole doesn't try to speak over. She just shrugs. Sam pushes the lever back up and pops a lid on the coffee cup. "But I don't mind it," she adds, handing Nicole the cup with a smile.

Nicole takes it, staring at the cup, her brain trying to compute what Sam just said.

"You don't mind what?" she asks as Sam starts on the next cup, adding a few pumps of flavoring. The syrup shimmers on the pump handle, and Nicole suddenly thinks about how Sam must smell—vanilla and sugar and coffee woven into her skin.

Sam pulls the lever down again, the noise loud. She keeps it down for a long time. Then she pushes it up, tops it with whipped cream (Don loves whipped cream), and brings it over to Nicole. Sam takes out a cardboard tray to hold this one.

"Don't mind seeing you," she says.

It feels like a hammer has come down on Nicole's head. "Oh," she says. Her eyes feel too wide-open. She has to remember to close her mouth. "Why?" It's a stupid question. She knows what's happening here. It just pops out of her in surprise. She wasn't ready for flirting. She needs to be ready; if she's ready, then she's a good flirt. Or she was. Hasn't done it in years.

Sam laughs. "You know, I'm part of this activist group; we could always use some legal help, if you can donate some time..." She takes a folded-up flyer out of her back pocket and hands it across to Nicole: STOP WAR-FOR-PROFIT. It looks like the sort of thing Nicole would have been handing out before law school. In college, she was cochair of the Black Student Alliance and the LGBTQIA+ Student Committee, as well as a member of Queer Peers, Queers of Color for Change, and Students Stopping War. But then she had class and studying, and changing the world fell by the wayside.

"Oh, I—" Nicole starts.

"I get it, you're busy. But just in case." Sam grabs one of the markers for writing names on cups and flips the flyer, writing a number on it. "Text me if you want to get together."

"For activism," Nicole says. She meant for it to be a question, but it sounds like a pronouncement.

"For activism," Sam says with a laugh, then pulls the handle down for the last cup. Nicole observes her for a moment and sees the hint of a tattoo peek from under the sleeve of her black T-shirt, notices her earrings—small silver skulls. This would never work. Nicole leans back from the counter slightly, thinking about it, about someone from work seeing her, the rumor spreading—*Nicole is dating the coffee girl, Nicole has a crush on the coffee girl.* She can't be seen in the office that way. She's not sure how homophobic the partners are, but even if they aren't, they place value on social standing. If Nicole were to bring a girlfriend to a company event, she'd better be working at a Fortune 500. She'd need to look impressive. Powerful. Dating the coffee girl from around the corner will just mean teasing, the insidious kind that seems good-natured at first and then creeps into who she is, the way to distinguish her from the two other Black women junior associates: *You know, the one dating the coffee girl.*

Not *you know, the one who found that ruling that helped us win the Henderson case.* Not even *the one who's so on top of everything*. You don't promote the one dating the coffee girl.

Sam puts the last of the coffees in the tray and smiles at Nicole. "These are yours."

"Yeah," Nicole says, taking them. "Thanks. For the flyer, too." She holds it up for a moment before folding it into her purse, then puts her hands on the tray of coffees.

They say nothing for a moment, both their fingertips resting on opposite sides of the tray. Sam is wearing tinted lip gloss, slightly purple.

"See you later," Sam says, turning around to make the next order. Nicole puts a twenty in the tip jar, far too much, her hands shaking. She takes a deep breath and puts her coffee cup in the tray before taking it away. Outside, the air is cold, and she realizes she's sweating.

There's another Nicole who would date Sam. The one who hadn't been buried under the work, who would hand out flyers with her, working for a nonprofit, saving the world. But the law became the world, and it self-replicates forever, never needing saving. *Her* world, the one she'd protect, is down to just three people. Five if she includes her parents. And she doesn't need to hand out flyers for them. But someone does need to cover the brunch bill.

She just needs to work. Become queen bee. That's enough to save the sliver of world she can still see through the slits between legal briefs. Later, when she's comfortable, working for Hollywood, making big money for a normal amount of work, then her world will get bigger again. That Nicole could date Sam, too. Maybe she'll still be around.

Nicole looks back briefly at the coffee shop window without thinking, her eyes pulled there for a moment, as though caught in a strong wind. She shakes her head before she picks out Sam. Nicole looks away. She has work. There's no time for this nonsense now.

4.
Ian

THE BOOKSTORE IS SLOW, BUT Ian doesn't mind that. It gives them time to read. They'd prefer to be the sort of artist who practices all day and performs at night, but they don't make enough for that. They actually have to ask Brandon to help out with their share of rent more often than they'd like because drag is fucking expensive—makeup, wigs, custom dresses. And the tips they make aren't really enough to break even on it. Brandon is cool, and generous, but Ian hates when they have to ask. So that, plus the ever-present student loan debt, means a bookstore job where they try to pick up as many shifts as they can.

It isn't a bad place to work. At other jobs they've had, reading when it was slow was discouraged; they were supposed to be folding shirts or cleaning. In a bookstore, though—at least this one—as long as they were behind the counter, ready to answer questions if a customer appeared, Kate doesn't mind them reading.

They're currently working through a mystery Ollie recommended. Gruesome, inspired by true events, kind of unputdownable, as much as Ian wishes they could. They have trouble not finishing things. They're a completionist. No matter how awful the TV series, how boring the book, how offensive the movie, they will finish it. The only time they're allowed to back out is the first ten pages, the first episode, the first date—that's just testing something, not committing to it. But once they're in, they're in. Even if the book is bad or, in this case, very weirdly gory and with some terribly written sex scenes, they have to know how it ends. And they're not going to look it up online; that's cheating. Get to the end—then they can make a complete, well-informed decision. *I hated this book, and I'm sure I hated it, because I read the whole damn thing.* That's what they'll tell Ollie tomorrow at brunch.

The phone rings, a regular just checking in on a cookbook she ordered last week that hasn't come in yet. Ian says they'll let her know soon as it does and leaves a Post-it on the desk as a reminder to whoever is here when it shows up. They read another few pages of the book, sneering at another sex scene where "her pudenda quivered," and then, blessedly, the bell over the door jingles.

It's a small bookstore, about the same size as the apartment they share with Brandon, but stuffed with ceiling-high shelves, so they can't see the door directly from the counter. Kate, the owner, put up a mirror in a corner, but it's bulbous, curved, so the faces coming in the door are distorted for a moment, supersized balloons. A blond mom and a blond kid, maybe four. The store doesn't have the best kids' section. Kate started it as a queer bookstore but branched out into—ew—heterosexual mainstream stuff to bolster sales.

"Hello?" the woman calls out.

"Welcome," Ian calls back in their best customer-service voice. "You looking for something in particular?"

The woman rounds the shelves, clutching her kid's hand

tightly as the kid tries to squirm away, toward the brightly colored art books, Ian thinks. The woman gives Ian a once-over, in their oversize cardigan and crop top, the multiple rings and necklaces, the long dangling earring, the visible tattoo of a thick black circle around their left hip that rises from the waist of their jeans and falls back down again.

"Hi," Ian says, smiling at her look, wondering where it'll fall. If anyone bothers staring at Ian, they're usually an out-of-towner, and that means they're either going to be so pleased to see some of the Brooklyn weirdness they came for, embodied in Ian, or disgusted. Real New Yorkers barely notice Ian anymore. Unless Ian wants to be noticed, of course.

"Yeah," the woman says, her eyes narrowing a little, landing in the unnerved-but-staying-polite category. "I apparently got the wrong book in the series for my niece's birthday, so I was just hoping you had the right one before I go to the party. Linus, stop pulling, please, there's no time to browse."

"Sure thing," Ian says. "What's the series?"

Ian doesn't even need to check the computer; they remember shelving it last week—the latest from the Princess and Powderpuff series. They walk over to the tiny kids' shelf and pick it out, then bring it back to the counter.

"Linus," the mom sighs as her kid finally breaks, dashing to, yes, the art books. Big brightly colored ones all stacked on a low shelf with one face out, covered in a photo of running paints in a rainbow: *QUEER COLORS: Contemporary LGBTQ Painters*.

"Lookit the paint!" Linus says, excited.

"Yes, but that book is too grown up, honey; it's not what we're here for."

"It's a great book," Ian says, ringing up the Powderpuff book, *very grown up* feeling like one of those phrases that could be homophobic, or could just mean she thinks it's too advanced. "*QUEER COLORS*, I mean. Some overlooked painters."

"That's nice," the woman says flatly. Linus is opening the cover of *QUEER COLORS* slowly.

"It's mostly photos," Ian says, swiping the woman's card. "Your kid might be inspired."

"I appreciate the upsell," she says, sounding tired. "But we're just here for this. I don't suppose you gift wrap?"

"Sorry, only for the holidays," Ian says. The receipt prints, and they take out a paper bag and put the book in it and hand it to her. "Hope this is the right one."

"Thank you," she says.

"Lookit!" Linus says. He's pulled the first few pages open and is up to a big full-page photo of a painting of two men kissing. Neck up, very modern style, in vibrant Vaporwave colors.

"That's a good one, right, kiddo?" Ian asks.

"I like the colors!" Linus says, excited someone responded.

"Come on, honey, we gotta go," the mom says, taking the bag from Ian and walking over to Linus. She closes the book.

"It's a great book," Ian tries again. "Mostly photos of art, not really too adult at all." That's not entirely true, but the kid likes a queer book—that should be celebrated.

The woman sighs loudly, intentionally. "No thank you. We're going, Linus."

She takes his hand and walks out.

"You seem homophobic," Ian says loudly, when they've opened the door.

The woman pauses for a moment but doesn't turn back, and the door closes with a shutter and a ring of the bell.

Ian knows they shouldn't have said that. But it's what she was dancing around, right? If she'd just been too rushed, too tired, or just didn't want to buy it, it would be one thing, but *too grown up* is like a jolt in Ian's veins. Too queer—that's what she meant, right? And Ian was supposed to call her out on it. It's where the conversation was supposed to end. And Ian's a completionist. So why do they feel even more annoyed now?

They sigh and pick their book back up, then put it down again and take out their phone instead.

"Bitch," they murmur to themself, checking the chat.

OLLIE

I love a party!

NICOLE

Won't a guy you just met think it's weird if you throw him a party?

They roll their eyes.

IAN

Stop talking about this like it's happening! We're not throwing a party!

BRANDON

But we could! They're selling streamers at the grocery! You love streamers

IAN

You want to have a party for the streamers?

BRANDON

Yes. Then it's not for Jon, we're just throwing a party and inviting him

IAN

Let's see if he texts you back first

They wait a moment, but there's no response. Maybe that was too cruel. Though it does mean this guy hasn't texted Brandon back yet. They never do. Ian doesn't know why—Brandon is cute, and there's gotta be some other guy out there who's just as in love with the idea of being in love as Brandon is. Why have they never met? They could hook up, decide it's love, have a few weeks of intense romance, realize they hate each other, and break up dramatically. Isn't that how it's supposed to go for guys like Brandon? Ian doesn't know why it hasn't yet.

Ian closes the chat and stares at their phone screen, their thumb hovering over the Instagram icon before tapping it. They switch over from their main account to one of the others, then from there go to Raphael's profile. Raphael is Victor's boyfriend. He's a big guy, lots of gym selfies, huge arms and chest, always mugging for the camera like he's butch, like his Instagram isn't filled with photos of him in a tiny red Speedo at the beach in Jersey, where he and Victor went over the summer. Ian doesn't hate Raphael; it's not his fault Victor cheated, ended things. But they do think of him with some contempt. And while making some inevitable comparisons. Ian is narrow, so femme that they don't even identify as male—though they are only into guys, and they think of themself as a woman only when in drag. They're nothing like Raphael, with that faux-gay-butch-dom-top-daddy thing that feels like it's trying too hard. Ian doesn't know how Victor fell for it.

Ian was never like Brandon. They do not fall in love. If anything, they were the one who never texted guys like Brandon back. Then, with Victor…it kept happening. And he made Ian laugh. And he was angry at all the same stuff, too. That's why Victor said he'd hooked up with Raphael, was leaving Ian for him—Raphael wasn't angry like Ian. He didn't make Victor feel angrier. Instead, he felt calm with him, he said. Happy. Things were just easier.

Ian didn't know what to say to that at the time, and Victor didn't give them a chance to respond, anyway. He just apologized again, crying, and left. The conversation was never finished.

Ian's hands move quickly now, leaving some hearts under the selfie of Raphael as this fake persona—Adam, some photo pulled from Google of a hot shirtless guy. They switch back to their main account, close it, open TikTok, switch to a different account, go to Victor's page, and feel their hand tighten around the phone as they watch a fan-cam-style compilation of Raphael, sparkly filters and all. Ian hates Victor for this. For being happy. And then they hate themself for hating Victor, and then they think about what it felt like dragging a key on Victor's car—some old one, his uncle's, fancy and sleek. Ian used to tease him about it. The car of a guy compensating for something. Victor always laughed at that. Until he didn't.

They start to leave a comment on the TikTok—*FAGGOT*—but delete it. This account is linked to his other accounts, and if

Victor blocks it, it'll block those, too. They need to write hate speech from their burner. They put their phone back in their pocket and reach for their bag, under the counter, where the burner is, but the back door to the office opens, and Kate comes out.

The door is right behind them, so they're suddenly too close, crowded behind the counter. Ian straightens up, stops reaching for their burner.

"You okay?" Kate asks. She's fiftysomething, a rail of a woman with short bleached hair and purple cat-eye glasses. "You look tired. Angry-tired. You yell at a customer again?" She folds her arms. This has been a sticking point with them lately. Kate likes Ian, but not enough that she'll let them drive off every customer. Only, like, one a week.

"No," Ian lies.

She sighs. "Did they deserve it?"

No, Ian thinks. It was just a tired mom rushing out of there. Ian knows that. But it was the way she was talking to that kid. That kid could be queer, and now he's going to think men kissing is "too adult" for him, and that might make him ashamed or scared, and thinking about it just feels like pressure building inside Ian's brain, pushing out their eyes.

"Just…stuff," Ian says, taking a deep breath. They spot the book on the counter. "My book isn't great."

She laughs, walking around them, in front of the counter. "So stop reading it."

"I—"

"I know. I'm kidding."

"I'm sorry," Ian says.

Kate nods. "It wasn't a regular, was it?"

"Tourist."

Her face goes blank, thinking about that, and then she smiles. "You'll get better, right? I'm not making a mistake keeping you on?"

"No," they say. They need this job. If they lose it, it'll be months before they can find another, and they don't think Brandon will float them on rent that long again. "I'll get better." Ian feels a faint prickling that could become tears, a tightness in their throat, and looks back at the book. It's such a bad book. It annoys them to no end, just thinking about how they'll have to finish it, and the prickling in their eyes goes away, the tightness in their throat moved to their jaw. What a fucking terrible book.

"Okay," Kate says. "I'm going out for lunch, the vegan place. You want anything?"

"Iced coffee," Ian says, without even thinking. They look up at Kate's smirk. "And I guess one of those little mushroom buns?"

"Sure," Kate says. "Have fun being angry at your book."

"I'm going to finish it," Ian says, picking it up, almost forgetting it wasn't the book they were pissed off at.

"I know you will," Kate says, walking to the door. "You can't help yourself."

The bell on the door rings, and Ian turns the page.

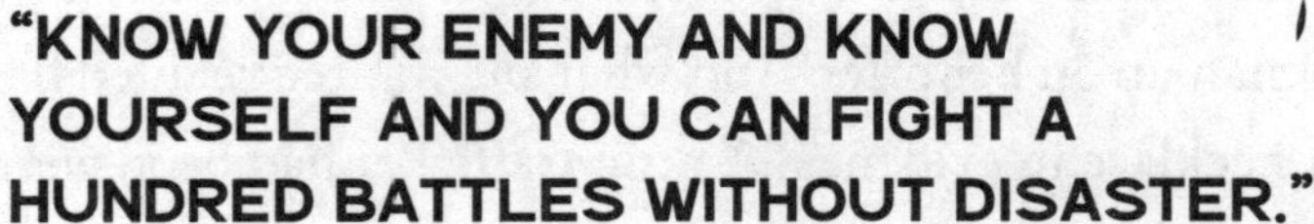

"KNOW YOUR ENEMY AND KNOW YOURSELF AND YOU CAN FIGHT A HUNDRED BATTLES WITHOUT DISASTER."

—SUN TZU

"WHAT DO YOU WANT YOUR life to be?"

That's what the woman had asked him, her eyes hidden by large black sunglasses. She'd told him her name, but it was obviously an alias, so he hadn't bothered to remember it. He knew then that even if he took her offer and came to work for her, he'd probably never learn her real name. She'd just go by an awesome title, like Contessa or Z. At the time he wondered if he would get a one-letter code name and what the coolest letter was. X, right? Or was X too obvious?

She'd paid for the drinks and gotten up and just left him at the bar, thinking. Wondering how much trouble he would get in if he did what she asked. None if no one ever found out, right? And he was—still is—a spy. A good one. Which is why he was wasted cataloging surveillance when he should have been out in the field. He'd had one glorious year before they pulled him—"too much risk-taking"—as if that weren't the point. And then they just had him sitting in a cubicle, filing reports on fieldwork other people did, and even that was boring. He was turning into his boss, a middle-manager type with no cool code name at all, who still drank Pabst even though they lived in Brussels.

Just a few hours back at work, and he knew he had to take the woman up on her offer. And what she wanted seemed harmless. A necklace in evidence. A drug trafficker had been wearing it, but it had nothing to do with the drugs. No one cared about the jewelry.

It was easy enough to take it. Janet, the guard for the evidence locker, liked him, so he just combed his hand through his wavy blond hair, smiled, and said he needed to check something for the reports. She let him in easy.

The problem was the Taser. One of the new Shoktek models from McClintock. It was in the evidence box and still loaded, and it's not like he could resist picking it up, right? Slipping the necklace into his pocket without the camera seeing was easy, done in a flash, but he should get to play a little, handle stuff like the Shoktek Seven. Just to get a feel for it, weigh it in his hand. So he picked it up, looked down the sight, imagined the jolt of shooting someone with it.

He didn't know Janet would be making her rounds just then. He felt caught in the act—did she see him sliding the locket into his pocket? It was too risky to wait and find out.

"Just doing my"—he fired—"rounds." The *s* sound fizzed into a seizure of noise as she hit the ground, body twitching with electricity.

So he ran. Because the cameras had definitely caught that. The woman in the sunglasses had told him to call from a burner anyway, and when he did, he told her he had the necklace, and she told him where to bring it—New York. Another little part of her test, the application to join. But that was easy. He had passports and go-bags all over the place.

It was on the plane that he actually thought to look at the necklace, to see what it was he'd taken. It was a dangling thing, like a bunch of coins on a string, frilly, but he didn't feel silly wearing it. Though, he had to admit, he was the kind of good-looking that could pull most things off. In the plane bathroom, he took it off, flipping through each coin-shaped bead, wondering if it was nothing but a test, a meaningless trinket. Then he found the drive—small, high-tech. He didn't know what it held, but he knew this was the real prize, and so took it out and put it somewhere new. Best to switch the hiding spot. He dumped the necklace when he got off the plane.

It was in the taxi from the airport that he decided—if he had risked his career, his life, to get this thing, he should know what it was, right? He pulled out his new burner and texted an old contact, wanting to meet up. Maybe he'd still turn it over to the woman in sunglasses; he wasn't sure. But he knew one thing: This was his ticket to get the life he wanted—the life he deserved.

5.
Brandon

IAN

How do I look?

BRANDON WAITS FOR THE PHOTO to load. Ian in their drag persona: Constance Leigh Cumming, with a short '20s-style blond bob in finger waves, and a long black sequin dress, posing on stage, light framing them perfectly as they make a sexy little moan face.

OLLIE

Fabulous!

IAN

They'd better give me a better slot after tonight.

Brandon knows Ian isn't on for hours, but any Friday-night slot is a good slot. He doesn't text that back right away though. He waits a minute, still a little angry about the text from earlier. Even if Ian was right. Jon never texted back. Brandon wonders if he'll see him tonight, walk into the lobby, maybe come over and apologize. *I dropped my phone down a sewer grate!* or something. Some excuse, some apology, something to show Brandon's not crazy for thinking they had something. He sighs, not sure.

BRANDON

You look amazing! Knock em dead!

Maybe Jon will just walk in, go to the elevator, and take it up to his room, not even looking at Brandon. Brandon shakes his head—he can't think that; that would be too much, too terrible, worse than vomiting in front of a guy, worse than…a lot.

It's quiet in the lobby again. Friday nights are usually busier, he thinks. People walk between the door and elevators, but no one is shouting, laughing, stumbling to the elevators like usual.

"You doing anything tomorrow?" Amber asks, interrupting the peace. She asks in a way that makes it clear she wants him to ask her the same question, so he just shakes his head. "I'm going to the museum. There's an exhibit at MoMA I want to see."

"Cool."

He wishes it weren't so quiet.

"It's nudes." She leans in to whisper the last word.

"Oh."

Blissfully, the phone rings. Brandon picks it up as fast as he can.

"Bergamot Hotel, this is the front desk. How can I help you?"

"Hanna," Hanna the maid says on the other end of the line.

She's never been one for pleasantries. "Room 310, a left-behind bag."

Brandon blinks, confused. Jon's room. "310 doesn't check out until Monday."

"Not what they told me. Late checkout today."

Brandon frowns and brings up the room status on the computer—she's right. Jon checked out an hour before Brandon came on duty tonight. Didn't even ask for a refund. And he left his bag behind? He had only the one bag when he checked in.

"All right, yes," Brandon says, realizing he's been quiet too long. "Bring the bag down here. I'll call—or, no, I'll run up and get it. That'll be faster."

"Okay," Hanna says, then hangs up.

"Left bag," he says to Amber, not looking her in the eyes. She might see whatever he's feeling on his face. What is he feeling? Worried, he thinks, though he has no idea why. Maybe offended, too—was the sex so bad, Jon checked out early? Did he leave because of Brandon? "I'm going to grab it."

"I can call him and—"

"No, no, I'll do it," Brandon says, a little faster and louder than he means to. Amber raises an eyebrow at him. "I mean, once I have the bag. I want to make sure it's not just, like, trash."

"Okay," Amber says, confused. She shrugs.

Brandon takes the elevator upstairs, feeling as impatient as he did last night, feet boosted, not quite running again to room 310. Hanna is already outside it, rolling her cart down the hall. The same bag Jon had around his shoulder last night is on top of it. Brandon pulls up next to her and takes it. She glances up at him and nods.

"Anything else in there?" he asks.

She raises an eyebrow at him. "You think I missed something?"

"It's just unusual," Brandon says quickly, forcing a smile.

"Nothing else. Extra towels—you brought him those, right?"

"Yes," Brandon says, feeling himself blushing.

She keeps staring at him. He stares back, unsure what she's able to read off him.

"Okay," she says finally, then pushes the cart away. Brandon stares at the door to 310 and then takes out his master key card and swipes it, going inside. He doesn't care if he offends Hanna. It's weird to leave a bag behind, and he's going to search for anything else.

Inside, he sits on the carpet, not wanting to dent the made bed, and opens the bag. A white T-shirt, a pair of black briefs, and…a phone. You definitely don't leave a phone behind. No matter how bad the sex was. Or maybe this is the opposite, like when a guy leaves something at your place so they have to meet you to pick it up later. It's never happened to Brandon, but he's heard it's a thing. Maybe this is like a glass slipper and Brandon is Prince Charming.

He takes his own phone out, pulls up Jon's number. Maybe he has two phones. Who else would leave one behind, except someone who has two, right? He can test it, he realizes.

BRANDON

You left your bag at the hotel

The message pops up on the screen of Jon's phone a moment after he sends it. Four unread messages. He tries sliding it open, but it needs a password, of course. So he must have two phones.

Or... Brandon isn't sure what the *or* is. If this is the phone he was willing to leave behind, what does it mean that it was the number he gave Brandon? Four unread messages means maybe he never saw Brandon's texts—that's good, right?

He stares at the phone, watches the screen go black again. He has no idea what this means. Maybe nothing. Ian would say it's nothing. Nicole would say it means Jon is an idiot. Ollie might believe the glass-slipper thing. Brandon almost texts them, but what for? He stands up, brushing his pants off, and then searches the room carefully, but Hanna was right, there's nothing else. He could go check the trash she took, maybe, but that would seem weird. It would *be* weird. He knows what he's supposed to do now: call the number on file for the reservation and let him know he left a bag behind, then put it in storage for two weeks, and then it's fair game for the staff to take.

Still, two weeks seems like a while. And Brandon has a connection with this guy. He could even be his Heimweh, maybe. One day. You can't wait for Heimweh—you have to go out and find it. He slips the phone into his pocket.

Back at the desk, he puts the bag down and looks up the number on file for the reservation. He picks up the phone and calls it, realizing only a moment too late that it could make his pocket vibrate, which would be hard to explain to Amber. But it doesn't. It rings a few times before being picked up.

"Yes?" It's a woman's voice. Angry.

"Hello, this is Brandon from the Bergamot Hotel, calling for Mr. Engle."

There's a pause. For a moment, Brandon thinks she's hung up.

"He's not available—tell me." Her words are clipped, but

the anger seems pressed out now. Brandon tries to remember what the rules are—this is the number on file, and that's what's most important. Most employees wouldn't know Jon's voice, after all. Wouldn't know he checked in alone. They'd just tell this woman.

"Mr. Engle left behind a bag when he checked out, which we found cleaning his room. We'd be happy to ship it to him, or we can hold it for—"

"I'll send someone," she says.

"Wonderful, we'll hold it for two weeks—"

"He'll be there soon." She hangs up. There's a *click* like a trigger being pulled and no bullet firing.

Brandon stares at the phone a moment.

"They coming to get it?" Amber asks.

"Someone is," Brandon says, hanging up. "Said he'll be here soon."

"Anything good in it?" she asks. Brandon raises his eyebrows. "What? You didn't look?"

"Just a tee and underwear," Brandon says, almost forgetting he's lying until he's done saying it. "She sounded irritated."

"Maybe this was his affair hotel," Amber says. "And she caught him or something."

"Maybe," Brandon says, feeling a sudden trickle of sweat between his shoulder blades. Is that what it was? He was just some quickie affair for a married bisexual—or closeted or something—guy?

"I think affairs are sexy," Amber says. "I'm always trying to figure out which of our guests might be having one."

"Ah...oh," Brandon says, not sure how to respond. He's

certainly played that game before, but he doesn't feel very sexy right now, having been a piece in it.

About half an hour later, the doors open, and a large man in a leather jacket walks up to the desk. He radiates danger. Intentionally, Brandon thinks. And then he spots the tattoo on his neck, thumbnail-sized: the emoji with hearts for eyes. Somehow that seems to take the bite out of him—until he seems to catch Brandon looking and shoots a smirk at him that almost makes Brandon take a step back. And wet himself.

"Hello," Amber says, apparently unfazed by the man's energy. "Welcome to the Bergamot Hotel. How can I—"

"Bag," the man says, holding out his hand.

"Oh. Mr. Engle?"

The man nods. Brandon swallows. This is definitely not Mr. Engle. Amber reaches for the bag. Brandon thinks about stopping her, asking who he is. He says nothing. Amber hands him the bag, and he snatches it from her, quickly looking through it. He frowns.

The phone. It's in his pocket, Brandon realizes. He should—no. This isn't Jon. Something feels wrong. This is not what Jon would want. He knows it. Jon would want Brandon to find him. So he says nothing, and the man with the heart-eyes tattoo leaves, taking the bag with him.

"Well, not an affair, I guess," Amber says when he's gone. "Or one gone really wrong."

"Yeah," Brandon says. "Really wrong."

6.
Ollie

"YOU TOOK HIS PHONE?" NICOLE practically screams. Ollie flinches. He's sitting right next to her, Brandon and Ian on the other side of the table at brunch. Pete, curled up under Ollie's chair, doesn't seem to notice the yelling. "Do you know what kind of trouble you could get in?"

"I know I could get fired," Brandon says, "but, I mean, I already fucked him at the hotel, so—"

"Forget getting *fired*," Nicole says, almost spilling her mimosa as she lets her hands explode in front of her. "You've committed theft! A phone might be expensive enough that it's a felony, too. Probably not. But if it's a work phone, there could be confidential company data on it or—"

"It's not a work phone," Ian interrupts.

"You're defending him?" Nicole asks.

Ian laughs, rolling their eyes. "Absolutely not. Stupidest fucking thing you've ever done, honey."

"Thanks," Brandon says, toasting.

Ian clinks their glasses, and they both drink.

"I think it's romantic," Ollie says. "Like Cinderella."

Brandon smiles hugely at this. "That's what I think!"

"Do *not* encourage this," Nicole says to Ollie, shaking her head. She looks like she's coasting that line between amused annoyed and real annoyed.

Ollie feels the urge to respond but instead reaches out for some of his bacon, breaks off a piece, and holds it under his chair. Pete gobbles it up.

"This is what's-his-name all over again but with criminal charges," Nicole says, not ready to let it drop.

"Which what's-his-name?" Ian asks, smirking.

"The one where he—remember—he wrote a poem about all the moments they'd had and read it aloud to him from outside his window."

"Marcus," Brandon says, lifting his chin a little, "and everything on that list was true."

"But it left off that he was straight and fucking half the girls in our dorm," Nicole says, pointing at him.

"Oh, that's not even my favorite." Ian waves his hand at Nicole like he's interrupting one good story with a better one.

"You have favorites?" Brandon asks, eyes wide in shock, or maybe hurt.

Ian nods. "Oh yeah. My favorite was Mr. Beard."

Brandon sighs softly, looking at his drink. "We had a moment. His hand was on my lower back. There was a spark, a thing!"

"He was our biology professor and pointing out the parts of the spine on you for the class," Ian says, smirking again. Ollie flinches, remembering the secondhand embarrassment. Brandon was talking about their "moment" for a solid month afterward. And he was so sincere about it.

"Doesn't mean we didn't have a moment," Brandon says, looking up but still a little hunched over with shame. He takes a breath, straightening up. "But Jon is different, anyway. We actually did have a moment. We had sex. He knew my tattoo was from DSLWLS. And he gave me his phone number."

"And then you took the whole phone." Ian pats Brandon on the back, as if proud.

"How do you know it's not a work phone, anyway?" Nicole asks Ian.

"You don't give a hookup your work number," Ian says simply, crossing their arms.

Nicole sighs, leaning back, and Ollie reaches his hand out to Brandon, who looks forlorn. Brandon grabs it for a moment and squeezes before letting his hand drop back down to the table, only to raise it again with his glass.

Brunch isn't supposed to be sad, Ollie thinks. Or angry. They've been coming here for years, this weird little café with endless mimosas and white wooden benches, the wallpaper all flowers and birds. It's not the kind of place that gets crowded for brunch, but the waitress knows them and their orders on sight now, which makes it feel special and means the food comes faster.

"I still can't believe you did it," Nicole says. "You should go drop it down a drain right now. If someone traces it..." She shakes her head.

"I just want to give it back to Jon," Brandon says.

"Then you should have given it to the guy who came for it."

"He said he was Jon. He wasn't." He takes the phone out and

puts it on the table, between all their plates of pancakes and eggs. "Is there some way to look up, like, who bought it? It has a SIM card or something, right? Can you trace that?"

"Me?" Nicole asks, half laughing. "I'm not a cop. I can't do that. But someone will."

"I might be able to do something," Ian says, taking it.

"Stop encouraging him," Nicole says.

"I'm not encouraging," Ian says. "If he finds this Jon guy, maybe he'll give the phone back. Jon probably doesn't want to explain why his hotel hookup has his phone either, right? Give him the phone, win-win. Everyone walks away not arrested."

"And maybe he'll be grateful," Ollie says, watching Brandon's face and wanting to cheer him up. "Maybe you guys will talk."

"Talk about pressing charges, probably," Nicole says. "The guy who came back for the bag could have been working for him."

"Okay," Ian says, swiping open the phone. "Password, of course. Could try to force it, but it might lock us out. I could reset it to factory, if you wanted, but that would erase everything. Then you'd have to restore it, which would take a while. Might not work unless I can access— Oh, but there are unread messages. He didn't set it to hide those; we can read them."

"They're from me," Brandon says, a little embarrassed, scraping some egg yolk with his fork. "You don't have to read them."

"One isn't," Ian says. "These other three are though… Oh, honey." They pat Brandon on the shoulder. "We gotta talk about your texting game."

"How do you know how to reset a phone to factory?" Nicole asks, suspicious. "Or hack a password?"

"What's the one other message?" Brandon asks, looking over

Ian's shoulder as everyone ignores Nicole's question. "From his wife?"

"Just from a number, no name saved. Same as yours."

"Maybe he didn't see them, so he never had a chance to enter my name," Brandon says quickly, defensively. "My texting isn't that bad." He downs the rest of the mimosa, probably trying to hide his blush and failing, Ollie thinks.

"'Let me know when you're up. We can do something fun. Again, I mean,'" Ian reads. "And 'sleep well?' the next morning."

"Ooof," Nicole says, cutting into her eggs.

"What?" Brandon asks, looking at Ollie.

Ollie makes himself smile. "I mean, it's sweet."

"Desperate, you mean," Ian says.

The waitress comes by and refills everyone's mimosa. Everyone drinks. Ollie gives Pete more bacon under the table.

"We really connected," Brandon protests, trying to take the phone back. "What's the last message anyway?" He grabs it from Ian. "It didn't pop up for me before. It's an address. And today's date. Two p.m."

Ollie's ears perk up, his body straightening. He suddenly wants to say something when he's been so quiet. "Address, date, and time? Sounds like a meeting." That's something for him to do—something for them all to do. Together.

"Yeah," Nicole agrees, then takes a long drink of her mimosa. "Maybe someone else he was screwing."

"But he'll be there," Ollie says, so excited that he points his fork at Brandon. "If he saw the message—and he had it set so he could read texts quickly off the lock screen, right? So he might have seen it, and he might be there today."

"I could give him the phone!" Brandon says, grinning. "But then why didn't he text me back?"

Ollie hadn't thought that far ahead. Hadn't even thought of finding this guy. It is romantic, returning the phone, and he'd love Brandon to be happy, but it's like his brain is running on autopilot: This is what they'd do in a podcast. A mysterious time and location—go to it. It's a clue. "We can ask him and find out," Ollie says, thrilled to be able to help Brandon in that way, too.

"You'll look like a crazy stalker," Ian says.

"And Ian would know," Nicole says, making everyone, even Ian, laugh.

"I'll go with you," Ollie says. "It's sort of where I walk the dogs. If you want, I mean."

"You walk the dogs on weekends?" Ian asks. "Aren't their owners home?"

"Some, but some like the routine for the dogs. And not having to pick up shit, probably."

"And some people work weekends," Nicole says. "It's very normal."

Everyone is quiet, looking away from Nicole, sipping their mimosas. Ollie looks at Brandon, waiting for him to say yes (he really hopes he says yes!).

"Let's do it," Brandon says to Ollie, breaking the silence. "I won't look as crazy if I'm with a friend. And then…and then"—his voice gets louder, his mimosa sloshing—"I can say we found the phone after we gave the bag to the guy! Like it had fallen out. And I was holding on to it because I didn't trust someone at work not to steal it. Yeah! That sounds believable, right?"

There's another silence no one seems eager to fill.

"Well," Brandon says finally. "Anyone else want to come?"

Nicole and Ian raise their glasses in unison, not making eye contact with Brandon.

"Fine," Brandon says, smiling at Ollie. "Just us, then."

"I have to work, anyway," Nicole says.

"You can't even take all of Saturday off?" Ollie asks. "We miss you." He reaches out and takes Nicole's hand and squeezes it.

"I wish. I miss you guys, too. But I just gotta—when I'm a senior associate, y'know? Then maybe..." Her eyes drift off, and she looks down, sad.

"What?" Ollie asks.

"I think—so there's the cute girl at the coffee shop by work, and I'm pretty sure she was flirting with me, but—"

"Ask her out!" Ian says, slamming the table. "You need to get laid more than anyone I know. More than Ollie even."

"Hey!" Ollie says, surprised anyone, even one of his friends, keeps track of his sex life. "Why me?"

"Sophie was four months ago, and you two lasted three weeks. Juan was, like, three months before that. Unless there's someone you haven't told us about?"

"That just means I'm right on track for someone new," Ollie says, making himself smile. He's been kind of lonely, he thinks, but it's not so bad. And he hasn't been so horny. At least not in a way a toy couldn't handle.

"You're depressed," Ian says.

"No I'm not," Ollie says quickly, wondering if he is and doesn't know it.

"I finished that book you recommended. Only a depressed person would enjoy that thing."

Ollie laughs. "Really?"

"And you're clearly stoned out of your mind," Ian adds.

"It's these new edibles. I didn't want to waste them, but they're so strong."

Nicole, still holding Ollie's hand, squeezes it. "It's okay. They're just trying to make us all as sad as they are since they still can't get over Victor."

"I'm over him!" Ian says immediately, slamming the table again. "I'm just still pissed at him."

"Then why didn't you ever call Tim back?" Brandon asks.

"Tom," Ian corrects. "Because we'd never work. He's too nice."

Nicole nods thoughtfully. "Yeah, nice is terrible."

"Oh, shut up," Ian says, laughing. "Did you even ask out coffee girl?"

"Her name is Sam."

"You know her name?" Ollie says, smiling.

"It's on her shirt," Nicole says quickly. She pulls her hand back, and Ollie feels the air rush in where she'd been holding it, colder than the rest of his arm.

"Still," Brandon says, pointing his glass at her. "You noticed it and remembered."

Nicole glares at him. "Fine, she's hot, so I remembered it."

"So ask her out," Ollie says. "What's the worst that can happen?"

"We make a date, but I have to work, so I reschedule, and then I reschedule again, and then she says to just forget it, and next time I have to get coffee, she gets a senior partner's order wrong and he decides to dump it on me in the cubicle before firing me but the story of me getting covered in coffee gets around the legal world and everyone feels sorry for me but no one will hire me, and I have to go back to living with my parents, who have more of a social life than I ever will again, and I end up selling cheap tights on TikTok as part of a pyramid scheme."

Everyone is quiet for a moment. Ollie feeds Pete another piece of bacon.

"Well, it's good you were thinking it through, I guess," Ian says.

Everyone laughs, and for a moment, Ollie feels the warmth of being with them, with his best friends, again. Teasing, wanting the best for each other, even demanding it. He's not lonely. Not when he's with all of them.

It ends too soon. And it always ends the same way. An alarm on Nicole's phone goes off, and she calls over the waitress with the bill and pays it, waving off the promises from everyone else to Venmo her with a "when you can." She gives them all a hug, says she has to get back to work. "Just trash the phone, Brandon. I know you're not going to, and I love you, but lawyer advice? Wipe your prints off it, and trash the phone."

Ian leaves a little after her—they have a shift at the bookshop—but reminds them to come to drag brunch tomorrow at the Wreck Center.

Normally, Brandon would head home, saying he's got stuff to do, though Ollie suspects he just goes on the apps and starts swiping. But today is special—today he's coming with Ollie to walk the dogs, then maybe check out this mysterious meeting and find his Cinderella.

"I like brunch," Ollie says as they walk outside toward the first of Ollie's dog pickups.

"Me too," Brandon says, wobbling slightly as he walks. "The mimosas there aren't great, but they're good enough."

"Good enough!" Ollie says at almost the same time as Brandon, who stumbles into him, laughing. Ollie laughs too. They walk quietly, and Ollie feels the mood shift, brunch behind them. He barely spoke during brunch, he knows. Did anyone else notice?

"Do you think Ian was right?" Ollie asks. "Am I depressed?"

Brandon is quiet for a moment, and Ollie focuses on Pete trotting ahead of them, little legs pumping.

"I think you'd know that best, right?"

"But from the outside?"

Brandon sighs. "I don't know. I mean, you're quieter than you used to be. And you seem—you used to keep lists, remember? Of all the stuff you wanted to do."

"That was transition stuff. Grow a beard. Karaoke a man's song in the right range. Top surgery."

"No, no, it started that way," Brandon says quickly. "But there was other stuff, too. Pick a major. Have a threesome."

Ollie thinks, listening to the pitter-patter of Pete's feet on the sidewalk. "That was kid stuff," he says eventually. "Checklists of like...adulthood."

Brandon makes a shocked face, and then a surprised laugh bursts out of him. "A threesome is on that list? Then I guess I'm still a kid."

"Maybe you should make a to-do list, then."

Brandon laughs some more, the easy, too-loud laugh of someone still drunk, and they walk quietly again. He knows Brandon didn't give him a real answer. Lists aren't related to depression. But he also knows when he stopped keeping them—after his dad's hit-and-run.

"I like Pete's feet," Brandon says after a while. "He's a good little guy."

"Yeah," Ollie says. "He's the best."

They arrive first at Samba the Pomchi's house, where Ollie has Brandon wait across the street as he takes Samba from the doorman. Ollie tells Brandon about his new podcast and his theories about the sister as they pick up the rest of the dogs and head for the address from the phone. Ollie can tell from Brandon's body language that he's becoming more anxious as they get closer. His legs bend a little more when he walks, the knees coming up too high, and he starts balling his fists and then shaking them out and putting them in his pockets. Over and over again.

"Hey," Ollie says, when all the dogs have fanned out in front of them, toes tapping on the concrete like rain on the window (except Harpo and Linus, whose owners walk their dogs themselves on weekends). "There's nothing to be nervous about, okay?"

"I mean, this is crazy, right? I know I said I felt like I had a connection with him, and I think I did, but what if he didn't? Maybe he wanted to leave everything behind and he'll think I'm some crazy stalker. I mean, I am a crazy stalker right now, right?"

"I think it's romantic." Ollie says, deciding it as he says it. "As long as you're not, like, expecting him to be happy. You're trying. You're going out of your way to do something nice for a guy you like. That's good, I think."

"I should have left the phone in the bag."

"Maybe." Ollie shrugs. "Still, what's the worst that could

happen? He sees you, takes it, tells you to leave him alone, right? At least then you tried. And you know he didn't feel the connection. There's nothing wrong with hoping for something great, if you can."

"'If you can'?" Brandon says. "That sounded pretty depressed, Ollie."

Ollie laughs. "I didn't mean it like that." He's pretty sure he didn't. "I just mean it's good to hope for love. I love how you never lose hope for it."

He looks up and sees Brandon isn't listening anymore. He's stopped short, staring across the street. They're at the address from the phone. It's a pretty boring T-shaped intersection, sort of out of the way and quiet, more in Boerum Hill than Park Slope. It's a weird place to meet up. No one is around; most of the buildings don't even have windows facing this way. Like an alley more than a street. There's a parking lot in one corner, the backs of some apartments everywhere else, a few stores across the street (including a weed one Ollie has been meaning to check out), and one of those old skybridges stretching over the alley. Ollie thinks they're so cool every time he sees one, though he imagines no one uses them. But Brandon isn't staring at the bridge; he's staring at two men under it, who are talking in quiet tones even as their hands dance loudly.

"That's him," Brandon hisses.

"Which one?" Ollie asks, looking at the two men—one is bearded, maybe in his thirties, very hot, and the other is older, balding, and thin in a drained way.

"Which do you *think*?" Brandon says back. "Should we hide?" He ducks behind the building next to them, still watching the men. One of them—the cute one, Jon—glances over and smiles at the gaggle of dogs but doesn't spot Brandon.

"He just smiled at me," Ollie says. The dogs start pulling at their leashes, confused as to why they've stopped walking. Zoey walks around Malkia to sniff at Brandon, wrapping Malkia's legs in the leash. "He seems nice. Go give him his phone."

"He's talking to someone though."

Ollie quickly moves to undo the knot that's forming, but Pete wants to sniff Samba's ass now and everything is braiding. "You want me to tell you when he's done?"

"Yes," Brandon says, leaning against the alley wall, out of sight.

"So I just stand here?" he asks, someone's leash wrapping around his ankle—he doesn't even know whose at this point. "Doesn't that look weird?"

"I don't know—pet one of the dogs or something."

Ollie shrugs, then frees his leg and kneels down to give Pete some chin scratches. He stays facing Jon and the other man. The dogs, feeling the leashes a little laxer, have started to pull out like a starburst. The men are talking louder, but they're still trying to whisper, so their voices sound blurry. He catches just a few words. "File." "Fun." Pete licks his nose.

Finally, Jon turns away, and Ollie is about to tell Brandon to come out of the alley, but then the older man turns and goes after him.

And then the older man's head explodes.

7.
Nicole

BATHROOM BREAK.

Nicole doesn't have to use the bathroom, but she likes to come in here every few hours and stretch, take a moment to check her phone, focus on a few deep breaths, and just close her eyes. Saying she needs a break wouldn't look good though, like she couldn't handle the job, and going to the roof or outside would imply she's a smoker, and she knows she's too young to be a smoker without looking like she's trying too hard. She could vape, but every time she's tried, she's felt silly, like a kid blowing on a bubble pipe, smelling like cheap candy. Not a good look either.

So the bathroom is her little getaway spot. The one a flight up is usually empty on the weekends, the partners all working from home. And it's a little bigger, too—eight stalls—so it gives her room to do a deep stretch, leg out at a 90-degree angle, foot touching the wall, hand on the peach marble counter for balance. She likes getting into her body to get out of her head. She used to do yoga, once. The treasurer of the Black Student Alliance was a part-time yoga instructor and would lead all the members in a free session once a week to stay grounded and refreshed. There's a pleasure in telling her leg to stretch out, hold, her toes to point, and all of it working. Everything going exactly as she tells it.

Next, the shoulders. She turns on her phone as she pulls her head to one side.

Seven missed calls.

Brandon, not in the group chat, weirdly texting just her:

BRANDON

SOS

SOS

SOS

NICOLE PLEASE

She frowns and straightens out her neck, then locks the bathroom door and calls him.

"Oh, Nicole, thank god."

"Brandon, what's going on?"

"A guy just got shot."

She shakes her head, assuming she heard him wrong or he's confused. His voice is high, fast, like that time they did Adderall in college. Everyone agreed Brandon wasn't allowed to again.

"What?" she asks. "What guy?"

There's the sound of barking through the phone.

"Hold on!" she hears Ollie say in the background.

"Brandon, Ollie is with you?"

"The dogs ran away!" Brandon says. "We've been chasing

them. Ollie said we had to. I think we should run, too. Somewhere else. Or…I don't know, Nicole. I've been calling and calling. He's dead!"

"Brandon, who? Who is dead?" She says it loudly enough that the tile walls echo, the words coming back at her. She walks away from the door, tries to remember to keep her voice low.

"I don't know!" Brandon says. "I was waiting around the corner so Jon didn't see me. He was talking to some guy. Ollie was watching and then the dogs started barking and Ollie screamed and I came out of the alley and Jon was running away and there was a dead guy in the street! His skull was, like…open, Nicole. It wasn't just blood, it was…"

"Okay," she says softly. "Brandon. Take a breath." She takes one, too. "Jon was meeting with someone, and that someone got shot?"

"Yes!" He sounds relieved.

"Why didn't you call the police?"

"I called *you*!" he shouts.

"*Why?*" She works hard to keep her voice low, but she wants to shout, she's so annoyed.

"You're a lawyer! I don't want to get in trouble. I still have Jon's phone, and—"

"What?" She leans against the wall, slides down to the floor. Of course he does.

"I don't want him to get in trouble!"

"Samba!" Ollie shouts in the background. Are they at a dance studio? Or are they babysitting?

"Who? Ollie?" Nicole asks, confused by all the noise.

"Sambaaaaaaaaa!" Ollie wails.

"Jon!" Brandon practically shrieks it.

"Jesus fucking Christ, Brandon." Her head falls forward, and she brings her hand up to rub her neck. Time to be a lawyer. Pretend he's the client. Protect him. "Okay. Take out the SIM card. You can do that, right?"

"I think so."

"Do that. Crush it." It's not evidence tampering because the phone has nothing to do with the shooting—shouldn't even be present. At least, that's what she'd tell a judge.

"Done." He sounds so proud. "Should I throw the phone away?"

"No," she says quickly. Fingerprints. Maybe if he tossed it in the water. But it still has those texts, evidence. At least if the police are looking for Jon now, they won't find Brandon instead. "Keep the phone now. I..." She sighs. Calling the cops would actually be easiest. Just tell Brandon and Ollie to relax, give a statement, say they happened to be walking along, they didn't recognize anyone, didn't know Jon, just saw some random guy get shot. But Brandon's a bad liar.

Brandon's crying now. He's trying to hold it back, she knows, but she's heard him cry too many times before. The soft sort of hiccup of a long sob. The way he sniffs twice in a row.

"Where are you?" she asks. "I'll come meet you."

"On the street. We have all the dogs back now." He pauses, and she hears Ollie's voice but can't make out what he's saying. "We're going to a dog park so they can run around more, get it out of their system, he says."

"Address."

She writes it down as he says it, then hangs up. Her eyes focus on the tile floor. It's possible this is all just regular old crime. A bad moment. Or something even sillier—a fight, Brandon and Ollie distracted by the dogs, confused. Ollie seemed pretty stoned at brunch, said his edible was powerful. Brandon could still be drunk. He had a lot more mimosas than anyone else; he always did.

Though the description of the skull felt…

She shakes her head. She has to go see everything for herself. Figure out how much trouble they're in. Then fix it. She could have already made it worse, telling them to take out the SIM card, crush it. It was just a gut reaction, and she was pretty sure of it at the time, but maybe if she'd thought ahead more… But it's not like lawyers are always about being the most legal. There's Ellen Kang, who represents some shady people—she must give them all kinds of counsel. Nicole knows she's not the first lawyer to offer legally nebulous advice. It was over the phone. There's no evidence she told him to do it.

She looks at herself in the mirror. Her face is skewed, worried, angry. She readjusts it into a professional smile.

Not many people would be worth this. But Brandon, Ollie, Ian—they've seen her at her worst, helped her through a lot. The breakup with Eva, that terrible time she tried acid, and the bad night. The smile in the mirror turns genuine for a moment, soft, as she remembers Brandon punching the guy who was trying to drag her out of the club. He socked him pretty well across the jaw, then hopped away, shaking his fist, flinching in pain. Had stunned the guy enough that Ollie could help her up and take her back to the party, hiding in the crowd, where they lost him. Ian took her to the ER, insisted she'd been roofied, and yelled at every nurse until they admitted her, did the blood tests, gave her drugs. All of them stayed by her bed. Refused to move.

She takes a breath and walks back to her desk, gathers her things up.

Don looks up from his desk across from hers. "Actually taking a weekend off, Nikki? At least part of it?"

"My mom was hit by a car," she says simply. She hadn't even prepared the lie. It just fell out of her. Easy. She always thinks of herself as a bad liar, but maybe she's more like Ellen Kang than she thought.

His face falls. "Oh god, Nikki, I'm so sorry. Do you need to fly down there? I can take you to the airport." He's getting out of his chair already.

"She lives in Washington Heights," Nicole says, smiling as politely as she can.

"Oh, right, I—" He sits back down. They both know who he was thinking of: Ashley, one of the other Black junior associates. From Atlanta.

"Thank you," she says, trying to keep her voice kind. "I'll be back soon."

"Take the weekend, Nikki," he says.

"Maybe." She throws her jacket on and heads for the elevator.

She maps the route in Incognito Mode and boards the 5 train headed to Brooklyn. The train is crowded with tourists, families, lots of small children. She tries to go over what Brandon said. Someone Jon—the guy he hooked up with, whose phone he still has—was talking to was shot. While they were talking? Could it have been Jon? Brandon said he had been around the corner. Ollie had been watching. Everything is coming to her second-hand. She needs to talk to Ollie. Look in his eyes to see how stoned he is. See the condition of the body. Then she can call the cops, maybe anonymously. She'll buy a burner phone if she needs to.

It's a nice dog park, sandy with a little fort in the middle for the dogs to hide inside and play on. There are two picnic tables to one side. A bunch of people are at one, packed around it like sardines and glaring at the other table, where Ollie and Brandon sit alone, Brandon with his face in his hands, weeping loudly. Ollie is watching the dogs with a vacant expression. She wonders if she just got dragged out of work because one friend is having a bad trip from an edible laced with something and convinced her other friend that a hallucination happened.

"Nicole!" Ollie says, waving.

She sighs to herself, then goes and sits next to him. "Let's avoid saying names aloud right now."

"Um..." Ollie says.

"Okay," Brandon says, looking up, then hugging her tightly. "I'm so glad you're here."

"Sit up," she says, trying to keep her voice gentle. "Speak quietly." She focuses on Ollie. "What happened?"

"We were going to see Jon—" Brandon starts.

"I need to hear it from him," Nicole says, nodding at Ollie. "He saw it happen, you didn't, right?"

"Okay," Ollie says, whispering with shaky breath. "Yeah, we were going to the address from the phone, and there were two guys talking. Brandon said the hot one was Jon. Brandon was behind a wall, told me to pet the dogs until..." He pauses, swallows. "You think the puppies are traumatized? Will their owners notice? I know pet psychiatrists are a thing, and I always thought they were a joke, but..." He stares off vacantly at the dogs, who are bounding around the fort, tongues long, tails wagging, playing some version of hide-and-seek.

"What happened next?" Nicole asks.

He keeps his eyes on the dogs as he speaks. "I was watching them. They were talking, quietly. But with their hands. I guess maybe they looked a little angry before..." He swallows. "And then Jon turned to go, and the other guy, he was going to go, too, the other way, but he changed his mind and walked back toward Jon, and then there was this soft crackle and..." He swallows. "His head just broke."

"Broke?"

"Part of it just flew off. But I couldn't...I didn't understand it because the dogs started freaking out. And Jon started running, and the dogs pulled in all directions and two of them got loose, so I had to run after them." He turns back to her. His eyes are bloodshot, watery. "Is Pete limping, you think? I feel like he's lifting his back leg a little."

"Focus." Nicole snaps her fingers in front of Ollie's face. "You chased the dogs. You didn't see anything else? Hear anything?"

"There was a sort of hum," Brandon says. "That's when the dogs went nuts."

"Ollie?" she asks.

He shakes his head. "I don't remember."

"Okay," she says. "Did Jon see you?"

"Yeah," Ollie says. "But he doesn't know me. He smiled at the dogs."

She turns to Brandon. "Did he see you?"

He shakes his head.

"And you have the phone?"

He nods. "I crushed the SIM card on the sidewalk like you told me." He takes it out of his pocket, offering it to her, but she leans back quickly, hands far away.

"You keep it for now. I think I need to see where this happened. Then we can figure out how to tell the cops."

"But Jon—"

"I don't give a fuck about Jon," she says, loudly enough some folks at the other picnic table glance over. She takes a breath. Brandon starts to cry again. "Brandon, you don't know this guy. I don't care how good the dick was, if everything you say is true, he's mixed up in something shady and dangerous. Best to get as far away from it as possible. Okay?"

He nods, looking at the ground. "I'm sorry. I know. I know it's crazy, I just feel bad." He takes a long breath that cracks halfway through, an aftershock from crying.

She puts her hand on his shoulder and squeezes. "I know. But none of this is your fault, okay?" She doesn't mention how he should never have taken the phone, how fucking stupid that was. "Let's go."

She stands, Ollie gathers up the dogs, and they lead her back to the alley. She keeps an eye out for cops, police cars, but the ones she spots are just patrolling, nothing extreme. And in a nice neighborhood like this, they'd send out a squadron for a mugging.

"How strong are those edibles?" she asks Ollie.

"Pretty strong," he says. "You want one?"

"Laced with anything?"

He's quiet for a moment, watching the dogs. "Maybe. The guy I bought them from said they were special. I didn't think that meant laced though. He's usually up-front about what's in stuff, but it's definitely a special kind of high."

"Not worn off yet?"

"Almost."

She nods. Unreliable witness. Tampering with evidence. Theft. Failure to notify police of a crime. Ollie's drugs probably don't come from a reputable dispensary if they're laced. She ticks off the crimes and problems in her mind. These are her friends. She'll protect them. She'll do what she needs to. It's not the kind of lawyering she wanted to do. But that's changed before; it can change again. She told herself she wanted to go to movie premieres and wear nice dresses. Well, Ellen Kang wears nice dresses. At the holiday party, she wore something bloodred. She looked amazing in it. Maybe Nicole could be more like Ellen. Maybe that's the kind of lawyer she really is, even if it's not what she wanted to do.

"Here," Ollie says, leading them down a side street that's mostly the backs of stores and a few apartment buildings. There's a skybridge overhead, casting a thick line of shadow, like someone is censoring the alley. There's no police tape, no crowd of bystanders. There's nothing.

"Where?" Nicole asks, not seeing anything on the street. "Where's the body?"

"Huh," Ollie says.

Then one of his dogs—the Afghan—lifts a fringed leg and starts peeing on the wall. Perfect.

8.
Ian

ANOTHER DAY, ANOTHER TERRIBLE BOOK.

The one the mom came into the store for: the latest Princess and Powderpuff. Ian picked it up almost as a kind of penance—they'd been rude, sort of, even if it was maybe deserved. And they were hoping maybe reading some cheerful kids' stuff would make them feel childlike themself, filled with wonder. But it doesn't. It's gender-drenched nonsense, like a pink toy aisle, and it makes them so sad thinking of all the kids forced to walk down this aisle or the blue one, like the walk through the long halls of a prison to their cells, the Barbies on the wall ringing cups against the bars. *Fresh fish!*

No, not sad, they decide, shrugging off that feeling or swallowing it deep down like a pill. It makes them angry. They don't want to be angry all the time. But things just keep making them.

Brunch was good this morning. Having brunch and being onstage are the only times they feel like they can be anything, like they're made of stars, and all the emotions swirl in them. Same as when they were back in dorm rooms, talking identity with friends, playing with the self, with performance, talking philosophy, discovering things. Ollie was always so good to talk to. Ian should try to have some one-on-one time with Ollie soon—though these days Ollie is so stoned, he probably wouldn't notice it was just them.

They're thinking about hurling the book across the bookstore, figuring out how to aim it so it doesn't hit any of the people browsing, when their phone vibrates in their pocket.

TOM

Hi! Your show last night was amazing

Ian smiles. Tom is really a sweet guy. Cute in a dad kind of way, scruffy, glasses. And the sex was good. But he's so nice, it's annoying. After the sex, Ian thought maybe they could click more, turned on YouTube to watch some stuff in bed together, cuddled up. And the algorithm—their algorithm, which should be all drag queens, makeup vloggers, and shirtless guys—showed some pseudo-right-wing bullshit. Ian blew up about it, ranted about how these machines are turning everyone into Nazis. The usual stuff. Tom just nodded, put his arm around Ian's shoulder, brought them close so they were leaning on Tom's chest, and clicked on a Trixie video.

"It sucks" was all he'd said about the algorithm.

Ian felt hot with rage, and now here they were, being comforted like a kid, and that just pissed them off more. They watched the video in silence, Trixie unboxing makeup, and they even laughed with Tom at the jokes, felt relaxed after. But that's not how it's supposed to go, is it? The rage can't just drift off, turn into vapor, and disperse. Rage is hot. It has to burn.

If it had been Victor, he would have raged right along with Ian, and they would have gotten each other riled up, written an angry Instagram post filled with swearing, and then had a sweaty round two.

Tom didn't get angry though. It made Ian feel like there was something wrong with them, seeing Tom's calm in the face of all their rage. So it wasn't going to work out. No matter how sweet, how cute, how good the sex.

TOM

The bit about vinyl almost made me piss myself

Or how good his taste is.

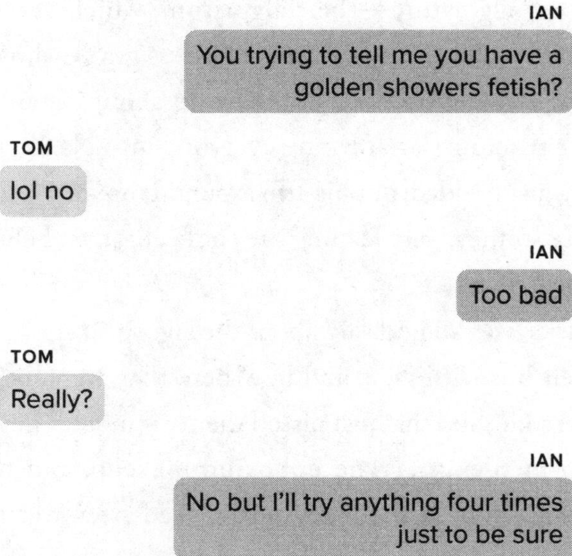

TOM

lol

So do you want to hang out again sometime?

There's this documentary on Jackie Shane playing at Alamo I thought you might be interested in.

Damn it, Ian has been wanting to see that.

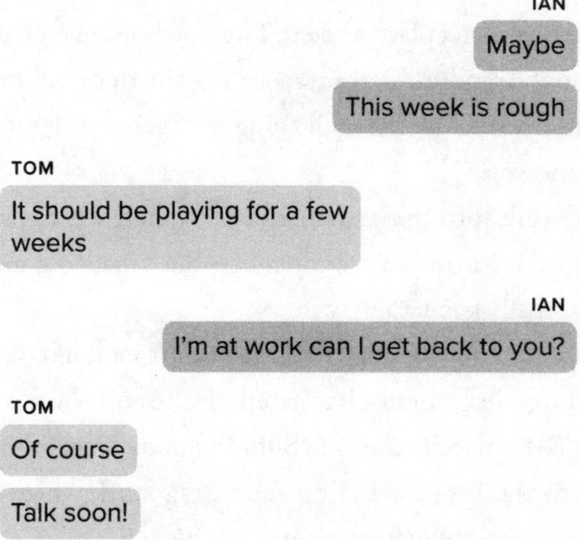

Ian puts the phone down, feeling their mouth corkscrew the way it does when they don't know how to feel about something. They don't mind how thirsty Tom is; it's kind of flattering. But it's not going to work out, right? They're just not compatible. He's so calm, so happy.

But if Ian can't find anyone else to go to the Jackie Shane documentary with them…

The rest of their shift goes quietly. They browse and pick out another book to read, a queer rom-com Brandon recommended. Brandon hasn't texted about his stalking with Ollie, not even by the end of Ian's shift, which feels kind of weird. Maybe he's crying it off, or maybe that means it worked perfectly and they're fucking at home. Ian hopes not; they really want to lie in bed for a while and just relax. They have drag brunch tomorrow, and that's always a lot. Fun, but a lot. Hard to relax when Brandon's head is banging against the living room wall though. But when they get home, it looks like Brandon's plan worked. The door isn't even locked.

"C'mon, Brandon," Ian says, closing the door behind him. "I get the undressing-in-the-hall thing is fun, but at least close the door behind you."

They walk into the apartment. It's quiet, which is weird—Brandon is, unfortunately, a moaner—but it's also a mess. They must have really been going wild.

Except, Ian quickly realizes, this doesn't look like the mess of people untangling themselves from clothes on their way to the bedroom. The place is trashed. Sofa cushions lifted, things taken down from shelves—including their drag stuff, which Brandon has always respectfully kept his hands off of.

"Brandon?" Ian calls. Nothing. Ian stares at one of their wigs, a black bob with silver streaks, lying on the floor like a dead dog. They go to pick it up and quickly find the box it came from, open on the sofa. "Brandon, what the fuck?"

Still nothing. They put the wig in the box. They're going to have to give it a good brush, along with the others dotting the room, splotches of different-colored hair like a clown tried to shave their pubes for the first time.

They knock on the door to Brandon's bedroom. "What is this mess?"

The door swings open. No Brandon. No one.

They take out their phone and open the group chat, looking for an explanation. Nothing.

IAN

I think someone robbed our place!

That's the only explanation, right? They feel the shock of violation, of being vulnerable. It's a cold liquid in their stomach, but then they boil it into a fury as they run to the boxes of jewelry in their room, check their laptop. They really can't afford to be robbed.

The jewelry is a mess, tangled, but nothing is missing. Not even the few expensive pieces. And their laptop is open but on the bed, next to a pair of nipple clamps they haven't used in forever. Nothing stolen. Just rifled through. Invaded.

IAN

False alarm

It's just a mess—were you looking for something?

They wait a moment, but the text stays unanswered. Why would Brandon go through their jewelry though? Why would anyone? It doesn't make sense unless—

Those nipple clamps were Victor's favorites. They'd bought them together, a simple silver pair with a chain between them. Ian would clip them onto him gently, but then later, when they were riding Victor, would tug the chain hard. That's what they remember when they see them—that's why they live in a box under the bed and haven't seen daylight in forever. And that's why they're laid out on the bed. A message. Revenge. For keying his car.

Ian feels themself smile but pushes that to the side. Victor could easily break in and would do this to fuck with Ian. It's amazing it took him so long to retaliate, honestly.

They glance at the time. Five. Not usual work hours, but Ian knows Victor's schedule. And just where to find him. They stomp out, door slamming behind them.

The U.S. marshals' office in Lower Manhattan is technically closed on Saturdays, but Victor comes in to do work. Raphael, his new boyfriend, is a bartender at some fancy restaurant and works Saturday afternoons until closing. And Ian knows Victor only ever cares about four things: his boyfriend, his car, his mother, and his work. He worked the Sunday mornings Ian did drag brunch when they were together. *If I can't be with you, might as well get something done.* Practical. Ian admired that.

Now though, from Raphael's and Victor's Instagrams, Ian knows Sundays are date days. They start at the gym, then brunch at their little neighborhood spot, LightBite, and then some fun activity, like a museum or matinee, or walk in the park, a nice dinner out, and bedtime. Raphael chronicles all of it, right down to Victor stripping down to his boxer briefs before he climbs into bed.

But today is Saturday. And Ian would bet money that Victor is here, at the lovely art deco building with the golden doorway.

They never visited Victor at work before or anything, but they met him outside sometimes, when they were trying to grab dinner together in between their mismatched schedules—Ian working weekends and nights, Victor working weekdays.

Ian marches in, shoulders back, jaw set like they're about to fight someone. Maybe they are.

The building isn't just the marshals' office. They have to find the floor and take the elevator. Funny for law enforcement to be here among dentists and printers, but the marshals aren't especially showy in New York. Most people forget they're here, putting people in witness protection, searching for the most wanted. Ian was not into the idea of dating a cop, but Victor always explained they weren't really cops, and Ian chose to believe it. Stupid. Of course they're cops. Who cares if they're hiding innocent victims, too? Trust a cop to cheat and then break into Ian's apartment as retaliation for a little light vandalism. Which Victor totally deserved. All seven times.

The door to the marshals' office is glass and locked, but there are lights on inside. Ian pulls on the doors then knocks, looking for someone. All they can see is the waiting room, blue carpet, beige walls, photo of the president on the wall. They really never should have dated a cop. They bang the door with both hands, and eventually someone comes to open it. Not Victor though. His partner, Willis. Ian met Willis only a few times. He's impossibly tall and narrow, with deep-brown skin. He always seemed nice, if a little standoffish. But from the way Victor talked about him, they're like family.

"Hi, Ian," he says, leaning in the doorway so Ian can't move past him.

"I'm here to see Victor," Ian says, trying and failing to keep their voice neutral.

"I sort of figured. What about?"

"It's personal."

Willis nods slowly, looking Ian up and down. "Maybe you tell me and I pass it along."

"What are you even doing here?" Ian asks, frustration rising. "This is when he does paperwork."

Willis cracks a smile. "We had to go over a few things. He's at his computer. I saw you on the camera." He points at a camera behind him, through the glass doors. "Said I had to use the can. Thought maybe he didn't need to see you."

"What's your problem?" Ian asks, folding their arms. "I'm allowed to talk to Victor."

Willis gives a faint smile. "Look, Ian, I like you. You're passionate and smart, and you know how to make Victor laugh. And what he did to you was cowardly, and believe me, I let him have it when he told me. Told him it was selfish."

"So nice of you to stick up for me." The sarcasm in their voice wavers a little, like a teenager with a cracking voice.

"But the thing is, he's happy now. No drama, no fighting, no on-again-off-again."

"We weren't like that," Ian says quickly, but the moment it's out of their mouth, they're not sure. They did fight a lot. But they always got back together—that was usually the fun part. Sometimes Ian would start fights just to get back together. They swallow under Willis's gaze. "Look, I'm not trying to get back together with him. This is about what he did today."

"Today?"

"Yeah. I guess he didn't tell you about that, huh?"

Willis considers Ian for a moment, then sighs. "All right, I'll send him out."

"Thank you."

"But, Ian, maybe take a breath. You know, about ten years back, I had to go to this anger-management class after...well, something I'm not proud of." He reaches into his wallet and takes out a card. "You ever want to talk about that, let me know."

"If I take the card," Ian says, voice a growl, "will you go get Victor?"

Willis smirks. Ian takes the card.

"Good to see you," Willis says, going back inside and locking the door behind him. Ian watches him move, too slowly, back into the office, feeling like a cat stalking prey. Then they sigh and lean against the wall opposite the door. They fold their arms again, trying to look angry, which isn't hard, and menacing, which is. Briefly, they wonder if they should text Brandon, or Nicole maybe, just a quick *hey, I'm outside the U.S. marshals' office about to yell at my ex*, in case Victor decides to arrest them or something. But he probably won't. Victor got angry a lot, but he was never a tough guy, never threw his authority around, except to get out of a speeding ticket once. Ian didn't even know what he did for a living until they'd already fucked a dozen times, and then it was kind of hot: Show me your badge, get out your handcuffs.

The door to the waiting room opens, and through the glass Ian sees Victor's face, polite but guarded at first, and then, after he looks through the glass and meets Ian's eyes, falling into something more resigned. Sadder.

Fuck him. Sad? He should be guilty.

He opens the glass door and closes it softly behind him. "Ian. You okay?"

Ian scowls, eyes prickling with tears that must be of rage, a thousand retorts on their tongue, saliva dripping like needles, hungry for everything they want to say. "No," they settle on. "You broke into my apartment. What did you take?"

Victor looks up and down the hallway. It's empty, but their voices echo off the polished floor. He's got a square face and a broad body, like he went pro after being a college quarterback instead of becoming a marshal. He's not in uniform now, just a white Henley and jeans. The Henley is so tight, Ian can almost make out his abs, and they hate themself for searching for them. Their eyes meet his, dark brown and probing. Confused. Innocent. Ian doesn't buy it. This was always the expression he wore when talking to other people, but Ian knows what he really looks like.

"I didn't break into your place, Ian. Why would I?" He sounds more confused than annoyed. That's not him.

"To get me back for keying your car."

Victor's expression changes. The soft, open look closes, a flower turning into a knife. The real him reveals itself: Creases sharpen in his forehead, and his jaw turns hard as he clenches it. "That's *you*? You've been keying my car?" He keeps his voice low, but it's straining. Ian likes this. Likes seeing Victor angry again. The real him.

Ian rolls their eyes. "Like you didn't know."

"I didn't. I thought it was some teenager. Why would you?"

Ian levels him with a glare. "Why do you think?"

Victor shakes his head, and the real face vanishes, turns back into the look he first had, sadder. "Ian, it's been a year."

"Since you cheated on me?"

"Since we ended." There's a flash of the real him at the reminder that he's the one at fault, but then it changes into something else. Sad again, though Ian doesn't know why. Ian hates this new expression on his face. An impostor.

"After you cheated on me," Ian says again, a little louder, hoping for another flash of the real Victor. There isn't one. Just a sigh.

"Yes. After I cheated. Which I apologized for. I can do it again if you want. But I didn't break into your apartment. Go talk to the cops. Ask for Lieutenant George Callas. Say you're a friend of mine, he'll help you out."

Ian scoffs at the fake kindness. "Sure."

"Ian." He pauses, wants to say something else, but instead shakes his head again. "Just…don't key my car again. I'll press charges."

"Don't break into my place again," Ian says. They shove off the wall finally, get close enough to Victor to kiss him. If he would just get angry again, like he should be, they'd probably make out. Duck into the bathroom for a quickie. Victor looks up, and his eye flash. So what if Victor has a boyfriend? He's cheated before. It would be only fair.

This is fucked up—the realization floods into Ian, cold water again, putting out the fire in them, steam rising. They take a step back. They want Victor to be angry at them so that they'll go fuck. So Victor will cheat on his boyfriend with them. This isn't who they are, right? It's not who they want to be, at least.

"Go talk to George," Victor says, his voice hard, not meeting Ian's eyes or seeing the steam there. He takes a step toward Ian, and for a moment, Ian feels it again, their bodies pulling toward each other, magnets of rage, tongues hot, fire on his breath begging Ian to reignite. They stare at each other. The hall is quiet. Then Victor steps back. Takes a long breath and holds it. "Bye."

He goes back inside. Ian goes to follow him, though they don't know why or what they'd say, but the door is locked again anyway, and Victor vanishes into the rest of the office without looking back.

Well, fine. Fuck him. He's clearly lying. Who else would want to break in and not take anything? Ian stares at the waiting room for the marshals' office a few minutes longer before going home.

There, they put on Olivia Rodrigo as loud as their speakers will go, take out some cheap bourbon, and drink it from the bottle while cleaning up the apartment.

9.

Brandon

THERE SHOULD BE A BODY. There was before. Brandon is positive there was one before. He can still see it in his head: the weird white shards stained with pink, like someone dropped a ceramic bowl of skinned peaches and everything had run together, sharp and fleshy and—

He stops, takes a breath, but can't take his eyes away from where the body was. Should be.

"Okay," Nicole says, in a voice that suggests she's humored them long enough.

"No," Brandon says quickly, turning to her, eyes finally peeling off the empty space. "I promise there was a body. Right, Ollie?"

Ollie nods, walking over to the spot where the body should have been. "It's wet here. Someone washed it."

"That doesn't mean there was a body," Nicole says, her expression already tired. "Maybe someone dropped a bowl of Jell-O and you two were high and drunk enough—"

"Peaches," Brandon says softly. "It looked like a bowl of peaches."

Nicole narrows her eyes at him. "Are you okay?"

Brandon doesn't have an answer for that. He thought he was. He thought he was better than okay—he was going to be Prince Charming! Jon was going to thank him for returning the phone, and they'd go on another date and another and get married and live happily ever after.

Except then there was the shattered skull on the ground, dropped peaches, and now it's gone. Is Jon in trouble? Could Jon be mixed up in this? No, Ollie said he turned away before the shot was fired. So Brandon needs to rescue Jon, right? That's what Prince Charming does. Destiny. It never runs smoothly. Maybe this is all just a trial for true love. Except it also feels like he's losing his mind.

"Did you take one of Ollie's edibles?"

His phone buzzes, and he takes it out.

IAN

I think someone robbed our place!

Brandon can't even try to think of that. Too many bad things are happening at once. They come in threes, right? Murder, theft—what's left?

IAN

False alarm

It's just a mess—were you looking for something?

"Are you really on your phone?" Nicole asks, hands on her hips. "You dragged me out of work for a nonexistent body, and now you're on your phone?"

"It was Ian," Brandon says, slipping the phone away. "I don't want to tell them because—" He looks back at the empty spot a body was lying on just a little while ago. "There was a body." He's almost positive.

"Because you're afraid you'll look ridiculous, you mean," Nicole says.

"Look," Ollie says, pointing at the asphalt in the street. The dogs are all sniffing the wet spot on the pavement but not stepping on it, like they're patrolling the border. "There's a little hole."

Nicole shakes her head. "It's a street. There are holes everywhere."

"This one is sharp, fresh," Ollie says, getting down on his knees, surrounded by the sniffing dogs. A big one about head level with Ollie licks him, and Ollie scratches him behind an ear, still staring at the street. Brandon goes over to look at the hole. Just a dent in the asphalt really. Nothing. If he imagined a whole body, that means he's losing his mind.

"Wait," Ollie says, standing and then lifting Pete, excited. "His limp!" He extends Pete's paw to Nicole.

"What? What are you doing?" she asks.

Brandon watches, also not understanding.

"Put out your hand," Ollie says. She does; Pete licks it. Ollie pulls Pete back, and Pete starts licking his wrist.

"What is going on?" Nicole asks, shaking her empty hand.

"Sorry," Ollie says, holding Pete's foot over her hand as Pete continues to lick him. Ollie pops something out from between Pete's toes with his finger. It bounces into Nicole's hand, white and pink like the inside of a peach.

Brandon lets out a deep breath, his posture dropping with

relief, his shaking legs going still. "Bone," he says, smiling as a wave of relief hits him. He's not losing his mind. Then he realizes that means they saw someone killed. His smile turns into a grimace. He was half hoping it was a hallucination somehow. But no, he saw a murder. He's a witness. It sinks into him and feels like something he needs to shower off, even though he knows he can't. "Yikes," he says. Everyone is quiet, politely ignoring that understatement.

Nicole studies the shard in her hand, her expression rippling with disgust, then worry, then landing on her determined expression, the one she always wore before talking to a professor about a grade.

"All right," she says, pocketing the maybe bone shard. "If you're right, to make an entire body vanish that quickly means major players. Scary big."

Brandon swallows.

"Like the mob?" Ollie asks, undaunted. Maybe even thrilled.

Nicole nods. "Or cartels. The government. Corrupt cops. Any kind of syndicate." She leans back on the brick wall, looking more tired than Brandon has ever seen her, even after that time she worked for three days with only one hour of sleep and a twenty-four-ounce water bottle filled with an unholy mixture of Red Bull, espresso, pureed ginseng, and cherry Coke Zero. "I don't really know; this isn't my field exactly. But I know making a body vanish is a lot of work."

"We need to find Jon," Brandon says, voice louder than he meant it to be. It bounces off the walls of the alley. One of the dogs whines. "He could be in trouble."

"No, we don't. He's clearly mixed up in this," Nicole says. "We need to keep you safe. Make sure no one saw you. Witnesses get offed all the time."

Brandon feels his body ripple with cold. Mixed up in this? He didn't shoot the guy. The guy he was with was shot. "He's in danger—we can't just leave him!" He doesn't say anything about true love or destiny or Cinderella; he knows what Nicole would say to that. Judging by her expression, she wants to say it anyway.

"*You're* in danger!" Nicole shouts, arms flying up as she pushes off the wall. "Who cares about some random hookup?" She shakes her head and leans back again, her eyes going somewhere else. "Should we go to the cops? That could be more dangerous. Maybe the phone… It had this location. Jon is probably part of this. But you can trade the phone for your life, maybe. I don't know…" She slides down the brick wall, ass on the sidewalk, and stares up at him. "How do you not get what is happening?"

"He gets it," Ollie says suddenly. "He's just in love."

"With a guy he met yesterday?" Nicole asks Ollie, dismayed, like Brandon isn't even there. Brandon huffs, and one of the dogs lifts its leg and starts peeing by his shoe, so he has to dance away.

Ollie shrugs. "Love is stupid a lot of the time. But he might be right. If we want to know if anyone saw anything, if anyone is in danger and from who, Jon might know."

Brandon shakes his head. He's not in love, and Jon isn't mixed up in this. Or maybe…maybe he is. Mixed up in it. This location was on his phone after all. He checked out so suddenly. Maybe it was to protect Brandon. He feels light inside realizing that. If Jon wanted to protect him, not ghost him, then Brandon needs to help him. For sure. They had a connection.

"So let's find Jon," Brandon says, reassured by his realization.

"Let's figure out who was murdered, and by who," Ollie says. "Let's solve the case. That'll help us find Jon. And it'll keep us safe, right?" He looks at Nicole.

"Maybe," she says, shrugging. "Let me..." She stands up. "There's someone at work who deals with criminal stuff. I can ask her for help. Until then, lie low. Act normal. Don't text about this. And don't tell anyone either; it could put them in danger, too."

"We need to figure it out though," Ollie says. "Look, this is definitely where the bullet hit the street. And judging from the angle, it was fired from..." He puts his finger in the hole, rotating it for a moment, and then takes his other hand and puts another finger on top of the one in the hole, pointing the other way. He then lowers his head to stare the way his second hand is pointing. Brandon can't decide if it looks more like that time they all tried to play Twister in college and Nicole said Ian was cheating—Brandon's still not sure if they were—or like the one time he tried to take hot yoga but it was all super-attractive men in their underwear doing weird bends, and he couldn't keep up and eventually farted the most foul-smelling gas of his life and had to leave and never return.

Ollie stands back up, pointing at a rooftop. The dogs have started to weave their leashes around him again, but he seems not to notice. "There. But they should have had time to line it up if they were prepared. It was a hasty shot, like they were—"

"Are you okay?" Nicole interrupts.

Ollie shrugs, eyes a little glassy. "Just solving the case."

"Let's leave that to the professionals," Nicole says.

"How did you know all that?" Brandon asks.

Ollie shrugs again. "Podcasts."

"He's stoned," Nicole says, shaking her head. "And you're

drunk. Neither of you knows anything. Maybe that wasn't even bone in the dog's toes—"

"His name is Pete," Ollie says.

"And maybe I'm losing my mind, too!"

Everyone is quiet for a moment.

"At least you got out of the office though," Brandon says, trying to cheer her up. "Got some fresh air."

Nicole sighs. "Go home, lie low. Call me if anything else turns up."

"Like what?" Brandon asks.

"I don't know, anything weird. A gun, a ransom note, a video telling you to keep your mouth shut. Anything that feels like it's part of this."

Brandon looks at Ollie, still not quite understanding. Ollie shrugs.

"Be careful," Nicole says, walking away. "And don't tell anyone anything." She steps artfully through the net of leashes and vanishes down the street.

"Do you think she believed us?" Brandon asks. "I don't know if I would."

"I think she did enough. She seems worried. You don't worry about something you don't believe."

Brandon nods. That sounds true. "Did I drag us into something scary?"

Ollie shakes his head. "Exciting." He has a look in his eyes that Brandon hasn't seen in a long time. Not that slightly glazed one he usually does. Something bigger, like when he was about to check something off his list. Something like his old self, which Brandon guiltily realizes Ollie maybe hasn't been in a while.

"'Exciting'? This seems bad." Brandon wonders briefly if this is down to his taste in men, if the universe isn't trying to tell him Jon is his true love, but rather the opposite—that he doesn't have a true love waiting out there for him, and in fact his endless quest to fall in love is less likely than someone getting shot on the street. He laughs suddenly.

"What's funny?" Ollie asks.

"Just that when I think I've finally met a great guy, someone's head explodes."

Ollie laughs. "That is pretty funny." He claps Brandon on the back and then pulls the dogs away from the street. Brandon goes after him. "Don't worry," Ollie says. "Maybe Jon is the guy for you; maybe not. But what's important right now is we find him and figure out who was shot, who shot him and why, who cleaned up the body, and what it has to do with Jon."

"I feel like you're making one of those bulletin boards with red string in your mind," Brandon says.

"I am!" Ollie says. "Once I drop off the dogs, I'm going to make one for real, too. There's an office-supply store two blocks from the Strongs."

Brandon sighs.

"Want to help?" Ollie asks.

Brandon thinks for a minute. He wants to find Jon, but he doesn't want to do whatever all this is. Not yet. His head hurts, and he's not sure if it's a hangover or something else.

"Maybe later?" he says. "I gotta nap. Eat."

"Oh, sure, sure, we'll regroup later. Text me—no, call me. That's what Nicole said. No evidence." He grins and leads the dogs away, leaving Brandon standing alone at the entrance to the alley.

Brandon walks home in a daze, wondering how much of what he saw was real. His body feels shaky, like he hasn't eaten, and all he can think of is Jon, next to him, holding his hand like they did in bed, whispering something in his ear: *They'll kill me next, then you.*

Brandon shakes his head, dispelling the fantasy, or whatever the fantasy turned into. He will not think, he decides. Much better to not think. He counts his steps instead, all the way back to his apartment, where he finds Ian on the floor, dusting under a shelf, the apartment spotless except for half a bottle of bourbon on the counter.

Ian looks up as Brandon comes in. They're wearing a pink wig. They sigh heavily. "You will not believe the day I've had."

10.
Ollie

OLLIE PUSHES THE ROLLING BULLETIN board down the street. He thought about getting a smaller one to hang on the wall, but he assumes that when the Strongs told him he could make the guest room "his space," they didn't mean holes in the walls or that impossible-to-take-down sticky stuff. Besides, this way, if he needs to, he can flip it around so people don't see it, or roll it somewhere else.

The office-supply store didn't have red string, but the Strongs have a crafting closet, and he bets he can find some in there, and they said, *Feel free to use anything. The space is so inspiring.* And right now, Ollie is feeling very inspired. It's probably indicative of something, his excitement over seeing a man's head blown off, the urge to solve this mystery. Maybe it has to do with the fact that he never really finishes anything anymore, and with a mystery, there's always a solid end point, a check on the list, a culprit unmasked. Maybe it has something to do with his dad. He can think about that later. After he's solved the case.

He finds red string in the crafting closet and brings it to his room with the bulletin board and some sticky notes and thumb tacks he bought. He wonders if he should feel more…something. Shaken? Brandon seemed shaken. But Ollie was mostly worried about the dogs. He hopes they don't have any trauma. The dead guy was dead. There was nothing to be done about that. But the dogs were all freaking out. There was no time to be shaken. And now, as he thinks back on it, the sound of the skull cracking, the blood on the street, the weirdly sweet metallic smell, it doesn't bother him. It's more like remembering a movie. A movie where he's the detective.

He starts writing down what he knows: Jon, the address, the phone. He constructs a timeline, best as he can remember it: Jon checked in, checked out early; they went to the address; the man died; they collected the dogs, went back; the body was gone. How long was that? The meetup was at two, and it's six now. It took them a while to catch the dogs and then longer before Nicole showed up, and then they went back to the body, talked, and Ollie went shopping and came back. So five? Four thirty? He's not sure. The edible has mostly worn off now, but it makes remembering what happened while he was on it a lot harder (he really needs to put those aside, stick to the gentler ones, especially if he's working the case).

He'd make a good detective, he thinks, standing back to stare at his work. This is a good start. In fact, all four of them together would make a great detective agency: Nicole could handle the legal stuff, Ian's stalking skills could find anyone and have apparently led them into some light hacking skills, and Brandon's taste in men would ensure a never-ending supply of clients—plus he's good with handling people, always sees the good in them. It's why he falls in love so often. Ollie would be the detective though. He thinks that might be something he could be good at. Well, he'll find out, anyway. But if he is, maybe they could do it together—that could be their thing: one big gay detective agency. And then they'd see each other more than once a week, have time to talk about things, real things again.

He's getting ahead of himself. He still has no idea what's going on (timeline or no) and there's no next episode coming, like on a podcast. He'll have to go figure things out himself. But first he should try to see if what he does know points him anywhere. And there's always one person he loves to unpack those podcasts with. He pops in an earbud and dials.

"Oliver! I wasn't expecting to hear from you."

"Hi, Mom."

"Wait, wait, the gals and I were just drinking margaritas and playing never have I ever. These ladies, let me tell you, are prudes. You know it's true, Steph!" she shouts to someone, then laughs.

Ollie laughs with her. Mom's retirement community sounds pretty wild. It's part of the reason he doesn't visit much and instead she comes into the city. If he goes there, he's afraid of what he might find out about her.

"We were just finishing up anyway though—let me go outside so we can talk. Bye, ladies! It's my son on the phone! See you tomorrow!" Ollie can hear other women saying goodbye and shouting, "Tell that good-looking son of yours hello!" and laughing. He wonders how much they know about him. "Okay, Ollie, it's quieter now. Did you call because you listened to the last episode? I think it was the sister. I thought maybe it was the mom because of her prescription, but after they revealed she'd lied about her piccolo lessons, I think definitely the sister. The timeline works now—she could easily have driven out to meet Kaylee at the lake, not knowing Sarabeth was going to be there, too, and drugged Kaylee with their mom's medicine, then, suddenly caught by Sarabeth, run her over with Kaylee's car before dumping everything in the lake and fleeing." His mom talks in a fast excited hush, words blurring together, but Ollie understands it all perfectly. They have these chats every week.

"I think the same! Unless the piccolo teacher was lying about her not showing up for the lesson—he had been Kaylee's teacher, too, and Kaylee had said she'd had a fling with an older man in high school."

"Oh, I forgot about the friend saying that. That's a good point. Plus, we're only four episodes in! They must have at least eight more big twists."

"Oh, at least." Ollie flops down on the mattress, staring at his bulletin board. Pete leaps up onto the bed next to him, walks in a circle a few times, and then settles into a bun. "So..." he says cautiously, wondering how to get his mother's opinion on his new case. Nicole said not to talk about it. So he won't (not for real anyway). "I was thinking of doing my own podcast."

"Oh, Ollie, how wonderful! You'd be great at it."

"Thank you. But I need to solve an unsolved case first, right?" He looks across at the bulletin board. An unknown case, really.

"Well, sure. You know, my friend Margaret, she says that her daughter's friend's aunt disappeared, and no one ever found her. People say she ran off with another woman, but no one could prove it. Or so I heard. You want me to get her name?"

"No, no, I found a case. These two guys said they saw a guy get shot, but when they went back, no body."

His mother gasps with excitement. "Oh, that's a good one, Ollie. What happened next?"

Ollie stares wide-eyed at the bulletin board. "...I don't know yet."

"Well, you've gotta find out!" She sounds so excited, like it's already a real podcast and it just ended on a cliffhanger.

"Yeah, but I don't know where to start."

"What do you mean, you don't know where to start? Of course you do! You talk to the witnesses, you go to the police for their report, and then you talk to local businesses to see if they recorded anything, just like in the podcasts."

Local cameras—that's a good idea. He should have thought of that (he was kind of stoned, but still).

"I know, I just don't know how to..."

"You go and you ask, honey! You make a list, and then you go and do it. Oh, I'm so happy you're doing something."

"I do stuff," Ollie says, voice too defensive, like he's a small child (he's her child, but still, he's an adult now, right?). "I dog walk."

"I know, I know, honey, but I mean something for you."

"Oh."

"You just haven't seemed too excited about anything lately. Haven't...taken much initiative. Which is fine! You can't force it. I'm just excited you found something."

"Well...maybe. I still need to do it."

"You will," she says confidently. He can hear her unlocking the door to her little condo on campus in the background. "I'll start finding you recording equipment so you can do it well. You want good sound quality; I hate those podcasts where everyone sounds mealy-mouthed. This one isn't in the Appalachians, is it? Those accents—"

"No, it's local."

"Great! Oh, this will be fun. I'll be your producer. Oh, or maybe your cohost. Does that sound fun?"

"Yeah," Ollie says, suddenly drowning in his mother's plans.

"You sound worried. Are you worried?"

"No, no."

She pauses, and he can see her pursing her lips. "Is this bringing up stuff about your father?" she asks, her voice softer, more nervous.

"No, Mom," he says quickly.

"All right!" She bounces immediately back to excited. "Well, get to work. I'll start reading microphone reviews."

"Yeah. Thanks, Mom."

"Anytime, honey."

Ollie clicks off the phone, still staring at the bulletin board. He tears his eyes away and goes over to the little Tupperware of edibles he put in the nightstand drawer. Pete looks up as he pops it open.

"I know, I should focus. But one more won't hurt."

The new edible hasn't even kicked in by the time he gets back to the street where the man got shot. Pete walks a little slower as they approach it, then pees against a hydrant. Ollie is pretty sure this is a bad idea—returning to the scene of the crime. But he's not the criminal, and they did it once already. Though Nicole told them to lie low, and this probably isn't that, but what is, really? Staying inside? He has dogs to walk.

Ollie looks around at any stores that might have cameras facing the alleyway. It's mostly the backs of buildings on this side, and he doesn't see any doors or cameras. But across the street, facing the alley, is that weed shop he keeps meaning to drop by: Paradise Planet. It's got a big neon sign with a green palm tree against a red circle on one side and a pink flying saucer beaming up a marijuana leaf and a cow on the other. The building itself is painted bright teal, the windows yellow. It's gaudy and weird and has two cameras over the door. Ollie grins and walks over. His little bin of edibles is getting low anyway, and here they won't be laced with anything.

Plus clues, maybe.

Inside, it has that heavy musk of dried pot mixed with the candy smells of the edibles. No one else is in here aside from the girl behind the counter, who glances up at him and then grins at Pete.

"Cute dog," she says.

"Thanks," Ollie says, walking over and trying not to stare at various boxes and bags of weed and weed-laced things, all set up on the pastel counters. "His name is Pete."

"Awww, hi, Pete," she says, coming out from behind the counter and kneeling down to pet him. Pete flops onto his back to give her better access, and she laughs, scratching him. "I'm Safiya."

She glances up at Ollie and smiles. She's pretty. Black wavy hair up in two topknots at the front and pouring down her shoulders. Olive-toned skin, heavy kohl, a black-and-white flannel over a crop top, a lot of earrings, a nose ring, and a thick lace choker over her Adam's apple. She's staring at him a little while, too, and Ollie realizes they've probably clocked each other. And that she's waiting for his name.

"Ollie," he says.

Safiya stands, nearly a foot taller than him in her platform shoes. "Nice to meet you, Ollie." She leans a little closer. She smells really good, like the shop. "We just got in these amazing gummies I've been trying to hold back for folks like me. Body high that triggers the best kind of euphoria. And they're pineapple."

"That would be cool..." he says.

She walks back behind the counter and takes out a large, square yellow gummy dusted with crystallized sugar. Fancy. Artisanal. And big enough that it's going to be several bites. He stares at it for a moment before looking away, back up at her. She's staring at him. Her eyes are golden.

"I will for sure take one," he says, taking out his wallet. "And maybe, if you can, some information?"

She tilts her head. "Like my number?"

Ollie feels heat rise in his face like a firework display going off all at once. "Oh, I mean..."

She laughs, but it's a little resigned. "Relax. It's okay. I'm not usually that forward, but you have a cute dog."

"Oh, well, it's not that I would say no," Ollie says quickly. "I just didn't think—"

"You were going to ask something else."

"Yeah." He feels sad saying it, but he's not sure why. He's usually not this bad at flirting, but he's never had to ask someone for their store's security videos before, so he might be bad at that. "I was going to ask if those cameras out front work and if I could look at the tape of earlier today if they do."

Her eyebrows rise, and she crosses her arms. "Oh. Huh." She

bites the corner of her lower lip, staring at him, evaluating. It's very hot. "What for?"

"Oh." Ollie nods; he should have been prepared for that response. "Well…I'm a detective." No, a bad lie. It comes out sounding like a question. "No, not really. I'm a dog walker. I'm trying to be a detective though."

She keeps staring at him, chewing her lip, gold eyes unblinking. "How many dogs?"

"What?"

"How many dogs do you walk?"

"Uh, seven," he says, not sure what kind of test this is.

"All at the same time?" She narrows her eyes.

"Yes? I mean, um, yes."

Her expression cracks into a faint smile. "That's probably pretty cute."

Ollie grins, more ready for the flirting this time. "It is. They fan out in front of me and pull me like a kite."

She laughs, the lip chewing sadly done. "Okay, so what do you want to see the tapes for, Detective Dog Walker?"

"I think something happened this afternoon that they might have recorded."

She smirks. "Yeah, I kind of figured. What happened?"

Ollie frowns. "Something bad."

"Bad?" She narrows her eyes. "You want me to help you out based on that?"

"For Pete?" Ollie asks, nervous now. She's getting defensive. "He has this thing he does when he runs where his butt kind of wiggles." Her expression relaxes. "Oh, and if you wake him up, he makes the cutest confused little 'rooo?' noise."

She grins at that, eyes going over to Pete. "He's trying to win me over with you. You think I should help him out?" Pete sploots on the floor. "Yeah, I think he's pretty suspicious."

"I'm not," Ollie promises.

Safiya looks up at him. She looks a little nervous now. "You're just trying to get some information?"

He nods. "To help my friend."

She sighs and glances at the door behind her, then leans over the counter a little, voice lower. "I didn't see anything but…someone else already came in, took the tapes."

Ollie feels his body sway with shock for a moment, and Pete leaps up, knocking his head into Ollie's shin. The world seems to steady. He kneels down to pet Pete, who immediately flops back, belly up. "Who took them?" Ollie asks, his voice weak.

Safiya comes back around the counter and sits on the floor next to him, petting Pete's tummy. "I had a dog, but she died a few months ago."

"Oh," Ollie says, trying to follow but still feeling the electric aftershock of knowing the tapes were taken. "I'm sorry."

"I'll tell you all about who took them, and throw in that gummy, too, if you take me out to walk dogs with you one day this week."

"Really?" Ollie asks, surprised.

"And buy me a coffee," she says, flashing him a smile.

"Deal," Ollie says.

She gives Pete's belly one more rub and stands up, going behind the counter and wrapping the gummy as she speaks. "Big guy, all muscle. He bribed my manager for the tapes, had lots of cash. I got really bad vibes off him." She puts the gummy in a small paper bag, then takes out her phone and slides them both across the counter. "Funny tattoo though."

"Tattoo?" Ollie asks. That sounds clue-like. Clue-ish?

"It was of the heart-eyes emoji, on the side of his neck. Didn't match his whole thing at all."

"Huh," Ollie says, not at all sure what that means. He takes her phone and quickly enters his name and number.

"Just don't get killed before you take me dog walking," she says.

"I'm trying not to get killed at all. And let's do a weekday—I have more dogs then."

"Sweet talker." She takes the phone back and types something. Ollie feels his own phone ping and takes it out.

UNKNOWN NUMBER

He laughs, saving the number as *Safiya*. "I'll text you the best times and where to meet. We can go to a dog park and play with them."

"Save that for the second date," she says, waving him off like she's scandalized. "I'm kidding," she says, straight-faced after a moment. "That would be amazing; don't save it for anything."

"I won't," he says, taking the gummy. "We'll do it Monday if you want."

"Yes please," she says. "Thank you."

"I'll text you where to meet," Ollie says, backing out but still smiling. It's that awkward walk-away moment, and he's never super sure how to handle it, so he focuses on Pete instead and says,

"C'mon, Pete, we'll see her in a few days." Pete follows him to the door, and Ollie looks back up once. "We're both looking forward to it," he says, then leaves. That was pretty smooth, he thinks.

Around the corner, he excitedly takes out his phone.

OLLIE

I have a date!

He grins and puts it back in his pocket before remembering everything else. He might have a date, but someone else has the tapes. Which probably have him and Brandon on them.

11.

Nicole

OLLIE

I have a date!

NICOLE FROWNS, ALMOST TYPING IN *How does lying low get you a date?* But she refrains. Ian is still on the chat, and it's best to keep them safe. She's at her desk in a nearly empty office, thinking of maybe going home before nine on a Saturday for once. She could text Ollie privately, but maybe it was just a dating app or something. Besides, this could all be nothing. She's still not convinced they actually saw anything. They probably just wasted her time, which pisses her off a little, but better safe than sorry. She said she'd look into it, and she will—she'll talk to Ellen Kang. Ellen represents all kinds of criminals—good guys, too. She even used to be an ADA, but somehow now she's the partner who works with folks like McClintock Arms, the Martin Pharmaceutical Company, and some people Nicole knows are crime bosses. She'll know if anyone is after Nicole's friends.

Nicole's not entirely sure how to broach it: *Hey, my friends think they saw a murder and then the body was removed, and I know you work with a lot of criminals, so maybe you could ask around and find out if they're crazy?* But if she makes the appointment for Monday now, she has all weekend to come up with a good story.

Maybe she'll just say she's interested in what Ellen does—fuck, maybe she *is*! She felt so in control while Brandon and Ollie were losing it. Well, while Brandon was. Ollie wasn't spiraling out so much as spiraling in, gathering all the information like it was a new pack of stray dogs for him to walk. But they were both looking to her for advice, and she gave it so easily. No researching, no helping someone else with case notes but, in the action, making stuff happen. It was overwhelming, but it felt good to actually be doing something.

She hasn't really *done* anything in years. In college she was going to save the world, be an activist lawyer fighting for change, but then law school made her realize she needed to be smart before she could be idealistic, and then the law firm just made her want a boring, comfortable life, which is better than the no life at all she has. Expectations lost their firmness bit by bit, a bowl of ice cream left out to melt into simple sweet soup.

But helping Brandon and Ollie? That was something outside all her expectations. And it felt good. But also terrifying. Maybe she's not ready to be Ellen Kang, but...she's not against learning more.

She goes upstairs to the partners' floor. Ellen Kang's office isn't one of the big ones—despite how much money she brings in, she's not a name partner. Her office is down a hall, out of sight, next to Jeremy Blatt, one of the oldest senior partners, who doesn't come in much anymore. They share a secretary, too, an older white woman named Cherie who always smells like cigarettes. But she's not in right now. Not shocking. Nicole should have emailed Ellen to make the appointment, but she wanted to beg a little, if possible. She sighs and turns to go back downstairs, when Ellen Kang's office door opens.

Ellen's head pops out, short hair a little tousled, wearing bright red lipstick and a smoky eye. She stares at Nicole, eyes narrowing, and for a moment, Nicole feels caught doing something wrong without knowing what.

Ellen shrugs, her long neck bobbing out the side of the door. "Cartoons," she says.

"What?" Nicole asks, confused.

"Just get in here." Ellen Kang's head vanishes back into her office. The glass walls' privacy screen is up, and the lights are out, so Nicole isn't sure what's going on, and for a moment, she's worried that Ellen Kang already knows everything somehow. That some crime boss has asked her to give Nicole a talking-to, get her to give up her friends, maybe even kill her. But she can't say no to a partner. So she walks into the office.

Ellen Kang's back is to her, a tight blue dress unzipped to halfway down her back.

"Zip it up, would you, Cartoons?"

"Oh." Nicole steps forward. Not an assassination, then. She zips the dress to the top, watching Ellen Kang's skin vanish under the blue fabric, feeling a strange thrill at having seen so much of it, at how smooth and pearly it was.

Ellen Kang steps forward and turns around. The blue dress is high-collared and sleeveless, a corset fit that flares out at the waist, a chain of pleating that creates a long loose shaft of a skirt. She looks gorgeous; it's a dress for a party, not work. But then, Nicole remembers, it is Saturday night.

"Thanks," Ellen says. Just Ellen, Nicole tells herself. She just zipped her dress up after all.

"Sure. Did you say 'cartoons'?"

Ellen smirks, going over to her desk. The office is plush, like all the partner offices, but more feminine than Nicole would have imagined, with a white armchair and ottoman with a lavender throw pillow, a soft pink rug. Ellen sits down in the armchair and starts putting on a pair of blue heels. "Sorry," she says, not looking up. "The partners don't know every junior associate's name, but you do earn nicknames from us after a while."

"And mine is Cartoons?" Nicole asks, wondering how bad that is.

"Someone noticed you're in the office more than anyone else," Ellen says, then looks up, a wicked smile on her face. "Except Saturday morning."

"I have a standing brunch," Nicole says, defensive. "I don't watch cartoons."

"Relax," Ellen says, standing. "It's far from the worst of the nicknames. It's cute, right? Reminds everyone how hard you work, makes you sound sort of innocent. Way better than Tuna Lunch and Pitstains."

Nicole frowns, knowing exactly which other associates she means. "Yeah."

"Your real name is...Nikki?" Ellen tilts her face slightly and squints with one eye, like she's expecting to get a slap for guessing wrong.

"Nicole."

Ellen nods. "I was Ellie for years at my first firm. Nicole. I'll try to remember it. Thanks for the help. I have a date, and this guy, I think he's just trying to show off, but it's some black-tie fundraiser, and I didn't want to go all the way back uptown to change, so I brought this dress. Thing is too fucking tight though."

"You look great." It comes out soft, more appreciative than it should.

Ellen looks Nicole over, as if evaluating how sincere she is. "Thanks." She leans back on her desk. "So what were you doing outside my office?"

Oh. Shit. She thought she'd have the weekend to come up with a story. "I was, uh, trying to make an appointment to see you."

"This about your mom? She okay?"

Nicole blinks, confused, until she remembers the earlier lie. That must have gotten around. "No. I mean, she's fine. Just grazed and sort of overreacted." Really, if her mom were hit by a car, Nicole wouldn't know for a few months until her mom casually mentioned it in a rare phone call, as if it were old, dull news.

"Okay, so?" Ellen asks.

Nicole is silent, trying to think. She has no story. She is unprepared.

"You okay?" Ellen asks.

"My mom wasn't hit by a car," Nicole says. This always happens. When she isn't prepared, she falls back on the truth. Not great for a lawyer. "I lied."

Ellen grins, as if this is fun. "All right, so what's the truth?"

"My friends..." Nicole sighs. "Two good friends. They think they saw a murder. They freaked out and called me. But when I went to see them, there was no body. There was evidence of one maybe having been removed though."

Ellen's eyes widen, not in shock exactly, more in curiosity. She adjusts an earring. A cat studying prey. "So you came to me? Why not call the cops?"

"I…know you work with a lot of larger organizations that keep track of crime in the city," Nicole says, the words coming out too slowly as she focuses on being careful.

Ellen laughs, crossing her arms. "Your euphemism is shit, but I like that you didn't sound judgmental when you said it." She picks a black purse up off the desk and walks past Nicole, out the door. Nicole follows, not sure if she's just gotten herself fired. "So you're worried your friends are witnesses and next on some kind of list, so you kept them from the cops. Solid call." Ellen says, headed for the elevator. "Sure, I can ask around about bodies vanishing." She says it like she's going to check the weather. They stop in front of the elevator doors, which reflect them both: Ellen all glamour, Nicole barely her shadow. Ellen leans forward and runs her middle finger over the corner of her mouth, smoothing out a lipstick smudge Nicole didn't even see. Then she leans back and hits the button. "For now, tell your friends to keep their heads down, out of sight. Let me know if anything else turns up."

"That's exactly what I told them," Nicole says, feeling proud. Her phone buzzes in her pocket. She ignores it.

"Well, good on you, Cartoons," Ellen says, getting into the elevator. "I'll be in touch if I hear anything." She hits the button in the elevator, and Nicole almost follows her in before realizing she just has to walk down one flight, and she's not really done for the day. Ellen turns around, looking like a sapphire set in a crown, and smiles as the doors close.

Nicole stands alone in the office for a moment, letting everything that just happened wash over her. *Good on you*, Ellen said. That felt nice. Knowing she told the boys the right thing to do. Hopefully it's nothing, hopefully Ellen tells her she heard nothing, and they can dump the phone and forget all about all this, just go on with their lives. That's the best outcome. If everyone just leaves this alone and forgets anything ever happened.

Her phone buzzes again.

IAN

A date? Well if you decide to steal their phone like Brandon, maybe we can start a collection

OLLIE

Not funny

Nicole sighs. Her friends aren't really great at leaving things alone.

12.
Ian

"YOU WILL NOT BELIEVE THE day I've had," Ian says with a sigh when Brandon walks in. They're still on their knees, cleaning up and looking for bugs or anything Victor might have planted. And they're wearing one of the wigs they found on the floor—a pink updo with a huge cotton candy–looking bun. Just to make the process seem less like a chore. It hasn't exactly worked. But the bourbon has. Though that might also be why it feels like Brandon is taking forever to answer. They'd understand him being stunned by the look—wig, briefs, and nothing else—but it's warm in the apartment, and why clean in clothes when it'll just make them dirty? It's not like Brandon hasn't seen them in their underwear before.

But no, Brandon *is* taking a while to answer. And he has a weird look on his face—haunted almost. Ian looks down at their underwear, making sure there's no awkward stains or anything hanging out—nope, they're covered. They look back up at Brandon. "You good?"

That seems to shake him out of it. "Oh, yeah, just…based on your texts, this is not what I expected."

He says it kind of funny, but Ian doesn't mind. They stand up and take off the wig, putting it on its stand on the shelf. They're all back in place now. "Yeah, it was..." They shake their head, not wanting to get into it being Victor, the confrontation—which will lead to the pitying look in Brandon's eyes, the group chat going pseudo-intervention as everyone tells Ian that this is what they get for being obsessed and keying a car now and then. Ian will tell him later. Maybe everyone at once, at brunch next week when they've had a few. "It's taken care of," Ian says with a shrug, then sits down on the futon. "How was your thing? You see your man? Play Prince Charming?"

Brandon stares a moment, and Ian is worried they've said the wrong thing and he's going to start crying. They love Brandon but really don't want to deal with that right now. "That bad?"

Brandon shakes his head quickly. "He just wasn't there. It was nothing."

"You were gone a while for nothing."

"Ollie and I walked for a while, and then I just...wandered around, wondering what I'm doing with my life."

"Awww, honey." Ian pats the futon next to them. "Honestly, same. Except I cleaned up instead of walking. I feel like maybe I'm making some bad choices lately."

"Me too," Brandon says, sitting down.

"But we can get better. Just gotta try," Ian says, arm around Brandon for a side hug.

"Yeah," Brandon says, laying his head on Ian's shoulder.

"Wanna order from that taco place and watch *The Nanny*?"

Brandon nods on their shoulder. Ian hugs him a little tighter. They know the world can be cruel to people who love love. The one time Ian really fell, it was more pain than anything else in the end. They can't imagine doing it over and over again like Brandon.

They grab their phone and order the tacos—Ian is happy Brandon went for that, since all the other delivery places are more expensive—and turn on *The Nanny*. It's not until halfway through the third episode and second taco that Ian sobers up enough to realize Brandon really is acting kind of weird. Not laughing at *The Nanny* as much, or Ian's one-liners. He's quieter, almost defeated. He doesn't even respond when Ollie texts about having a date and only manages a slight smirk when Ian texts back making fun of Brandon while sitting next to him on the sofa. Ian isn't sure what to say. This Jon guy was another schmuck who ghosted Brandon, but until Brandon says something about it, Ian doesn't want to go into "you're better than that bitch" mode. But they will, soon as Brandon says he's ready for it. For now, though, there's tacos and TV.

Ian goes to bed first, since they have to be up early for drag brunch at the Wreck Room, but they can tell Brandon's still upset, and there's really only one thing he can be upset about. "I don't know what's going on with that guy, but if it's meant to be, I'm sure you'll find him again." They give Brandon a tight hug. What else can they do?

Brandon is quiet for a moment before saying, in a strange voice, "Maybe."

Drag brunch is more of a family-friendly event, so Ian's usual combination of filthy stand-up and their lip sync to "HOT TO GO!"—which involves faking a lot of orgasms—isn't really the vibe. Instead they have a bit they do lip-syncing to "Surface

Pressure" from *Encanto* while juggling a bunch of plates of fake food like an overwhelmed waitress, dressed in a fun '60s number, and then a backup role when Cheong Mendes does his "A Girl Worth Fighting For" number, from *Mulan* (Constance is the girl). Otherwise, it's mostly joking with customers, walking that line between funny, mocking, and flattering without being too sexy about it, which admittedly is difficult when you look as good as they do. They have regulars: some cute families who love to come see "Miss Constance" sing, and some straight girls and gay boys who are fans of their evening shows, too. It's busy, hectic, but fun. And the tips are good.

There's a good-looking guy sitting in their section today—alone though, which is weird. No one goes to brunch alone, especially not drag brunch. And he orders only coffee. Ian wonders if he's a talent scout, but he's so big and square-jawed, kind of rough, not at all what Ian thinks of talent scouts being. And the weird emoji tattoo on his neck makes him look even rougher. Which Ian likes, of course. They try to be a little flirtier with him, then a little funnier, but his expression stays sort of at a half smile, the kind where Ian can't tell if it means anything. They hope this isn't a prelude to a hate crime or anything, but he's gone after their solo and leaves an adequate tip, so maybe he was just looking for some coffee. Who knows? New York takes all kinds. Funny tattoo though. Which is what they text the group about when they have a break.

IAN

Weird guy in my section today

big and mean but ridiculous emoji tattoo

OLLIE

Was it the heart eyes?

BRANDON

Heart eyes?

They text it almost simultaneously.

IAN

WTF? Is that some popular new tattoo I don't know about?

The chat goes silent. Ian watches both Brandon's and Ollie's "…" appear and disappear a few times, but no one says anything. Very weird, in an itchy, people-are-talking-about-me way that Ian hates. Did they do something wrong?

IAN

What's going on?

NICOLE

I have no idea about the heart eyes tattoo guys?

BRANDON

You said not to tell!

IAN

Tell what?

They feel very anxious now. Why would they be left out? Have they been secretly annoying these people they thought were all their besties, the few people in the world who would never get really annoyed with them, never abandon them?

NICOLE

Great job, Brandon

Maybe Ian has done something wrong. Maybe it was the car keying, the rage. They should have known no one could handle it, Victor couldn't, and they're just going to keep doing this with everyone in their lives.

Ian types in *Are you mad at me?* but it sounds so pathetic, they delete it immediately.

OLLIE

No one is mad at you Ian

Ian smiles a little at that. Trust Ollie to know them best.

NICOLE

No texting

facetime now

Ian swallows as the chat turns to a video call, something they usually save for special occasions, like New Year's, if they're not all together. Faces pop up in a pyramid of screens, Nicole and Brandon on top, Ollie on the bottom, and Ian's own face in the lower right, still in full drag. Nicole looks like she's in a bathroom, Brandon is at home on the futon, and Ollie is somewhere Ian doesn't recognize, but it looks soft and white like heaven.

"Everyone alone?" Nicole asks.

Ian looks behind them. The dressing room has people going in and out, mirrors for doing makeup everywhere, clothes strewn around. They duck into the bathroom and lock the door.

"Now I am. What's going on?" they whisper. They don't know why they're whispering; it just feels like they should.

"You look great," Brandon says.

"The makeup is giving," Ollie adds.

Ian doesn't need compliments right now, but they check themself in the screen and fix where a lock of their wig is coming loose. "I know. Now what the fuck is going on?"

"Do we need to talk in code?" Brandon asks.

"I honestly am not sure," Nicole says.

"Okay," Ollie says. "So it's about yesterday, when Brandon, or, I guess…B?"

Brandon nods on-screen.

"When B and I went to…play Prince Charming. Return the glass slipper."

"Just say it," Ian says, unclear on why a code is warranted. "What is going on?"

Brandon flinches.

"Code," Nicole says. "Just trust me."

Ian nods. They're outnumbered, but they hate this. It feels silly. Their fingers tap the wall they're leaning against.

"And we found him at the…palace we knew about," Ollie continues slowly, trying to think of code phrases.

Nicole sighs, kneading the spot between her eyes.

"But once we were there…" Ollie shakes his head, unable to find words. "There was a sudden change in someone's status."

"Oh, Jon has a boyfriend? Sorry, Brandon," Ian says, still confused.

"No," Ollie says quickly. "Not Jon. We saw someone else, and they—"

"We saw someone's peach get blasted," Brandon interrupts, eyes wide.

Ian frowns, still confused. "You saw someone get fucked in the ass? It's New York, who cares?"

"No, not the ass," Brandon says, horrified. "No, no."

"Oh no," Ollie says. Pete barks somewhere off-screen.

"A peach is an ass." Ian is getting frustrated now. "What else could 'blasted' be?"

"He got shot!" Brandon says.

"What?" Ian feels their head starting to hurt. "Like a load? On his ass? I'm so confused." The annoyance is really boiling in them now. "Why are we even talking like this?"

"Stop," Nicole says, voice cold with authority. "It's best if you just say it clearly."

"But what if someone is listening?" Ollie says.

"Then we're screwed anyway." She takes a breath and looks at the camera, chin level. "Yesterday, when Brandon and Ollie went to track down Jon"—her voice is the same one she used while giving presentations in school—"they saw him meet with another man. Who was shot in the head by an unknown assailant."

"What?" Ian swallows. "Is he okay?" They were already sweaty from working and the lights, but it dried a little, turned sticky, and now they're sweating again, extra oily.

"No," Brandon says, eyes wide.

"And you didn't tell me? What the fuck?"

"I told them not to," Nicole says. "To keep you safe."

Ian nods. From Nicole, it makes sense. And they appreciate it. But she should have known better than to think Ollie and Brandon could keep this a secret.

"So I'm guessing from the poor attempt at code that you didn't go to the cops?" Ian says.

"They called me," Nicole says as Ollie opens his mouth to respond. "And they took me to where they saw the shooting, but the body was gone."

Ian shakes their head, not sure what to do with this. "So what does this have to do with the guy in my section?"

Nicole frowns. "That, I don't know."

"That guy was the one who picked up Jon's bag when we called the number he'd left," Brandon says. "That tattoo anyway."

"And yesterday, when I went to see if there was video of the alley—" Ollie starts.

"You what?" Nicole interrupts, voice higher than Ian has heard it in years. "After I told you to lie low?"

"I wanted to figure out what was going on!" Ollie says back.

Ian would normally enjoy watching this sort of drama unfolding, but with murder in the mix, it's not the usual sort of low-stakes amusement. "So why was he in my section?" they interrupt. That's the important thing. Are they in danger? Suddenly it hits them—the break-in. "Was he who trashed our place?"

"Someone trashed your place?" Nicole asks quickly, eyes narrowing.

"Oh," Brandon says, as if realizing something. "Could that be related to our thing?"

“Of course it could!” Nicole looks like she wants to reach through the screen to strangle Brandon.

“Ian said they had it figured out,” Brandon says, defensive.

“I thought it was Victor, getting me back for keying his car,” Ian explains. “I kind of went to his work and yelled at him.”

Nicole sighs.

“You saw Victor?” Brandon asks, softening. “How did that go?”

“Well, I accused him of breaking into our place, and it sounds like he didn’t, so I’m guessing not well,” Ian says, a cold flush of embarrassment sweeping through their body. They must have looked insane to Victor. A year of nothing, and they show up out of the blue and admit to keying his car and accuse him of something he didn’t do. Great. Just great.

“Maybe it’ll help you find closure,” Ollie says.

“I don’t really care about closure right now,” Ian snaps, voice harder than they meant. “Am I in danger? How does he know where we live and I work?”

“Yeah, that part is scaring me, too,” Brandon says, standing and putting the chain on the door in his little video screen.

Nicole shakes her head. “I don’t know. But home isn’t safe right now. You need to find someplace else to stay.”

“Come here!” Ollie says, almost bouncing. “There’s a study with a pull-out bed, and the master bedroom. We can have a slumber party!”

“Ollie, you understand they’re hiding from a potential murderer, right?” Nicole says slowly.

“No reason we can’t make it fun.”

“It sounds safe,” Brandon ventures. “Just until we can figure it out. Did you talk to that person at work yet?”

"Yeah," Nicole says. "I'll call her once we hang up."

"So do I just leave?" Ian asks.

"No," Ollie and Nicole say at the same time.

"You have to act normal," Ollie says.

"I…agree." Nicole sounds surprised as she says it. "The more innocent you look, the less likely he is to take interest in you. You just happen to live with someone who just happened to see something, and you're all going to go about your business without mentioning it. You are no danger to anyone."

"Okay…" Ian says, tugging at a poster for a gay dance party someone taped to the door in here. It's got a photo of bears in jockstraps, ass to ass.

"Go home after work, pack a bag, and you and Brandon go to Ollie's together."

"Take a weird route," Ollie says. "In case you're being followed. Subways are good. Get on the train last minute like you just realized it's the one you wanted."

"Sure," Brandon says. Ian is happy to note that he looks as shell-shocked as they feel.

"Okay," Ollie says, then gives them the address. "See you later!"

Everyone hangs up, and Ian takes a deep breath alone in the bathroom. They're going to kill Brandon.

Someone knocks on the door, and Ian leaps away from the wall like they heard a gunshot.

"Constance, you in there? We need you for the finale number."

Finale number. Fuck, is everything just going to sound ominous now?

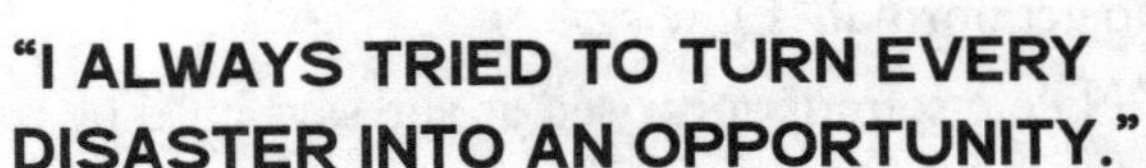

"I ALWAYS TRIED TO TURN EVERY DISASTER INTO AN OPPORTUNITY."

—J. D. ROCKEFELLER

THINGS AREN'T GOING QUITE HOW he expected. RIP Fred—but that's why you need to make sure you're not followed. But he's had to go to his second-choice hacker: Sean.

Sean always asks for too much money and gets ahead of himself with plans and ideas. And his online handle is SeanCode-y, which is terrible. Plus, they had really awkward sex that one time. He didn't even look like a Sean Cody guy with his shirt off! He's not bad looking, but scrawny. It's false advertising.

Still, Sean is good at hacking, so he's here, outside Sean's weird little apartment in Alphabet City. Sean is on the top floor, in the corner, his peephole replaced by a small camera most people wouldn't even notice. There's no bell, so he just knocks, pulling up his collar to cover his neck a little, then maintains sexy eye contact with the camera.

After a moment there's the sound of locks turning—one, two, three, four, five, and six (a new one)—and the door opens to Sean smirking.

"You're in a lot of trouble," Sean says. "I bet they have a million guys looking for you. Or one really good one."

He shrugs, gives his most charming expression. "You going to turn me in?"

"I guess that depends on why you're here," Sean says, walking backward into his apartment. He follows. Sean is in a lavender hoodie with two anime boys kissing on it, a pair of blue plaid boxers, and white gym socks. He hopes he won't have to fuck him again. Sean kisses so weird, his tongue a quarter inch out of his mouth, lips clamped around it, like he wants you to pull it out or something.

"I need you to find out what's on this flash drive," he says, taking it out. "It's why I got in trouble."

"You stole something from the company, and you don't know what's on it?" Sean laughs, incredulous, and opens the door to his office, a white room wrapped in computer screens and other equipment, wires everywhere, windows with black drapes over them, so the only light comes from the screens and a standing lamp in the corner. "I knew you were crazy, man, but that's pretty stupid."

"It was an impulse," he lies. "They didn't even know it was there. Someone just walked in on me at the wrong time. Otherwise no one would have known."

"Bad luck?" Sean asks, sitting down at his computer and extending his hand.

"Yeah," he says, handing him the drive.

"And yet you look thrilled," Sean says, pressing a few buttons and slipping the drive into the computer.

He puts his hands in his pockets and grins. He is thrilled. This is the kind of shit he signed up for. On the run. Dealing with hackers. People getting shot for no reason. He's having fun.

"Shit, this thing is locked tight," Sean says, looking at the screen. "It's going to take me a while. You want to come back?"

"Nah," he says, leaning against the wall. He stayed at some cheap hotel by the airport last night; it was hard to find places that still took cash. Slept terribly, worried there were bedbugs, and spent most of the night watching the news to see if there was anything about him. There wasn't. Makes him wonder how Sean knows. But hackers always know everything. In any case, he doesn't have anywhere to go but here, and besides, he's not sure he trusts Sean to be left alone with the drive. He loses that, he loses everything.

"You sure? I can call you when it's done."

"I'm between phones," he says. True. He didn't want to be tracked, so he left his behind. He uses a virtual phone number for most stuff, so he can just log in when he gets a new burner.

"All right, then settle in," Sean says, turning back to the computer. "I'm assuming the plan is to auction this off and go halfsies?"

It's not, but if he says that, Sean will ask for money up front, and he doesn't have that right now. "Seventy-five, twenty-five," he says instead. Maybe it is the plan, after all. Depends what's on it. He already double-crossed the company. Why not double-cross the woman, too? She didn't even tell him her code name, after all. That's no way to earn trust.

Sean spins back around in his chair. "Sixty, forty," he counters.

"Okay," he says. "But you gotta let me take a nap somewhere."

Sean smirks again. "You know where the bedroom is. I'll call you when it's all set up."

"Thanks," he says, glad there's no flirting. He walks down the hall to the bedroom, which is thankfully much less a hacker stereotype than the office. There's film on the windows, so they look frosted, but there's light and a nice green carpet and some framed prints on the wall of nude men who all look...well, they all look kind of like him. Maybe he should be insulted Sean didn't go for some sexual tit for tat.

But he's too tired to care. He lies down in the bed and takes a deep breath. With other guys, he wouldn't do this, but Sean isn't someone who would kill a man in his sleep. And he needs somewhere safe to rest. Like Sean said, they've sent out the cavalry to hunt him. They shouldn't find him here though. At least, he hopes not as his eyelids grow heavy. For now, this is fine.

When he wakes up, it's dark outside. His face is stuck to the pillow with drool. He really crashed. But that makes sense; it's been a busy few days, lots of adrenaline, lots of fun. He needed to recharge.

He pads out of the bedroom, uses the bathroom, and walks back to the office, where Sean is in the same position and outfit.

"Perfect timing, my guy." He taps a few buttons. "The auction is live."

Shit. Auction? He feels his adrenaline kick in, head lighter, vision tunneling on the computer screen, where there's an auction site up. He didn't mean for this to happen yet. "What?"

"Cracked it twenty minutes ago. This is going to make us both private-island rich." He tosses him a phone. "Here, a burner so you can watch the numbers go up. Already flooded the dark web, letting people know. Like, seven cartels are bidding, three anonymous groups I think are governments, and even the McClintock family is interested."

"Sean, I didn't tell you to do that." He looks down at the phone. There it is, a screen with an auction happening. Several groups are registered to bid, but none of them have yet. That's a good sign.

Sean spins in his chair. "How else do you let criminals know there's an auction?"

He sighs. "Take it down."

Sean frowns. "What?"

"I don't even know what it is yet; you should have told me. I can do the selling."

"So, what, I just hand it back to you, and you leave and never call me? You think I'm an idiot? We auction it off—trust me, that's the best way—and set up payment so it goes to an account I control and then we'll split, and then you can turn the drive over. We'll both be at the meet. That way we both have skin in the game."

The phone vibrates and he looks down. The first bid: fifty million dollars. He feels his eyes go wide.

"Told ya."

"What even is it?"

"Key to the private data of Velvet Alley, that dark web trading site," Sean says, grinning.

Fuck. That feels bad. That's bad, right? That's where terrorists sell briefcase nukes—and kids. Why would the woman want that? The only people who should have that are people who would stop it…like maybe the government. Who he stole it from. That's, like, full traitor shit. Which he guesses he sort of already knew he was, but he thought he was bringing the woman some banking info or something. Kid stuff, not…fuck. This isn't James Bond stuff. This is stuff the villain does.

"Take it down," he orders Sean.

"What? Fifty million! And that's just the first bid." The phone buzzes again, and he glances at the screen. Ninety million. "See?"

He takes a step toward Sean, not sure what he should be doing right now or why it feels like he has a headache somewhere that isn't his head. Like he pulled a muscle somewhere he has no name for, but it aches all over and itches, too. "Take it down, Sean."

"Sure. For ninety million."

He glares at Sean, but he can feel a shock of electricity in his veins. No. He will not lose control to this twink hacker. He reaches over Sean and tries to mess with the computer, stop what's happening, undo it, even. He might be able to. He's not a good hacker, but this is just taking down an auction site.

Sean tries to push him off, but he elbows him with enough force that he rolls away. "Fuck!" Sean clutches his newly bloody nose. "What the hell?"

"I'm taking it down," he says, frantically trying to figure out the computer. There should be a take-down-post button or something, right?

To his side, Sean has grabbed a box cutter from the drawer and is clicking it out, blade by blade, pointing it at him. "Stop it! We're going to be rich. Leave it alone."

"Don't," he says, glancing at him, then back at the screen.

"You literally just stole this, and now, what, you're too good a person to auction it off?"

"I don't know!" he says. That's part of it. The other part, he realizes, is fear. "This is some deep shit, man. If we do this, they'll come after us forever. We'll never be safe."

The phone buzzes again. "Two hundred million," Sean says. "We can be safe with a hundred million each."

He presses a button, but it doesn't work. Out of the corner of his eye, he sees Sean step closer to him, blade out. Adrenaline is running through him like a wild animal. He tries another button, then a menu. He should have paid more attention in the tech briefings. Sean steps closer again.

"Just stop," Sean says.

"No," he says, voice louder than he wanted it to be.

Sean lunges at him. He's surprised enough that the blade manages to poke him in the shoulder, but then his instincts kick in. He twists Sean's hand so he drops the box cutter. Sean cries out in pain. Then, without even thinking, he swings Sean forward. A hard blow to knock him out.

Except he swings him into one of the parts of the computer. It's harder than it looks. Metal case, not plastic. And Sean's head hits the corner with an unpleasant *crack*.

He kind of thought it was a bunch of separate computers. But they must be connected, because all the screens go black. *Fuck*. He looks over at Sean. Blood runs down his face. He hadn't meant to ram him into anything that hard. Sean came at him with a knife though. So it was self-defense. Yes. He steps back and takes a deep breath.

"Sean?" He frowns, checks for a pulse, breath. Nothing. He closes Sean's eyes, which are going glassy, and walks softly out of the room, shutting the door behind him. Sean wanted to sell this stuff off. That makes him the bad guy. He stopped him. So it's...he's...

He leans against the wall in the hallway and takes a deep breath to slow his heart. People will be coming here. Sean is good, but not good enough to fend off whole governments. Putting that auction up was like raising a flag with a giant target on it. They will trace it back here and break in and find the body and the drive, and maybe that's all that needs to happen. He can vanish, live off the grid, get a job as a lumberman in Canada or something... It sounds awful. But the woman probably won't be giving him a job after all this. And the company definitely won't be taking him back.

The phone in his hand buzzes again. He didn't realize he was still holding it. Six hundred and fifty million. Private-island rich.

It's so quiet all of a sudden. The whirring of the computers was loud, filling the place with white noise. But now all he can hear is his own heartbeat, his breathing.

What is the life he wants? That's what she asked him.

He swallows and turns off the phone. Then he goes back into the office, reaches around Sean's body, and takes out the drive. He'll think about what to do next. He just needs to lie low. Figure it out.

13.
Brandon

BRANDON KNEW OLLIE WAS A dog walker for the wealthy, but this place is a lot richer than he imagined. It feels like a museum, the spotless white walls, the high windows, the track lighting spotlighting various key elements of the house: a pale modernist painting, an old-looking vase, a very high-tech air fryer. Pete is chewing on some blue toy in a dog bed big enough for a dozen more dogs on one side of the living room. Ollie is hugging both Brandon and Ian as they stand paralyzed in the entryway.

"I'm afraid if I move, I'll get my poor all over this place," Ian says, voice wheezing from how tight Ollie is squeezing them.

Ollie laughs. "It's fine, come on, come on, just leave your bags there. I want to show you something."

"Why does he seem so happy?" Ian whispers to Brandon as they follow Ollie up the stairs.

Brandon shrugs. He doesn't know. He barely understands how *he* feels right now. He's worried for Jon but also scared for himself and his friends, guilty over what he's gotten them into but also eager to actually make sure they don't abandon Jon in case he's the love of Brandon's life. Every choice seems like a bad choice. Or at least a dangerous one. And Brandon suspects they are not a group well equipped for danger.

"Look," Ollie says, opening the door to a room with a large bed and a larger corkboard covered in Post-its, photos, and red string.

"Uh-oh," Brandon says under his breath.

Ian snickers. "Why is Lady Bunny up there?"

"To represent Jon," Brandon says, understanding immediately. He walks closer to the board, studying it. Not much yet. A timeline, from Jon checking in, to the emoji-tattoo guy in Ian's section at brunch this morning. Emoji tattoo—helpfully identified by a printout of the heart-eyed emoji—is linked to three of them now, at three times. This, Brandon has to admit, isn't bad work. It's just scary, seeing it all laid out like this and still having no idea what any of it means.

"I should never have hooked up with a guest," he says, feeling tears coming on. He turns away, sniffing them back.

"Hey," Ian says, rubbing his back. "Yes, it was stupid. So, so stupid. But no one could have seen *this* coming."

The tears are streaming now. Brandon wipes his eyes with his wrist. Ollie grabs a box of tissues and hands them to him. Brandon takes one and loudly blows his nose. It's the softest tissue he's ever felt—better than most cloth napkins. "And I shouldn't have taken his phone."

"Again, I agree," Ian says. "Completely insane stalker-level stuff that would probably get you arrested. But not"—they gesture at the corkboard—"this kind of insane. This isn't on you."

Brandon sniffs again and looks up at Ian. Reliable Ian, looking unimpressed as always. It's reassuring. And Ollie, excited but in a way that reminds Brandon of college, of Ollie and his lists, leading the charge to get something done. "I'm sorry," he says to both of them. "I'm so sorry we're all mixed up in this."

"Are you kidding?" Ollie says, taking Brandon's arm and squeezing. "This is the most exciting thing to happen to us in ages."

"Yeah, love to be worried I'm going to die. So fun," Ian deadpans. They cross their arms. "How high are you?"

"Just a little," Ollie says as Brandon walks toward the corkboard, staring at it. "This girl I met, Safiya, she gave me one she liked, and since I'm seeing her tomorrow, I wanted to make sure I tried it before—"

"I just want to make sure Jon is safe," Brandon interrupts, eyes still on the terrifying corkboard. "I don't care about all…this." He gestures at the web of red string.

"And I just want to make sure *we're* safe." Ian crosses their arms.

"Solving the case will do both those things," Ollie says.

Brandon looks at Ian. They stare back, silent words passing between them: *Solving the case sounds like it'll put everyone in more danger.*

There's a low chime that takes Brandon a moment to recognize as a doorbell.

"That must be Nicole!" Ollie says, heading back downstairs.

Brandon feels a wave of relief as he and Ian follow, like a slight lightness in his chest. Nicole will fix it. Nicole is a lawyer. She knows how to take care of messes like this. It's her job.

"I have no idea what's going on," Nicole says as Ollie opens the door for her, her body wound tighter than it got before the

LSATs, like her shoulders are trying to become earrings. She pauses, taking in the house. "Jesus, Ollie, what is this place?"

"The Strongs' house," Ollie says. "And Pete's."

"Maybe I went into the wrong line of work," Nicole says, looking around. "Should be a house sitter."

"Did the person at work have any information?" Brandon asks, trying to move into Nicole's roving gaze. They need to get back on track, or they'll spend hours on this house.

"Not yet," Nicole says, eyes focusing back on him. "I texted her about the tattoo though, right after we got off the phone. Something memorable like that might help us figure out who he is and who he works for."

"We don't even know what he's doing," Brandon says. He wants to collapse, but he sees no chairs. There's the entry foyer with the dog bed and stairs, a giant kitchen to the left, and wide-open darkness to the right. "Is there somewhere to sit?"

"Oh, yes, let me show you your rooms," Ollie says, flipping a switch and lighting up the other side of the room, which is also white, with a giant fuzzy rug, and several leather seats around a glass table. The glass in the tall windows goes from blackout to clear, letting in some light from outside, too. Bookshelves are on one side of the room, filled with books that are all clothbound in black and white, with several glass pieces of art spread among them.

"We're sleeping here?" Ian asks.

"Don't be silly," Ollie says, walking through the living room and pressing on a wall Brandon assumed was just an architectural feature. But no, it slides away, and there's another white room, this one with one of those wall-mounted TVs that look like framed art, a large wraparound white leather sofa, and a white marble coffee table about the size of his and Ian's apartment. "This sofa pulls out into a bed. So one of you can sleep here."

Brandon wants to collapse, but the leather on the sofa looks pulled as tight as a facelift. He stares at it warily.

"And the other bedroom is the master. They told me not to use it, but we'll just clean up before they get back."

"When do they get back?" Nicole asks. "How long is this viable?"

"Three weeks," Ollie says. "Two and a half now."

"Oh great," Ian says. "Plenty of time to get murdered. At least the bloodstains will be impossible to get out of all this white."

Brandon laughs but feels tears coming on again. This is all his fault. And he still doesn't know what's happening with Jon. He gives in and flops onto the sofa. It holds firm for a moment, then relaxes slightly, the leather so much softer than it has any right to be. He grabs one of the throw pillows—not white, but the palest blue—and hugs it to his chest.

"I guess that means you're taking the master," Ollie says to Ian.

Ian rolls their eyes. "At least I'll die in luxury."

Nicole's phone beeps, and she looks at it.

"Something from the lawyer?" Brandon asks, hopeful that somehow this has all been fixed.

"Not the Mafia," Nicole reads. She looks up at them. "So that's something, I guess. But that reminds me, we all need to download this app to text on. Show me your phones."

Brandon takes his phone out, and so do Ollie and Ian, and Nicole has them download a texting app.

"It's double encrypted, and no one has access to the messages but us, so it's a lot safer to text there."

"And it has GIFs!" Ollie says, texting them all an image of a cartoon hippo waving and saying *hello friends!*

Brandon hearts it, the emoji popping up on the side.

"We should break into *Jon's* phone," Ollie says. "If we want to know who that guy is, there'll be more clues in there."

"How?" Nicole asks, shaking her head. "I mean, it's not legal, so we shouldn't, but we've certainly already broken enough laws." Her head is tilted down, almost like she's talking to herself. "So I'm not against it." She looks back up. "You know a hacker?"

"I brought my laptop, and…I might know how to get in." Ian won't meet her eye. "Could take me a while though."

"How do you know how to hack a phone?" Nicole asks, raising an eyebrow.

Ian shrugs. "Seemed like something worth knowing after…" Their eyes drift to the ground.

"Oh," Nicole says, voice a little soft. "That's… Obviously cheating is bad, but I feel like hacking a partner's phone is probably—" She cuts herself off with a shake of her head. "Know what? We're past that. It's useful. Brandon, give them the phone so they can hack it."

Brandon reaches into his pocket. He doesn't want to give it up. This is his one connection to Jon now. And yes, Jon led him and all his friends into whatever they're into now, but he was still so handsome, and sweet, and maybe Brandon's soulmate. It really felt like they could be—

"Brandon," Nicole repeats, hand out for the phone. He sighs and gives it to her, and she hands it to Ian. "Get to work, hacker."

"Work." Brandon feels the word hit him like a live wire. "I have work tonight. Do I go? Not go?"

"Go," Nicole says confidently. "We should act normal."

"What if the emoji-tattoo guy comes by?"

"Treat him like you would any other guest."

"What if he asks for the phone?"

"Tell him you don't know what he means, no phone was left behind."

"What if he asks why I was near a shooting?"

"Tell him you have no idea what he's talking about, and text me. If he gets violent, call the cops. If you feel afraid walking home alone, text us; someone will come get you. But the important thing is to act innocent."

"I am innocent," Brandon says. "We're all innocent. Even Jon."

Nicole raises an eyebrow. "We don't know that yet."

"You need to eat, too," Ollie says. "Let me order pizza. Sleepover!"

"I am not sleeping over," Nicole says flatly.

"Well, at least stay for pizza," Ollie says. "Oh! And I want to show you my—"

"Murder board," Ian interrupts.

Brandon snorts. Then he feels like crying again. His stomach rumbles. He hasn't eaten since last night, and it's close to six. They spent a few hours packing stuff up and took a while to get out here. At least he doesn't have to be at the hotel until nine. Maybe food will help his mood stabilize enough for work.

Ollie gives them a full tour, each room more violently white than the last to the point where Brandon wishes he'd brought his sunglasses. Pete follows them around, and Brandon wonders how this little dog can live in this pale house without getting dark fur everywhere. The game room on the second floor is amazing.

They could throw a great party here. As long as there was no red wine. When the pizza arrives, Ollie checks the camera on the door before opening it, which makes Brandon feel a little safer.

They eat in the kitchen, Ian typing away on their laptop and sometimes watching a tutorial video on how to hack, which Brandon didn't know existed. Nicole goes back to work after one slice of pizza, and Ollie is texting a lot, sometimes looking up at everyone and smiling, making sure they're eating.

"I'm just so happy we get to hang out," Ollie says. "I wish you didn't have to work. We could watch a movie. Can you call in sick?"

Brandon opens his mouth, about to say yes.

"Nicole said to act normal," Ian says first, eyes still on the laptop. "And I'm going to be at this all night. This isn't a slumber party, Ollie." They say it so coldly that even they flinch and glance up at Ollie. "Maybe tomorrow night?" They offer an uncertain smile, and Ollie nods, satisfied.

"Definitely tomorrow," Brandon says, reaching out and squeezing Ollie's shoulder. It could have just been a slumber party if not for what he's gotten them all into.

"If we live that long anyway," Ian says, turning back to the computer.

Brandon washes up and packs up his suit for work. Act normal, Nicole said. So he'll do that, even if it's terrifying. She's giving orders, asking around. Ian is hacking. Even Ollie is making a murder board. What is Brandon doing, aside from worrying about everyone—Jon included? He feels useless, he realizes. Not just the one who got them all into this, but the one who can't do anything to get them out. He needs to help out more. Maybe there'll be something at work.

"Got it," Ian says, when Brandon is almost ready to leave. He rushes over to the kitchen counter, where Ian has the phone and computer hooked up. "I'm going to set up a VPN before I let it connect to the internet, hold on..." Brandon watches Ian open a few programs, set some dots around a globe. "That'll keep anyone tracking it from finding us, at least for a little bit. I think we should connect it to the internet for only, like, two minutes at a time. Otherwise, Airplane Mode, okay?"

Ollie and Brandon nod, looking over Ian's shoulder as they turn the phone's internet on. They wait as Ian scrolls through files, texts, contacts. But there's nothing. It's all empty.

"Did you mess it up?" Ollie asks quietly. "It's all right if you did, you're new to this and—" He stops talking as the phone dings. A small icon on it lights up. It has a little red notification in the corner: **1**

Brandon gasps, unwillingly and loudly enough that Ian snorts.

"It's a virtual phone number," Ian says. "Works even without the SIM. This is just coming in even though it's from yesterday, so he hasn't logged in with this number anywhere else."

"Does that mean he doesn't have a phone?" Brandon asks, worried.

"What's the message?" Ollie asks. Ian clicks.

PRIVATE NUMBER

You can still make this right

"Well, that's ominous," Ian says.

"It's from right around when that guy got shot, too," Ollie adds.

Ian looks up at Brandon. "Sorry, sweetie, looks like your boy is definitely part of this."

Brandon feels his hands tingle, and he clenches them into a fist and shoves them in his pocket. "Could just be a coincidence. We don't know what that message is even about."

Ollie and Ian exchange a look, and Brandon knows what they're thinking, but he refuses to believe that Jon is a criminal. It just doesn't make sense. And Brandon wouldn't feel that connection with a criminal, right?

"Turning off the internet," Ian says, putting the phone in Airplane Mode. "I changed the code to three, two, four, six—fags. Easy to remember." They grin.

"I was sure there'd be another clue," Ollie says, disappointed.

"I'm going to see if I can find out who made the reservation," Brandon says, deciding it suddenly. They're all doing so much. He has to do *something*.

Ian and Ollie look at him, evaluating. "Is that allowed?" Ian asks. "Or is that something you could get fired for?"

"It's on the computer. I have access; I just need to make sure no one notices. And I got us into this, so...I should try."

Ian smiles. "Good luck."

"You'd better go. Remember, hop on the train last second."

"Right," Brandon says, nodding at them both and heading out the door.

Getting to work isn't so hard. He gets on the train at the last minute like Ollie told him to, only tripping a little as he steps on, looking all around him, but he doesn't see anyone following him.

But would he? He doesn't know. Probably not. He's never been aware of anything before. He's stumbled into more walls than a woman in a rom-com. So, if he's being followed, he won't know it. He looks around at everyone on the train, trying to see if they're looking back at him. One old man glares at him. Or maybe that's just his eyes. Brandon quickly looks away, swallowing, sweating.

The old man doesn't get off at his stop, so maybe it's just paranoia. Brandon doesn't know at this point, but at least at the hotel, he'll be behind a counter. He has a good view of the room. And no one is going to come for him in such a public place, right? At work he puts on his suit and stands behind the desk with Amber, who smiles at him expectantly. Is she in on this somehow? Did Heart-Eyes pay her to watch him?

"Do anything fun this weekend?" she asks.

Brandon almost laughs but manages to keep his face calm as he shakes his head.

"I saw that art exhibit. You know, the—" She leans forward, whispering, "Nudes." He blinks, wondering if this is code, then remembers it's just Amber. She's not watching him. She wouldn't be able to keep it a secret.

"You don't have to whisper it. No one is even in the lobby." He gestures at the empty waiting area.

"Oh." Amber leans back, pouting a little. "Fine. Well, it was really interesting. And *erotic*," she says loudly enough that it bounces off the mirrors. Brandon sighs. He needs to get her out of here to grab a look at the computer alone. Amber takes his sigh as a request for elaboration and continues. "They were all modern artists, a mix of photography and oil and charcoal. Even some sculptures. Anything, as long as it was a naked body." She giggles. "Sounds like my dating profile. You think I should be an artist's model?"

Brandon smiles weakly. "I'm glad you had fun. I'm going to restock the water bottles."

There's still plenty of water left, but there's another computer in the back office, and the night manager usually doesn't show up until ten. The back office is painted white with a plain desk, somewhere between the fancy lobby and the blank burrows under the hotel. But the computer isn't logged on. Brandon has no idea what the password could be. He tries *Bergamot*, and then the night manager's name—Tod, ugh—but neither works. He tries them again with *123* after each of them, but nothing.

BRANDON

Ian, how do I figure out the manager's computer password?

IAN

What kind of computer is it?

BRANDON

A mac. Older, but not like really old.

NICOLE

So we're all just becoming criminals. Cool.

IAN

Look at his calendar or in his drawers, then? Sometimes people write them down.

Brandon checks the calendar and then opens the desk, where he finds a neat little card with the password on it.

BRANDON

Thanks!

OLLIE

You know, we'd make a great detective agency

Brandon ignores that and goes into the reservation database, finding Jon's information. There's a credit card on file, but he can't access that without another password, and he's already been in here long enough that Amber must be getting suspicious. Instead he just takes a photo of the screen—the contact phone number he called, the name Jon Engel, and the check-in and -out dates with a note in the comments: checked out early due to work schedule change.

Well, that's good to know. If it was work, then it wasn't because of Brandon, and maybe he'll text back and—

Brandon shakes his head, remembering everything that's happened. Still, maybe it's all just a series of misunderstandings. Jon will think it's so funny when they find him and Brandon tells him everything. *You left your phone, I wanted to give it back, we saw a guy get shot, but then the body disappeared!* Oh, they'll laugh and laugh.

Brandon logs out of the computer, grabs a case of waters, and walks back out to the front desk.

"That took a while," Amber says.

"I just needed a moment," Brandon says, trying to keep his voice deadpan like Ian does. "After you talking about your naked body."

Amber looks shocked for a moment. "Aren't you gay? I would never talk about this stuff with a straight guy."

Brandon sighs again, wishing he were straight. "I was kidding."

"Oh." She forces a laugh that becomes a real laugh. At least he got some information. They can find Jon now, maybe. Or at least get closer. He watches the doors for anyone coming in, anyone outside the glass windows watching them, but people walk by without even glancing at him.

Amber goes on about her trip to the art show as Brandon tries to tune her out. Sunday nights are usually pretty quiet. A lot of people check out on Sunday morning, but not many check in late on Sunday night. Just one older man clearly here for business who complains about his flight delays. Otherwise it's quiet. Brandon texts the photo to the group when Amber is on a break.

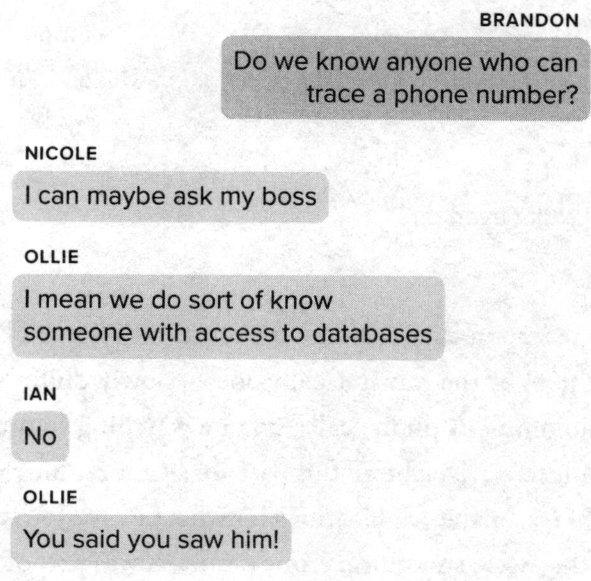

IAN

Yeah because I thought he'd broken into our place. I screamed at him. I don't think he wants to help us out right now.

NICOLE

I will ask my boss

IAN

Great, I'm going back to bed and putting my phone in sleep mode this time

OLLIE

I guess I should go to sleep too. You remember the code on the lock to get back in Brandon? I pulled out the bed in the den for you and put down sheets and pillows.

BRANDON

Thanks! I'm good, don't wait up for me.

OLLIE

Night everyone!

No one responds, and Brandon pockets his phone. The rest of the night goes by the way it usually does—slowly, dully. No weird tattoos, no ominous phone calls, no one watching him with any particular interest. Maybe all this paranoia is for nothing. He tries to think of reasonable explanations for what he saw: Jon is a movie star, and they were shooting a crime drama. It was part of a globe-spanning game of paintball Jon plays with his wealthy friends who have too much time on their hands. Something. Brandon knows it wasn't paintball though.

But he also knows Jon couldn't be involved in anything really bad. The man Brandon met that night was kind and funny. You know a person after you make love to them, right? Your souls intertwine or something? He'd never say that aloud, but it feels true. He intertwined with Jon. He's a good guy. And Brandon just wants to see him. The thing that makes him feel craziest is Jon just leaving, like there wasn't something between them. There had to be. Otherwise, what is all this chaos leading to? With everything that's happened, it has to be true love. Heimweh.

He gets off at six in the morning and rides the train home surrounded by men going to work. He really has to get on a better shift. In the huge white house, everyone is still asleep. Ollie doesn't have to walk the dogs for a while, and Ian doesn't have a bookstore shift until later and isn't performing at the Wreck Room until Thursday. Just Brandon awake in the house, and Pete, who ran downstairs when Brandon came in but thankfully hasn't barked, just stares at him in the dark, that weird chew toy of his dangling from his mouth. He pats Pete once on the head, hoping that will appease him, but Pete keeps staring. Brandon swallows and walks past.

The phone—Jon's phone—is still on the kitchen counter. They probably shouldn't have left it out. Brandon takes it. It's his, sort of. It's Jon's, but Brandon has to be the one to return it—that feels right. It's his glass slipper. He goes to the den, where the white sofa is now a big white bed with fluffy pillows. Brandon strips down and gets under the covers. This is more comfortable than his bed at home. That's not right.

He puts Jon's phone on the nightstand next to his. Then he takes it in his hand, slides it open. Ian said they could connect it to the internet for only a few minutes, but maybe something will come in. Maybe Jon is out there somewhere, under the same stars, thinking of Brandon this very moment, and if they could just connect—

Brandon turns the phone's internet on. Nothing. He stares at the screen a moment. The wallpaper is a sleek black marble pattern with a gold border. Kind of reminds him of the hotel lobby.

Then a text comes in—sent earlier tonight.

AVERY

Excited to see you!

And a photo. Well, that's something.

14.
Ollie

OLLIE WAKES UP AND LISTENS to the house. Nothing aside from Pete snoring in bed next to him. Brandon and Ian must still be asleep, which makes sense. So Ollie goes about his normal routine. He's meeting Safiya this morning, after he's picked up all the dogs, so he takes a little extra care with the sea fennel and oud body cream (he doesn't want to smell like a soap store, just nice). He has a little cereal before heading out and leaves a note for Ian and Brandon, telling them he'll be back later and where everything is so they can make themselves breakfast. He loves that they're both here. Sure, the Strongs probably wouldn't love it, but they didn't say anything about guests and told him to make himself at home, and nothing makes him feel more at home than having his friends over.

Outside the air is brisk and smells like the decay of leaves, earthy and sweet. He knows he should be more afraid. There's a voice in the back of his mind just screaming about the huge man who has a video of him witnessing a murder. But he also has a to-do list of things to figure out: Who is the man? Who does he work for? Who was the target? He made the list last night. First one he's made in over a year, and it felt like putting on his favorite sweater again after losing it for a decade. Like he was home. Having everyone in the house added to that, too. It's like college again: everyone together, and everything he has to do and think about laid out, ready to be tackled. It's just there's murder this time.

He picks up his puppies like any other day, except he's not listening to a podcast. He's listening to the streets, the children laughing, the puppies panting, and, most importantly, footsteps. Streets have a particular echo and rhythm, and a man as big as the one Safiya described probably would walk pretty heavily. But Ollie doesn't hear or see anyone following him. Just a normal day.

He texted with Safiya last night and arranged to meet her at the Prospect Park Dog Run. The puppies shouldn't go in the water—their owners don't like the cleanup—but there's a huge lawn usually brimming with dogs and surrounded by trees where maybe he and Safiya can sit down and chat while watching them play.

He finds a good spot, far from the beach so they don't run off, and unhooks all of them from their leashes, taking out a variety of balls and toys to toss. They're already running circles around him, mingling with other dogs, ears flopping, drool dripping, by the time Safiya shows up. She walks onto the lawn looking like a supermodel in a long black Muppet-fur coat belted at the waist and huge black sunglasses. She waves at him, wearing black driving gloves, too. Ollie walks over to her, and he's worried there's going to be an awkward moment, trying to figure out if they're going to shake hands or what, but she goes for a hug right away, leaning over to wrap her arms around him, and he hugs back. A hug was what he was going to go for, too.

"There are so many dogs." Her smile is huge as she looks around. "Which ones are yours?"

Ollie points them out, calling them over for Safiya to pet. She seems so happy, scratching each of their chins and butts, calling them adorable and introducing herself to them with "hellos," and "nice to meet yous," and even an "I love your collar, I have one just like it" for Pepper. None of them act weird; they all just accept the scritches and happily play fetch with her when Ollie hands her a few toys.

"This is so fun," she says, tossing a tennis ball and watching all the puppies gallop after it. "Thank you for inviting me. I know I sort of forced you to."

"You didn't force me at all," Ollie says, next to her.

"I mean, I said you had to if you wanted information for your case. I'm like a femme fatale. But for dogs."

Ollie laughs. "I was getting up the nerve to ask for your number anyway. You just beat me to it and suggested the date idea. Took a lot of work off my shoulders."

She smirks, throwing the ball out again and grinning hugely as the dogs run after it. "I am known for that. My manager never even leaves the back room. I'm the one doing all the hand selling."

"Thanks for that gummy. I took it yesterday; it was amazing."

"So good, right? My body feels so connected and in place when I take that one. And my brain just relaxes and thinks, you know? I always feel like I'm putting off just thinking about stuff, but when I take one of those, it's like I finally have the space and I can remember a poem I read or a movie I saw and really consider it."

"Poems? That's cool. I don't know many people who read poems."

"Really? Oh yeah, I love poetry. I read this one the other day, just this part in it I loved: 'What part of me is the seed? Not my skin, because it cracks, but doesn't blossom. Not my mind, because it blossoms, but doesn't close. Not my soul, because… because…' And that's just the end of the poem. It fades like an echo. I love it."

"That's beautiful," Ollie says, turning the words over in his head. "I mean, maybe no part of us is a seed. Maybe we're more like mushrooms, y'know? Spores, mycelial networks all connected."

She turns to him. He can barely see her eyes through the sunglasses, but she looks pleased. "That's good. I like that."

"Thank you," Ollie says, leaning slightly closer. She smells better than yesterday, the sweet earthiness of the pot now mingling with something like oranges and jasmine. Perfume? Did she put on perfume for him?

"I'm going to think about that later. Mushrooms." Samba has brought over the tug rope, and Safiya pulls on the other end. Samba pulls back, tail wagging. "So this what you do? Dog walker, detective, poet?" she asks as Samba keeps playing tug with her.

Ollie shrugs. "I'm the same as you; I just like to think about things."

"That's the poet part. And you love dogs, so that's the dog walker. But what's up with being a detective but not?"

"Oh." Ollie tosses the tennis ball for the other dogs, who seem uninterested in the tug-of-war. Pete plops down at his feet, worn out. "I'm just working this one case. For a friend. But I do love true-crime podcasts."

She laughs. "Really? Those things creep me out."

"That's what my friends say. They make me feel safe, weirdly."

"Really?" she asks again, then playfully growls at Samba, who growls back, tail wagging like a cheerleader's pom-pom. "How?"

"I think it's just…bad things happen. A lot. But seeing them laid out neatly makes them feel less chaotic. A case to solve, instead of another terrible thing that happened."

She nods, quiet, and drops the rope suddenly, letting Samba run off with it, triumphant. "Something terrible happen to you? You don't have to tell me."

"No, it's fine. My dad. A year back." Saying it makes him even more eager to solve Brandon's case—their collective case, really—as quickly as possible. Ollie knows what it feels like when things aren't solved and instead just fade away, dissolve, and no one even seems to remember except you.

"I'm sorry." Her voice is tissue paper crinkling delicately around the topic. "I guess you were close?"

Ollie nods. His mouth won't do anything. He really didn't want this to come up on date one. He should have brushed off the question. But it spiked back into his brain when she asked, an iceberg under the surface, like it had been waiting.

"That sucks. I'm sorry." She picks up a Frisbee toy and sends it sailing high into the sky, and all the dogs in the park, an army of them, look up, watching it soar.

Ollie watches it with the dogs, then throws his shoulders back. First date. He used to have a checklist for these. He should focus on that.

"So what *is* your case, anyway?" She leans closer to him, eyes peeking over the sunglasses.

Ollie watches Linus sniff the butt of another dog, not one of his puppies. He feels a slight trickle of sweat on his neck, even though it's chilly. He shouldn't talk too much about the case. He could put her in danger.

"Just something my friend thought he saw. I think it's probably nothing."

"I mean, it's not." She says it simply, like it's obvious.

"What?" He looks at her. One of her eyebrows is up.

"I told you, some big guy came and took the exact same tapes you were looking for. Whatever your friend saw probably happened."

"Maybe," Ollie says.

"Definitely. Or maybe he saw something but didn't understand it. What did he think saw, anyway?" There's a faint edge to the question.

"I thought you didn't like murder podcasts," he says, smiling.

"This isn't a podcast. At least not yet, I guess." She sighs and lies back on the grass for a moment, staring up at the leaves. Silence hangs there, waiting for him to fill it. Zoey comes running back with the Frisbee. Ollie takes it and tosses it, a shorter distance than Safiya did.

"A murder," he says, giving in.

"Fuck." All around them the barking dogs suddenly sound farther away.

"Yeah."

"Well, I hope he's wrong. I don't need violent crime where I work." She props herself back up on one arm, looking at him. "So solve it for me, okay? Tell me what you find out."

Ollie laughs, but it sounds a little sad. "Sure."

They play with the puppies until they and the dogs are all exhausted. They talk about other things from Ollie's first-date list:

Where they're from (Ollie is a local, but Safiya is from Michigan), where they went to school (Ollie to Oberlin, Safiya to UCLA), and what they majored in (both in philosophy, which they agree is useless). They swap hobbies (Ollie's true crime, Safiya's pottery) and favorite books and movies (more true crime from Ollie, and he worries briefly if he's boring before remembering he likes high fantasy, which Safiya also likes, along with rom-coms), and by the time Ollie has to bring all the puppies back, he feels like this is someone he knows and likes. She feels like a new friend, and then when she smiles and kisses him lightly on the cheek as she leaves, she feels like maybe something more. She smells good, and her lips are soft on his skin, a little sticky from lip gloss. He would like to kiss her, he thinks. He'd like to touch the skin over her ribs, hear the sound she makes when he does.

That's the best place to leave a first date, he thinks. The feeling of friendship, but filled with sexual tension. Waiting on the edge of something. He drops each of the puppies off, feeling a little dance in his steps, that little bouncing thrill of something new and exciting in his blood, like he's uncovered some new part of himself through her. Something new to investigate.

He checks his phone as he walks Pete home.

NICOLE

How'd the date go, Ollie?

IAN

He's still out walking the dogs so I think it's going well.

Or she's killed him.

NICOLE

I want the deets!

Ollie grins. Even amid everything, his friends are happy for him.

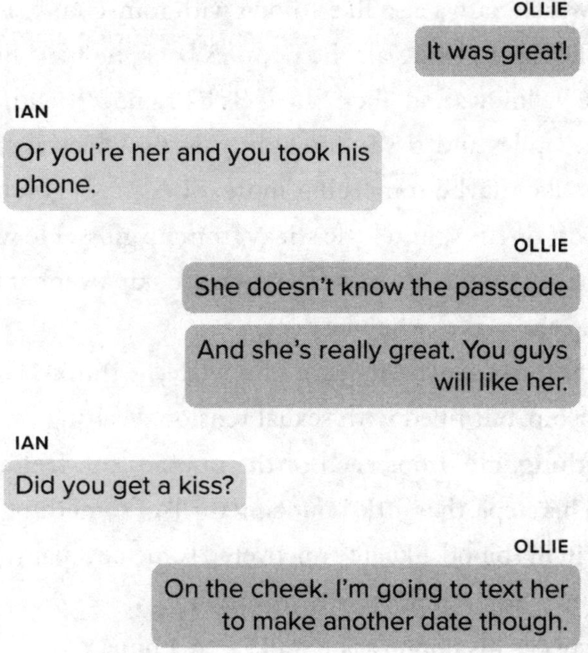

He closes up the group chat and opens the one with Safiya.

OLLIE

I had a lot of fun

Any chance you want to see me without the dogs?

He looks at the text, but it goes unread.

"She's on the train, probably, right?" he asks Pete. Pete blinks. They keep walking.

By the time he makes it back home, it's almost noon, way later than usual. He lets himself in, excited to tell Brandon and Ian about the date, but finds Brandon alone at the kitchen table in his underwear, a soggy bowl of cereal in front of him, holding Jon's phone and staring at it. His eyes are distant, and he's chewing his lower lip. He doesn't even turn as Ollie comes in with Pete. Still worried about everything. But probably Jon, mostly. Ollie feels almost guilty after his date.

"Hey," Ollie says as Pete goes over to his bed and gnaws on his teething ring.

Brandon turns with a start. "Oh, hi." He pauses, considering Ollie. "I should show you something."

"Okay," Ollie says, walking up to him slowly, like he might run.

"I didn't show Ian, I knew they'd—I knew what they'd say. But I don't think it's that." He holds up the phone.

AVERY

Excited to see you!

And under that is a photo of a woman, maybe late twenties, holding up a smiling baby.

"What do you think it is?" Ollie asks.

"I think it's a friend, not his wife, like Ian would say. I just think she'd text more if she was his wife and he was on a trip."

Ollie nods. He's not sure what this is yet, but it means something. "So what do you want to do?"

"Look—" Brandon pulls up the photo, zooming in behind them. "That's the *Alice in Wonderland* statue in Central Park. Let's go."

Ollie grins. "To look for clues?"

Brandon nods. "Let's go, detective. I mean, after I put on pants."

15.
Nicole

NICOLE BARELY SLEPT, TRYING TO catch up on the amount of work she normally would have done over the weekend, her phone by her side in case Ellen texted with some new information. But the phone was silent all night. Ellen had said to lie low, act normal, so that's what Nicole does. She washes up, pins on her wig, and picks out one of her nicer suits, the one that makes her ass look great—professionally, of course—then goes into the office at six, like normal.

There's plenty of work to do, research for the senior associates and partners, case dockets to update, argument notations to check, coffee to get. She looks at her phone as she waits in line: nothing from Ellen, and nothing from her boys either. She guesses it's because they're having that big sleepover. Maybe she should have stayed over, too. It would have been fun. Like college again. She opens the group chat, not sure what to type as the line moves forward. *Good morning*? *How did everyone sleep*? It all feels weirdly motherly. She's not their mom, even if she does sometimes feel like the one responsible one. Then she remembers Ollie's date. That's something.

NICOLE

How'd the date go, Ollie?

IAN

He's still out walking the dogs, so I think it's going well.

Or she's killed him.

Nicole snorts a laugh. But Ian isn't wrong. Who is this girl?

NICOLE

I want the deets!

Oh god, that sounds terrible. She grimaces at herself. But better than outright asking if the girl is suspicious. She shakes her head. She hates the idea that she's distrustful of everyone now. *Just let Ollie have his fun date.*

"Something bad in the text?"

Nicole looks up. She's at the front of the line. Sam.

"I just texted something that didn't sound like me."

"What?"

Nicole sighs. "A friend went on a date with a girl I don't know anything about. I said I wanted the deets."

Sam throws her head back and laughs. "Yeah, that doesn't sound like you."

Nicole raises an eyebrow. "You know that from the way I order coffee?"

"Yes. Just like I can tell you're here just for you because you have your relaxed expression, not the one where you're repeating orders in your head. And I happen to know your order is a large black with a shot of espresso, a pump of cinnamon, and hazelnut milk." She holds up a cup, already filled, for Nicole.

Nicole is impressed but tries not to show it as she takes the cup. Instead she just smiles and sips, paying. "So what should I have said?" she asks. "How do I ask my friend to tell me if this girl is actually worth his time and not just…hot and slick?"

Sam leans on the counter. "I think just let your friend trust his instincts. All romance is a risk. Better to dive in than stand on the sidelines, right?" Her lipstick is a deep burgundy today, and when she smiles, there's a flash of white teeth. Nicole leans forward, sipping her coffee again. It tastes perfect. Sam stares at her, and Nicole opens her mouth slightly.

"Excuse me, are you done?" the man behind her in line asks.

Nicole blushes furiously, turning away from Sam and nodding at the man in line. "Yeah, sorry," she mumbles, stepping to the side. "See you later," she throws at Sam, suddenly needing to get out of there. She forgot there was anyone else in the shop. She forgot it *was* a shop. And that's just mortifying. She needs to stop coming back here. But the coffee is the best in the area.

She sighs, smelling the cinnamon in her coffee as she takes the elevator back up to the office, looking at the rest of the texts—Ollie is going to ask her out again. Good. Nicole is glad things can seem normal amid everything. Normal would be nice, right about now. She sits back down at her desk, sipping her coffee and wondering if Sam tastes like coffee. Wondering what her order is. She's probably one of those people who order an espresso with a slice of lemon. Or maybe she's a tea drinker. Nicole frowns, realizing she doesn't seem to know Sam as well as she knows Nicole. But that's by choice, Nicole tells herself. She shouldn't be thinking about this at all. She should be thinking about work. Or the fact that there might be a large man with an odd tattoo trying to kill her friends.

She sits down at her desk and opens her email; Don managed to send her three emails with various research requests while she was gone, and she's cc'd on dozens more. She knew she should have asked if he wanted anything before she went out. She gets to work. She wanted normal—well, she's getting it.

"Come on, we're doing lunch."

Nicole looks up a few hours later, startled. It's after noon now, and Ellen is there, in sunglasses and a bright red trench coat over a black suit.

"Oh," Nicole says, not sure what's happening. "All right, let me just ask Don—"

"Don," Ellen shouts down the hall into his office. Don pops his head out. Ellen never comes down here. "I'm taking Nicole for the day." It's not a question. She looks at Nicole through the sunglasses for a moment, then turns and walks, leaving Nicole to scramble to get her coat and bag and follow.

"Something smells like cinnamon," Ellen says in the elevator. "That you?"

"My coffee."

"Spicy and bitter. Fun."

Nicole pauses but then just asks it: "Did you find something out?"

"Yes. But let's discuss over lunch. Fewer ears."

"Okay." Nicole feels worried now. And also, she realizes, excited. Shady meetings to exchange information away from spies at the office? That's pretty good stuff. Not at all what she thought she wanted, but now that it's here, her body tingles, like her wig and suit could fly off at any moment and something else could emerge. Something more like her.

But she doesn't say any of that. It would be unprofessional. The suit stays on.

"How was the fundraiser?" she tries instead.

The elevator doors open, and they walk out into the building lobby.

"Oh, it was awful," Ellen says, smirking. "I mean, the cause was very good and all. Environmental conservation." She squints, trying to remember. "Plants, I think, not animals. Pretty sure. But the guy was just…ugh." They're outside now, Ellen walking quickly enough that it feels like she's generating a wind as Nicole tries to keep up. "I didn't have high hopes for him, but sometimes you just say yes because you never know, right? Well, I was wrong. I knew he was a dud. Should have trusted my instincts."

Nicole laughs, a little shocked at the honesty. "Sorry."

"Don't be. The food was all right, at least. Usually these Goody Two Shoes events have some sort of garden salad and then fish, but it was a pretty decent steak." Ellen cocks her head. "It definitely wasn't a fundraiser for animals."

"Well, that's good."

"Still," she says, stopping at the glass door to one of the dark expensive restaurants in the neighborhood, a block and a half from the office, "this place is better."

The hostess nods at them as they come in and doesn't even say anything, just starts walking. Ellen follows, and Nicole follows both of them, like the caboose in a train. She passes by this place all the time but has never come in. Low lights, a long bar, dark wood, black leather. This is an old-school expensive restaurant, not one of the modern ones that are all light and white walls. It smells like decades of scotch.

The hostess takes them through a pair of curtains in the back to a small private room with a round table, one dim lamp hanging over it, a black leather bench circling it, so tight that when sitting, you can lean back on the walls. The hostess lays down two menus and walks out without saying anything.

"The steak is good," Ellen says, sliding off her coat and sitting down. "You eat meat?"

"Uh." Nicole pauses, the question unexpectedly stymieing her when it comes from Ellen. Something about the way she asks it, like she's asking something else. She swallows. "Yes."

"And they make a great Manhattan, too. I assume you drink?" She raises her eyes at Nicole, who is still standing. She quickly takes off her coat and sits down opposite Ellen.

"Not usually while I'm working."

Ellen snorts. "You told your friends not to call the cops when they saw a murder. You really going to tell me you're a rule follower?"

"Well, when it comes to work, I don't want to—"

"Relax. I checked you out of the office. You're not due back till tomorrow."

Nicole smirks. "So I'm a library book."

"Something like that. So what's your drink?"

"Martini," Nicole says. She doesn't really have a drink, but she's always wanted to drink more martinis. "Vodka. With a twist."

Ellen smiles. "Okay, not bad." She takes off her sunglasses and hands Nicole a menu. Nicole looks it over. Everything is meat.

"So can we talk about what you found out yet?"

"First I need you to promise never to text about that tattoo again."

"Oh," Nicole says, swallowing. "All right."

"That man is dangerous. Former special ops turned freelancer. His name is Arthur Nuys."

Nicole laughs.

"Something funny?"

"The guy with the heart-eyes tattoo is named Art Nuys? It's like Doctor Seuss."

Ellen shrugs. "I'm guessing it was some sort of joke with his squad that turned into a dare to get the tattoo. That's how a lot of those guys end up with funny ink. Even mine was on a dare."

She pauses, the silence filled with the invitation to ask what and where her tattoo is. Nicole has experienced this pause before. It's always a come-on. She's not sure what's happening. She remembers Ellen's smooth back. No ink there. She wonders where it could be and looks Ellen up and down in the dim light: Chest? Legs?

"What's yours of?" Nicole finally says, half swallowing the words as they come out, afraid she's misread it.

Ellen leans forward, half whispering, "A stiletto. It's on the side of my hip." She leans back again. "You have any?"

Nicole blushes, not wanting to share the swallow on her shoulder, which was definitely not a dare but which she had agonized over for all of freshman year. What should it be? How should it look? Where should it go? She even got a temporary tattoo that she had Ollie help her reapply every few days to try out for a month before finally going through with it. It's cute, but she suspects Ellen would find it childish. Especially considering the freedom and soaring to new heights she hoped it would represent do not seem to have come to pass yet.

The curtain to the room parts before she has to answer though. A waitress comes in, notepad ready.

"I'll have a Manhattan," Ellen says, her eyes still on Nicole, who suddenly can't look away. "She'll have a vodka martini with a twist. I'd like a steak frites, medium rare."

"And you?" the waitress asks Nicole.

Nicole keeps her eyes on Ellen. No one has ever ordered a drink for her before, aside from a few skeezy guys. It was hot. Like twinge-between-her-legs hot.

"The same," Nicole says, glancing down at the menu. She doesn't know what she's doing now. This is her boss! She tears her eyes away from Ellen to look up at the waitress. "Thank you. Where's the bathroom?"

The waitress shows her the bathrooms down the hall, and Nicole locks herself in for a moment before taking out her phone.

NICOLE

Tattoo guy is dangerous. Ex special forces turned freelancer.

Also I think my boss is hitting on me.

IAN

That's terrifying and hilarious

I mean the ex-special forces thing is terrifying and the boss hitting on you is hilarious.

NICOLE

I figured. Why is it hilarious?

IAN

Because you sound like Brandon

BRANDON

Hey! A guest isn't the same thing as my boss!

OLLIE

Is she hot?

I assume she

NICOLE

She is

BRANDON

Go for it!

IAN

Do not take relationship advice from Brandon

Brandon disliked "Do not take relationship advice from Brandon"

NICOLE

I won't

I'm just shocked

OLLIE

Why? You're amazing and beautiful

Nicole smiles and takes a deep breath. Okay, she'll go back out there, ignore the flirting. Get any other information she can.

NICOLE
I gotta go

IAN
Have fun fucking your boss

NICOLE
Shut up

She puts her phone away, washes her hands, and goes back to the small private room, where a martini is waiting on the table and Ellen has rearranged herself, lying back, legs crossed, the long line of her neck glowing as she sips her Manhattan.

"You all right?" she asks, raising an eyebrow.

"Yes, sorry. My friends texted."

Ellen narrows her eyes, sitting up straighter. "They're lying low?"

"I told them to." She sits down and sips the martini. It tastes somehow purer than any drink she's ever had, like she's drinking from the source of all martinis, a waterfall somewhere. "They're not great at it."

Ellen frowns. "They get involved with dead bodies and then don't have the sense to lie low?"

Nicole shrugs, suddenly feeling very small. She sips her drink but can feel Ellen's eyes on her, questioning.

"You know, I grew up in California," Ellen says, voice softer. "My parents owned a dry cleaner. But now look at me." She gestures at her face, smiling. "Sometimes we rise above. But you have to want to."

"Yeah," Nicole says, nodding. She knows what Ellen is saying, and part of her is thankful for the advice, the mentoring. But what exactly is she asking Nicole to do? She leans back farther into her chair, and the leather squeaks. "Do you ever see your parents?"

"The holidays. And we text now and then. I appreciate who they were, but my life now—if I tried to include them, it would just be embarrassing for all of us. I have friends, colleagues, and people who understand me so much better than they ever could. And I don't let them drag me down into their drama."

"Drama?"

"Oh"—Ellen sips—"family gossip, arguments. If they ever really need help, I help them, of course, but all their little complaints? I've made it clear I'm not the one they should go to. Boundaries."

"Oh, yeah." Nicole sips again. "That makes sense."

"My point is, find people your level. You don't have to give up old friends, family. But...people your own level will make you feel more at ease. More like yourself."

"I don't know if they came to me with a little complaint," Nicole says, catching her drift. "They saw a body."

"That disappeared," Ellen says, taking the olive out of her drink and popping it in her mouth. "And now they're out gallivanting when they should be hiding. It just feels... a little silly."

"Yeah," Nicole says, drinking again, hoping to drown the pit of shame in her stomach.

"And you're not silly," Ellen says, laying her hand on the table, reaching out to Nicole. Her red nails glint in the light.

"But they could be in real trouble."

Ellen pulls her hand back and takes out her phone. "Maybe. Let's find out."

16.
Ian

IAN HAS BEEN IN UNPLEASANT situations before. Hookups that turned awkward, a sex party they thought they'd try out and quickly discovered they didn't care for, a terrible tucking incident that came to head during a performance, STI exams, having to tell former partners they might have crabs… The list goes on. Most of it they can handle with grace and humor as long as no one is being an asshole. Then they can handle it with rage and attitude.

But they're not sure how to handle texting Victor. They're up early for work and keep glancing over at the phone as they eat some weird health cereal they found in a cabinet; it tastes like he imagines the cabinet does. He doesn't like this house. The whole place feels like an insane asylum, or maybe an old-age home, like everything here is supposed to be calming, as opposed to actually lived in. They finish the cereal, still looking at their phone.

NICOLE

How'd the date go, Ollie?

Ian looks around. Brandon is still asleep in the den, but Ollie has been gone for a while.

IAN

He's still out walking the dogs, so I think it's going well.

Although, these days, maybe they shouldn't be so sure something that looks good is good.

IAN

Or she's killed him.

NICOLE

I want the deets!

Ian frowns at that. It doesn't sound like Nicole. But maybe it's like a forced smile, trying to calm all of them down as they wait for a man with a ridiculous tattoo to shoot them all in the head. Blast all their peaches.

OLLIE

It was great!

IAN

Or you're her and you took his phone.

OLLIE

She doesn't know the passcode

And she's really great. You guys will like her.

Ian smiles. They're happy for Ollie. He deserves a new partner, or at least a fuck, or maybe just a kiss. All of them deserve at least a kiss, right? Like a good, soft kiss that makes everything in your body melt away, and you don't feel scared or sad or angry, just safe. Ian hasn't had one of those in over a year.

IAN

Did you get a kiss?

OLLIE

On the cheek. I'm going to text her to make another date though.

Ian smiles, putting their bowl in the sink and going up to the master bedroom. Even the walls are covered in white fabric. Absolutely mental-hospital chic. They get dressed and take the train to the bookstore, opening up and closing the last few messages they sent to Victor, eleven months ago: You really hurt me.

And his response: I'm so sorry.

And now Ian has to apologize.

But at the bookstore, they have to open, and a bunch of parents are there with their kids. The cool kind of parents who buy their kids the gay art book. A lot of the parents are queer themselves. Ian wonders if that's in the cards for them. They ring up a picture book for a pair of hot, bearded literal DILFs and their adorable little daughter, who is in a purple tutu. They've thought about kids before—Victor had always wanted kids. Ian isn't opposed, as long as it's a long way off. Once they have an established drag career. Once stuff stops pissing them off so much.

But they like kids. Kids are so honest and genuine. Ian never gets mad at them.

Not babies though—babies are gross.

Maybe adoption?

Ian shakes their head, ringing up another book for another DILF and his wife and their little stroller gremlin, who starts chewing on the board book immediately. But once the morning rush is over, and it's just them and Kate, Ian's eyes keep flitting back to their phone. To Victor's message. *I'm so sorry.* Ian took that as a challenge—made sure he was sorry. Victor has probably blocked them by now, right? That would make it easier.

"You keep staring at your phone," Kate says as she shelves some new books. It's below her pay grade, but Kate likes putting the new books on the shelves herself, seeing what's being bought or handled in the space more intimately, instead of just looking at sales numbers on a sheet. She says it helps her figure out what titles to buy next and what to return.

"I have to text someone."

"You're usually good at that."

"I have to text an apology."

Kate laughs, throwing her head back. The laugh goes on longer than Ian thinks it should. And then it keeps going, ending in panting. "Oh," she says finally, making her face expressionless like she didn't just cackle at them for ten minutes. "Sure. That's hard."

Ian rolls their eyes. "I apologize to you all the time."

“I sign your paychecks. You kind of have to.”

Ian sighs. She’s not wrong. “Fine, whatever. I guess I won’t do it, then.”

Kate laughs again. “Sure, there ya go. Get angry and defensive and don’t apologize to someone else because of something I said. Seems healthy.”

“Well—” Ian says. She is, once again, not wrong. “Yeah. Sorry. See? There, I apologized.”

Kate shelves a few more books, then walks over to the counter. “What are you apologizing for?”

Ian sucks on their lower lip, not wanting to reveal the whole story to Kate. Because she’d probably think they’re nuts. “I accused them of something they didn’t do.”

“Oh, that’s easy,” Kate says. “Just say, ‘Hey, sorry, I was wrong.’ You can do that, right?” She asks it like she’s asking a six-year-old.

“Unclear. I’ve never been wrong before.”

Now Kate rolls her eyes and gives them a stare that they know means a biting critique of their character is imminent, but they’re saved by the chime of the door opening as a couple of old dykes walk in, regulars who come in once a month, looking for the new queer releases or recommendations from Kate. A couple, Ian assumes, one with short, nearly shorn hair, the other with a faux-hawk, always wearing leather jackets, no matter the time of year.

Ian smiles politely, but they know Kate has this one, and she’s soon chatting them up about all the new books, so Ian pulls out their phone again. Since they’ve been using this new texting app, Ian hasn’t seen normal texts in a while. Beneath the energetic group chat is something from Tom. Shit. They should get him an answer. They do really want to see that movie, but…

"Can you put these aside for us?" one of the old dykes asks, placing some books down on the table: a pierogi cookbook, a naming book for dogs and babies, a hard sapphic noir with a vintage cover, and another pierogi cookbook.

"Of course," Ian says, thumping the pile to the side of the counter.

"Don't mind them," Kate says. "They have to send an apology text."

The trio of older women chuckles together. The one at the desk pats Ian on the hand. "Once you do it, it'll be over," she says.

"Or it'll blow up," the other says.

"Yeah," Ian says. "That's the fear. Well, that and I'm broken forever." They smile, making it a joke, but no one laughs.

"Aw, honey," the customer by the counter says. "Nothing is broken that can't be fixed."

Ian nods. That's true. In one of their art-history classes in college, they did a whole section on kintsugi and became obsessed with it, buying up dozens of cheap ceramic pots at dollar stores and then throwing them on the floor so they could repair them in art class. Beautiful cracks all over. None of them ever came out looking great though. Their teacher said something breaking naturally wasn't quite the same as shattering it against the wall just to see it break. Ian nodded, but still doesn't really believe it.

They flick past Tom's message, scrolling back to the last ones he and Victor sent.

VICTOR

I'm so sorry

IAN

The stuff you had at my place is in the dumpster by the bad sushi place.

Ian frowns reading those over. They feel the righteous rage that they had typing it out—how angry they were. It blossoms in them like a rose of fire. But they feel something else, too. A little shame, but that's easy enough to shrug off. Something else, something like a pit opening under their feet that they're going to fall into and never get out of, just them alone in the dark forever.

"Putting this one aside too!" one of the dykes says, putting a dark-academia horror romantasy on top of the other ones. "Your boss has the best recs."

"She does," Ian says. "So do you two though. Thanks for the advice."

"We love to help out family. You probably don't know that term. That's what we all called each other in the seventies. 'Family.' Not sure why we don't anymore."

"Gay Republicans, probably."

She snorts and pats them on the hand again, then goes back to Kate, who has a new book out to show the customers. Ian turns back to their phone.

IAN

So turns out someone else broke into our apartment

Sorry for accusing you

I think it was just less scary imagining it was you

I was really scared

They stare at the words they just sent, feeling queasy all of a sudden.

"You do it?"

They look up to find both customers and Kate staring at them, eyes wide and too warm.

"No."

"They did," Kate says. "They just feel weird about it."

"Shut up," Ian says.

"Isn't she your boss?" one of the old dykes asks.

"I can tell you to shut up, too." Ian is pretty confident they can get away with teasing these customers.

They all chuckle. "Well, good for you. Apologizing is hard but…needed," one of the customers says.

"Yeah." Ian doesn't meet any of their eyes. "Thanks."

Their phone buzzes and they look down.

VICTOR

What?

Who?

Did you talk to George?

I'll kill whoever did this

Ian smiles, a warm feeling in their stomach. Victor still cares. Murderously.

VICTOR

Was it Brandon's newest crush or something?

He didn't bring home a con artist again did he?

IAN

Something like that

"Ooooh, they're texting someone back now," one of the old dykes says. Ian glances up and glares, and all three of them burst out laughing as Kate takes them to the far end of the store to show them more books.

IAN

We don't want to go to the cops

An idea crosses their mind. Ollie pointed this out yesterday—Victor can run phone numbers.

IAN

But could I ask you one favor?

VICTOR

Is that why you apologized?

IAN

No I just thought of it

Sort of a lie, but not really. It's not why they apologized anyway.

VICTOR

What is it?

IAN

All we have is this guys phone number

Can you run it? Get us an address, maybe a real name?

The ellipsis appears and disappears, then shows up again.

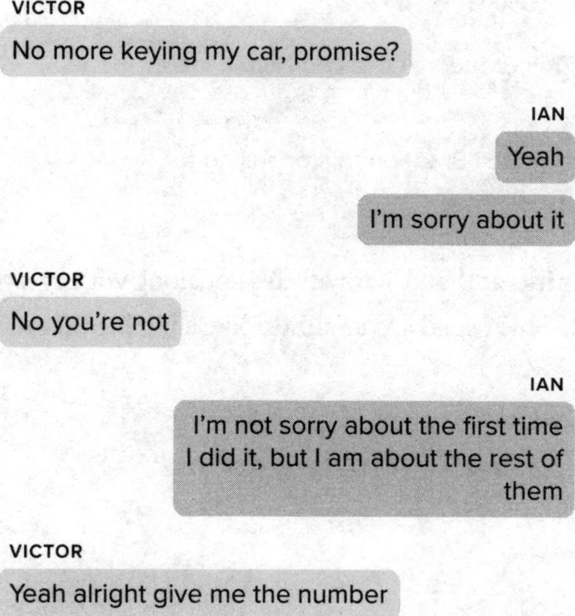

Ian pulls up the reservation Brandon took a photo of and sends it.

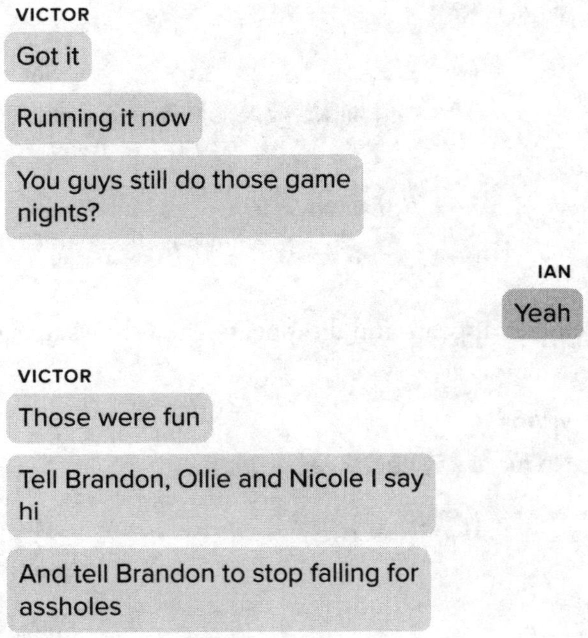

Ian smirks at that. Victor always got along with everyone, genuinely liked his friends. Was almost like a big brother to Brandon.

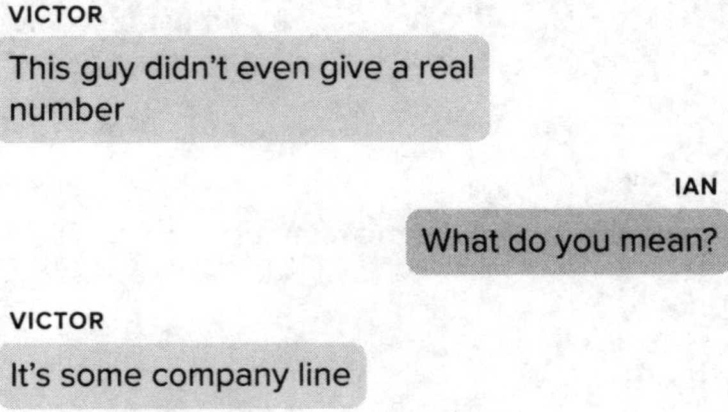

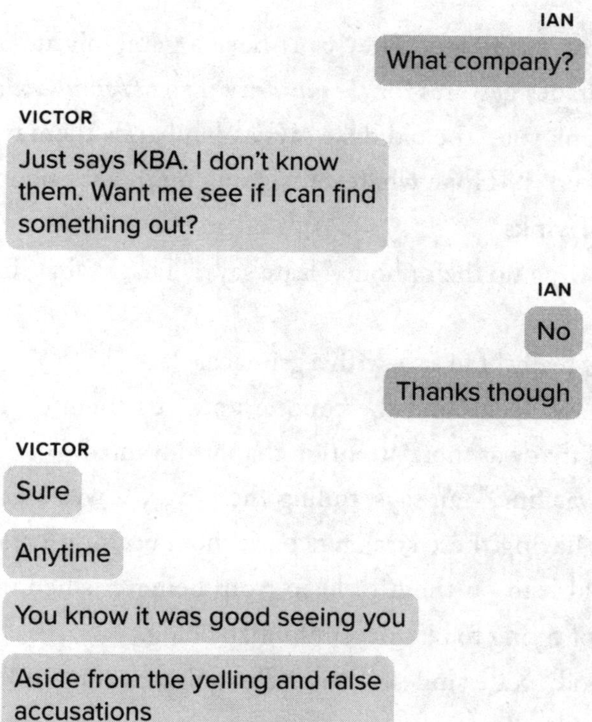

Ian's body suddenly fizzes like shaken soda. Good to see them? What does that mean?

"Okay," one of the old dykes says, putting seven more books down on the counter with a slam that startles Ian away from the texts. "I think we're done for now."

Ian rings them up, glad for a reason to put down their phone, which suddenly feels radioactive. They have no idea what to say to Victor. Maybe he was just being polite, *good seeing you* as a way of saying goodbye. And with a little dig at the end. Very Victor.

Very hot.

Maybe they should have a game night. They can invite Victor, and—Ian stops the thought, shaking their head. They are hiding out. There was a *murder*. People could be hunting them, like the heart-eyes-tattoo guy. They can't have a game night. Are there even charades gestures for *the murderer is right behind you*?

"Thank you," the old dyke says as Ian hands them two heavy bags of books. "Hope whatever is going on in your phone works out." She winks.

"Blowing up their phone," Kate says. "That's what they call it, right?"

"Not really," Ian says with a grimace.

Kate walks around the counter and pats them on the back. "Sorry if that was more attention than you wanted."

"It was fine," Ian says, rolling their eyes. It was kind of nice, actually, having these strangers back them up for no reason, like Ian could lean on them to keep from being crushed under the burden of trying to be a decent human being.

"Good." Kate smiles. "I think I'm going to run out for coffee. You want anything?"

"Where are you going?"

"That one with the cocoa-nib cold brew."

"Yes please. That. Biggest size they have."

"The usual, got it." She shrugs on her coat and walks out.

Ian's phone buzzes and they look down, wondering if Victor is actually elaborating a little. But it's the group chat.

NICOLE

Tattoo guy is dangerous. Ex special forces turned freelancer.

Also I think my boss is hitting on me.

Ian feels instant whiplash, the terror from the first part of the message vanishing in the laughter of the second as they try to imagine Nicole dealing with work and romance mixing. Assuming she means the boss that she mentioned the other day, the woman. A man would be icky. They suppose any boss hitting on someone who works for them is icky, but if it's queer, it's somehow funnier, too. Because it's Nicole. Stumbling into romance. The only way she was ever going to find it, with her life choices.

IAN

That's terrifying and hilarious

I mean the ex-special forced thing is terrifying and the boss hitting on you is hilarious.

NICOLE

I figured. Why is it hilarious?

Ian thinks, trying to nail it down.

IAN

Because you sound like Brandon

They can hear Nicole laughing at that one.

BRANDON

Hey! A guest isn't the same thing as my boss!

OLLIE

Is she hot?

I assume she

NICOLE

She is

BRANDON

Go for it!

Oh gods, no. Ian can't handle two of their friends being that person who fucks at work.

IAN

Do not take relationship advice from Brandon

BRANDON

Fair

NICOLE

I won't

I'm just shocked

OLLIE

Why? You're amazing and beautiful

NICOLE

I gotta go

IAN

Have fun fucking your boss

NICOLE

Shut up

Ian laughs, wondering how insane Nicole's day is right now. How insane everyone is. It's funny how the fear seems to have faded somewhat, or how they've become more accustomed to it. That's probably not a good sign. Ian takes a deep breath. Should they be more terrified? Less? They have no idea. Maybe Nicole will figure it out. She's the only competent one.

They stare at their phone a while, wondering exactly how to say what Victor found out without it being a big deal that they texted. But it's impossible, of course.

IAN

I texted Victor. The phone number that made the reservation is registered to a company—KBA. That's all he would tell me. Didn't know what they are though.

And I don't want to talk about it

Victor says hi and he misses you guys and game night, though

They stare at their phone for a moment longer, but their messages stay unread. They feel a faint relief but also a sudden well of loneliness. They want their friends to ask how they are and tell them it's okay to text Victor and that maybe they'll get back together or they definitely won't—something. They want to be comforted.

Gross. They put their phone down. They need to find something to read.

The door chimes as someone comes in. Ian glances up at the mirror in the corner. It distorts the man, but one thing is terrifyingly clear: the heart-eyes emoji tattoo on his neck.

17.
Brandon

BRANDON IS RELIEVED THAT OLLIE believed him. He knows that if he'd shown the text and photo to Ian or Nicole, they would have told him Jon was married and closeted, that's his wife in the photo with the oversize sunglasses and pink lipstick, his baby in the dinosaur onesie. Brandon was a dirty little fling, they'd say, and tell him to forget Jon. But Brandon knows it was something else. Or at least, he's pretty sure. None of this makes any sense, and he's aware that at this point, he's very far into lovelorn-fool territory, maybe further than any other time he's been here (pursuing a guy even after seeing someone murdered is probably worse than the three months he spent dating a guy who wouldn't even kiss him because it might distract from his tuba career—probably).

He needs to understand what's going on. Not just with him and Jon but with the tattoo guy and the dead guy, and if he and his friends are in trouble, or if Jon is in trouble. Brandon needs to save everyone. That's what Prince Charming does, right? Slays the dragon and hands over the glass slipper—or phone in this case. Those might actually be two different stories, he realizes. But the principle still applies.

"What are you thinking about?" Ollie asks him as they hang on the pole of a crowded 3 train heading to Central Park.

"Just trying to understand what's going on."

Ollie bounces on his toes, holding the pole, a grin spreading over his face like a flood. "Yeah. It's fun, right?"

"I don't know. I know you think it is. This is the happiest I've seen you in ages. Which is kind of concerning."

Ollie scrunches his face. "Why?"

"'Cause normally people would be worried, not happy. It's like you're rushing into this, like you don't"—Brandon leans in so the people around them can't hear—"care if you get killed."

Ollie shakes his head. "No, no, it's not like that." He pauses, like he's trying to figure out what it *is* like. The train stops, people get off and on. Ollie still doesn't say anything.

"Well, I'm glad you're coming with me anyway," Brandon says. "I mean, if we are going to"—he leans in again—"die, then at least I'll be with a friend." He straightens up, spinning back a little on the pole. "And it'll be for love."

An old woman on the train behind them snorts a laugh behind her sunglasses. Brandon ignores her.

"For love," Ollie says with a nod.

It's noon by the time they make it to the *Alice in Wonderland* statue in Central Park. They decided to walk from the west side, Brandon forgetting the statue is on the East, so he's a little sweaty under his fall wool coat and a little hungry, too. None of which is aided by the shrieks of the children running around them. The statue is large, bronze, and swarming with children like bees on a honeycomb.

Around that is a walkway lined with benches on which various parents and nannies sit, watching either their kids or their phones. Grass and trees spread out beyond that, more people lying on them, even in the fall, with blankets and juice boxes as needed.

Brandon takes out the phone. He saved the photo, and now the two of them huddle close to stare at it. Most of it is the baby. The woman holding the baby is half hidden behind them and her sunglasses. She's white, with long, straight brown hair, but so are a lot of the women around here.

The baby is also white and looks to Brandon like…a baby. He's not even sure how old the baby is—newborn to two years old, Brandon can never tell. Only when they're walking around and talking a little. Then they're moved from *baby* to *kid*, which is a whole new category of confusion where he can't tell their age until they've hit puberty and acne marks them as teens.

Ollie looks up, scouring the area of the park. "Okay, the baby has a sort of oval face, brown eyes, a little hair on top, sort of blond. I'm guessing boy, or at least has been assigned boy, from the blue onesie, and probably like eight months?"

"Yeah, that all sounds right," Brandon says, hoping he sounds convincing.

"The photo was taken from a little way away—" Ollie zooms in to make the photo larger. "See, they're on the grass, not a bench, and there's a tree, so from the angle…" He turns around, watching. "I'm going to guess it was taken over there." He points at a shady spot. "Think moms have spots they always go to?"

Brandon shrugs as a small child runs into his legs, not looking where she's going. She's one of the ones who seem unsteady on their feet, just learning to run. She's got one tall pigtail on top of her head, and as she tumbles backward, her purple dress falls back over her face, and she lies there on her back, crying.

"You okay there, little one?" Brandon asks.

"Pepper, are you all right?" a woman asks, running over to sweep the child into her arms. She turns on Brandon, glaring. "You should be more careful."

"I was just standing," Brandon says, taking a step back. The woman's energy is terrifying.

"Yeah, looking at the kids," says another woman behind him. Brandon turns, startled. She looks like someone copied and pasted the other woman and applied a filter: same sunglasses, same puffy-sleeved top, same blowout, just all in different colors. "What are you two doing here anywhere? You babysitters?"

"Um, no," Brandon says, just as Ollie says "Yes."

Both women cross their arms in unison.

"Oooooh, that's Mommy's mean face," says a little girl behind the second woman, her hands on her cheeks.

"Harpo, go play with Zoey. Mommy is dealing with predators," the woman says, eyes still locked on Brandon.

"Whoa," Ollie says, "not a great word to throw at queer people!"

The woman turns pink. "I'm not homophobic!" she declares quickly, defensive. "My dog walker is trans!"

Brandon looks at Ollie, afraid to say anything to that, wondering if this woman somehow doesn't recognize her own dog walker, but Ollie shakes his head.

"We are looking for a friend," Brandon says quickly, his concierge instincts kicking in. He's dealt with unhappy customers before, and he's good at it. He's good at making people happy. He takes the phone and holds it up like he's on a game show. "Here she is. Avery."

The first woman leans forward to study the photo. "Weird for you to have a photo of a baby like that."

"I'm sure you have photos of you just like this on your phone," Brandon says, voice soothing. "Who could resist showing off their kids, right?" He smiles widely.

The second woman sighs. "Just stop staring at our kids."

"We didn't mean to," Brandon says. "They just looked like they were having such a great time. It made us feel like kids again."

Both women soften at that.

"Any chance you know where Avery is?" Brandon tries.

"She usually sits down there," the second woman says, waving in the direction of the trees Ollie pointed at.

"Thanks," Ollie says warily and starts to walk over. Brandon hurries to follow, feeling happy he de-escalated. He looks again at the photo on the phone. White woman, straight brown hair—but that could be any of the four women in the shade of this large tree. They're all in pale puffy-sleeved tops and jeans, too. Is that a uniform?

"You handled that really well," Ollie says.

"Thank you." Brandon feels a little warmth.

"But let me do the talking with Avery. I have an idea."

"What—"

"Avery?" Ollie shouts before Brandon can finish his thought. One of the women looks over, confused. Ollie trots over, Brandon following, amazed at how easily that worked. They're really going to find Jon, and they just had to endure some angry white women to do it.

"Um, hi," the woman says from her blanket. The baby is asleep next to her, and she's scrolling through her phone. "Do I know you?"

"This is so awkward," Ollie says, squatting and speaking in a low voice. "But my friend here, he hooked up with your friend Jon the other night, and they accidentally traded phones. Jon said he was meeting his friend Avery by the *Alice* statue today, so we just thought...let's hope, right?"

The woman peers up at them over her sunglasses. "I don't have any friends named Jon."

Well, fuck. He shouldn't have let Ollie charge ahead.

"Really?" Ollie reaches up, looking at Brandon. "Phone?" Brandon hands it to him, and he shows the woman the phone. "That's not you and this adorable baby?"

She smiles slightly. "Yeah, but I sent that to a lot of people," She glances up at Brandon, then does one of those full-teeth awkward half smiles that Brandon knows he does all the time. "Oh."

"What?" Brandon asks, shaking out his hands, which have formed fists in his pockets without his realizing.

"I think..." Her shoulders hunch, awkwardness flooding off her. "I think maybe my friend Connor gave you a fake name. Sorry."

Brandon feels something like a hangover suddenly grip his body; he's sweaty, nauseous, sounds too loud everywhere—the birds, the babies, the gossiping moms, all of it is too loud, and he wants to get away and go cry somewhere. "Oh," he says. "That's fine."

She shrugs again, still shrinking into her body. "I'm really sorry. He's just in town from Brussels, where he works. Or worked. I don't know. Connor is always all over the place. Don't take it personally. He, like, falls in love with people for one night and then never speaks to them again."

"It's fine," Brandon says. The grass feels like it's sinking under him. That would be nice. To be swallowed whole by the earth.

She takes a deep breath, and her body seems to unfold again, the discomfort over, dissipating, or maybe transferring from her to Brandon, who wishes he could fold up into a square, a sandwich without a crust, and be eaten by one of these children. "But he's not here. I told him my schedule, so I thought he'd come by this week, but he's probably drunk at Deep Dive."

"Deep Dive?"

"Gay bar we used to go to in college. So trashy. I loved it. He always wants to go back there when he's in town. But I told him I can't just hit a bar in the middle of the day." She nods at the baby. "I'm a grown-up now."

"Yeah," Ollie says, voice wary.

"You can leave me the phone though, and your address, and then maybe he can send you yours." She holds out her hand, and Brandon takes a step back, not wanting to give up yet, no matter how awful all this is.

"We'll try the bar," Ollie says. "I don't want to know how much it costs to mail a phone."

"True," she says. "Well, sorry. If he shows up, I'll tell him you're looking for him…" She looks at him.

"Brandon," Brandon says. He feels like a shadow on the grass at this point. He's surprised he still has a name.

"You're so his type." Her voice walks the line between appreciative and mocking.

"Thanks," Brandon says. He stares at her for a beat longer before Ollie takes his arm and leads him away.

"You okay?" Ollie asks, when they're far from the screaming children and cackling parents.

"I'm so confused," Brandon says. "I know we had a moment.

Why would he lie about his name? He checked in under it, we joked about—" Brandon shakes his head. "Wait, he had an ID with that name! He couldn't have been lying."

"It could have been a fake ID," Ollie says.

"To check into a hotel? Why? It's not like he knew he was going to seduce the concierge."

"Maybe he'd seen you from afar and made a plan," Ollie says. "To have one perfect night with you."

Brandon smiles. He knows Ollie doesn't believe that—Brandon doesn't even believe it, as much as he wants to. It would be nice to believe, right? That this was all some fantasy of Jon, or Connor or whoever, to create this night with Brandon, to have him—but then why leave the phone? Unless that's part of it...like a scavenger hunt...that this woman could be in on...to find Heimweh.

That's too crazy though, right?

"I just felt like we had a real connection," Brandon says, instead of letting the crazy fall out of his mouth. "I know we did."

"You've said that."

"I know. Let's just find him. I'll show you, prove to you we do." He feels something in him straighten out, some firmness in his spine that wants to show Ollie he's right. Jon is special.

"Okay, but—" Ollie starts.

"If it was all some quick thrill, fine. Then I can move on."

"I was going to say we should also find out about the guy who got shot."

"Right," Brandon says, remembering. "That too."

"And I believe you," Ollie says suddenly. "I think you had a connection. Maybe it was like she said and he just fell in love for one night, but there was something there, and he's worth finding to figure out what it is. Even if someone hadn't died."

Brandon looks over at Ollie, who is beaming at him. "Thanks."

"You believe in love," Ollie says, squeezing Brandon's shoulder. "It's one of my favorite things about you, so don't give it up."

Brandon smiles. Yeah, it is one of his best traits. Then he narrows his eyes at Ollie. "Is this about your date this morning?"

Ollie grins, but Brandon feels his phone buzz, and Ollie takes his out before he can answer.

NICOLE

Tattoo guy is dangerous. Ex special forces turned freelancer.

"I could have told her that," Brandon says. They're walking through the middle of the field by the pond but stop to text.

NICOLE

Also I think my boss is hitting on me.

"Oooooh," Ollie says.

IAN

That's terrifying and hilarious

I mean the ex-special forced thing is terrifying and the boss hitting on you is hilarious.

NICOLE

I figured. Why is it hilarious?

IAN

Because you sound like Brandon

"Rude," Brandon says.

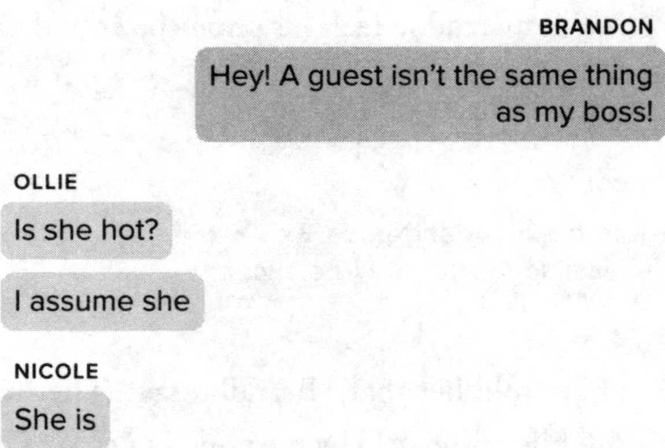

Brandon meets eyes with Ollie. They're both thinking the same thing: Nicole needs some love in her life!

BRANDON

Go for it!

IAN

Do not take relationship advice from Brandon

Brandon sighs.

"They're just teasing," Ollie says.

"No, they're right."

BRANDON

Fair

NICOLE

I won't

I'm just shocked

OLLIE

Why? You're amazing and beautiful

"Should we tell them Jon's name might be Connor?" Ollie asks.

"Not yet," Brandon says quickly. The teasing is going to be bad, and he wants to find Jon—or Connor, whatever—first. Ian and Nicole do not think Brandon's belief in love is one of his best traits.

NICOLE

I gotta go

IAN

Have fun fucking your boss

NICOLE

Shut up

"So," Brandon says, "want to go see if Jon is at this gay dive bar?"

"Already found it online. Let's go."

18.
Ollie

DEEP DIVE IS ON THE Upper West Side, not quite close enough to Columbia to be a popular college hangout but still close enough that the few folks who are inside on a Monday afternoon are mostly college guys and older men who come to leer at college guys, which some of the college guys seem to know and appreciate. But the vibe is definitely dark, dirty, dive. Not in the sexy way. It just sort of smells stale.

"What do we do if we see him?" Brandon asks in a whisper. Ollie was wondering that himself, going over ideas in his head—confrontation, interrogation, seduction (Brandon would have to be cool with that, of course), or maybe just seeing how he reacts to Brandon and playing it by ear—but with Brandon, a plan is needed. Otherwise he'll spill everything immediately, and if Nicole is right about taking the phone being a felony (and she probably is), that would be bad.

"Just pretend we're bumping into him," Ollie says. "See if he looks happy."

Brandon nods. He's got that nervous look, his hand flexing again. "How will I be able to tell?"

Oh. Poor guy. "Just trust your gut. And don't mention the phone. Just be cool."

"Right," Brandon says, his chin rising far too high in his attempt to be confident. "Cool."

"You're looking at the ceiling."

"Yeah."

Ollie thinks back to his podcasts, what the reporters on them say they do to find people they want to interview. "Let's get a drink. Don't look around too obviously, just take everything in."

"Sure..." Brandon says, immediately looking around.

"Just sit down," Ollie says, walking to the bar. "Order whatever you'd normally get."

"Can I have a cosmo?" Brandon asks the bartender, who sighs and nods.

"A seltzer for me," Ollie says, smiling. "Now look at me, I'll scan the room," Ollie says, turning on the cracked-leather stool to face Brandon.

"This feels so weird," Brandon says.

"Why? We're just two friends talking at a bar."

"I feel like everyone is looking at us."

"They're not." Ollie's eyes are scanning behind Brandon. The bar isn't huge, but it's not small, and it's dark, with strange columns placed almost at random. When they have their drinks, Ollie stands. "Let's go get a table." Then he leans in to whisper, "Look to the left as we walk."

Brandon nods and looks to his right as they head to the back of the bar.

"Other left," Ollie hisses.

"Oh, that's him," Brandon almost shouts as they pass a man alone at a dark table, staring at his phone.

Ollie feels the case crack open in his chest, pouring adrenaline into his limbs. They did it! They followed the clues and found him!

Brandon doesn't move. He looks frozen by shock, like a dog unsure what to do once they've caught their own tail.

"Say hi," Ollie whispers, which is enough to let Brandon off the leash.

He bounds over to the admittedly very handsome man at the table. "Jon!"

The man doesn't look up until Brandon is standing over him. Ollie stays close, just behind Brandon. He honestly didn't think it would be so easy. The adrenaline starts to fade a little. Is this it? What's next?

The man glances up, and Ollie can see his face calculate something, maybe Brandon's voice and the name Jon rushing into his ears with the new context of Brandon standing before him. Then he smiles. It's a really beautiful smile.

"Brandon!" Jon (or should it be Connor?) says, standing and giving Brandon one of those hugs that go above one shoulder and under the other, latching around like they're going to kiss. Brandon looks ready to. They definitely have a connection (sexual, at least, if not the romantic one Brandon seems to want). Ollie turns away for a moment, just in case they want to, but when he turns back, they are full-on making out.

He clears his throat, and Brandon and pulls back, blushing. "This is my friend Ollie."

"Hi," Jon says. "I'm…an idiot who lost his phone after he got Brandon's number. Jon." He holds out his hand to shake Ollie's. It's a charming handshake somehow, firm without being show-offy. He seems really great. But also his friend who directed them here said his name was Connor. So something is definitely off.

"I was wondering why you didn't text," Brandon says. Ollie can't tell if he's suddenly become really good at playing along or is just swept up in a fantasy and has forgotten about the exploding head.

"I just lost my phone." Jon shakes his head, holding up the one he was just staring at. "This is my new one. I was trying to download my backups, but I'm not good with tech." He pockets the phone before Ollie can get a look at the screen. "But, wow, you wandered into my favorite bar. It's fate, right?" He kisses Brandon again.

"Yeah," Brandon says, eyes gleaming. "Fate."

Ollie believes in love. He believes in fate. He believes in hoping for all the good things to happen while knowing they might not—and that terrible things happen every day. But right now, he is concerned that maybe Brandon has forgotten everything that led him to find "Jon"—like how he's lying about his name.

This isn't fate. It's an investigation.

Ollie sits down at Jon's table as though they've been invited. The kissing at least implied it.

"So, Jon," he says, sipping his seltzer and leaning in. If there was a light he could point at Jon's face, he would. Interrogation. He briefly considers using his phone flashlight but decides that might be distracting. And Jon is still standing. This is backward. He shouldn't have sat down. "What brought you to Brandon's hotel?" And what made him check out early, he hopes, is implied.

Jon shakes his head as Brandon nuzzles his neck. "Ugh, it was a work thing, and then it was canceled, and I thought they were sending me somewhere else, but then it was back on, and I'd already checked out of the hotel—" He sighs, sitting down. Brandon sticks to him as he does, holding his hand. He looks like he wants to leap into Jon's lap but settles for sitting pressed against him, chin on Jon's shoulder. "You ever feel like the world is conspiring against you?"

"All the time," Brandon says dreamily, hair standing on end from the making out like Jon is a cartoon socket he stuck his… finger in.

"What do you do that's so chaotic?" Ollie asks, leaning farther across the table. Brandon raises Jon's hand to his lips and then weaves all his fingers through it.

"Art insurance." He says it so naturally, Ollie wants to believe him. Jon turns to Brandon and brings their interwoven hands to his chest, smiling. "I go around all over the place and work with local authenticators to determine insurance plans for art, but usually in private collections, not museums or anything. It's sort of fun to see the art, but the part I do is really boring. Just numbers."

"So what happened that your schedule got all confused?" Ollie says, wishing Jon would turn back to him so he could look into his eyes. But he's locked in with Brandon now. They're barely moving, just gazing at each other, which is somehow more disturbing than when they were making out.

Jon pauses and sips his drink, something frothy looking. "Oh, just—the piece wasn't where they thought it was, so I was going to leave, but then the owner brought it back to the city, and I had to stay. Just…moving pieces. Or a moving piece." He smirks at his own joke, then finally turns back to Ollie. "What do you do?"

"Dog walker," Ollie says with a shrug.

"And house sitter," Brandon adds. "He's house-sitting this giant, like, mansion in Park Slope. We're all staying there because—" Ollie watches Brandon pull back, eyes wide, as he seems to remember everything.

"I was scared," Ollie shrugs, covering for Brandon. Jon is suspicious, and Ollie wants to know why that man got killed, but he's not going to out Brandon as a stalker and ruin the *very* obvious chemistry they have. "Huge empty house at night. Way more fun with friends."

"Sounds like a slumber party," Jon says with a giant smile.

"That's it exactly," Ollie says. Maybe that's an opportunity for more interrogation. "We're even doing game night tonight."

"Oh!" Jon turns to Brandon, excited. "Like the one you told me about, with the trivia?"

"Yep," Ollie says as Brandon's eyes go wide. "You should come."

"I have work tonight," Brandon says, frowning. "I didn't think you meant tonight."

"Call in sick," Jon says. "I want to spend as much time with you as I can before I have to go home."

"Where is home, anyway?" Ollie asks. "How long are you here for?"

Jon laughs. "You doing the friend-interrogation thing?"

Obviously. Ollie must have a confused look on his face because Jon smiles and waves him off.

"No, it's sweet. I'm originally from the Bay Area, and I live in London now. I'm not sure how much longer they need me here, but"—he glances at his phone, which he holds beneath the table—"probably not too much longer." He turns to Brandon. "So I want to spend that time with you. See what fate keeps bringing us together for."

Brandon flushes pink in the light. He looks so happy that Ollie wants this all to be real for him, even if he's still deeply suspicious of what Jon isn't telling them. Like why his friend Avery said his real name was Connor.

"Okay, I'll call in sick."

"I'm going to go use the bathroom," Ollie says, standing. Brandon and Jon barely notice as he makes his way to the back and locks himself in the one-toilet bathroom. There are already a few unread messages.

IAN

I texted Victor. The phone number that made the reservation is registered to a company—KBA. That's all he would tell me. Didn't know what they are though.

And I don't want to talk about it

Victor says hi and he misses you guys and game night

OLLIE

IAN! Are you okay?

He waits a moment, but Ian doesn't respond.

NICOLE

We can talk about it if you want

I hope it helped you find closure

OLLIE

Or reopen something!

NICOLE

Ollie...

OLLIE

Who knows?

NICOLE

Well, we're here when you're back on your phone

OLLIE

Hopefully just busy at work, right?

But I have news!

We found Jon!

Oh but his real name might be Connor

NICOLE

You found him?

Are you okay?

Real name?

OLLIE

Yeah, Brandon is talking to him right now. Or kissing him.

They're kind of cute together

NICOLE

Oh Jesus

OLLIE

And he was living in Brussels. At least according to his friend. He says London.

NICOLE

So he's lying a lot

OLLIE

Or his friend is

NICOLE

The EU is in Brussels.

How did you meet his friend?

BRANDON

It's a long story

NICOLE

Are you being careful? Heart-eyes is dangerous.

OLLIE

We are, promise!

Oh, and I invited him to game night tonight at the Strongs'

NICOLE

What?

That's insane

Like completely insane

OLLIE

It's a great way for us to get him alone and question him

NICOLE

Ollie! You're not a detective! This isn't one of your podcasts! This is what the podcast is about—a bunch of innocent twenty-somethings all get wrapped up in something and murdered! And you just chose the crime scene!

Though we're all queer so probably no one will do a podcast about us

I feel like Ian should chime in here to back me up or say that dead bodies in a rich person's house means we will be a podcast.

OLLIE

Oh, Ian you should bring Victor, since he misses them!

And Nicole you can bring your boss

NICOLE

Absolutely not

OLLIE

Or the coffee girl!

NICOLE

I'm putting my phone down now. Please don't bring the man who people get murdered around.

OLLIE

Eight tonight! Bring snacks!

NICOLE

I cannot believe I'm doing this.

Ollie smirks, putting the phone away. Perfect. Just what a detective would do, right? A dinner party turned fact-finding turned accusation maybe? In any case, it'll all come out one way or another—who Jon really is, why that man was shot, if they're in danger—and then maybe Ollie can make sure they're not. Once he has all the info, he can save everyone.

19.

Nicole

WHILE THEY WAIT FOR THEIR steaks, Ellen shows Nicole how to research criminal activity. Not the laws but the activity itself, through NYPD accounts and crime bulletins, neighborhood watch groups, and key organized-crime reporters on social media. Nicole takes notes. It's exciting, this new form of research. But most of the research, it turns out, is person-to-person. Ellen calls people—actually calls them, not texts. Police officers, criminal defense lawyers, even someone who talks about "the family" once, which Nicole assumes is the mob. She puts every call on speakerphone and introduces Nicole as a colleague, which gives her a warm feeling in her stomach, better than the one from the martini. But they don't find anything out.

Her phone chimes, but she ignores it, trying to stay professional. Ellen glances at it.

"If it's your silly friends, they could be in trouble."

"Uh, right," Nicole says, picking up her phone.

IAN

I texted Victor. The phone number that made the reservation is registered to a company—KBA. That's all he would tell me. Didn't know what they are though.

Oh shit. She tries to keep her face calm. Texting an ex is probably the kind of silly drama Ellen would tell her to avoid. The message is from a while ago, too. Nicole feels a heavy hit of guilt for having ignored it. She keeps reading until she hits a text that makes her eyes go wide.

OLLIE

We found Jon!

She glances up again but keeps her mouth shut for the moment.

OLLIE

Oh but his real name might be Connor

NICOLE

You found him?

Are you okay?

Real name?

OLLIE

Yeah, Brandon is talking to him right now. Or kissing him.

They're kind of cute together

NICOLE

Oh Jesus

OLLIE

And he was living in Brussels. At least according to his friend. He says London

NICOLE

So he's lying a lot

OLLIE

Or his friend is

NICOLE

The EU is in Brussels.

EU is spy stuff, intelligence stuff, probably. Especially when coupled with a fake name. Brandon always knows how to pick them, but this is top-tier.

NICOLE

How did you meet his friend?

BRANDON

It's a long story

NICOLE

Are you being careful? Heart-eyes is dangerous.

OLLIE

We are, promise!

Oh, and I invited him to game night tonight at the Strongs'

She almost chokes on her drink, and Ellen looks over, her stare lingering for a moment, disapproving, before Nicole turns away, back to her own phone to fire off what she knows is a lecture, but come on, Ollie is being insane right now. A party with a man with two names who maybe got someone killed?

OLLIE

And Nicole you can bring your boss

Nicole almost chokes reading that but covers it with a fake cough. Ellen glances over but doesn't say anything.

NICOLE

Absolutely not

OLLIE

Or the coffee girl!

NICOLE

I'm putting my phone down now. Please don't bring the man who people get murdered around over.

Nicole shakes her head, confused, and then texts with Ollie as he explains and conjures up a game night over her objections.

OLLIE

Eight tonight! Bring snacks!

She sighs, knowing she has to go.

NICOLE

I cannot believe I'm doing this.

She puts down the phone, wondering how to tell Ellen everything. Not about the party. Ellen would tell her to stay away, and Nicole knows she can't do that. She can't abandon her friends when they might be in danger. All she can do is try to help them now, try to figure out what's going on.

"What's KBA?" Nicole asks.

Ellen takes a long swig of her drink and leans back. "Private security. Private espionage. Private army, really. Why?"

"An army?"

"For hire."

"They made the reservation for Jon—who also goes by Connor and worked in Brussels. EU, right?"

"Shit," Ellen says, her face going a little pale. "If KBA made the reservation, then your friend's hookup is either working for them, which means he's dangerous, or had a deal with them, which means he's in a dangerous situation."

Nicole sighs. Of course.

Ellen blows her bangs off her forehead, a long exhale pointed up, her lower lip jutting out a little. It's weirdly hot. "The EU thing tracks, too. He could be one of theirs, coming back from a mission over there. He could be a diplomat or courier meeting with them on behalf of our or another government. Though then he'd be doing an American accent for no reason. You said he was American, right?"

Nicole nods. "Pretty sure." Brandon would have gone on about his sexy accent otherwise.

"So state, or CIA maybe. But the worst possible thing he could be is someone who decided to go work for KBA." She finishes the rest of her drink. "They're notorious for recruiting via turncoat. Bring us these files, this code name, whatever, and you get a job with us. We keep you safe from the people you turned on, get paid an absurd amount, life of adventure, that kind of thing. But these are bad people. That life of adventure is usually political assassinations and warmongering."

Nicole stares and realizes she hasn't moved in a while. Her body feels leaden. Even her arm is stiff as she reaches out and grabs her drink. She just means to sip it, but as it touches her tongue, she keeps pouring it down her throat, thirsty.

"Yeah, now you're getting it," Ellen says.

"So what do we do?" Nicole says, almost slamming the glass down. Her voice sounds breathy.

"I'm going to reach out to some contacts and see what's going on. You..." Ellen tilts her head. "Research. Use Incognito Mode on your phone. KBA is run by Carter Kells and Judith Battle. I want you to look into where they've been recently, what they've been talking about, put together a picture of what they're saying their company goals and expectations are this quarter."

"They're publicly traded?"

"Oh yeah," Ellen says. "Why wouldn't they be?"

"I don't know," Nicole says. "Just seems in bad taste."

Ellen smiles at her. "You're cute."

Nicole looks down to hide her blushing cheeks. "So you want me to look at what their public plans are for the company?"

"And the subtext. From there we can try to figure out how this links in. Hopefully I find something out, too."

The waitress comes back in with their meals. Nicole and Ellen are silent as the food is laid out before them. Ellen lifts her glass. "Another round for both of us, please. We're going to be here a while."

"We're not going back to the office?" Nicole asks.

Ellen cuts into her steak slowly, parting the cut of meat to show the pink flesh within. Steam rises and clouds the metal of the knife. "Nope. Trust me, it's better if nothing we do is on the company Wi-Fi now."

Nicole swallows.

"Eat. It's good. And I like watching a woman eat a steak. It's hot."

Nicole starts to blush again but shakes her head. "You're kind of my boss."

Ellen grins. "True. You gonna go to HR?"

"Maybe," Nicole says, cutting into her steak. She should, she knows. But her body is tingling. She takes a bite. The steak melts in her mouth, deliciously rich and smoky. "I guess it depends how you look eating yours."

"Well, now I just want to eat you," Ellen says, voice low in a way that makes Nicole's skin tingle. "But let's have lunch and try to save your friend first."

Nicole feels goose bumps rise on her neck. That's how to flirt. Although doing it with her boss was probably a bad idea. But Ellen is sexy, and she's at the top of the field Nicole wants to be in. She's smart, self-assured, glamorous: Why shouldn't Nicole be with her? Maybe Nicole can learn something about having a social life. It's not like she's Brandon—her boss isn't a client.

It's way stupider.

But she hasn't slept with her yet. Just flirting. She eats as Ellen takes out her phone, typing frantically into it. Research, right. She pulls her eyes away from Ellen's hands—short red nails, soft-looking skin—and takes out her own phone and goes into Incognito Mode, looking into KBA and its bosses. Technically Kells is the CEO, British, former diplomat, which Nicole assumes means MI5. He's got a knighthood and some long family history that makes him fourth in line to be a duke. Battle is the COO, Texan, did a stint in the army, then moved over to the State Department. There are no photos of her on the website, and the only one Nicole can find online has her blurry behind Kells, just sunglasses and a smudge of pale skin. Aside from brief bios on the company page, it's hard to find out much else.

They seldom do public appearances unless they're defending themselves from accusations of being part of a variety of terrible things: violent regime changes, stolen weapons of mass destruction, genocide. Then it's all Kells, very smoothly explaining that KBA provided aid to key clients who may or may not have done terrible things, but doesn't everyone deserve to feel safe? It makes Nicole's steak lose its flavor.

They haven't been accused of anything in six months, and then it was of being involved in an African warlord's consolidation of power around a rare-earth-minerals mine. That could involve the EU, but she's not sure why people would be killing over it now. So she follows the advice Ellen gave and looks for information they released to shareholders. It takes a while to find anything, during which she eats, and drinks, and occasionally looks up at Ellen, who is typing on the phone but sometimes is looking up at her. She shifts closer to Ellen when she's done eating. She feels warm from all that meat inside her and wonders if Ellen can feel it radiating off her. Ellen leans toward her but keeps typing on her phone. Nicole wonders if the flirting was just for fun, the way some people flirt like a game, and now she's back to work, or if she's just really good at compartmentalizing her various desires.

Most of what Nicole finds for shareholders is about earnings and losses, which she's pretty expert at scanning through, but there's one statement in a financial article, a quote from Battle: *We hope in the near future to greatly expand our client base. Such rapid growth may incur more expenses but of course will result in greater long-term profitability. If we can, we'd love to partner with every player across the globe.* Nicole scowls at that. So they provide armies to two countries and then have their own guys fight each other? She sighs. They'll make a lot of money.

In college, she thinks, she would have known about KBA already. There must be protests against them somewhere. She would have been involved. *War profiteers paying for more war!* She would have tried to be interviewed by anyone who would talk to her, explaining how if you pay people to fight, they're going to make more reasons for more fights, and the bigger they are, the more at war the world will be, and the more profit they'll make.

"They're talking about expansion," Nicole says. "More clients."

"That could mean a lot of things," Ellen says with a sigh. Her phone rings and she looks at it, eyes narrowing. "I should take this one privately."

"Okay," Nicole says. "Does it have to do with—"

"Something else," Ellen says, rising smoothly and walking out of the room.

Nicole turns her eyes back toward her own phone. What has

she really found out? Not much. She wishes she were better at this. Ellen is smart, and maybe Nicole could be like Ellen, right? But… maybe not.

She opens her research back up again. But it's not enough. Looking at their statement to shareholders was smart, but she wonders if there's some other angle. That's all couched in investor speak, after all. They're for people who want to make money but don't care about how. But there are people who care about how. She used to be one of them.

She fishes the flyer out of her purse. She didn't throw it out, which she's sure Ollie and Brandon would say means something but which she knows just means she never cleans out her purse. There it is: STOP WAR-FOR-PROFIT. The people who watch the people who make money are the activists.

She takes a deep breath and types in the number.

NICOLE

Hi, this is Nicole

From the coffee shop

The lawyer

Oh god, why is she still typing?

NICOLE

You gave me the flyer?

SAM

I remember

The cute lawyer

Nicole bites her thumbnail. No way is she telling anyone about this. She's already flirted with her boss today. Must be something about her friends being in mortal peril. Or about her actually doing something for once. It's making her heartbeat rise.

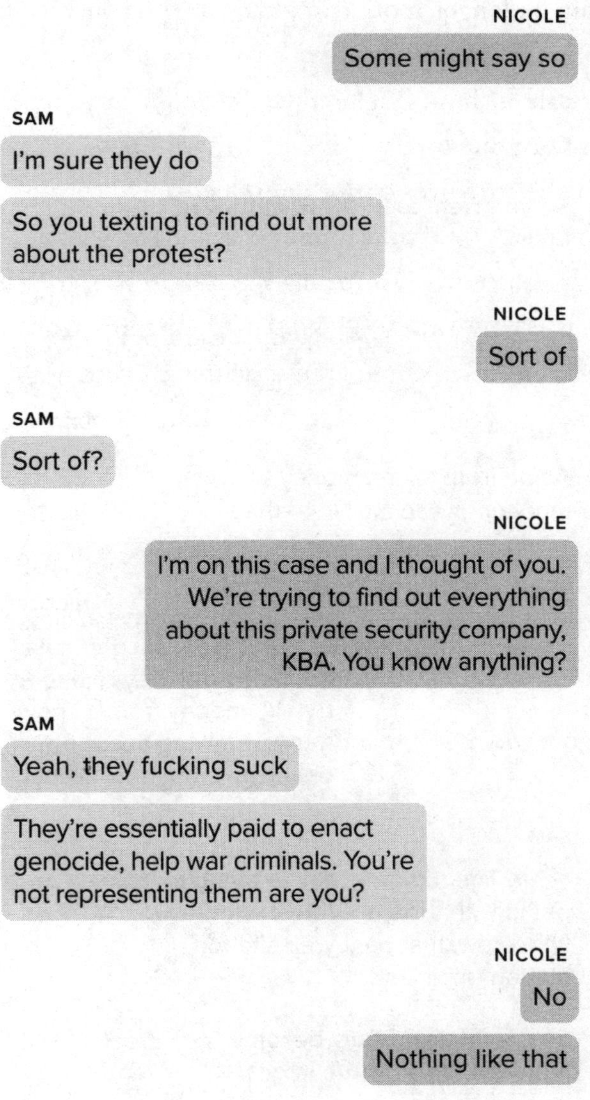

But I'm trying to figure out what they might be up to now

We think they might be interfering with a case

It's a lie, unless a case is her friends' lives. But she doesn't want to put Sam in danger, too.

SAM

Okay, good

So you want to know what they're up to?

NICOLE

Like what they seem to be doing, in terms of business

SAM

Aside from taking money to kill innocent people all over the world?

NICOLE

Maybe? Or if there's a particular part of the world they're eager to take money from. I know they've been talking about rapid expansion and new clients.

SAM

Yeah. The rumor is they're trying to get in with folks on Velvet Alley—you know, that dark web site for human traffickers?

So they'd essentially become a private army for the largest

criminal trade network in the world. It would go beyond being paid war profiteers, they'd be helping one side start wars, then helping the other end them.

Just an endless cycle of violence.

NICOLE

How would they do that though? Don't they have competition?

SAM

I don't know

That's just what a whistleblower said—they want Velvet Alley's business

But no one knows who runs it

So hopefully it's a bluff or a sales pitch

Or maybe the whistleblower is a plant

Sorry. With KBA it's hard to know what's real

NICOLE

No this is all useful

Thank you

SAM

My pleasure

Anything else you want?

Nicole stares at the phone, not sure what to say to that. Ellen comes back in suddenly, the curtains to the room letting in a cool breeze.

"Find anything else out while I was gone?"

"KBA might be trying to partner with or take over Velvet Road."

Ellen narrows her eyes, considering that. "Hmmm, okay. That's interesting. Where'd you get it?"

"Activist I know," Nicole says, feeling guilty about not responding to Sam.

Ellen sighs. "So just rumors. Still, it's something."

"You find anything else out?"

Ellen shakes her head. "I think we're at the point where we wait for someone to get back to me. But that's good work, Nicole. Smart thinking."

Nicole glows. "Thanks. So, do I just go back to the office?"

"If you want." Ellen smiles, hand on her hip. "Or, y'know, I live nearby. We could wait at my place."

20.
Ian

IAN STARES AT THE BULBOUS reflection of Heart-Eyes for a heartbeat, then ducks down behind the counter. They know this isn't a long-term plan, but it's the first thing they can think of. Hide. Maybe they can text for help? Except their phone is still on the counter. Heart-Eyes would definitely notice a hand popping up and grabbing it.

They listen to the sound of the door closing and footsteps coming farther into the store. They stop, then pace for a moment. Maybe he'll leave. For a moment, there's silence. Then the sound of a page turning. Is he...browsing? Ian waits a minute or so more, or it could be an hour, they're not sure. Then they hear it again, another page turning.

They wonder how they can get out of this. There's the back room, but the door is closed, so while they could crawl to it, opening it would still attract attention.

There's the sound of another page turning.

If he were here to kill Ian, he'd be tearing the place apart, right? Maybe they should just stand up?

Seems insane. But so do all the other options. So they take a deep breath and stand.

There he is, standing in the middle of the store, heart-eyes tattoo facing Ian. He's flipping through *QUEER COLORS*. He glances over as Ian pops up, gasping slightly. "Oh, you scared me. Drop a contract or something?" His voice is softer than Ian expected. In the light of the shop, and without the distraction of performing and waitressing, they can take in more of him in the light, too: tall, broad-shouldered, all muscle. White, maybe thirties with brown hair and blue eyes. Ian doesn't think they're the eyes of a killer. Not that they would know.

Heart-Eyes looks back at the page of *QUEER COLORS* and seems to really take it in. He smiles a little. It looks natural on him.

"Earring," Ian lies, tapping the one that dangles. "Found it."

"It's pretty," Heart-Eyes says, looking over at them.

"Can I help you find something?" Ian asks, swallowing down their nervousness. Trying to treat this as normal.

Heart-Eyes smiles, looks back at the book, flips the page. "This is really lovely work in here," he says. He walks over to the counter, still staring at the piece on the page: a pastel of two men sixty-nineing. "I like art. It's my name, so I tried to avoid it a lot, but as I get older, I find I like museums more and more. I wish I hadn't been so insecure as a kid, y'know? Maybe I'd be a painter now."

"It's never too late to start," Ian says. They can feel their hands shaking, so they lay them on the counter. "We have some great introduction-to-painting books. Even some coloring books if you want to start small."

Heart-Eyes looks up and smiles, and Ian's heart beats faster. Is this guy about to kill them with a highbrow erotic coffee-table book? But Heart-Eyes just puts it gently on the counter. There's a dent from his fingers in the cover though. Strong hands. Maybe he's trying to hold back his anger.

Ian tries to remember if he heard the *click* of the door locking when Heart-Eyes came in. If they just run and try to open the door, will they have to unlock it first? How fast can a man this big chase after them?

"Yeah, a coloring book sounds fun. Where are they?"

Ian steps out from behind the counter, still trying not to shake too obviously, and leads him over to the adult coloring books, some of which are very adult. Heart-Eyes smirks, taking down a Tom of Finland coloring book and flipping through the very explicit drawings. His smile grows wider.

"I'm a Kinsey two," he offers, still flipping. "I hadn't even heard of Kinsey, until this sex worker I'd hired in the UK—beautiful, and she had this friend—asked if I wanted some company. He was a man."

Ian nods, not sure what to make of this. Ian eyes the muscles in his arms and then legs. He could definitely run fast. And he's tall enough, his arms long enough that he could probably just reach out and grab Ian's collar if they tried to run. Especially if the door is locked.

"We had a great time. I mean, sure, in the military I'd fooled around with guys, because that's what there was. Always had fun, and I wasn't one of those men who wouldn't bend over or suck a dick or kiss, y'know? I liked everything. But didn't realize there was a scale for it until then. We were taking a break, me and these two good-looking Brits, and just talking, and that's how they taught me about it. Kinsey two, we decided. Maybe three."

He closes the book and pulls out another, this one Georgia O'Keeffe. He nods as he flips though. His nails are short and clean, which feels like a serial-killer thing on a man this big, though Ian isn't sure why. "Then there was this other sex worker in Vegas. They really are the smartest people, you know. And I told her I was a Kinsey two, and she laughed. She was trans, had a dick, which I didn't mind, and *she* said she thought I was pansexual but heteroromantic. Said maybe I wasn't even really heteroromantic, it's just I felt I had to be because of societal pressure, y'know?" He looks up at Ian as if expecting an answer. Ian nods.

"So I don't know," he says, turning back to the coloring book. "I know it's bad to try to put yourself in a box, but it's comforting, too. The sex worker, the second one, she said I should think of myself, think of everybody, really, as fluid, always evolving and changing, and being open to attraction or falling in love with whoever. So that's what I try to be." He looks up and breaks into a wide, almost-innocent grin. If Ian hadn't gotten a text earlier saying this man was a dangerous merc, they might almost be charmed by all this, would probably be flirting a little. So they smile, try to act normal.

"I'll take these two," Heart-Eyes says. "And the art book. Thanks for the recommendation. I just need to find some crayons or pencils or something."

"We sell those, too," Ian says numbly, walking over to the kids' section and picking up a small box of pre-sharpened colored pencils.

"You're amazing," Heart-Eyes says, taking the box.

"Just happy to help," Ian says instinctively, walking back over to the counter, terrified of how their back is to this man, how vulnerable they're letting themself be. But anything else would be suspicious. Heart-Eyes follows them and puts the pencils and coloring books on top of *QUEER COLORS*, then slides them over to the register. Ian rings them up and takes the offered credit card, noting the name: Arthur Smith. He should let the others know that.

"Hey," Heart-Eyes says, after Ian has handed him the bag of books. "Thanks for letting me ramble. I know it was oversharing."

Ian forces a smile, trying to act normal, and shrugs. "No worries, we love it when our customers are inspired to open up to us."

Heart-Eyes grins. "Any chance I could get your number? I mean, like I said, trying to be open to whatever happens, and what's happened is I think you're cute."

Ian feels their eyes go wide. If they say no, do they get killed? But if they say yes, that feels like an invitation to violence, too, right? They know better than to date someone dangerous. They're supposed to be the dangerous one in the relationship.

No, wait, that's probably not good either.

"You don't have to say yes," Heart-Eyes says after a moment.

"Sorry," Ian says, forcing that smile again. "I was just taken aback. We're not supposed to give our information to customers though. Sorry." Two sorrys. That's a record—just make them nervous, and apparently apologizing is easy. But they sigh in a way that they hope sounds sincerely wistful, like Brandon would if a handsome customer came in and asked for his number.

Heart-Eyes nods. "I get it. Well, thanks for all the help today anyway."

"Sure," Ian says. They stare a moment at each other before Heart-Eyes takes his bag of books and leaves.

Ian counts to sixty in their head, then screams. Which is just when Kate walks back in, holding two coffees. She startles back, spilling some coffee on the floor. Ian stops screaming, and they look at each other for a moment.

"Got a bad text back, huh?" Kate asks, moving past them warily. "There's a pillow in the back I use to muffle my sobs, if you want it."

Ian does a quick calculation in their head—as much as they want to tell Kate everything, that would be putting her in danger, so instead they just take a deep breath and shake their head. "Just needed to get that out."

"I hear ya," Kate says, handing them their coffee. Ian takes a long sip of the coffee, wishing it were spiked. "My treat because I need your help unloading stock," Kate adds. Ian frowns; so much for texting everyone immediately. They follow her to the back room, which is half office, half storeroom, a desk in one corner and then boxes and boxes of books. "New releases," she says, pointing. "Get 'em all on the shelves."

Ian sighs.

"I'll buy you lunch, too, from that sushi place you like."

Ian smirks. "For doing my job?"

"For doing the part you don't like."

"Fine." Ian turns away to hide their smile. The tips at the Wreck Room weren't good the other night, so they were probably just going to skip lunch today. And tomorrow. Somehow it's like Kate always knows. They hate that they need the charity but are glad for it anyway.

They grab a pair of scissors off the desk, slice open the first box, take the books out in a pile, and walk back into the front room to start shelving them. Kate turns back to her computer to work on the billing.

They work for a few hours, brain half reading titles and finding the right spots for them on the shelves, and half replaying that exchange with Heart-Eyes. Was it just a coincidence that he came into Ian's bookstore? Are there two big scary men walking around town with the same awful tattoo? They try to remember exactly what he looked like at brunch, but aside from a vibe and the tattoo, they can't conjure up his face clearly. Ian knows everyone has at least one doppelgänger in life, but with the same tattoo?

Still, he didn't seem violent. Dangerous, sure, any guy that big could be dangerous, but there was so much less menace once he started talking. Except about being a Kinsey 2. That's definitely the most menacing Kinsey rating.

They go on shelving for a while, pausing to sip their coffee and ring up customers as they come in. They're still not sure what to text the group: that the scary guy showed up and bought some books while talking about his sex life? Half the customers who come in here talk about their sex lives. Still, they should probably say something, right?

"Lunch!" Kate says, emerging from the office. "You got almost everything shelved, nice."

"I'm not that bad at this job," Ian says.

Kate shrugged. "I got you the California roll and the Philadelphia roll."

"And—"

"And the gyoza. I know your order."

Ian grins. "Want me to go pick it up?"

"How many books left to shelve?"

Ian nods at the small pile.

"Just take care of those first."

"Thanks." Ian grins and finishes shelving. They're eager for the walk to the sushi place. Fresh air might clear their head. Outside, they pull out their phone, still not sure what to say to their friends about Heart-Eyes. The city is cool and breezy, and they walk with their eyes on their screen.

Then, a block from the bookstore, a car pulls up suddenly in front of him. The door opens, revealing Heart-Eyes inside, grinning. He holds a gun pointed at Ian.

"Get in," he says.

Ian swallows, eyes darting down the street. No one can see Heart-Eyes. The windows are tinted and he's leaning back. Ian could try running, but that would probably be bad, too. So they get in, legs shaking.

Heart-Eyes reaches over them to slam the door shut, and the car starts moving. There's a privacy screen up, so Ian can't see the driver.

"What do you want?" they ask, voice quivering.

Heart-Eyes puts the gun in a holster under their coat. "Relax. Just want to talk. This would be easier if you'd just given me your number. Why didn't you? Not your type?"

"Uh—"

"It's okay if I'm not. Just curious. It's a shame, you're cute. I liked your act at brunch. That red dress looked real good on you."

Ian swallows. "Thanks."

Heart-Eyes shrugs. "Hey, no worries. I'm just—ah." He takes a vibrating phone out of his pocket and hits Speaker. "Someone wants to talk to you, Ian."

"Okay…" Ian says.

"Hello," says a voice from the phone. Feminine. "So nice to speak with you, Ian."

"Um, hi," Ian says, staring at the phone in Heart-Eyes's hand as though it might show them something beyond a blank lock screen. "Who is this?"

"That's not really what you should be asking, I'm afraid."

Ian is scared but still frowns. If there's one thing they hate, it's being told what to do. Except by Kate. "No?"

"No, you should be asking why someone like me would go to all this trouble just to talk with you. How did someone like you get wrapped up in this?"

Ian sighs. They know how: Brandon. Good thing they love him. "Bad choices?" they say instead.

The voice chuckles and Heart-Eyes laughs, too. "They're funny," the voice says.

"Cute too," Heart-Eyes adds.

"Can we just get to what you want?" Ian asks. "I have no idea what's going on."

"No, you probably don't, poor thing," the voice says. "And I am sorry for that. So let me tell you what's happening in brief: We asked a friend to bring something to New York. A little zip drive. Simple thing. He checked into a hotel we paid for, where he met your roommate, Brandon Weissman, and then vanished. But his phone stayed at the hotel. We thought that was curious, so Arthur here followed it. Brandon seemed to have it on him. We're not sure if that was some hilarious mix-up, or intentional, but in any case, Arthur followed it back to your place, which he investigated thoroughly."

"That was you?" Ian asks, glaring. "I had to clean for hours."

"Sorry," Heart-Eyes says, maybe even sincerely—Ian can't tell with him. "I tried to be gentle with the wigs."

"We needed to make sure you weren't in on this," the voice says. "But then the phone moved again. Brandon led us to our friend. Arthur tried to…retrieve our property but, sadly, made a miscalculation."

"I fucked it," Heart-Eyes says.

"Yes you did," the voice says.

"'Fucked it'?" Ian asks.

"There was this other guy," Heart-Eyes says, shaking his head as if disappointed. "Moved at the last second."

Ian swallows, understanding. "You shot the wrong man."

"Fucked it," Heart-Eyes says with a nod and a sigh.

"In any case," the voice continues, "our friend escaped with the zip drive, and Brandon fled the scene without meeting him."

"And there were a lot of dogs," Heart-Eyes adds. "Cute ones."

"The phone went dead a short while later. We're honestly not sure what to make of all this. But you, being Brandon's roommate, might know something. And we'd love to know what you know."

"Honestly, much less than that," Ian says, leaning back. Ian almost snorts at how little they and their friends know, apparently. But one thing is for sure—they have nothing Heart-Eyes and this woman on the phone want. May as well tell them everything and hope they laugh enough they decide not to kill anyone. "Brandon met this guy at the hotel, like you said. Jon. They hooked up, and Brandon is, like, in love with him."

"Wait," the voice says. "He slept with a guest at the hotel he works at?"

"Yep."

"And now is in love with him because of that one night?"

"Yep."

"I'm not sure I believe this."

"Trust me, I don't either, but it's classic Brandon."

"Kinda sweet," Heart-Eyes interjects.

"So, when someone who wasn't Jon picked up the phone, and then someone else who wasn't Jon came for his things, Brandon hid the phone. Thought maybe he'd slept with a married man. Wanted to give him the phone back. Said he'd be like Prince Charming with a glass slipper."

"Christ," the voice says, exasperated. At the same time, Heart-Eyes says, "Aww."

"Yeah," Ian says. "There was a meeting place on the phone, Brandon went there, saw someone die, and we've all been freaking out since then. We want nothing to do with this, I promise."

"But why would our friend—Jon, you called him—decide to run from us after meeting Brandon? And put our zip drive up for auction?"

"I have no idea," Ian says. "Brandon is great, but he's never chosen anyone who fell in love with him the way he falls in love with them before. Maybe he finally got it right."

"You think Jon is in love?"

Ian shrugs. "No clue."

"If he is, he'll find Brandon again, won't he?"

"Honestly, I hope not. Brandon deserves someone not being hunted by scary people with guns."

"You showed them your gun?" the voice asks.

"They didn't respond to my flirting!" Heart-Eyes says, looking mildly crestfallen. "Still not sure why."

Ian almost feels sorry for him. "You're cute, but Brandon already described your tattoo, so I figured it wasn't genuine."

"It was," Heart-Eyes says. "Work and play can go together." He smiles in a way that's almost sexy. Ian tries not to smile back. That would totally make them Brandon.

"I told you, you need to get that thing removed," the voice says.

"It's sentimental," Heart-Eyes says. "I'll just switch to turtlenecks. I can pull off a turtleneck, right?" he asks Ian.

"Sure," Ian says, not sure how else to respond. "Don't go with black though, too obvious. Blue is more your color."

"In any case," the voice interrupts, "we have a simple request. Arthur here will give you his number. If Jon turns up, please let him know when and where. And if, by any chance, you find that zip drive, I'd be happy to reward you very generously."

"Will you hurt my friends?"

The voice laughs. "A bunch of twentysomethings in way over their heads? No. No need. No one will believe this story. I barely do. And cleanup would attract more attention. As long as you fulfill your end of the bargain, you'll be safe. And if you find that zip drive, you can be more than fine."

Ian rolls their eyes. "Sure."

"Ten million dollars. Think of how that could kick-start your drag career."

Ian goes silent, brain whirring at the number. Student loans done, easy. Their friends' loans, too. Custom gowns and wigs. They could quit the bookstore job, open their own club, perform as a headliner every night, hire a publicist. An image of success flies up in their mind. They don't know Jon. They don't know what's on this zip drive. They know all this is sketchy as fuck, but…for ten million…

"Think about it, Ian," the voice says. "What do you want your life to be?"

"I..." Ian shakes their head. They want to get less involved in the drama, not more, but their life could change. What do they want their life to be? "I'll think about it."

"That's wonderful to hear. And, of course, everything I said about not hurting you or your friends? That goes out the window if you try to warn your friends about this or tell anyone about our chat. Then I'll have Arthur here sink all your bodies in the East River." Ian looks up at Heart-Eyes, who shrugs apologetically. "This has been a nice little chat. Thank you. Goodbye." The line clicks off, and Heart-Eyes puts the phone away.

"So, can I give you my number now?" Heart-Eyes asks, hand open for Ian's phone.

"Do I have a choice?" Ian asks, opening their phone; they have like a million texts. They swipe those away and hand it to Heart-Eyes.

"Awww, don't be like that," Heart-Eyes says, entering his number as Arthur Smith, then sending a heart emoji. "Think of it this way: Sure, this is a scary situation for you, but it could be a fun story to tell our grandkids."

"You're way too thirsty," Ian says, taking the phone back. "You'd have a better shot if you played hard to get."

Heart-Eyes shrugs. "What can I say? I don't usually have much time to make an impression. Where can we drop you?"

"Sushi place, Wassup B, just a few blocks from the bookstore."

The car turns, but Heart-Eyes stays silent, looking out the window. Ian is almost offended.

"Anything else you need from me?" Ian asks.

“Nope,” Heart-Eyes says. “We’re good.”

“Was she lying? Are you going to kill me and my friends?”

Heart-Eyes shakes his head, a small smile on his lips. “Nah, she was right. Too much trouble. And besides, I could never kill someone as pretty as—” He stops mid-sentence, turning his smile into a scowl. “No.”

“Someone as pretty as me?” Ian asks, laughing.

“You told me to be hard to get, so I’m doing that.”

“Great,” Ian says. “I do like a man who can take orders.”

The car pulls to a stop in front of Wassup B. Heart-Eyes turns to look at Ian and wiggles his eyebrows. “I was in the military.”

“Tempting,” Ian says, opening the door. “Maybe if you were wearing the uniform.”

They get out as Heart-Eyes laughs and close the door. The car drives off. Ian watches it until it’s around a corner and out of sight, then screams again.

21.
Brandon

THIS IS FATE. JUST DAYS ago Brandon was saying they should have a game night to meet Jon, and now they're going to! He reads over the texts as Jon gets them another round from the bar, grinning because Ollie thinks he and Jon are cute but then frowning because Ollie is calling Jon Connor. Maybe Jon is his middle name or something. People can call themselves whatever they want, right? So, no matter what's going on, this is something good. And yeah, someone's head got blown off, and there was brain on the ground, but Jon will tell Brandon about that when he's ready. It must have been so traumatizing for him, after all. That's not second-date territory. And that's what this is, right? A second date, sort of?

"So are you sure I won't be crashing?" Jon asks, setting another cosmo down in front of Brandon and sitting next to him, thighs pressing together.

"Absolutely not," Brandon says, letting himself lean into Jon. He's morning-blanket warm. "We have people at game night all the time. Ollie will probably bring the new girl he's seeing, right?" he says as Ollie comes back and sits down.

"What?" Ollie says.

"I was telling Jon about game night and saying he won't be crashing."

"Oh, no, not at all," Ollie says with a smile. "Everyone is really excited to meet you."

"And you might bring that new girl you had a date with," Brandon says. "Then it's everyone meeting everyone's new... people." Too soon for *boyfriend* probably, though the word wants to explode out of his mouth, tinted bright pink from the cosmo. Jon squeezes his thigh. Soon.

"That's not a bad idea," Ollie says, nodding. "We should probably go clean up, buy snacks and drinks though."

"Oh," Brandon says, disappointed to be leaving Jon after finally finding him.

"I can help," Jon offers. "Why don't Brandon and I handle the shopping and bring food and drinks to the party?"

Ollie's eyes narrow. He's suspicious, Brandon realizes. Or maybe just being an overprotective friend. And Brandon gets it. It's sweet. But he can handle it. He saw brains splattered on the street; he can deal with shopping with a guy he admittedly doesn't know so well and who might be—but probably isn't—mixed up in something dangerous. Brandon has made plenty of bad choices and survived before. Maybe this will finally be the time he makes a bad choice that turns out to be a good one. Jon might also be—and hopefully is—Heimweh.

"Yeah," Brandon says, wrapping his hands around Jon's arm. It's so muscular. "We can handle the shopping. I wouldn't know how to clean that place anyway."

Ollie holds his stare a moment longer, then nods. "Sure." He stands, still looking wary. "No red wine."

"I would never," Brandon gasps. In that house?

"See you later, then," Ollie says, almost nervously, before walking off.

"Alone at last," Jon says, arm wrapping around Brandon's waist. "I still can't believe you just walked in here."

"Yeah," Brandon says. He thinks about telling him everything for a moment, but it's a lot. The phone, tracking him down, talking to his friend. He almost wants to say it all right now. He can feel Jon's phone in his pocket. But better to wait, have an amazing night, bond even more with him, and tell him later, tomorrow, next week, next year, on their ten-year wedding anniversary. Whenever it goes from sounding like a stalker to being a cute story. He'll play it by ear. "Just lucky, I guess."

"Me too," Jon says, kissing Brandon. The kissing is better than Brandon remembers. The sex was so rushed before, they didn't really get to experience lips on lips, tongue on tongue, the smell and taste and warmth of him. So they do that now, and it's like a shot of champagne, all fizzy and light, and then a bite of dark chocolate, coating his tongue. They make out at that table in the back for a while, but also not long enough.

"You want to go to the bathroom?" Jon asks.

Brandon bites his lip. He does. But he shakes his head. "You can stay over tonight, after game night," he says. "It would be nice to have you naked somewhere I don't feel like we're in a rush." He reaches out and runs his hand down Jon's chest—god, it's so muscular.

"Mmm, good point," Jon says, kissing Brandon's earlobe. "Okay, we can wait," he whispers. Brandon is way too hard for this. He leans back and downs some of the cosmo. "What did your friend mean about red wine?"

"Oh, the place he's house-sitting for these rich people is fancy. And the whole house is white. White furniture, carpet, everything."

"Ah, so nothing that stains."

"Exactly," Brandon says.

"But the house isn't his, or yours? No one knows you're staying there?"

Brandon shakes his head, confused as to why that matters. "No, I guess not."

Jon grins widely. "How fun."

Brandon shrugs, happy Jon is happy. "It's pretty cool. Oh, I have to call work, call in sick."

"Go do that. I'll settle the tab and meet you outside."

Brandon smiles. A man hasn't bought him a drink in what feels like forever. "Okay."

Outside, the air smells clean and fresh, like autumn and love. A few leaves drift from a tree and swirl around him, red and gold. Magic. He calls in sick, faking a hoarse voice and getting away with it pretty easily.

He watches Jon through the window to the bar as he pays and then checks his phone and smiles. He comes outside and extends his hand, and Brandon takes it, Jon's chunky rubber bangle resting on his wrist. They're holding hands! On a perfect fall day.

"I'm so glad you walked into my bar," Jon says. "What were you even doing there?"

Brandon swallows. Ollie was the one with the good cover story. "We were just out enjoying the day," Brandon says. "Ollie's a dog walker, so he has the afternoon off, and we thought we'd just, like, go out."

"Nice," Jon says. "Lucky for me."

"And me," Brandon says. "I wish you'd left a note or something for me."

"I was worried you'd get in trouble."

"I get it," Brandon says.

"Plus I thought I could text you. Did anyone find my phone in the hotel?"

Brandon swallows again, pulling on Jon's hand so they start walking. "A maid found some stuff. It's in the lost and found, if you want to go get it."

"Eh, later," he says. "For now, let's go shopping. I think we should make the party DSLWLS themed."

"Oh," Brandon says, "like those weird little cream puffs they eat in that café?"

"Windbeutel," Jon nods. "There's gotta be someplace in NY that sells them, right?"

Brandon shrugs and goes to take out his phone, almost taking out Jon's accidentally. He's really not made for keeping secrets. "Let's find out," he says, heat rushing to his cheeks. They google and find a place in Brooklyn that makes German pastries, so they take off for it.

"Oh, and we can get beer and Jägermeister," Brandon says as they walk.

"Maybe more options than that. My treat. Let's go all out."

Brandon laughs. "Are you rich, too? That would make you too perfect."

Jon grins and puts on a pair of sunglasses. "Nah, not rich. But I might be coming into some money soon."

22.
Ollie

OLLIE ISN'T TOO SURE ABOUT leaving Brandon alone with Jon or whatever his name is, but getting him to a game night is enough of a win that he's making himself okay with it. What's the worst that happens, they fuck in the bathroom? They had very get-a-room energy, as his mother would say (he should call her, but after the party). It's more important he prep for game night—game night could solve this whole case.

Back at the Strongs', he looks over his board, moving the red string and putting up a new Post-it: *Connor?* Why use a different name? Sure, maybe he does that with hookups, but to have a fake ID for it? Unless trolling hotels for concierges is his fetish. Ollie's heard of weirder. But that combined with him talking to the man who got shot makes the whole thing feel like even more. A conspiracy. Guns, fake names, hotel hookups—it's just like the *Behind Closed Doors* podcast, where it turned out the husband was a former KGB agent who had fled to the U.S., changed his name and given up that life until the drama following his and his wife's key party. It's spy stuff. Or it could be a con-artist thing, maybe, like in *Two-Faced and Three-Assed*. But either way, what's the angle? What could Connor/Jon want with Brandon? Maybe he's planning to use Brandon as a drug mule, like in *Open Heart, Open Throat*. Drugs would make sense with the shady meeting with a guy who got shot. He adds a new Post-it: *Drugs?* And takes a step back. There's one more thing to consider.

Ollie puts another Post-it up on the board: *True love?* Maybe Jon really did fall for Brandon in one night and all this is him trying to get out of his old life. Ollie smiles to think about it. Brandon deserves that kind of love. But Ollie needs to make sure they know about Jon's past—so they can help him escape it, maybe. Victor works for the marshals. If Ian is back in touch with him, maybe he can help find Jon a new life—though then maybe Brandon would have to go with him. Ollie swallows. He doesn't want that.

And what does the private military Nicole mentioned have to do with any of it? Or the EU?

Ollie sighs and sits back down on the bed. Pete was curled up sleeping and lets out a soft, surprised bark before trotting over and laying his head in Ollie's lap. Ollie absently pets him while staring at the board. He has to figure out what's going on. He has to solve the case. And he has one big chance to do it: game night.

The games are usually trivia, celebrity, and Pictionary. Since Ollie is hosting, that makes him trivia master—which means he needs to come up with the categories and questions, and that's where he will lay his trap. This is just like the end of the *Play Stupid Games* podcast, where they killed the trivia-night host at the bar in that small town in Idaho. Except Ollie's not going to get himself killed, of course. What's important is having questions that only some types of people would know—like, EU stuff, spy stuff, drug stuff. Stuff that Jon would only really know if he was into one or more of those things. Theories that can be tested in the form of questions, and Jon's answers will paint a picture of who he is. And once Ollie knows that, he'll be close to solving the case.

He thinks. Certainly it'll make him give something away. Ollie isn't so sure what's going on at this point, but if he can figure out exactly what kind of trouble Jon is mixed up in, he can tell Nicole, and then Nicole can fix it. Somehow. Either tell them to go to the cops, or the FBI, or maybe to the heart-eyes-tattoo guy and give him whatever he wants so that everyone gets left alone. Hopefully Jon too. And then everyone will be safe. Case closed.

But to pull this off, he needs to figure out exactly what trivia questions to ask, and that means research. Also he should probably clean the house, and he still has to walk the dogs again. He makes a list on a new sheet of paper and pins it to the board: *Dogs, research, clean, write trivia.*

A text comes in as he smiles at the board.

SAFIYA

What kind of dog should I get?

Ollie smiles wider and looks at Pete, wondering if he has an opinion. Pete drools on his leg.

OLLIE

Depends on how much time and space you have and what you want.

SAFIYA

Not much of either.

Nevermind I shouldn't get one.

OLLIE

Some dogs are okay being left alone for a while, and small. A few are even both.

SAFIYA

Like lap dogs?

OLLIE

Yeah. Think the store would let you bring a calm dog in?

SAFIYA

Probably not. I can ask.

OLLIE

Well, you can always come walking with me if you want.

SAFIYA

I'll keep that in mind.

OLLIE

Want to come to a party tonight?

He knows he shouldn't really ask this early in the relationship, despite Brandon's suggestion, but he can't help himself. He likes her. He wants to see more of her. Even if it's too soon. She'll probably say no.

SAFIYA

What kind of party?

OLLIE

Game night. I'm housesitting this fancy, like, mansion, so I'm hosting a little game night. Trivia, Pictionary, celebrity. Snacks, drinks, probably pizza.

They always order pizza, which suddenly makes Ollie nervous about the white carpets. The Strongs didn't explicitly say no parties, but they definitely implied no stains. White pizza maybe. No toppings.

SAFIYA

Sure!

OLLIE

Really?

SAFIYA

Thought I'd say no?

OLLIE

Kind of. I just worried it was too much too soon.

SAFIYA

Nah. I don't care about rules. Just go with my gut. And my gut says Pete will be at this party.

Ollie laughs, making Pete's ears perk up questioningly. Maybe he knows they're texting about him.

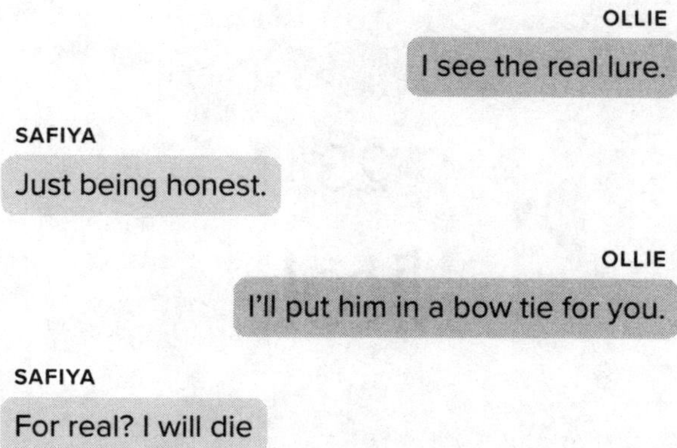

Ollie swallows at the word, wondering if inviting her to the party where he's trying to dig up dirt on someone potentially involved in murder is actually a very bad idea.

Well, too late now.

OLLIE

Please don't

But I'll see you tonight!

He texts her the address and then flips back to his list. He has a lot to do before what he hopes will be a really fun party.

23.
Nicole

NICOLE HASN'T HAD SEX IN well over a year, but she's pleased to find she's still pretty good at it. Or at least, that's what Ellen's various noises and dirty talk suggested. Yes, sleeping with her boss is a transcendently bad idea. That said, it was a good time, some much needed de-stressing, and she doesn't think Ellen is the type to hold it against her. She's not even sure Ellen is the type to remember they did it. Ellen is all business and glamour, after all. Yeah, she's a lawyer for shady people, but she's a high-powered lawyer who goes on fancy dates, has power, comfort, and a social life. That's everything Nicole wants. And if Ellen likes Nicole, maybe that means she can get there one day, too.

Nicole sits up, looking for her clothes. It's dark. Ellen didn't turn the lights on in her apartment when they came in, and all the window shades are drawn, just cuts of afternoon light coming in through the floor-to-ceiling windows, drawing lines over the bed that Ellen now lies out on, snoring softly. Nicole has to pee, and she still has more work to do to make sure her friends are okay. Oh god, her friends. They cannot know about this. The mocking would be even more than she could handle. She'll reveal it in a year or so, offhand at brunch, like she thought they already knew. She can call it her *Brandon moment*.

She finds her purse at the door to the bedroom and pulls out her phone to use as a flashlight. She shines it around, looking for her underwear.

The apartment, revealed in pieces by the light, is not quite what she expected. It's expensive, the walls in the bedroom are covered in silk, the furniture all looks high-end, sleek, sophisticated. The kind of apartment Nicole wants to have when she's rich and successful.

But it's also a sty. She thinks the floor is parquet but can't be sure because it's literally covered in clothes. Nice clothes, expensive things that should be hung up. In the bedroom, it looks like the clothing flood started in a pile on an Eames armchair, but then toppled and coated the room. There are legal papers and files amid the clothes on one side of the bed, buried like ancient relics. Lots of the clothing still has tags on it, too, and on the console in the corner is a mountain of receipts from eBay and other auction sites. Ellen seems to like bidding.

The open living room and kitchen are safe from clothes, and here Nicole can see the parquet floors, but there's a smell, probably from the various take-out and pizza boxes stacked on the kitchen counter, coffee table, and sofa, each in various states of emptiness, strewn among more legal documents and fanned-out books, notes written on them. There's a console on one side of the room covered in open boxes and weird antiques pushed up against each other—lamps, candlesticks, letter openers. The boxes have more of the same, with receipts from more auction houses in them. It's got baby-hoarder vibes. Ellen works, eats, takes off her clothes, and bids on a worrying amount of crap online. But there's no evidence she does anything else.

Nicole eases back into the bedroom and tries the master bath, where there's a wet towel on the floor and another in the bathtub. No toilet paper either, so she makes her way back out to the living room, trying a few doors there—one is locked, but the other is a bathroom that is notably tidier than the rest of the house, except for the layer of dust on everything, including the toilet paper. No one has been in here in a while. She's happy to break it in though and sits down to pee, dusting everything with toilet paper first, like it's a public restroom or something.

Is this really the fancy high life that Ellen is living? Can't she hire a maid?

She washes her hands, sneezing from the dust on the faucet. Outside, there's faint light coming from the bedroom, and she makes her way back there. Ellen is still in bed, propped up on one shoulder now, staring at her phone, but rolls over when she senses Nicole to smile at her.

"Hey. I know it's pretty bad. My maid quit a few weeks ago."

Nicole shrugs, trying to be cool. All this built up in a few weeks?

"I know, I know, I'm a mess." Ellen sits up. "There's just not much time to clean, you know? I'm working until three a.m., in the office by ten, trying to have a personal life. You'll see when you get to my level. There's no time for stuff like cleaning. Or finding a new maid."

Nicole sits down on the bed. "I thought getting to your level meant more free time."

Ellen laughs loudly. "Sure." She glances down at her phone again.

Nicole tries to hide her frown. Doesn't more power mean more time for life? Isn't that why she's been putting so much of herself into her job now? As a sort of loan so that she can have a great life later? Ellen's life—or at least her apartment—is not the glamour Nicole wants for her own future.

"Is that work?" Nicole asks, looking at Ellen staring at the screen. She sits down on the bed, peeking over Ellen's shoulder. "Something to do with—"

"No, no." Ellen clicks the Lock button but not before Nicole sees a full-screen Chibi character. Ellen did not seem like the anime type, and Nicole doesn't know enough about Japanese animation to know who it was, but she feels her eyes going wide with confusion.

Ellen seems to spot this and smiles, maybe a little embarrassed. "It's an auction I'm watching. I love to win stuff. No better feeling."

That seems like a lie, but from the apartment, it's a believable one—this place is filled with *stuff*. Never fuck your heroes. Ellen loves to win—auctions included—so much that she's essentially just packing her house with crap. If that's what gets you to the top of your field, winning at work, Nicole isn't sure she wants to have that drive. But she does believe, based on everything else in here, that Ellen might be bidding on some anime auction just to win it.

Ellen points at Nicole's phone. "How about you? Your friends find anything out?"

Nicole leans back, opening the phone. No new messages, but she decides to tell Ellen that they actually found him. She'll probably tell her not to go to the party, but Nicole thinks she can make a case for it. "Apparently they found him and they're having a party tonight."

"Oh, sure," Ellen says sarcastically. "A party. Sounds fun." She props herself up on her arms to peek at Nicole's phone.

Nicole glances over and considers pushing a loose strand of hair out of Ellen's face but doesn't. Too intimate, somehow, even after what they just did. This woman is her boss. "I know, they're all out of their minds. I guess the plan is to try to figure stuff out about him at the party."

"Okay." Ellen runs her tongue along her teeth, really considering it. Nicole hadn't expected that. "I guess that's better than just letting him vanish again. But with KBA on his trail—"

"I know. It's dangerous." Nicole lets her head fall back onto the headboard.

Ellen turns, back going straight as she looks at Nicole. "Where's the party?"

"A friend is house-sitting. Fancy place in Brooklyn." There's a beat, a moment, as they look at each other when Nicole knows she can ask Ellen if she wants to come with her. But she lets it pass. There's too much mess here—both figurative and literal. Is this what crawling to the top of her career looks like? Queen bee? So much for work-life balance.

"Sounds fun," Ellen says, turning back to lie down on the mattress again.

"Why would he come to this party though?" Nicole asks. "If he's in intelligence, and all this is spy stuff, why go to a house party with a guy you just met?"

"Good place to hide, potentially," Ellen says.

Nicole considers that and decides it makes sense, and she hates it—this guy is using her friend's crush on him. "Maybe. But we still don't know what's going on, just that he was working in Brussels and KBA made his reservation, which he left early."

"So figure it out," Ellen says, still staring at the ceiling. "Interrogate him at the party."

"Interrogate?"

"Get him alone, dress it as looking out for your friend." Ellen's hand rests on her bare hip, right over the stiletto tattoo. It's smaller than Nicole thought it would be, but just as sharp looking as she imagined, yet right now, it's almost delicate looking, not like something Ellen might stab her with.

Nicole nods, not letting herself reach out to touch Ellen, even though she suddenly wants to. "Yeah, that could work. Should I tell him I know about KBA?"

"Maybe. But carefully. He could run. Or get violent. I don't want this to end in a hostage situation."

Nicole swallows. "Good point." Though can she trust someone whose apartment looks like a crime scene?

"Text me the address so I know that if something goes down there, it's a problem. I'll monitor the police scanner tonight. Be careful."

Nicole nods, trying to ready herself for this. Put on her armor. Despite being naked. Which makes her realize the other thing: "Did you want to talk about…?" she asks, trying to sit as professionally as she can while also naked in bed.

"The sex?" Ellen tilts her head, confused. "It was great. No complaints. Why?"

"Just—you're my boss, it could be weird—"

"No, no, no," Ellen interrupts quickly, hand flying up to stop her. "I'm your boss's boss's boss. And don't worry, there's no quid pro quo here. If we end up in this position again, sounds fun, but you'll never have to if you don't want to, and it won't impact anything at work."

Nicole takes a deep breath. Good. She could be lying, but good. "Thanks."

"Just don't tell anyone about what a mess my place is. Looks like I don't have my life together, y'know?"

"Yeah," Nicole says. "I promise."

"Okay, so I'm going to make a few calls for some other cases. But why don't you shower off if you want to? Or keep working on KBA until your party."

"Sure," Nicole says.

"We okay?" Ellen asks. "Feels like something's off."

Nicole nods, though she knows Ellen is right. She's just reevaluating her entire life based on Ellen's apartment. Sort of hard to say that out loud though. "Just sort of confused about how I got here, going to a party with a probable spy." *Sleeping with my boss whose glamorous life turns out to look like it could end up on a hoarding TV show.*

Ellen gets out of bed and stretches. "Yeah. Sometimes it feels like everything is out of your control. You just need to step back and ask yourself: What do you want your life to be? That's how I got where I am."

"I guess I should figure that out, then," Nicole says with a smile. She thought reaching Ellen's level would mean more balance, more time for a life—but based on this apartment, Ellen doesn't even have time to hang up her clothes. Maybe that TV-lawyer idea is better. Or maybe—she suddenly has a flash of Sam, the protest poster, her dark lipstick. Maybe Nicole should never have drifted away from that.

"Well, let me know how I can help. But I'm going to go make those calls now."

Nicole lies back in bed, staring at the ceiling as she hears Ellen unlock the door in the living room. It's a good question: What does she want her life to be?

24.
Ian

IAN WALKS INTO THE BOOKSTORE, carrying their sushi. They're not quite sure how they got back here. They remember being dropped off and going into the sushi place. They must have gotten their order, and hopefully paid, and walked back here, but all that is blank in their mind. Instead, they're thinking about the voice on the line, the offer of millions of dollars, their life changing. All they need to do is find some zip drive, apparently. But is that voice on the line good or bad? Is giving her this zip drive—if they even find it—something that will hurt people? Certainly they don't seem nice. Well, Heart-Eyes was kind of sweet. Dangerous, for sure, but kind of hot and really open and—

Ian shakes their head. Not what they should be thinking about right now.

"Why are you just standing there?" Kate calls from the counter.

"I don't know," Ian says.

"I'm hungry."

Ian walks to the counter and sets down the bag of sushi, hoping it's their order.

"You look dazed," Kate says, tearing the bag open and pulling out the food.

"Bumped into someone unexpected." Ian isn't sure what else to say: *Took a super-fun ride around the nabe while being held at gun-point because of someone else getting laid?*

"Was it who you were texting? That would be funny."

"No," they say quickly. Not Victor. Though Victor might know what to do in this situation. He's in law enforcement; he could protect everyone, right? Except then Ian wouldn't get the money. That money could change their life. If the woman on the phone can be believed, anyway. She might just tell Heart-Eyes to kill everyone.

Kate dishes out the food as Ian lets their mind spin.

"Eat," Kate says, pushing Ian's sushi toward them. "You look shell-shocked."

"What would you do with ten million dollars?" Ian blurts out.

She laughs. "Why?"

"Just wondering."

"I guess...I'd buy a place for the store. The rent here is killer. An apartment too. Maybe one big building, live on top, bookstore on the bottom. That would probably be all of it. Maybe put a little aside so the margins aren't so tight. Donate the rest to good queer causes." She dips a sushi roll into the wasabi and pops it in her mouth. "What about you?"

"Custom dresses," Ian says immediately. "Maybe try to buy a club, like in La Cage. Be the headliner and run the place, produce really high-quality shows, with really talented people, like *NightGowns*. Better wigs. Better place. Pay off my student loans. Not have to worry about..." They sigh. "A lot."

Kate pats their shoulder. "I wish I could give it to you, kid."

Ian nods. It's within their grasp. A whole new life. Well, maybe. They eat quietly, only half paying attention to Kate telling them about the new releases she's excited about. When they're done, Ian pulls out their phone and sees all the messages: people asking how they are, which makes them smile, and Ollie and Brandon finding Jon. And a party tonight. Well, that could make it easy to look for the zip drive the woman on the phone wanted, right? If they're willing to try. Which is dangerous.

A few teenagers come into the bookstore, going over to the queer YA section and looking at the spines.

IAN

You know how you said you missed game night?

We're having one tonight, if you want to come

Ian watches Victor's "..." appear and disappear a dozen times. They don't blame him. But if they're going to have a party with some guy on the run for stealing a zip drive that Ian might try to steal themself, it's a good idea to have someone with a gun on their side, too, right? Like a bodyguard.

VICTOR

Are you asking me out? I'm still with Rafael

Ian frowns, feeling mild embarrassment.

IAN

No

You can bring him if you want

Ian hopes he does not want.

VICTOR

He has to work tonight

I don't know

Ian glances up at the teens, now reading the back of a book together. Cute.

IAN

I'm bringing a date

I was just inviting you because you said you missed everyone

And to show you I'm sorry

But I get it

VICTOR

A date?

IAN

You're surprised? Fuck you

VICTOR

lol no

Sure it would be nice to see everyone

I miss those disasters

IAN

That's us

VICTOR

Should I bring anything?

Ian almost types *your gun*, but that would probably be suspicious.

IAN

Nah, but let me give you the address. It's where Ollie is housesitting. Fancy mansion

VICTOR

I'll bring cheese then

Cheese is fancy

Ian laughs. That was a joke of theirs, how cheese was the fanciest gift you could ever give anyone. They can't even remember where it came from, but sometimes they'd just text each other different types of cheeses, trying to find more and more obscure ones to show how fancy they were.

IAN

What kind?

VICTOR

Camembert?

IAN

Not Gruyere?

The "…" appears and vanishes again a few times.

VICTOR

I'll see what they have at the store. See you tonight!

Ian texts him the time and address, then moves on to the next issue—they said they had a date. A lie, but easily fixed, hopefully.

IAN

Hey want to come to a party tonight?

TOM

Tonight?

IAN

Yeah, my friend is housesitting this fancy place, so is throwing one of our game nights there. So not like, crazy trash the place party.

Sorry for the short notice. It's kind of spur of the moment

TOM

To invite me?

Ian frowns. They deserve that. What's one more apology?

IAN

I'm sorry I didn't text you about the movie. Life has been pretty crazy

TOM

But now you're inviting me to a small game night

IAN

Yeah

TOM

As a friend, or like as a date?

IAN

I thought that was obvious

TOM

It isn't, and you still haven't told me

IAN

Sorry!

Yes, a date. I am asking you to be my date to this silly game night.

TOM

Then yes, I'd love to

IAN

I know I'm a mess, sorry

But I'm hot and funny, right?

TOM

At least one of those

IAN

Hey!

Ian laughs. The teens look over at them, then at each other, disapproving.

Ian is smiling as the teens bring a book. Adam Sass's latest, which they ring up and hand back over, still smiling. When they leave, Ian opens up the group chat.

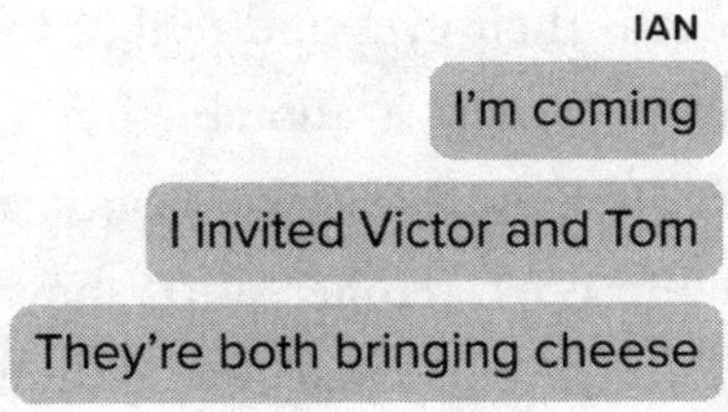

25.
Brandon

"TIME FOR TRIVIA!" OLLIE ANNOUNCES. They've all gathered in the game room upstairs, where there are several white chairs and a loveseat surrounding a white marble table on a white rug. Brandon and Jon were very careful, only buying pale beers, seltzer, tonic, vodka, gin. Brandon decided he didn't even want to risk white wine. Clear only. And for food, there are the German pastries, some vegetables with a yogurt dip, and crackers, thankfully, because three people brought cheese! And cheese probably won't stain anything either.

It's the four of them, plus Ollie's date, Safiya, with Pete curled up in her lap, wearing a polka-dot bow tie, chewing on a rubber ring; Victor, who greeted all of them with a huge hug before looking deep into their eyes and telling them how much he missed them; and Tom, who is adorable but a strong contrast to Victor, soft looking and professorial in a cardigan and polo next to Victor's tank top and open flannel shirt, showing off all those muscles. Everyone is drinking, snacking, even chatting a little. Everyone has been introduced.

But best of all, there's Jon, his arm around Brandon's shoulders, warm as Brandon leans into him on the loveseat.

"I worked hard on these," Ollie says, laying down stacks of note cards in the categories he created as he reads them off. "International Diplomacy. Hand-to-Hand Combat. Guns. Street Value of Drugs. Identity Theft. And, of course, our old standby: Porn Stars Who Are Couples in Real Life."

The room is quiet. Aside from the last one, these are not the usual types of trivia categories they have at game night. Brandon looks at Ollie, who is standing proudly, hands on hips.

"Well..." Nicole says. "The porn star couples better include some lesbians this time."

"You guys have gotten into some intense stuff," Victor says. "But I feel like I could do well with guns."

"Do you know about guns?" Jon asks from beside Brandon.

"He's a U.S. marshal," Ian says quickly.

"Huh," Jon says. Brandon can feel him tense up a little.

Tom giggles, a little high-pitched. Brandon wonders if he knows Victor is Ian's ex.

"Don't worry, I'm off duty," Victor says.

"Well, I work at a weed shop," Safiya says, "but the street value of drugs isn't quite the same. Just in case you were trying to win my affection with that one." She raises an eyebrow at Ollie.

"That would be unfair," Ollie says, winking at her.

"I don't mind," Safiya says. "I want to win!"

Ollie laughs. "We don't really keep score."

"No?" Jon asks, looking at Brandon. "How do I get my prize?"

"I guess just be very impressive." Brandon does his best flirty shrug, though they already decided Jon would stay over tonight.

He just has a backpack, not the one he had when he checked in, but Brandon doesn't want to ask about that. He must have bought it when his trip got extended, right? There's admittedly a lot Brandon doesn't want to ask, and he knows that's foolish, but he just wants to enjoy this. They had an amazing time wandering the city, talking about DSLWLS, tasting various German pastries, dolloping cream on each other's noses. It was a perfect afternoon. Something out of a rom-com. His friends would mock him relentlessly, and Brandon knows there are questions that need to be answered, but right now he is so happy. And he just wants to stay that way as long as possible.

"Ew, no flirting," Ian says.

"None?" Tom asks, trying to be coy, Brandon thinks, but sounding too nervous.

Ian rolls their eyes.

Ollie claps his hands. "Okay, let's do trivia!"

"These categories are ridiculous," Nicole says, glaring at Ollie. "We don't know any of this stuff."

"We'll learn!" Ollie says. His grin is growing forced, rigid. "The rules, if people don't know, are easy—shout out the answer fastest. First correct answer gets to pick the next category. Nicole, why don't you pick first?"

Nicole sighs and leans back into the sofa. Must be hard for her being the only one without a date. Brandon needs to find her someone.

"Porn Stars Who Are Couples in Real Life," Nicole says with a shrug.

Ollie lifts the top card and reads it: "Which twink couple has shared scenes in only two films—*Naughty Stepbrothers: Volume*

17 and *Heart Throbber*—but met on the set of *Open-Him-R: An Oppenheimer Porn Parody*, where they had no scenes together?"

"Not lesbians," Nicole says.

"They're in there, I promise," Ollie says.

Brandon glances at Jon. He knows the answer but is afraid if he says it too quickly, then he'll look like an oversexed pervert, and that's more of a third-date reveal.

"Oh, oh," Victor says. "I know this one. One of them is Justin Justins. And the other is..." He shakes his head, squinting.

"Starts with an *s*," Ian prompts, something they used to do all the time when they were together. Brandon wonders why they invited both Victor and Tom, and why they're crammed between them now. Like a test, but Brandon isn't sure for who.

"Oh, Stephen Hole!" Victor finishes.

"Correct!" Ollie says. "You get to pick the next category."

"Yes!" Victor does a fist pump and slaps Ian on the back, which Tom definitely notices. "Well, let's go with guns, then. I know about weapons and lifting." He flexes, grinning. Ian laughs, and Tom frowns slightly, though Brandon isn't sure anyone else sees it. Maybe he'll need to help Ian figure out their love life, too.

Ollie picks the top card in the Guns category and reads it: "What brand of pistol is most commonly used by German BND agents?"

Brandon frowns. He doesn't even understand that question, but he's starting to understand the reason for the unusual categories.

"I know this one," Jon says, raising his hand slightly. "Do I just say it? Glock."

"Correct!" Ollie says, his smile a little manic now.

Brandon swallows. "You know guns?"

"It's what Ingrid uses in DSLWLS, remember?"

Brandon smiles. He's right. A Totally Normal Explanation. He glances at Ollie and raises his eyebrows. Ollie's smile fades slightly.

"You pick the next category," Ollie tells Jon.

"Pick drugs," Safiya says. "I want to know something."

Jon laughs. "Okay, drugs."

This is all such a setup. Brandon should tell Jon everything. The truth of how they found him, what they saw. He's going to figure it out anyway—Ollie's scheme isn't subtle. He squeezes Jon's hand, the truth now rising in his throat. But not here. Especially not in front of Victor—who knows what he'd do? Later, if Jon doesn't figure it out. Hopefully he won't.

"What is the approximate street value of one gram of cocaine?" Ollie reads.

"One hundred fifty to two hundred dollars," Tom answers immediately and with calm assurance. All eyes turn to him.

"Correct," Ollie says softly.

"What did you say you do for a living?" Victor asks, leaning toward him.

"I'm in marketing," Tom says, smiling. His back is weirdly straight.

Victor narrows his eyes. "Marketing what?"

Tom nods. "My newest account is Dudches"—he points at Victor like he's selling him on something—"an anal-douching kit for bros."

Victor's eyes narrow even more.

"So," Ian says brightly, leaning forward between Tom and

Victor so quickly, their drink sloshes and threatens to spill for a moment. "Jon! Where have you been staying since you checked out of Brandon's hotel?"

"A few cheap hotels, wherever I could get a reservation," Jon says with a shrug. Brandon watches Ian. He can understand wanting to get attention somewhere else, but why on Jon?

"He's staying back at Hotel Brandon tonight though," Brandon says, squeezing Jon's thigh.

"Oh, so your stuff is here?" Ian asks. "I didn't notice."

"I don't have much," Jon says, with a laugh that sounds forced.

"Tom, you pick the next category," Brandon says.

"Go for international politics," Nicole says, looking up from her phone. "None of us know anything about that."

"Okay," Tom says. "International politics."

Ollie takes the card off the pile with a flourish. "Operation Mincemeat was a World War II plot to do what?"

"Oh." Jon sits up, excited, hands bursting out like he's onstage. "It was when they planted fake papers on a body and dropped it in the water around Spain to look like a pilot had washed ashore with invasion plans for Sardinia, so Hitler would move his troops out of Sicily. Ian Flemming worked on it," he says, turning to Brandon.

"That's correct," Ollie says, that manic look back in his eye, now with a giant grin to match. Brandon shifts uncomfortably, trying to settle back into Jon.

"Pick drugs again," Brandon whispers to Jon, wanting to get attention off him.

"Let's go back to drugs," Jon says, nodding.

Ollie takes the top card, eyes still on Jon, unblinking. "The street value of one pill of ecstasy."

"About seventy dollars," Tom says quickly.

"Correct," Ollie says, turning back toward Tom with the rest of the room, except for Nicole, who's looking at her phone. Probably doing work. Again.

"I'm going to the bathroom," Ian announces, standing. Brandon doesn't blame them; this is getting awkward.

Ian leaves, and Tom, oblivious to the stares, smiles at Ollie. "Let's do drugs again."

Ollie takes a long sip of his beer and picks up the next drug card. Tom knows the street value of a kilo of cocaine but thankfully, Safiya knows what a dime bag of Kush costs and announces it before Victor can arrest Tom.

"Let's do Identity Theft," Safiya says, petting Pete. "That sounds fun."

"All right," Ollie says with a smile, then plucks a card up. "Which state do the highest percentage of fake driver's licenses claim to be from?"

Brandon looks around. No one seems to know.

"Texas," Jon says casually.

"Correct," Ollie says proudly.

"Let's do Hand-to-Hand Combat," Jon says.

Brandon frowns; he really doesn't love this.

"What do you do for a living?" Victor asks, turning his attention to Jon now.

"Insurance," Jon says. "Art stuff. It's boring."

"He told us all about it," Brandon says quickly, feeling like he's helping someone lie.

"What hand-to-hand combat technique includes moves like Irimi Nage and Ikkyo?"

"Aikido," Jon says quickly.

"Guns, martial arts, fake IDs," Victor says. "You know a lot."

"Not as much as Tom does about drugs," Brandon says, forcing a laugh, like it's a joke and not just an attempt to divert attention. But Victor keeps staring at Jon.

Jon shifts so that Brandon has to move away. "I just like spy movies. I think I'm going to go get another beer from the fridge," he says, before downing what's left in his bottle.

"Oh, great, I'll go with," Nicole says, standing. Brandon's shocked she even heard anyone talking, she was so in her phone. "I could use one, too." She's drinking a vodka tonic, and Brandon has never known her to be a beer drinker.

"I can just get you one," Jon says.

"No, no, let me stretch a little. I sit down all day."

"Okay," Jon says, and they leave together. It's just Brandon, Ollie, Safiya, Victor, and Tom now.

"So how did you and Ian meet?" Victor asks, turning on Tom.

"Oh, I liked their show at the Wreck Room."

"Should I pick a category instead of Jon?" Brandon asks. Ollie is staring out the door Jon and Nicole just left through.

"So you just went to talk to them after the show?" Victor asks Tom, leaning closer to him.

"Yeah," Tom says brightly, apparently unaware of Victor's interrogation.

"Sure, you pick," Ollie says to Brandon, distracted. "I'm sure everyone will be back soon."

"Porn stars, then," Brandon says. "Only one I know."

Ollie picks up the card and sighs. "Of course, it's when Nicole is out of the room. But...these two porn stars have worked together in over twenty films, starting with *The Birthday Cake* and most recently *WLW 17*."

The room is silent.

"So none of us are into girls except Ollie?" Safiya says after a minute. "Feels unbalanced."

"So what did you talk to Ian about after their show?" Victor asks Tom.

"Just fan stuff. How funny they were. One thing led to another, and...now here we are. How do you know Ian?"

"We were together for a year," Victor says. "I'm with someone else now, but I still care a lot about Ian."

"Where's your someone else?" Tom asks, sounding a little nervous again.

"Working."

Brandon stares at Ollie, who stares back and then looks at Safiya, who shrugs. Not how anyone wanted the night to go.

"Well," Ollie says, "maybe we should wait for everyone else?"

"I'll go see if they need help," Brandon says, popping up, eager to leave. What is taking Ian so long in the bathroom, anyway? Brandon smiles at Ollie, who sits next to Safiya as Tom and Victor stare each other down. Brandon hopes it doesn't come to blows; Victor might kill Tom.

He leaves the game room and walks out into the hallway. White carpet, white walls, but all gray because the hall lights are out. He makes his way over to the stairs and hears voices. It sounds like Nicole and Jon.

"...I know what you're—" Nicole is saying.

Brandon speeds up, almost tumbling down the stairs into the kitchen.

"Hi!" he says loudly, interrupting and smiling at Jon, who won't meet his eyes, then glaring at Nicole. They're facing each other in front of the fridge, like a standoff interrupted. Nicole's jaw is clenched, her hand curling tightly around the corner of the counter. "You missed the lesbian question, Nicole. No one knew it."

"Shocking," Nicole says, eyes still glued to Jon.

"What are you two talking about?" Brandon asks.

"Just getting to know each other," Nicole says, using her strangely emotionless professional voice.

"Cool," Brandon says, staring at Jon. "Well, want to go back upstairs? I just wanted to get a seltzer."

"Yeah," Jon says, "I just need to grab something from my bag." He nods across the living room at the den, where Brandon put his backpack earlier. He walks over to the hidden door and opens it.

"Were you interrogating him?" Brandon hisses at Nicole.

"Yes," she whispers. "Brandon, I get you like this guy, but *come on*. He's dangerous, and he's lying to you."

"We don't know that," Brandon says quickly. "Jon could be his middle name that he goes by now. And he could work in art insurance. The head..." He has a sudden flash, a bowl of peaches, closes his eyes, shakes it off. "It might have been wrong time, wrong place."

"Well, that's all I'm trying to find out," Nicole says. "I'm looking out for you."

"I can look out for myself."

She laughs and takes a swig of the beer she's holding. "Sure."

Brandon crosses his arms. "You're just jealous I'm actually getting some."

Nicole licks her lips, about to say something, when Jon's voice comes from the den:

"What are you doing in here!?"

"Sorry, sorry," Ian says, half running out of the den, Jon following them. Ian suddenly falls to their knees on the rug, like they tripped or—

"Whoa!" Nicole shouts. "Do not push my friend!"

"He didn't push them," Brandon says quickly. Jon wouldn't have.

"He didn't—" Ian says, getting up, just as Ollie and everyone else come downstairs. Victor takes one look at Ian getting up, Jon behind him, and runs over, standing between Jon and Ian.

"What is going on?" Victor asks, eyes on Jon. "Who even is this guy?"

"He's my—" Brandon starts, then stops himself.

"Oh Jesus," Nicole murmurs.

"It's fine," Jon says, one hand open and up, the other holding his beer. "I just found Ian in our room and asked them what they were doing."

"I just got turned around," Ian says quickly. They're standing up now, and Brandon watches them tuck something deeper into their pocket.

"Okay," Ollie says. "So it's all fine! Let's go back upstairs and keep playing. You missed the lesbian question, Nicole."

"I really need more lesbian friends," Nicole says.

"No, I want to know what this guy was doing to Ian," Victor says.

"Victor, relax," Tom says. "You just said—"

"I look out for my friends," Victor says, voice rising dangerously.

"And that means protecting them from drug dealers and whatever"—he spins on Jon—"you are."

"I'm not a drug dealer,"Tom says, laughing in a nervous way.

"And I'm just a guy," Jon says, backing away. "Relax, man."

"Victor—" Ian says, putting their hand on Victor's shoulder.

"Watch yourself," Victor says, reaching out and shoving Jon's shoulder slightly, causing his beer to splash up all over his face. Brandon grits his teeth, annoyed. Even Victor is ganging up on Jon now? Why can't any of them just let him be happy for at least a little while?

"Fuck," Jon says, then pauses for a moment again.

"What the hell, Victor?" Brandon asks, shoving himself between him and Jon. "Don't be an asshole."

"He pushed Ian!" Victor shouts back, a little spit flying from his mouth and hitting Brandon's face. "I'm not letting this guy hurt anyone." He's weirdly angry.

"He's not going to hurt anyone," Brandon says, his voice much louder than he means for it to be. "Just cool down!" He says it at Victor, but he means it for everyone—they're all so keen to see the bad in Jon instead of just letting Brandon be happy for, like, five minutes. One good game night—that's all he wanted. One night to show Jon that his friends were cool, and his friends that Jon was cool, and then after, tomorrow, he'd have asked Jon about the…other stuff. Jon made him so happy today, just shopping and joking, and flirting and kissing and nerding out about DSLWLS. He felt like home—like Heimweh—but now it's like everyone is trying to take that away instead of trusting him to handle this.

"'Cool down'?" Victor shouts back. "Fuck you, 'cool down'!"

Brandon rears back. Victor would get mad at stuff, he and Ian could rile each other up, seemed to delight in it, but Victor has never been mad at him. They've always been friends—Brandon was sad to cut him out of his life. But now he's huge, looming, eyes bright and bloodshot. He's almost scary. So Brandon does the thing that seems most sensible for making someone snap out of it: He throws his drink in Victor's face.

And then, as the liquid flies through the air, he realizes what he's done. And how very, very stupid it was.

The liquid hits Victor's face with a soft splash, and his eyes go wide, staring at Brandon. Brandon stares back, wondering if he's about to die.

"Cool down?" Brandon says again, hoping it'll work.

"Okay," Ollie says, waving his arms. "Let's all just relax."

"I think it's a little late for that," Ian says, looking at Brandon with disbelief that Brandon understands—he has no idea why he did that either. "What the fuck, Brandon?"

"He shoved Jon!" His voice comes out very high. It's a weak defense.

"Jon shoved Ian," Nicole says. "C'mon, Brandon—"

"No, I didn't," Jon protests.

"He—" Ian starts.

"Please!" Ollie shouts again, but then Jon starts explaining the situation again, Brandon talking over him.

"He just went into the room to get something, and Ian was there and then they left and Ian tripped!" Brandon says, pointing at Victor, who has been telling his own side of the story, all their voices overlapping. Nicole is rolling her eyes, Ollie is holding his hands up, and Ian is trying to talk to everyone. But it's just a mess. No one listens.

No one ever really listens to him, Brandon realizes. They always make fun of him and his love life, ranking their favorite mistakes of his, joking about how quick he is to fall in love. Like they're better than him. But they always give each other chances—no one is telling Ian they shouldn't have invited Victor. No one is telling Nicole not to flirt with her boss or the coffee girl. Why is it always Brandon?

"Why don't any of you give Jon a chance?" he asks, just as there's a lull in the overlapping arguments. It sounds so sad when he says it. He looks at Ian, then Nicole, then Ollie. None of them will meet his eye. "I really like him and you're all here snooping"—he points at Ian—"or interrogating"—he moves to Nicole—"or trying to be smart and find stuff out but just embarrassing yourself," he says, hand landing on Ollie. They all think he's such a mess, he can't be trusted with his own love life. They're supposed to be his friends, but they seem so intent on making him unhappy.

"I'm just trying to solve the case!" Ollie protests, but it sounds weak.

"Case?" Tom asks, but everyone ignores him.

"He's trouble, Brandon," Nicole says. She's gotten closer to them from the kitchen but still hovers on the periphery, like she's too good to actually wade in. "Can't you see that?"

He closes his eyes, takes a breath. He can see that—tomorrow. Tonight he just wants to be happy, and they won't let him. They won't even talk to him about it.

"Oh, like you would know, with your nose in your phone all night. Texting your boss? Yeah, you want to talk about bad romantic decisions, how about that one? Or you"—Brandon turns to Ian—"bringing the guy you say is 'too nice' but is *clearly* a drug dealer and the ex you were hate stalking until today to the same party?"

"Fuck you," Ian snaps.

Brandon sticks his chin out. Maybe he's being mean, but they started it.

"It's like the moment I find something that makes me happy, and not just the butt of all your jokes, you need to do everything you can to take it away from me," Brandon screams at the room. Tears are running down his face.

"Hey," Jon says, taking Brandon's arm softly. "Hey, it's okay." His voice is like a hug.

"He's dangerous," Nicole says, now her turn to point, at Jon. "Look what he did to Ian!" It suddenly sounds so sad and desperate to Brandon.

He turns away, looking at Jon. Jon, who actually wants him to be happy.

"Let's clean you up," Brandon says, marching Jon toward the den, getting between him and Victor. "I think we're done for the night." He says it as hard as he can make it. Then he pulls Jon back into the den and slams the door.

Outside the den, he hears some murmurs, but no one calls for them to come out, and Brandon sighs as Jon peels his shirt off.

"Sorry," Brandon says. "I don't know what all that was."

"It's fine," Jon says with a shrug. "Your friends are...protective. But I'll win them over tomorrow. I'll make breakfast. That usually works; I can cook a nice omelet. Victor won't be here though, will he?"

"He's Ian's ex, so I don't think so." Unless they get back together. That's what Ian really wanted, probably. "We haven't seen him in a year. I think maybe he was feeling... I don't know. Not that I'm excusing what he did." He hates that this is how everything happened. He wanted to impress Jon, not have him attacked or fight with everyone or... It's just been a disaster.

"It's fine," Jon repeats.

"Are you sure? I mean—"

"Brandon," Jon interrupts, unbuckling his belt, "I've met a lot of people, and I've been in fights and I've been accused of things, and you know what? This was nothing. Just some drunk guy feeling protective. So I'm fine. Are you fine?" He pulls down his jeans, revealing sleek black briefs.

Brandon admires his body, all thoughts gone for a moment. "Uh, yeah."

Jon grins at him, shrugging off his various bracelets and laying them with his shirt on the bed. "I'm going to wash off. You want to join me?"

"Yes," Brandon says quickly.

Jon grins and takes Brandon's hand, pulling him for a long kiss. He tastes like beer and salt, and Brandon melts into him. Jon's thumb rests on the tattoo on Brandon's hip. Heimweh. He's so perfect.

Jon turns on the shower in the den bathroom and gets under the water as Brandon struggles out of his clothes, tripping on his underwear briefly before joining him in the shower, closing them in the bathroom, like their own little world, far away from the chaos that just exploded in the next room.

Jon kisses him deeply, pulling his naked body into his. Brandon lets his hands trace Jon's body, his hips, his abs, his ass. He's so gorgeous. He's into DSLWLS. He's got a real grown-up job. It's ridiculous that he'd want to be with Brandon, but here he is.

Although Brandon is sort of lying to him. Maybe that's the catch.

They kiss, tongues in each other's mouth, steam and hands wrapping around Brandon. He moans slightly as Jon kisses his neck.

"Wait," Brandon says, pushing Jon away for a moment. Jon smiles at him, water pouring off him, his expression all sex. "I need to tell you something."

26.
Ollie

"TIME FOR TRIVIA!" OLLIE ANNOUNCES. He's very proud of everything he's come up with. He spent almost the entire day preparing these questions, googling things even when he was out walking the dogs. He almost let Linus wrap a curious child in his leash. But it'll be worth it for when he unmasks Jon and solves the case! Though, at this point, he's not so sure what the case is. He's been so focused on Jon, he doesn't know anything about the dead man. But Jon is the only lead he has, so if he just reveals a little more about himself, maybe Ollie can figure out exactly what happened that day, and if Jon needs protection or, more likely, if Brandon needs protection from Jon.

Everyone has settled in nicely, too. Brandon was kind enough to bring only pale snacks, and almost everyone else brought cheese, which was weird, but who doesn't like cheese? Even Safiya brought some cannabis-infused pepperjack they sell at the store. She'd shown up before anyone else and given him a kiss on the cheek, which had thrilled him, and the cheese, which had been more confusing—she said it had one of those strains that makes people more alert and competitive, perfect for game night. Though, now that he thinks about it, Ollie doesn't think he told anyone it was laced. He was too busy trying to set up and talk to her and maybe get another kiss. He glances at the block of pepperjack. It's half-gone.

He lays out the categories, announcing them as he goes and watching Jon's face for any reaction, but there isn't any. Could he really be an innocent in all this? Wrong place, wrong time, happens to use a fake name with hookups? But then why is he here? Shouldn't he have gone to the police? Maybe he did. Ollie is prepared for that, too. The Pictionary cards he made are all police and shooting related: reporting a crime, witness statements, attempted murder. Very different than the usual kind of Pictionary clues they come up with—Ollie can draw a variety of sex acts and positions with his eyes closed at this point. But it'll show how much experience Jon has with things he might have done post-shooting. And for celebrity, Ollie looked up a variety of famous spies and assassins to put in the bowl.

For now though: trivia!

"Well, I work at a weed shop," Safiya is saying, "but the street value of drugs isn't quite the same. Just in case you were trying to win my affection with that one." She raises an eyebrow at Ollie.

"That would be unfair," Ollie says, then, before he can help himself, winks. Oh no. That was so cheesy and terrible.

Safiya grins and winks back. Okay, not so bad, then.

"I don't mind," she says. "I want to win!" Maybe she's been the one eating the cheese.

But they start with porn stars, of course. If Ollie left that one out, it would make people suspicious. But when Victor gets it, they move right to Guns—perfect. And Jon gets it! Ollie stares at Jon, feeling like he's learned something. Brandon can see it, too, he knows. Until Jon mentions that comic. Okay, plausible, but then he knows about Operation Mincemeat, too. He knows stuff. Identity Theft, Hand-to-Hand Combat... He knows something from every category. So he's not an innocent victim, right? It couldn't just be wrong place, wrong time.

Ollie realizes nothing he's learning is very specific, but he still feels on steadier ground now—Jon is a criminal, or spy, or something. (He's also learning Ian's date is probably a drug dealer, but that's not important right now.)

What's most annoying is how few people are staying. Ian leaves to go to the bathroom, and/or abandon the weird tension between Victor and Tom, and doesn't come back. And then Jon and Nicole go to get beers—which Nicole doesn't drink. With Jon gone, Ollie isn't going to find out anything new either. They need to finish up trivia and move on to the other games, more tests, more information about Jon. Ollie picks up the lesbian-porn-star-couple question he wrote just for Nicole (well, and himself) and reads it. The half-empty room goes quiet.

"So none of us are into girls except Ollie?" Safiya says after a minute. "Feels unbalanced." She giggles. She looks so cute giggling.

"So what did you talk to Ian about after their show?" Victor asks Tom.

"Just fan stuff. How funny they were. One thing led to another, and...now here we are. How do you know Ian?"

"We were together for a year," Victor says. "I'm with someone else now, but I still care a lot about Ian."

"Where's your someone else?" Tom asks.

"Working."

This is not great. Ollie looks at Brandon and then Safiya, then at the cheese she brought (even less of it now) and back at her. She shrugs, still petting Pete.

"Well," Ollie says, "maybe we should wait for everyone else?" And hopefully give everyone time to mellow out a little.

"I'll go see if they need help," Brandon says, popping up and practically running from the room. He's clearly wanted to since Jon left.

"I haven't seen you at any of Ian's shows," Tom says to Victor. He's getting condescending, while Victor is just looking angrier.

"I haven't been in a while," Victor says.

Ollie swallows. "This cheese is good, right?" he says, cutting a slice off the weed pepperjack. "Safiya brought it from her store. The weed just tastes a little grassy, right?"

Victor turns to Ollie as he pops the slice in his mouth.

"The cheese has weed in it?" Victor's anger seems focused more on Ollie now.

"Just a little," Safiya says, leaning back from him, wary.

"You drugged us without telling us? I could get fired for this." His face falls, and he rubs at his temple, anxiety washing over him, and Ollie starts to feel guilt in him like worms.

"What?" Safiya says, now scratching behind Pete's ears. "It's legal."

"In New York, but I'm a federal employee. If they randomly drug test me tomorrow, I'm screwed."

Ollie and Safiya exchange a glance. Safiya grimaces.

"Sorry," she says quickly. "I didn't know. I thought everyone knew the cheese—" She shakes her head, frowning. "Okay, wait, I know this. You need to drink lots of water, work out. It should be out of your system faster that way. Do they randomly drug test you a lot?"

"No," Victor says.

"What if someone calls something in?" Tom asks—trying to tease, Ollie thinks, but badly misreading the situation.

"Fuck you," Victor says, standing. "I came because I missed these guys and Ian asked me to and I thought we were all going to be friends, finally, but..." He shakes his head, falling forward slightly, head in hands. "I cheated on Ian, you know. I'm an asshole. And I mean it, I care about them, but we're not good for each other." He looks up. He's so much sadder than Ollie remembers him. When he and Ian were together, it was, well, yeah, a lot of drama. But when they weren't fighting, they were crazy about each other.

Tom sighs and gently pats Victor on the back, which makes him twitch and look up at Tom, who pulls the hand back. "I didn't mean I would."

"Then what did you mean? And what's your deal? I need to protect Ian, to make it up to them."

"I'm not dangerous, I promise! And I'm not a cheater."

"You do know a lot about drugs though," Safiya says nonchalantly as she scratches Pete's ears.

"My roommate in college was a dealer," Tom says. "I haven't actually done much besides some edibles. Oh, and once I took a mint from his tin before a date, but it turned out it wasn't just a mint."

"What was it?" Safiya asks, leaning forward.

"Acid." Tom laughs. "I thought this guy I was on the date with was supernaturally hot that night. Not so much the next morning."

Safiya laughs, and even Victor snorts, his posture loosening a little. The pressure in the room seems to go down a little.

"We all missed you," Ollie says, not sure what's happening. This was supposed to be a big detective night. He reaches out and pats Victor on the knee, but Victor grabs his hand.

"Thanks," he says. "I really missed you guys, too."

"Why don't we get you that water?" Safiya says, putting Pete on the floor and standing. "Everyone is downstairs anyway, so maybe we can go refill our drinks and stuff?" She reaches out for Ollie's hand, pulling it off Victor's and squeezing.

Ollie looks up at her, so grateful. He wants to kiss her so badly.

"Yeah," Victor says, standing. He heads out into the hall, and Tom follows with a shrug. Ollie hangs back for a moment, holding Safiya's hand.

"Thanks," he says to her softly. Pete wanders through their legs, going downstairs with everyone else. "This is not the night I thought it would be."

"Might be my fault. The cheese can be a little weepy, too. I didn't realize you hadn't told them it was laced."

"I was so focused on the games."

"I was distracted by Pete." She grins. "And you, of course."

He goes for it: He leans in for a kiss, on the lips this time, not the cheek. She lowers her chin to let him but doesn't lean in, and when he wraps his arm around her waist, she doesn't step closer, so it ends up being soft, lips brushing sweetly, but maybe not the sexy open-mouth action Ollie was sort of hoping for.

She's smiling when they break apart though. "Let's go find Pete."

As they step into the dark hallway, Ollie hears voices downstairs. Victor and Tom are just in front of them, and when they get into the wide-open kitchen and living room, Ollie is sure they all see the same thing: Ian on the ground, Jon looming over them like he maybe just hit them. Ollie gasps at the image, and that seems to reaffirm the scene for Victor, who charges forward.

"What is going on?" Victor demands, chest out. "Who even is this guy?"

"It's fine," Jon says, one hand open and up, the other holding his beer. "I just found Ian in our room and asked them what they were doing."

"I just got turned around," Ian says as they stand up.

"Okay," Ollie announces, desperately trying to keep control. "So it's all fine! Let's go back upstairs and keep playing. You missed the lesbian question, Nicole." This is bad. Ollie had a whole plan for the night, and the feeling he has now—like the moment before a bar fight breaks out—is not part of that plan.

"No, I want to know what this guy was doing to Ian," Victor says.

"Victor, relax," Tom says. "You just said—"

"I look out for my friends," Victor shouts at him. "And that means protecting them from drug dealers and whatever"—he spins on Jon—"you are."

"I'm not a drug dealer," Tom says, laughing.

"And I'm just a guy," Jon says, backing away. This is the most nervous Ollie has seen him. His charm flickers for a moment, and Ollie can see him deciding between trying to talk his way out or fight. "Relax, man."

"Victor—" Ian says, putting their hand on Victor's shoulder.

"Watch yourself," Victor says, reaching out and shoving Jon's shoulder slightly, causing his beer to splash up all over his face.

"Fuck," Jon says, then pauses for a moment. Ollie swallows. Is he going to punch back? But he just pulls up his tee to wipe his face.

"What the hell, Victor?" Brandon asks, standing between him and Jon. "Don't be an asshole."

"He pushed Ian!" Victor shouts back, face turning pink. "I'm not letting this guy hurt anyone."

"He's not going to hurt anyone," Brandon yells back. "Just cool down!"

"'Cool down'?" Victor asks, even louder. "Fuck you, 'cool down'!"

Then, wildly, Brandon throws his drink on Victor. Ollie feels his eyes widen in shock as the liquid flies through the air, like it's in slo-mo, a paper towel commercial where something is about to stain a carpet. He really hopes nothing is about to stain anything.

It splashes on Victor's face and the carpet, but thankfully it's clear. Good thing he made sure it was only gin and vodka, Ollie tells himself.

"Cool down," Brandon repeats, calmer. His face is all *Real Housewives* aside from the eyes, which are too wide, stunned by what he's done. Victor also looks stunned.

"Whoa," Safiya says.

"Okay," Ollie says, waving his arms. "Let's all just relax."

"I think it's a little late for that," Ian says. "What the fuck, Brandon?"

"He shoved Jon!" Brandon sounds borderline hysterical now.

"Jon shoved Ian," Nicole says. "C'mon, Brandon—"

"No, I didn't," Jon protests.

"He—" Ian starts.

"Please!" Ollie shouts again, but everyone is talking over each other, words and bodies forming a knot in the middle of the room, almost shaking the walls as they pull everything inward. Ollie instinctively puts a hand up, as if to protect Safiya from the gravity.

"Is it always like this?" she asks him.

"No." He can't hide the sadness in his voice.

"Why don't any of you give Jon a chance?" Brandon's voice is hoarse from screaming, so raw that everyone goes quiet. He locks eyes first on Ian, then Nicole, and finally Ollie. He looks so hurt, Ollie drops his gaze to the floor. "I really like him, and you're all here snooping"—he points at Ian—"or interrogating"—his hand flies over to Nicole—"or trying to be smart and find stuff out but just embarrassing yourself," he says, hand finally landing on Ollie in a way that feels like a punch.

"I'm just trying to solve the case!" Ollie protests, but it sounds weak.

"Case?" Tom asks, but everyone ignores him.

"He's trouble, Brandon," Nicole says. "Can't you see that?"

"Oh, like you would know, with your nose in your phone all night. Texting your boss?"

Nicole frowns.

"Yeah, you want to talk about bad romantic decisions, how about that one? Or you"—Brandon turns on Ian—"bringing the guy you say is 'too nice' but is clearly a drug dealer and the ex you were hate stalking until today to the same party?"

"Fuck you," Ian says, but their eyes flick to Victor, who looks back at them, confused.

"I think maybe I should go," Safiya whispers in Ollie's ear. Ollie doesn't say anything, waiting for Brandon to tear him down next, but he doesn't even seem to spot Ollie. Which somehow hurts even more.

"It's like the moment I find something that makes me happy, and not just the butt of all your jokes, you need to do everything you can to take it away from me," Brandon screams at the room. Tears are running down his face.

"Hey," Jon says, taking Brandon's arm. "Hey, it's okay."

"He's dangerous," Nicole says, now her turn to point at Jon. "Look what he did to Ian!"

That seems to remind Victor about the push, and he puffs his chest out again.

"What does 'too nice' mean?" Tom asks quietly.

"Let's clean you up," Brandon says, getting between Jon and Victor. "I think we're done for the night." He pulls Jon back into the den and slams the door.

Ollie forces a laugh, too loudly, he knows. He wants to go knock on Brandon's door and make it all better. But Nicole and Ian look angry. "Well, that was dramatic."

"Oh, shut up, Ollie," Nicole says, taking a long swig of her beer.

"Are you okay?" Tom and Victor ask Ian, voices overlapping. They meet eyes for a moment, and then Victor backs up, letting Tom step closer to Ian.

"I'm really fine," Ian says, laughing. "Victor, you shouldn't have pushed him. I just tripped. It was all just…a misunderstanding."

"Was it?" Nicole asks. "Or were you snooping?"

"Like you wouldn't?" Ian shrugs. "We're all doing it. Brandon was right."

"Because he's bad news!" Nicole says again. "Are we all forgetting what Ollie and Brandon saw?"

"This is why I was trying to be subtle," Ollie says.

Nicole throws her head back and cackles. "You think that was subtle? Jesus, Ollie, you were as subtle as a car crash."

The words *car crash* evoke images for Ollie, memories. His dad on a slab in a dark room. He hadn't had his license on him, was just out walking the dog, so Ollie did the ID. Bodies are so fragile. He feels Safiya put a hand on his shoulder from behind and looks over at Nicole, who seems to have realized what she said, her face falling.

She shakes her head. "I didn't mean—"

"It's fine," Ollie says. It's not. All the excitement of the case is gone. He needs an edible. A strong one.

"Hey," Victor says to Ian, hanging his head. "Can we just, talk?" he asks Ian. "Privately?"

Ian bites their lower lip and nods. "Yeah, sure. I'm staying in the master bedroom, upstairs."

"Thanks."

Ian leads Victor upstairs, leaving Ollie alone with Nicole, Safiya, and Tom, who watches them go, frowning.

"Don't worry," Safiya says to Tom. "I think they just need to talk."

Nicole throws Safiya a skeptical look.

"Why don't we set up Pictionary?" Safiya says, her hand on Ollie's arm. "We can go back upstairs…"

"You think Brandon and Jon aren't coming back out?" Ollie asks her. He was hoping to apologize.

"Maybe after they've fucked," Nicole says, taking a swig of beer and frowning at the taste. She puts it in the sink. "Maybe everyone will come back to the game room, all tension just screwed out of them."

Ollie frowns at Nicole, nodding at Tom, whose eyes are still on the stairs, where Ian and Victor have vanished.

"Sorry," Nicole says flatly. She sighs. "No, you're right. I'm fucking everything up. Let's go set up for Pictionary. Cheer us up. Or celebrity. But Pictionary we can do with only four people. Girls versus boys."

They all walk back up to the game room. The house feels noisier now. Soft murmuring. The sound of water. Ghosts. Nicole sets up the little white marker board while Ollie takes out his cards of things to draw: cops, spies, violence. He's not going to learn anything without Jon here though. He takes a thick slice of cheese.

"Where's Pete?" Safiya asks, settling back into her chair. At least she's stayed. If she left, Ollie would have failed at everything tonight.

"Probably still downstairs. I'll go get him," Ollie says. Maybe he can coax Brandon and Jon back to the game. Apologize.

Downstairs, he goes over to the den and knocks on the door. No answer. He pushes the door open a little, eyes closed, but all he hears is the shower going, so he opens his eyes: lights on, clothes on the floor—the shower. He swallows and retreats, just as Pete zips into the room, carrying his teething ring. Ollie doesn't want to walk farther inside, so instead he just leaves the door open a little and retreats to the game room.

"No Pete?" Safiya asks with a frown.

"He was in the den," Ollie says. "Sounds like Jon is...washing off. And Brandon is helping."

Nicole snorts. "Called it."

But then the door opens, and Ian walks back in. They sit down next to Tom, but with a little space between them. "Victor is going home," they say, voice neutral in a way Ollie can tell is taking some effort.

"Oh," Ollie says. "Well, that's all right. It was good to see him, right?"

"Sure," Ian says.

Nicole takes a sip of her drink.

"So, Pictionary?" Ollie asks. "Want to make teams? Nicole had said boys versus girls, so Ian, whatever you're feeling."

"Whatever," Ian says.

"Be on my team," Tom says, reaching out his hand to close the gap and squeeze Ian's thigh. Ian looks down at it but doesn't shift. "Yeah. Boys."

"I kill at this," Safiya says to Nicole as they sort themselves into different sides of the room.

"Yeah, let's destroy them," Nicole says, sipping again.

"You go first, then," Ollie says, offering them a stack of cards.

Nicole draws one and frowns but flips the timer and starts drawing.

"Oh, pigs," Safiya says. "Police, I mean. Police station. Someone talking? What is this? Someone—"

There's the sound of a door slamming downstairs, loud enough that they can hear it. Everyone stops, looking at each other.

"Victor wouldn't have done that," Ian says. "He wasn't angry anymore."

Ollie stands, a bad feeling creeping up his spine, and starts down the stairs, everyone following him. The front door is closed, but standing in front of it, dripping and in just a towel, is Brandon, who turns as they come down the stairs. His eyes are red with tears.

"He left."

27.
Nicole

"TIME FOR TRIVIA!" OLLIE SAYS, his excitement already cloying. Why is he even doing this? Why did he decide to invite this deeply suspicious man over to a home that's not even his? Isn't he worried about how much it would cost to get blood stains out of the furniture here? As he lays out the trivia categories, she sees an answer forming: Detective Ollie interrogating via game night. It would be clever if it weren't so direct. She wishes he'd asked for her help.

On the flip side, it's nice to see him interested in something again. Barreling forward, checking things off—like the old Ollie. And he brought a pretty cool-looking date. Nicole doesn't think an interrogation of a possible spy is what she'd call second-date material, but it's his life.

So she jokes about the porn stars and watches Jon react to the questions, just like she knows Ollie is. Of course, if he is a spy, keeping his face blank should be easy. So him not giving anything away aside from knowledge about guns, drugs…it means nothing. Him spending the night is news though. She doesn't love that.

Unsurprising, but why would Brandon still be all over this guy? She sighs, hiding it with a sip of her drink. She knows the answer to that. Brandon being Brandon. In love with a smile and willing to do anything for that love. She's almost jealous, aside from the fact that it's currently putting them all in probable danger. She can't even ask out the coffee girl, and the only danger there is getting teased a little at the office.

Though she did sleep with her boss. That might have been brave. Or just stupid.

Her phone buzzes as they play, and she glances down at it.

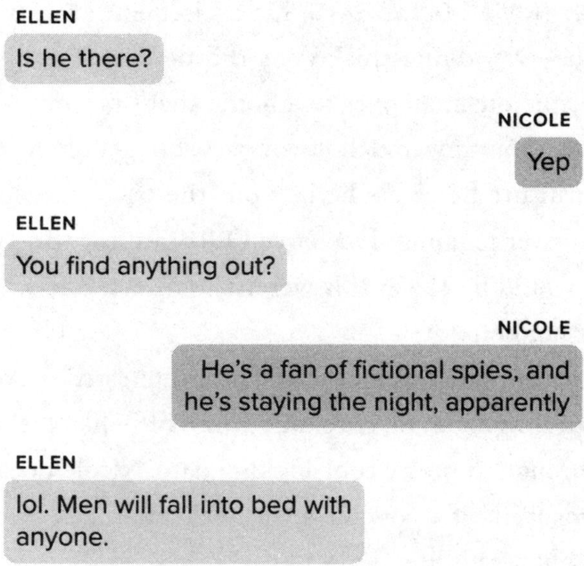

Nicole smirks, then remembers the weird smell in Ellen's kitchen. It's not just men who make choices that land them in bed with questionable people.

NICOLE

Yeah

ELLEN

Let me know if anything changes
or you find out anything else

NICOLE

Will do

Nicole tucks her phone back in her pocket, frowning. Ellen is supposed to be working on finding out if it really was KBA who killed the guy, and who the dead guy was, and why anyone wanted him dead, but she's checking in about Jon. Probably trying to cover all her bases, which means she hasn't found much.

"Tom, you pick the next category," Brandon says.

"Go for international politics," Nicole says, deciding to help Ollie out. "None of us know anything about that."

"Okay," Tom says. "International politics."

It's a softball though. There's a movie and a Broadway musical about Operation Mincemeat, not that Nicole has ever seen either of them. Ollie looks suspicious when Jon gets it, but it doesn't really mean anything. She goes over everything in her head again—someone shot near him, reservation made by KBA, two names. It really doesn't come to anything. Is it possible this is all just some weird misunderstanding and she's totally overreacting? Ellen definitely didn't seem to think so, and Ellen seems a lot smarter than Nicole feels. So maybe not. She remembers what Ellen said: talk to him, pretend she's looking out for her friend, and just interrogate. More directly than Ollie is.

She sees her opportunity when Jon gets up, probably

uncomfortable with the tension between Ian's two boyfriends—no idea why they brought both of them. Insane choice. But then, most of Ian's choices are insane where Victor is concerned. She smiles and says she wants a beer, too. Which is a lie, beer is gross, but she's doing what she needs to.

She follows him downstairs, the dark in the hallway suddenly making her aware that this guy is wrapped up with a private military and she's about to try to get some information out of him. He could be a trained killer. Who knows?

"So, you and Brandon hooked up at his hotel, huh?" she asks as they get into the kitchen.

"Oh, yeah." He smiles a little. Looks genuine. "Did he tell you the whole story? I did the whole 'I need a towel thing' like I was in a porno."

Nicole laughs. That would seem romantic to Brandon. "Well, you're here now, so seems like more than just a seedy hookup." She opens the fridge and takes out two beers. "Not everyone gets a game-night invite."

"Really?" He leans in to take the beer, pops the cap off on the counter. "Then who's the drug dealer? And the marshal? Weird combo."

She shrugs. "I said not everyone gets an invite. Not that we invited the best people."

He laughs, leaning back, not eager to go back upstairs. Perfect.

"Are you the best people?" Nicole asks. "Not to be the protective–best friend stereotype, but you're only here for a while, and Brandon is sweet, so—"

"You want to know my intentions with your friend?" Jon asks, grinning.

"I guess."

He sips his beer, and she mirrors him, trying not to grimace at the taste. "I get it. You're a good friend. You all seem to be really good friends. And, honestly, I don't have any bad intentions or anything, but I also don't know if this is like a fling, a couple days that we think about for decades or try to forget, or maybe something more." He shrugs, face too charming. "I'm just playing it by ear. But I'm open to anything. It would be fun to find my soulmate in a hotel on a work trip. Good story."

Nicole smirks. "So, art insurance?"

"It's not as exciting as it sounds. And you're a lawyer?"

"Also not as exciting as it sounds," she says.

He laughs and holds out his bottle for a toast. She clinks her bottle on his and takes another bitter swig.

"Although I do get to work on some interesting cases," she says, deciding on a different track. "My colleague is working on a case against KBA, this private military group." She watches him carefully as he says it. He blinks and quickly takes another swig at the mention of KBA, chin up, face away. Calculated to cover his surprise, maybe. "They're war profiteers, not great people," she continues.

He shrugs, face too charming again. "Never heard of them."

"Well, it feels good to try to take them down anyway," she says.

"You think you'll win? A private army sounds pretty powerful, right?"

Nicole smiles, trying to look just a little menacing. "My boss is very good at her job."

They lock eyes for a moment, both holding their beers, lights dim, dark house around them. She remembers the bad night, suddenly. The man who was chatting her up, how she'd told him she was gay and locked eyes with him, and she'd seen something then that she sees in Jon now: something cold and broken. She shouldn't have taken her eyes off the man chatting her up, but she was nineteen and using a fake ID and worried about a million other things, so she didn't notice when he spiked her drink. Her boys saved her. Maybe now she can save them.

"I know—" she begins, but there's a *clang* from the den, and they both look over. The door is closed.

"Should we check that?" Jon asks.

"Probably just the dog," Nicole says.

"I thought he was upstairs," Jon says, turning like he's going to head back up, like he wants to escape.

"I know what you're—" Nicole starts, but then there are loud feet on the stairs, and Brandon is there, smile too bright, eyes only for Jon.

"Hi!" he says.

Damn. She has no idea how to fix this now. Brandon looks so head over heels. And she wants him to be happy, but this guy is bad news. "You missed the lesbian question, Nicole. No one knew it."

"Shocking," Nicole says, still staring at Jon.

"What are you two talking about?" Brandon asks.

"Just getting to know each other," Nicole says, keeping her voice light as she finally turns to him.

"Cool," Brandon says, staring at Jon. "Well, want to go back upstairs? I just wanted to get a seltzer."

"Yeah," Jon says, "I just need to grab something from my bag." He walks over to the hidden door and opens it.

"Were you interrogating him?" Brandon hisses at Nicole.

"Yes," she whispers back. "Brandon, I get you like this guy, but *come on*. He's dangerous, and he's lying to you."

"We don't know that," Brandon says quickly. "Jon could be his middle name that he goes by now. And he could work in art insurance. The head— It might have been wrong time, wrong place."

She sighs, a million things she wants to say: *Just trust me. I know best. Get your head out of your ass*. But she knows just saying it won't be enough. "Well, that's all I'm trying to find out," she says instead. "I'm looking out for you." She sounds like she's begging.

"I can look out for myself."

She laughs and takes a swig of the beer just to make her mouth do something else. "Sure."

Brandon crosses his arms. "You're just jealous I'm actually getting some."

It's delivered like a slap, like he wants to hurt her—and that does make it sting a little. She could tell him she just got laid a few hours ago, but what does it even matter? It's not about that. It's about Jon. She opens her mouth to tell him that, but then Jon's voice comes from the den:

"What are you doing in here?"

"Sorry, sorry," Ian says, half running out of the den, Jon following them. He looks so menacing chasing after Ian that she takes a step forward, ready to get between them, but then Jon pushes Ian down, and they fall with a thud so heavy, the track lighting shakes a little, like rain on the roof. She swallows, a trickle of fear coursing down her chest. This was a bad idea. But maybe seeing Jon's violence is enough to convince Brandon how dangerous he is.

"Whoa!" Nicole shouts. "Do not push my friend!"

"He didn't push them," Brandon says.

"He didn't—" Ian says, getting up, just as everyone else comes downstairs, Victor practically jumping the banister to get between them and Jon. Well, good, someone knows he's bad news.

"What is going on?" Victor asks. "Who even is this guy?"

"He's my—" Brandon starts.

He stops himself, but she can tell he was going to say *boyfriend*. After one hookup and some shopping today. "Oh Jesus," Nicole murmurs.

"It's fine," Jon says, one hand open and up, the other holding his beer. "I just found Ian in our room and asked them what they were doing."

"I just got turned around," Ian says, standing.

"Okay," Ollie says. "So it's all fine! Let's go back upstairs and keep playing. You missed the lesbian question, Nicole."

"I really need more lesbian friends," Nicole says, realizing it suddenly. Surely a bunch of women wouldn't be this insane. Then she remembers Ellen's apartment. No, they could be. With her luck, they would be.

"No, I want to know what this guy was doing to Ian," Victor says.

"Victor, relax," Tom says. "You just said—"

"I look out for my friends," Victor shouts at him. "And that means protecting them from drug dealers and whatever"—he turns on Jon—"you are."

"I'm not a drug dealer," Tom protests, maybe with too much vigor.

"And I'm just a guy," Jon says, backing away. "Relax, man."

Nicole thinks about shouting, accusing, telling everyone he's obvious trouble, but at this point, that would just further drive Brandon away. She stays silent.

"Victor—" Ian says, putting their hand on Victor's shoulder.

"Watch yourself," Victor says, reaching out and shoving Jon's shoulder slightly, causing his beer to splash up all over his face.

"Fuck," Jon says, pulling up his tee to wipe his face, showing off some skin. Brandon stares.

"What the hell, Victor?" Brandon asks, standing between him and Jon. "Don't be an asshole."

"He pushed Ian!" Victor shouts back. "I'm not letting this guy hurt anyone."

Nicole rolls her eyes. Victor's not wrong about Jon being trouble, but he's acting like an overprotective boyfriend.

"He's not going to hurt anyone," Brandon yells back. "Just cool down!"

"'Cool down'?" Victor asks, even louder. Nicole opens her mouth to stop this, but not fast enough. "Fuck you, 'cool down'!"

Brandon throws his drink on Victor. Nicole stares, jaw dropped. She almost wants to laugh.

"Cool down," Brandon repeats, quieter. Both he and Victor look shocked.

"Whoa," Safiya says, speaking for all of them.

"Okay," Ollie says, waving his arms from atop the landing. "Let's all just relax."

"I think it's a little late for that," Ian says. "What the fuck, Brandon?"

"He shoved Jon!" Brandon is shrieking now.

Nicole doesn't understand how he doesn't see what's really happening. "Jon shoved Ian," she tells him. "C'mon, Brandon—"

"No, I didn't," Jon protests, voice angry now. She turns to look at him, and he's glaring.

"He—" Ian starts.

Ollie shouts something, but Nicole isn't paying attention. Her eyes are locked on Jon, whose eyes are locked right back on her.

"What's your problem with me, anyway?" he hisses.

"Oh, like you don't know?" she asks. Around them, people are shouting.

"I don't!" he says back. "I haven't done anything."

Nicole throws her head back in a cackle. The audacity of this man. "Haven't done anything?" He's the reason some poor guy got shot, the reason they're all in danger, that she had to leave work, that she idiotically hooked up with her boss—none of it would have happened if not for him. And he thinks he hasn't done anything! He's going on about Ian in the den. She opens her mouth, ready to spit venom, but Brandon screams out first:

"Why don't any of you give Jon a chance?" He sounds so hurt, Nicole feels guilt crack in her chest like an egg. He locks eyes first on Ian, then Nicole. His eyes are watering, and she realizes for a moment how it must look to him, her coming down so hard on Jon, a guy he really likes. She's not being protective or even overprotective. She's being cruel. "I really like him, and you're all here snooping"—he points at Ian—"or interrogating"—his hand flies over to Nicole—"or trying to be smart and find stuff out but just embarrassing yourself," he says, hand finally landing on Ollie like he's choosing them all out of a lineup as the criminals who attacked him.

"I'm just trying to solve the case!" Ollie whimpers.

"Case?" Tom asks, but everyone ignores him.

"He's trouble, Brandon," Nicole says, but it sounds weak, even to her. "Can't you see that?" She's not wrong. But she knows this has been the wrong way to tell him.

"Oh, like you would know, with your nose in your phone all night. Texting your boss?"

Nicole flinches at that—she was blaming her bad choice on Jon in her mind a second ago, but she knows it's all her. She looks away.

"Yeah, you want to talk about bad romantic decisions, how about that one? Or you, bringing the guy you say is 'too nice' but is clearly a drug dealer and the ex you were hate stalking until today to the same party?"

"Fuck you," Ian says, but their voice is soft, fuzzy.

"It's like the moment I find something that makes me happy, and not just the butt of all your jokes, you need to do everything you can to take it away from me," Brandon screams at the room. Tears are running down his face.

"Hey," Jon says, taking Brandon's arm. "Hey, it's okay." She sees it then, the charm, how safe Brandon must have felt with him, how special. She hasn't been making any of her friends feel that way recently. She was thinking of them the way Ellen did—as silly. Kids she has to clean up after, not the friends she should be working with.

"He's dangerous," she says, pointing at Jon, pleading with Brandon. "Look what he did to Ian!" She's bad at this. She's been too aloof for too long. But she needs him to listen.

Brandon looks at her a moment, and she thinks maybe he'll finally believe her, finally see what she wants to show—that she cares about him, that she worries, that she just wants him safe. But he sneers.

"Let's clean you up," Brandon says, getting between Jon and Victor. "I think we're done for the night." He pulls Jon back into the den and slams the door.

Nicole sighs. That all could have gone a lot better.

Ollie laughs loudly. "Well, that was dramatic."

"Are you okay?" Tom and Victor ask Ian, voices overlapping. Oh Jesus, now this?

"I'm really fine," Ian says. "Victor, you shouldn't have pushed him. I just tripped. It was all just...a misunderstanding."

"Was it?" Nicole asks. "Or were you snooping?" She wouldn't judge them if they were. She hopes they have information.

"Like you wouldn't?" Ian asks. "We're all doing it. Brandon was right."

No, no, no. She might regret how they're treating Brandon, but that doesn't mean they can trust Jon. "Because he's bad news! Are we all forgetting what Ollie and Brandon saw?"

"This is why I was trying to be subtle," Ollie says.

Nicole throws her head back and cackles. "You think that was subtle? Jesus, Ollie, you were as subtle as a car crash."

There's a beat in her mind before she realizes what she's said. A moment where it just seems like any old comeback, something she'd say at brunch, before she remembers and it pours down on her like a pipe just broke over her. She's such a bitch. She's a bad friend. "I didn't mean—"

"It's fine," Ollie says. She can tell from his expression that it isn't.

She keeps staring at Ollie, who won't meet her eyes, as Ian and Victor walk off.

"Don't worry," Safiya says to Tom. "I think they just need to talk."

Nicole tries to catch Ollie's eye with an expression hopefully conveying exactly how ridiculous that sounds. A little inside joke to show how sorry she is. But he only frowns.

"Why don't we set up Pictionary?" Ollie says. "We can go back upstairs..."

"You think Brandon and Jon aren't coming back out?" Safiya asks.

"Maybe after they've fucked," Nicole says, taking a swig of beer, now an instinct. It's disgusting. She puts it in the sink. "Maybe everyone will come back to the game room, all tension just screwed out of them." She knows she's being mean, crude. She's just so angry. Why can't Brandon just listen to her? "Sorry," she says. "No, you're right. Let's go set up for Pictionary. Or celebrity. But Pictionary we can do with only four people. Girls versus boys."

She tries to look cheerful as they head upstairs, but she knows everything is bad now.

She takes out her phone.

NICOLE

Dude is no good

ELLEN

You find something out?

NICOLE

Just looked in his eyes. He just pushed a friend. I feel like we should call the cops or something.

ELLEN

No don't do that.

He could get violent.

Nicole frowns, feeling like that's even more of a reason. She puts her phone away and sets up the little white marker board upstairs, which has been fussy since Ian knocked it over three parties ago and now needs some finessing. Setting it up feels like penance, and she keeps glancing over at Ollie, who is shuffling cards.

"Where's Pete?" Safiya asks.

"Probably still downstairs. I'll go get him," Ollie says quickly, clearly eager to get away from Nicole.

Nicole sits down, her phone buzzing.

ELLEN

Maybe you can convince him to leave

Let me know if you do

"Who's that?" Safiya asks.

"Just work," Nicole says.

NICOLE

Ok I can try

"You're smiling too much for it to be work."

"I'm not smiling," Nicole says, glancing up.

"Well, you're frowning less," Safiya says.

Nicole snorts.

"Are most game nights like this?" Tom asks.

No. Normally they're fun and warm and feel like everyone together in the dorm again. But tonight feels cold and shattered. Ice on the floor. But Tom doesn't need to know that. So Nicole shrugs. "Depends how much people are drinking."

"I probably should have made sure Ollie told everyone about the cheese," Safiya says.

"What about the cheese?" Nicole asks.

They explain, Nicole very happy she was focusing on the Gruyère because it was closest to her, and then Ollie comes back, and they split into teams, and Ian comes back in, looking sad. So much for a reunion there. She tries to look sympathetic. But Tom seems nice, and Victor and Ian clearly have too much stuff. Ian just needs a clean slate. No mess.

She should text Sam. Thank her for the advice earlier. She shakes the idea out of her head and tries to turn toward the Pictionary board, but Safiya isn't even done drawing her first clue when there's the sound of a slamming door downstairs. They all go to check, but Nicole knows what to expect—she feels a swell of guilty relief like a balloon inside her, seeing Brandon in a towel, wet.

"He left."

He's crying, like real ugly crying, and it hurts Nicole like an ache, but she's also so glad Jon is gone.

NICOLE

He just left.

Maybe all this can finally be over.

28.
Ian

"TIME FOR TRIVIA!" OLLIE'S VOICE is so shocking, Ian is almost knocked back. They're nervous. This is all a terrible idea. Some hot guy with a woman on the phone offering him obscene amounts of money to steal a drive from someone who has already been around one murder—which was probably committed by said hot guy—in a house they don't know while a bunch of people are over, including their law enforcement ex and some hookup they've been blowing off.

They are never judging Brandon's bad choices again.

Okay, that's a lie. But they'll try to be more sympathetic, because they're realizing right now how easy it is to just make a bad choice in the moment because it feels like you have to, like your body will burn up if you don't, and then suddenly being stuck with it. At least when you key a car, it can be repainted. Ian's not sure what kind of damage tonight will leave, but they're pretty sure it won't be fixable with some paint and a buff.

Ian doesn't know what's going on with the trivia categories, maybe something to impress Safiya, who looks way too cool for

Ollie, frankly. Thankfully, Nicole chooses porn stars, so they don't all embarrass themselves immediately.

"Which twink couple has shared scenes in only two films—*Naughty Stepbrothers: Volume 17* and *Heart Throbber*—but met on the set of *Open-Him-R: An Oppenheimer Porn Parody*, where they had no scenes together?" Ollie reads.

"Not lesbians," Nicole says.

"They're in there, I promise," Ollie says.

Victor shifts next to Ian. It's weird how familiar that feels, from the old days when he would come to these parties and they'd get competitive, desperately trying to outdo the others, annoyed at their own losses, stoking some kind of flame they'd take to bed afterward with such strength that Brandon made a rule that they'd go back to Victor's place after game nights.

"Oh, oh," Victor says. "I know this one. One of them is Justin Justins. And the other is..." He shakes his head, squinting.

Ian smiles—Victor almost has it. "Starts with an *s*," Ian says. They don't even think about it; it's just out like an old habit.

"Oh, Stephen Hole!" Victor finishes.

"Correct!" Olly says. "You get to pick the next category."

"Yes!" Victor does a fist pump and slaps Ian on the back, just like old times. There's even a moment when his hand rests there, in the middle of Ian's back, and drifts lower before Victor seems to realize and pulls it back. "Well, let's go with Guns, then. I know about weapons and lifting." He flexes, grinning. Ian laughs to cover the cauldron of feelings they're having from all this.

They go through another question, Ian trying to lean away from Victor and more into Tom, who smells mildly like cheese.

Which isn't bad. But Victor smells like sweat and that weird smoky cologne he always uses, and it's not the same.

"What is the approximate street value of one gram of cocaine?" Ollie reads.

"One hundred fifty to two hundred dollars," Tom answers immediately, not even shifting next to Ian. Ian looks at him. They would not have taken Tom for a cocaine user. But surprises can be fun. Not that Ian has touched the stuff. Well, not after the third time. But they don't judge others.

"Correct," Ollie says softly.

"What did you say you do for a living?" Victor asks. Ian watches Victor's hackles go up, that suspicious look in his eye, competitive, protective. Seeing it feels like a lighter flicking on in the dark, their pupils needing to adjust.

"I'm in marketing," Tom says, smiling.

Victor narrows his eyes. Ian bites their lower lip. "Marketing what?"

Tom nods. "My newest account is Dudches"—he points at Victor like he's selling him on something—"an anal-douching kit for bros."

Ian did not know that. They're all for anal hygiene, but this is the least-sexy thing they've ever heard. Victor is glaring even more. Ian feels their blood tingle, the urge to kiss Victor rising. Or slap him. This has to stop. And besides, they have something they need to do. Maybe. Sort of. They tap their foot slightly, nervous about that. Victor leans into them, thigh on thigh, and their foot stops on its own.

"So," they interrupt, turning their attention away from Victor's sexy glower. "Jon! Where have you been staying since you checked out of Brandon's hotel?"

"A few cheap hotels, wherever I could get a reservation," Jon says with a shrug.

"He's staying back at Hotel Brandon tonight though," Brandon says proudly.

"Oh, so your stuff is here?" Ian asks. Perfect. "I didn't notice."

"I don't have much," Jon says.

"Tom, you pick the next category," Brandon says. Looks like he doesn't like the attention on Jon. Which Ian understands. The more you interrogate a bad decision, the harder it becomes to justify. That's why Ian doesn't want to look at Victor or Tom right now.

There's another question, then back to drugs, when Tom announces the price of ecstasy this time. Maybe Tom is more fun than Ian thought? Like, he seemed sweet, but if he can hook Ian up with a little ecstasy, he could be more fun. But Victor is glaring again, which is somehow an even more potent drug, and besides, Ian knows what they need to know. It's time to try to find that zip drive.

"I'm going to the bathroom," they say, then make a quick exit. Outside the rest of the house is dark, light from the game room cutting white lines in black velvet. It's a good look. Ian pads down the carpeted stairs, then over to the hidden door to the den. They're not entirely sure why they're doing this. The money? Maybe. That can't be ignored, as much as they wish it could. It's life-changing; even if they split it with their friends—and they probably would—it's a huge amount of money. They could all buy an apartment together and throw wild parties. They could have a club downstairs. It could be so many things, so many opportunities opening up.

And then there's the thrill of just ending all this drama. Handing off the zip drive and being free and clear. Safe. All their friends safe, too. If they can believe the woman on the phone, anyway. But all this madness that Brandon has swept them into, Ian could sweep them out of. That plus a shitload of money? Hard to look away from. So they might as well try, right? At worst, they find nothing and then someone kills them trying to get to Jon tonight. Or maybe Jon walks in on them and kills them. Or maybe they find it and turn it over to Heart-Eyes and they all get killed anyway. But if they're going to be dead in any scenario, they want to go out trying to do something. Anything. Or maybe fucking Victor, even though they know that's a bad idea. Maybe Tom? No, the bloom is off the rose with Tom. He's cute and nice, but there's no spark, not like there is with Victor. Maybe Ian needs a little rage, a little brokenness to want someone. Maybe they should go to therapy. If they survive.

The den isn't big, so it shouldn't be too hard to find Jon's stuff. The sofa is still pulled out into a bed, though it's way nicer than their futon. It's way nicer than Ian's normal bed, they think, sitting down on it. It's nicely made—Brandon always does that, a hotel thing—and nothing is under the sheets. They open a few cabinets but just find wires, books, notepads, photo albums filled with pictures of a wealthy white couple in exotic locations, smiling like they came with the frame. Well, that and pictures of food. Just them and food. Very weird. Ian almost wants to go through all of them because of how weird they are, it's like art, but they shake their head, putting them away. Next, they check the bathroom, but aside from Brandon's toiletry bag, nothing's there.

It's just a bag, right? Where would he put it? Did he try to hide it? If he did, then the zip drive must be in it.

There are suddenly voices outside, muffled through the den door. Shit. Ian looks around, wondering if they need to hide. Maybe they can just say they got turned around and decided to use the bathroom in here? Maybe no one will come in.

Just in case, they dive under the bed. It's tight, that weird geometry of collapsing legs and springs that makes the space under the bed more awkward than being on top of it. It feels like being under some kind of bridge. But there's a bag that Ian doesn't recognize as being Brandon's.

Outside, the voices continue but don't get closer, so Ian shimmies to the bag like a worm and unzips it. Clothes, some with tags still on, all very basic-looking tees and pants. All black briefs—a classic for the unimaginative gay. Ian checks the side pockets and finds a phone. Weird for him not to have it on him, but maybe he's the kind of guy who doesn't like screens mixing with social time. Or maybe it's a criminal thing. He left another phone in his hotel room, after all. Ian feels around the rest of the bag, but there's nothing else aside from a receipt for the clothes. He must have a wallet, but that could be on him. And the zip drive must be on him, too, or hidden somewhere else entirely. So much for easy money.

Still, the phone is something. Ian rolls on their back and opens it up. Password, of course, but Ian still remembers the original password from when they hacked the last phone and types it in. It works. People are so reliable except when they're not. The phone doesn't have anything on it though, not even email, aside from one app, something Ian has never seen, called *Connor-auction*, with the icon that usually means the app is broken. Ian frowns, not sure what that means. But it's time to leave. They shimmy back out from under the bed but kick one of the metal pieces as they do. It makes a sound like a gong, and they freeze in place, only their head and hands out from under the bed.

The voices outside get louder, like someone is walking this way. Ian contemplates getting back under the bed, but they've already searched everywhere. They have Jon's phone. And if they're caught under the bed, it looks a lot weirder than if they're just in there, like they got lost. So they quickly get out from under the bed, scraping their ankle on the underside as they do so.

The door opens just as they stand up. Jon stands in the door. He's bigger than Ian remembered, or maybe it's just the light from the kitchen behind him. He looks large, mean, and suspicious.

"What are you doing in here?" he demands.

"Sorry, sorry," Ian says, pushing past him, trying to get away and keep the phone hidden, half up their sleeve. Jon turns to follow them, and Ian walks faster, glancing back, and then feels their foot catch on the rug in the living room. They focus on hiding the phone, not staying up, and fall with a bit less grace than they'd like. But the phone stays hidden in their sleeve.

"Whoa!" Nicole shouts from the kitchen. "Do not push my friend!"

"He didn't push them," Brandon, also in the kitchen, says. And he's right; Jon might be scary, but he didn't push Ian.

"He didn't—" Ian says, doing their best to rise with some dignity, but the scrape on their leg hurts, and they limp slightly as they step forward. When they look up, everyone is there: Ollie, Tom, and Safiya watching them from the stairs like Ian is onstage and just fell during a routine. But Victor is already beside him, heat radiating off his body.

"What is going on?" Victor asks, that sexy fire in his eyes. "Who even is this guy?"

"He's my—" Brandon says.

"It's fine," Jon says, one hand up, smiling at Ian like nothing weird is happening, even though Ian knows it is, has Jon's phone. "I just found Ian in our room and asked them what they were doing."

"I just got turned around," Ian says, shrugging and then hooking their hands in their pockets so they can hide the phone in one.

"Okay," Ollie says. "So it's all fine! Let's go back upstairs and keep playing. You missed the lesbian question, Nicole."

"No, I want to know what this guy was doing to Ian," Victor says. He's in full defensive pit bull mode. It's hot.

"Victor, relax," Tom says. "You just said—"

"I look out for my friends," Victor shouts at him. "And that means protecting them from drug dealers and whatever"—he spins on Jon—"you are."

"I'm not a drug dealer," Tom says with a reedy laugh. Hopefully after tonight, he'll think Ian is insane and Ian won't have to blow him off anymore.

"And I'm just a guy," Jon says. "Relax, man."

"Victor—" Ian puts their hand on Victor's shoulder and squeezes slightly, starting to tell him to relax, that they just tripped.

But Victor barely seems to register it. "Watch yourself." He reaches out and shoves Jon's shoulder slightly, causing his beer to splash up all over his face. Starting a fight.

Ian feels their toes curl. They should not be so into this.

"Fuck," Jon says, pulling up his tee to wipe his face.

"What the hell, Victor?" Brandon asks, standing between him and Jon. "Don't be an asshole."

"He pushed Ian!" Victor shouts back, face turning pink. "I'm not letting this guy hurt anyone."

"He's not going to hurt anyone," Brandon yells back. Ian tries to put their hand up, but Brandon's rage vibrates through them, pinning them in place. He sounds so hurt. And Ian knows why—he loves Jon. That stupid love you feel after a few right moments. Ian remembers when they felt it for Victor, remembers what it was like being in love. They'd respond just like Brandon is. Even if Jon is a spy or a traitor or whatever that woman with the sunglasses said, it doesn't matter. Ian could tell Brandon everything, and for Brandon, it wouldn't change a thing. Ian feels guilty for a moment, but also jealous. They miss being that in love.

"Just cool down!" Brandon says to Victor, which is way tamer than Ian would have been.

"'Cool down'?" Victor asks, even louder. "Fuck you, 'cool down'!"

And then Brandon throws his drink on Victor. Full *Real Housewives* style. Ian almost wants to applaud.

"Cool down," Brandon repeats, calmer. Ian feels themself grinning. They know they shouldn't—this is all very, very bad—but just watching it, it's kind of a great show.

"Okay," Ollie says, waving his arms. "Let's all just relax."

"I think it's a little late for that," Ian says, almost laughing. "What the fuck, Brandon?" They mean it like *what the fuck made them go full soap opera*, but it sounds like they're angrier than that.

"He shoved Jon!" Brandon shrieks, the soap opera dialing up to eleven.

"Jon shoved Ian," Nicole says. "C'mon, Brandon—"

"No, I didn't," Jon protests.

"He—" Ian starts to try to make it clear that this is all a big overreaction again.

"Please!" Ollie shouts again, but now Victor is repeating what he saw in a fast voice, Jon speaking over him, saying what actually happened—he found Ian snooping and Ian tripped. Ian tries to cut in with "yes" and "I tripped," but no one is listening to anyone now. So, instead, they look at Victor, face red, sweat on his brow. If they were still together, they'd be naked by now.

"Why don't any of you give Jon a chance?" Brandon screams in a quieter moment, and everyone turns to him. Maybe everyone else hears it now, too, the sound of being in love.

Ian tries to smile, to tell Brandon that they get it, but this isn't healthy, Jon is scary—can't he just step back from the love for just a moment? But Brandon's eyes are so hard and cold and filled with a fury that Ian can see their reflection in them, and they look away.

"I really like him," Brandon says, "and you're all here snooping"—he points at Ian—"or interrogating"—his hand flies over to Nicole—"or trying to be smart and find stuff out but just embarrassing yourself," he says, his gesture ending at Ollie and then dropping to his side like he just fired three bullets out of it.

"I'm just trying to solve the case!" Ollie protests, but it sounds weak.

"Case?" Tom asks, but Ian doesn't want to even try to explain.

"He's trouble, Brandon," Nicole says. "Can't you see that?"

"Oh, like you would know, with your nose in your phone all night. Texting your boss?"

Ouch, that one is rough, especially coming from Brandon.

"Yeah, you want to talk about bad romantic decisions, how about that one? Or you." Brandon turns on Ian, and Ian shivers.

"Bringing the guy you say is 'too nice' but is clearly a drug dealer and the ex you were hate stalking until today to the same party?"

That was uncalled for—in front of all of them. Ian feels a rage rising to meet Brandon's, but all they can manage is "Fuck you." And then they look at Victor, part of them hoping Victor will be smiling, but he just looks confused. It feels like a slap, and Ian turns away.

Brandon is crying now. "It's like the moment I find something that makes me happy, and not just the butt of all your jokes, you need to do everything you can to take it away from me,"

"Hey," Jon says, taking Brandon's arm. "Hey, it's okay."

"He's dangerous," Nicole says, now her turn to point at Jon. "Look what he did to Ian!"

Ian sighs; they really fucked it all up. They go to say something, but again, they're too late, as Brandon shoves past them, getting between Jon and Victor.

"Let's clean you up. I think we're done for the night." Brandon pulls Jon back into the den and slams the door.

Ollie laughs, almost manic. "Well, that was dramatic."

"Oh, shut up, Ollie," Nicole says, taking a long swig of her beer.

"Are you okay?" Tom and Victor ask Ian, voices overlapping. Ian smiles a little at the thrill of that. Even with everything going on, being fought over feels good. Which is fucked-up, they know. Then Victor backs up, letting Tom step closer to Ian, and Ian feels disappointed. Even more fucked-up. They really need to make better choices.

"I'm really fine," Ian says, forcing a laugh. "Victor, you

shouldn't have pushed him. I just tripped. It was all just...a misunderstanding."

"Was it?" Nicole asks. "Or were you snooping?"

Ian rolls their eyes. "Like you wouldn't? We're all doing it. Brandon was right."

"Because he's bad news!" Nicole says again. "Are we all forgetting what Ollie and Brandon saw?"

"This is why I was trying to be subtle," Ollie says.

Nicole throws her head back and cackles. "You think that was subtle? Jesus, Ollie, you were as subtle as a car crash."

Ian almost gasps. Sure, sometimes—a lot of times—they're all pretty mean to each other. But tonight it feels like everyone has been cruel. Except them, right? They look up at Tom and Victor, both looking between each other and at Ian. No, they realize. They've been cruel, too.

"I didn't mean—" Nicole says.

"It's fine," Ollie interrupts in a numb voice.

"Hey," Victor says, his dark brown eyes searching Ian's. "Can we just talk? Privately?"

Ian bites their lower lip and nods. "Yeah, sure. I'm staying in the master bedroom, upstairs."

"Thanks."

Ian leads Victor upstairs, almost feeling like they should take his hand, be coquettish. But that's not the energy Victor has. The fire in him has faded a little, and when Ian closes the bedroom door behind them, Victor doesn't make a move toward them. Instead he just sits down on the bed, puts his head in his hands, and cries.

Ian sits down next to him, not sure what's going on. Their

body tingles with the fight that almost broke out, the theft they committed, Tom and Victor's sniping, all of it so chaotic and hot, an engine revving up to full speed.

"I'm sorry," Ian says, not entirely sure what they're apologizing for. "I don't know Jon. I didn't invite him."

Victor shakes his head. "That's not it. He's an asshole, but that's not—" He stops himself with a deep breath and looks up at Ian. "I shouldn't have come tonight."

"Why not?" Ian says, leaning into him slightly. "You've been great."

"I thought we could be friends, you know?" He wipes a tear off his cheek with his hand. "I thought maybe you'd forgive me for what I did."

Ian shakes their head, confused. "What have I done that makes you think I haven't?"

Victor smiles a little. Ian loves his smiles. He goes from this slab of muscle and fire to something so soft, and every smile feels like it's just for Ian. "No, that's not the problem. The problem is I still feel that..." He rubs his chest. "Between us."

"Is that bad?" Ian asks, leaning even closer, close enough to smell the gin on Victor's breath.

Victor stands quickly. "Yes, of course." He looks at Ian, pleading. "Don't you get it? Didn't you see who I became down there? I haven't been that guy in a year. But us, all that fire, it turns into rage. I just get so angry."

Ian stands up, moving closer. "I know. It's a spark between us. It's special."

"No." Victor steps back, shaking his head. "No, Ian. It's not a spark. It's a bomb. I don't want to be that guy downstairs who wanted to start a fight. And you, somehow, always bring that out in me." He starts to cry again and wipes away both his tears. "I care about you. I want to be friends. But this was too much, too soon, I think. I should go."

"Wait," Ian says, reaching out, but Victor is faster, out the door like a snuffed candle. Ian follows him and watches him go down the stairs, and they wait for the rage to swell up in them. Victor cheated, ended their relationship, and now, just when it's clear they should be together, that there's still something between them, he leaves again, abandoning them in a dark hall. Why is he always leaving Ian? Because something in Ian is broken, they know. That rage Victor doesn't want to feel? Ian is addicted to it. It's so much better than what they could be feeling otherwise, the flood of sadness that's always at the edges of them. They hold it off with fire.

So that's what they do again now: *That asshole*, they tell themself. *That fucking coward.* They clench their jaw, and their hands turn to fists, and they march down the hall back into the game room. Ian's not sad now. Fuck Victor.

Everyone looks up as Ian walks in, but they keep their face steady, neutral. The best rage is the kind that isn't too obvious. They sit down next to Tom and announce it: "Victor is going home."

"Oh," Ollie says. "Well, that's all right. It was good to see him, right?"

"Sure," Ian says. *That asshole.*

"So, Pictionary?" Ollie asks. "Want to make teams? Nicole had said boys versus girls, so Ian, whatever you're feeling."

"Whatever," Ian says. They are totally going to key his car later.

"Be on my team," Tom says, suddenly taking Ian's hand.

Ian looks down at their hands meeting and feels nothing. No fire. Just meat.

"Yeah. Boys," they say.

Safiya and Nicole start, but then there's the sound of a door slamming downstairs, loud enough that they can all hear it. Everyone stops, looking at each other.

"Victor wouldn't have done that," Ian says. "He wasn't angry." *Asshole.*

Everyone clambers downstairs, eager for whatever new drama is unfolding. The front door is closed, but standing in front of it, dripping and in just a towel, is Brandon, who turns as they come down the stairs. His eyes are red with tears.

"He left."

Ian takes a deep breath, seeing in Brandon everything they're feeling, too—like they're naked and wet and abandoned. That's what they would become if they let the sadness flood them. Better to be fire.

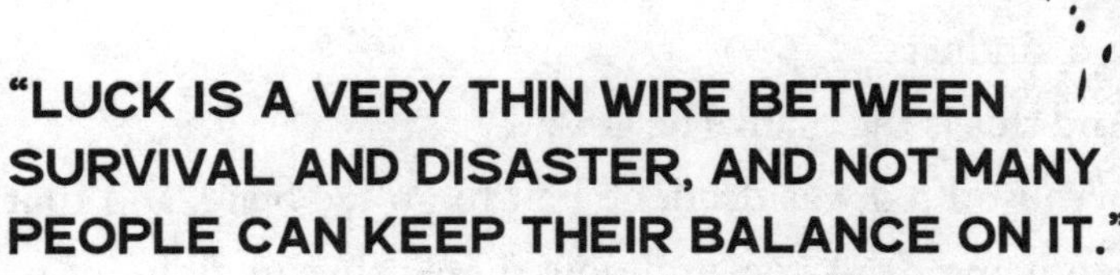

"LUCK IS A VERY THIN WIRE BETWEEN SURVIVAL AND DISASTER, AND NOT MANY PEOPLE CAN KEEP THEIR BALANCE ON IT."

—HUNTER S. THOMPSON

HE HAS FUCKED THIS UP royally.

Well, no. That was this fucking twink. Brandon told him everything in the shower—how they'd brought his phone to his meetup with Fred, then used it to stalk him and "bump into him" at his bar. He's been played. Who's the spy here, really? Him or some twink with a nice ass?

He works it all out as he furiously gets dressed, not bothering to towel off, just throwing on his clothes, his bracelets, grabbing his bag as Brandon pleads with him to stay: When he checked out and they called the woman up, she started tracking his phone. Followed it, or assigned someone to follow it, maybe back to Brandon's place, and then to the meet, where they were aiming for him but hit Fred. This twink almost got him killed! And that was after he did the nice thing, checking out early so he didn't get too attached. It should have been a fun roll in the hay with the help—a classic spy move, one of the main pleasures of being in the field: sex with random hotties who throw themselves at you. Then vanish, leaving behind only a memory of the best sex they've ever had. No relationships, no serious heartbreak. It's why he checked out at all—to make sure Brandon knew it was a one-night thing. It was a kindness.

And this is the thanks he gets.

Because Fred was dead, he had to go see Sean, and that led to Sean being dead, too, and now there's this auction out in the world, and the woman must know it's him. Maybe everyone knows it's him.

Bumping into Brandon seemed so lucky. He needed somewhere to lie low and was running out of cash, so staying with some pretty young thing with no connection to him? Who wasn't even staying at his own place, but some swanky town house? A dream. A five-star locale and decent sex on top of it. All he had to do was give Brandon the boyfriend experience. And the truth is, he loves giving guys the boyfriend experience. He's good at it. And it always feels good, like maybe they really are boyfriends, before he ghosts them. It was going to be a perfect few days until the auction was over.

And now? Now he's storming out of the fancy town house as the decent sex cries behind him. He needs to find somewhere else to stay, but first he has to walk off this rage. That's what it feels like: rage. At Brandon, at his weird friends, at himself. He's so angry, he doesn't even notice the van slow down beside him until it stops and slides open, and there's a hand on his mouth from behind him and the sweet smell of chloroform.

He wakes up in an empty gym. He knows the scent of it—sweat and industrial air freshener–before he opens his eyes. And then it's the classic setup: one light on over him, zip-tied to a chair and gagged. Three scrawny guys looking him over, one with a baseball bat. Boring really.

The gym looks long abandoned, a few free weights piled in one corner, indents in the floor where the expensive machines used to be. Nothing useful for getting out of this. Though he could probably crack a skull with one of the weights if he could get to it.

"Okay," the scrawny guy in front says, "now that everyone is awake, which one of you is Connor?"

He blinks, not sure what he heard, then turns his head as much as he can. There, on another chair to his right, equally tied and bound, is that guy from Brandon's party. The one who pushed him—Victor. His eyes are wide with confusion, staring back at him.

He tries to speak through the gag, tell them Victor is Connor, but his voice is muffled, of course. The head scrawny guy steps forward.

"Nod your head yes or no. Are you Connor?"

He shakes his head no. So does Victor.

"Well," the scrawny guy says, taking a gun out from under his jacket, "we were told Connor was coming out of the address you both walked out of around the same time. We were watching, and with the timing of texts, we weren't really sure which of you it was. Now, the one of you who isn't Connor, we're going to kill. Connor might get to live a little longer. So let's try this again. Nod your head yes or no. Are you Connor?"

He nods. Victor doesn't move at all. Connor doesn't usually use his real name, but it's easy enough to shrug back on. The man with the gun smiles, focusing his attention on Connor. He pulls the gag out of his mouth and holds up the gun to his forehead. Connor has had guns pressed to his forehead before though. He finds the cooling touch of the metal almost soothing. This is the fun part.

"So you know what we want," the man with the gun says. "Where is it?"

There's a way to break zip ties if you pull your wrists with just enough force at just the right angle. Connor tries to remember that angle as he talks.

"Who are you?" he asks. It's weird that they didn't find the drive on him. He's still dressed though, so maybe they didn't really search him, figured he'd have hidden it somewhere. He can use that.

"It doesn't matter who we are. What matters is the bidding is a little high for our tastes now, so we thought we'd just take it."

Connor looks them up and down. Not KBA, not enough cool. American. Two of them are white, one Black. Their jackets are plain, not leather, not suits. One has a tattoo on his forearm, but it's of a cross, not a gang symbol. The gun is nice though. Well kept. And he knows the maker.

"McClintock, right?" Connor guesses. Surprise passes over the face of one of the guys in the back. He got it in one. "Sure, a gun manufacturer could make a lot of illegal money with that information. Take over the Velvet Alley, dominate the global black-market weapons trade, I get it." To his right, he can feel Victor staring at him. But Victor is as good as dead, so it doesn't matter what he knows.

The man with the gun cocks the trigger. "Then you know why we want it so badly."

"Sure, sure," Connor says, leaning into the gun slightly. "Of course, if you kill me, then you won't know where it is."

To his right Victor is trying to speak through the gag. Connor ignores him, focusing on his wrists. He remembers the angle. Just one sharp pull and—

The zip tie snaps. It stings like hell, but Connor ignores that. He moves his hands fast. He grabs the gun from his forehead and spins it, pointing it at the man who was holding it a moment ago. This is the *really* fun part. He pulls the trigger.

The man is close enough that when his head explodes, it splatters on Connor's face. Some of it gets in his mouth. Gross. He wipes his eyes off, but the other guys are running forward now, and he's still bound to the chair at his legs. Fuck. What's the angle for breaking zip ties around the ankles? Oh wait, he can just slide those off. Right. He stands.

Just as the guy with the bat swings at his head. The movement means he gets smacked in the stomach, the bat thrusting it up into his throat. He collapses in pain, almost vomits. His hand releases the gun, and the other guy picks it up, pointing it at him. The one with the bat hits him again.

"Where is it, asshole?" the one holding the gun asks. His voice is faint through the ringing in Connor's ears from the gunfire. "We're not giving you another chance here. No answer, and the next bullet goes in your hand. Then your other hand. Then your knees. After that, your junk."

Connor snorts a laugh and spits blood. He pushes himself up onto his knees and glares at the one holding the gun on him. "I don't know what you're talking about."

The man fires. Connor knows a bullet was fired, his ears are ringing even louder, but he's not sure where. Then he feels his left hand go cold. And then roar with pain. He looks down at the blood pouring out of it.

“What the fuck?” he screams, clutching it. There’s a lot of blood and it just keeps pouring out and it hurts so much. He can’t move it. Is that bone? “What the fuck?” he repeats.

“Told you,” the man with the gun says. “Where is it?”

“Fine, fine,” Connor says. This has all been a disaster anyway. He holds up his unshot hand. “The bracelet. The teal one. I cut a little pocket it in for a zip drive.”

The one with the gun nods at the one with the bat, who carefully steps forward and pulls the bracelet off, then looks at it, pulling at it and frowning. He shakes his head at the one with the gun. He cocks the trigger.

“It should be there!” Connor shouts. His hand hurts so much. And what if they really do shoot off his junk? He can’t be a cool spy without his junk. What would the point even be? “Look!”

“It’s just got some bite marks,” the man with the bat says.

Through his gag, Victor starts to laugh.

29.
Brandon

BRANDON SHOULD HAVE KNOWN BETTER. He stands there, sobbing in just a towel, in front of his closest friends and two people he just met today. Of course, this is how it ends. He doesn't deserve love. He's such a fucking idiot.

"Hey," Ollie says, hugging Brandon. "It's okay." Nicole and Ian join in the hug, surrounding Brandon like the shell of an egg. Brandon lets himself lean into them, crying.

"I think maybe we should go," Safiya says softly outside the egg. Brandon barely registers it as she and Tom leave. For a little while, the only sound is of Brandon's tears and water dripping on the floor. He keeps his head down to hide the horrible contortions of his face as he wails. He knew it was insane, but if it was insane, it had to be worth it, right?

"Hey, it's okay," Nicole says, squeezing his arm. "You're going to be okay."

"You deserve someone who won't walk out like that but will talk with you," Ollie says.

“He lied about his name, and he is wrapped up in dangerous, sketchy stuff,” Ian says.

Brandon knows they’re all right. But it still feels like a cannonball in the gut. Like shattering. He looks up at all of them, a halo around him, and forces a smile. “Yeah,” he says softly. “Sorry I yelled at you.”

“We deserved it,” Nicole says. “Go get dressed; I will make us all some strong drinks.”

Brandon nods again, happy to be given a task, goes into the den and towels off, and puts on his clothes, then pads back out. Nicole has made everyone vodka sodas, and they’re talking in soft voices.

“You don’t have to whisper,” Brandon says.

They all pause for a moment, exchanging glances. “Are you sure?” Ian asks, eyebrows up. “We’re talking about how much trouble Jon is.”

“Connor,” Ollie corrects. “His name is Connor. I don’t think Jon was a nickname. It was an alias. He knew all about guns, hand-to-hand combat, and he was there when a guy got shot. He was drama, Brandon, the bad, dangerous kind.”

“That might all be coincidence,” Brandon says. He knows they’re trying to help, but he would really prefer them just telling him he’s amazing and will find someone better. Trashing Jon just makes him feel stupid.

“I talked to him, dropped some info about KBA to see how he’d react,” Nicole says. “I did a lot of research with Ellen today, so I had some specifics to press him with. He covered, but I didn’t buy it.” She sips her drink. Everyone is quiet.

“Okay,” Ian says suddenly. “I should tell you all something. Today Heart-Eyes came to the store.”

"What?" Ollie screams. At the same time, Nicole says, "Jesus." Brandon doesn't say anything but feels his eyes bug out.

"He came to the store and flirted a little—"

"Tell me you didn't," Nicole interrupts.

"I didn't!" Ian glares at her. "I'm not Brandon."

"Ouch," Brandon says, then sniffs.

"Too soon," Ollie says quickly.

"Sorry." Ian reaches out and squeezes Brandon's arm. "I love you. And it's not like I'm doing much better."

Brandon nods, and Ian slides their hand down Brandon's arm to squeeze his hand.

"What about Heart-Eyes?" Nicole asks, voice loud.

"Yeah," Ian says, frowning. "So he asked for my number and left when I didn't give it to him. Then, later, when I went out for lunch, he pulled up beside me in a car and made me get in with him."

"Made you?" Ollie asks.

"With a gun."

The only sound is Pete padding across the room with that blue thing in his mouth.

"Okay," Nicole says.

"Yeah. So, in the car, he wasn't actually so scary," Ian says.

"Jesus, Ian—" Nicole starts.

"I didn't!" Ian's hands fly up, breaking with Brandon's. "I did not screw the trained killer. I'm just saying he seemed, like, reasonable as mercenaries or whatever go. And he called someone, a woman, and she told me that Jon had agreed to bring them something on a zip drive, but hadn't, and asked me to bring it to them instead, if I could find it. For ten million dollars."

The room is quiet again. Even Pete is frozen by his water bowl, staring at Ian.

"Ten million," Brandon whispers. "What's on that zip drive?"

"I don't know, but they undersold me," Ian says, pulling a phone out of their pocket, opening it, and holding it up for them. It looks like an auction site, but the current bid is being held by a large chibi character. Weird. And the current bid is a number Brandon thinks is too high to be actual dollars.

"That's the site that was on Ellen's phone," Nicole says, eyes wide with shock. "She didn't say anything about this."

"How did you see it on her phone?" Ollie asks.

"Whose phone is this?" Brandon asks, taking the phone from Ian.

"Jon's. Connor's. Whatever. I took it," Ian says.

"Now *you* stole his phone?" Nicole smirks, then shakes her head. "This is bad news."

"Did Ellen show you the auction?" Ollie asks, one eyebrow raising.

"I saw it, okay?" Nicole frowns.

"You fucked her!" Ian shouts.

"Can we focus on the more important thing?" Nicole says, her expression professional.

"I'm so glad I'm not the only one making bad decisions," Brandon says.

"Focus!" Nicole says, clapping. "Ellen knew about this auction, and she didn't tell me. She was who we were trusting to keep us safe." She frowns more, thinking.

"The woman on the phone said we'd be too messy to kill," Ian says.

"Glad our being messes finally has an upside," Brandon says, not sure if he's going to laugh or cry.

"Did you find the zip drive?" Ollie asks Ian.

Ian shakes their head. "No money for us."

"Awww, you were going to split it?" Ollie asks.

"I thought maybe we could all get a place together," Ian says, rolling their eyes. "Don't make it a thing."

"Awwww," Ollie repeats, drawing it out more this time.

Nicole starts pacing, sipping her drink. "Ellen lying to me means she had her own agenda. She didn't even hide the auction from me. She was so confident, she played me..." She sighs. "I'm an idiot."

"But Jon is gone," Ian says, rubbing her shoulder. "And the woman on the phone said we're safe. So that doesn't matter. It's over, right?"

Nicole stares at each of them in turn, thinking. "It doesn't feel like it. I don't like being played like this. We should talk to someone. Victor maybe."

Ian sighs. "I don't know if he wants to talk to us. I did invite him in case Jon got violent though."

"What?" Brandon asks. "Really? You guys think my taste in men is that bad?"

They all exchange glances again.

"We should really have talked about all this before the party," Ollie says. "We could have worked together."

Nicole takes a sip of her drink, nodding. "Yeah, we fucked that up."

"We're better as a team," Brandon says. They are. Together, maybe, they could have figured everything out, and Brandon wouldn't have ruined it with Jon.

"Yeah," Ian says, rolling their eyes. "Could have kept me from embarrassing myself in front of Victor."

"What did you two talk about, anyway?" Ollie asks.

"Let's clean up," Ian says, standing. "We can do group therapy later."

Nicole goes over and locks the front door and puts the chain on. "I'll crash on the sofa tonight. I just think we should all be together. I don't believe we're just done with this."

They head up to the game room and clean up, and as Nicole reads out the unplayed trivia questions, and everyone laughs at Ollie's obviousness—*What is CIA training like? Name three famous spy ciphers.*—Brandon starts to feel like he's crawling out of a pit back toward normalcy. He knows later, when he's alone in the den, he'll be crying again. A lot. But with his friends, he knows he can get through it.

And yeah, maybe Jon was bad news. Brandon isn't suited to a life of crime. But it was so good to feel like he was special. He starts to cry again a little, collecting beer bottles, and Nicole wordlessly hugs him tightly, and then Ian and Ollie surround him, too. He'll be okay. He can get through this.

After they've given the game room and living room and kitchen a thorough going-over, Nicole makes another round of drinks, and they sit down in front of the TV in the living room. It's late, but Brandon doesn't want to go cry in bed just yet, and he can tell his friends know that. So Ian turns on *The Nanny*, and they all spread out on the sofa, watching and laughing, even Nicole, who is clearly lost in thought.

It's the third episode when Ian's phone rings. They pull it out and smile slightly, standing to leave the room. "It's Victor," they say, as some sort of explanation.

"You never told us what you two talked about," Nicole says.

Ian shrugs, putting the phone to their ear as they leave the room. "Yes. Who is this?" They stop, and Brandon and the others turn to watch Ian, their face now concerned, walking back over. They press Speaker and hold the phone out.

"—matter who this is," a male voice says. "What matters is we have your boys."

"Boys?" Ian asks.

"Victor and Connor," the voice says. "And Connor isn't doing so well, probably because of all the bleeding."

Brandon feels sick. He feels a heavy weight splash down in his stomach, pushing everything else out, even air. He can't breathe. He looks up at his friends. They all look the same.

"So here's what's going to happen: You're going to bring us the Velvet Alley data. And then we're going to let everyone go."

"What?" Ian says. "We don't have it."

The voice laughs. "Yeah, Victor figured it out. He saved his own life. Said he wouldn't tell us if we didn't promise to spare him. And you. Sweet, right?"

"They could kill us anyway," Nicole says, so softly that the phone can't pick it up.

"How can we trust you?" Ian asks. "How do we know you won't kill them and us anyway?"

"Mmmm," the voice says, as though they hadn't considered that. "I guess you can't. But don't worry, one dead body is enough to clean up for now."

"One?" Brandon mouths, eyes wide. "Who?"

Ian shakes their head.

The voice gives them an address in Williamsburg.

"The gym?" Ian asks.

"Uh, yeah, it's an abandoned gym," the voice says, clearly bewildered that they know the place.

"It closed?" Ian asks. "I had a threesome in the locker room there, but I guess that was years ago."

There's silence as Ian seems to realize what they've said, and the voice takes a moment to process it.

"Look, just be here by midnight. No one else."

"There are four of us," Ian says.

The voice sighs. "Fine. You four. That's it."

"Where's the zip drive?" Ian asks.

"Victor says check the dog. Hope he's right. Otherwise he and Connor are dead."

Then the line goes silent.

30.
Ollie

OLLIE TURNS TO LOOK AT Pete, who is happily lapping up water, his teething ring dropped next to him. Ollie's heart is beating furiously. He's scared—for Victor, for all of them—but also maybe… excited? He swallows that down (he'll think about it later). For now, he walks slowly toward Pete, who doesn't even glance up. Behind him, his friends are watching silently. He can almost hear them holding their breaths.

He picks up Pete, who looks at him, mouth dripping, and starts licking his face.

"Who are these guys?" Nicole asks. "Was that Heart-Eyes?"

"No, totally different voice," Ian says.

"Did you eat it?" Ollie asks Pete, turning him around, looking for something. "Your bow tie?" But no, the bow tie looks normal.

"That thing!" Brandon shouts suddenly. "It looks like Jon's bracelet."

Ollie doesn't remember Jon's bracelet but puts down Pete and picks up the toy. Except it's not the toy. Sure, there are some bite marks on it, and it looks similar, but it's not the same one Pete has been chewing. And on the inside, there's a little pocket cut into it. Ollie tears it open, peeling away the rubber, to reveal a zip drive, which he holds up, triumphant.

Everyone stares for a moment.

"The guy on the phone said it was Velvet Alley, the online black market."

"People were bidding millions of dollars for that," Ian says. "I don't even get how it can fit on there."

"Maybe it's just a key," Nicole says with a shrug.

"It doesn't matter," Ollie says. "These are bad guys, and they want it. We can't let them have it."

"But they have Victor," Ian says.

"And…" Brandon starts, then sighs. "This is all my fault. I should never have slept with a guest."

"I don't think anyone could have seen this coming," Nicole says, patting him on the back. "Though that was a really stupid idea."

"We can try to save Connor, too," Ollie says, knowing Brandon might be heartbroken but still soft-hearted. And Connor made him happy. That's worth saving. "We might send him to prison, but he shouldn't die."

"Yeah," Brandon says. "Thanks."

"Victor is the priority," Ian says. "He's innocent. All we need to do is give them that, right? Do we even know it's dangerous?"

"Velvet Alley is dangerous," Nicole says. "They traffic weapons, people. It's all bad news. And I don't think people taking hostages are planning on shutting it down." She shakes her head. "Ellen and I were just…" Her eyes go far away as the sentence drifts off.

"So we should just destroy it?" Ollie asks. That's what feels right.

"Then how do we rescue anyone?" Ian asks.

Everyone is quiet. Ollie doesn't want to turn this drive over to anyone except maybe Victor, or someone in law enforcement they can trust, if that person exists.

"Another client," Nicole says suddenly. Ollie looks at her. She's focused now. "That's who has them. Someone else bidding on the data, some client of Ellen's. That's how she was using me. I was the lookout; I just didn't know it."

"What?" Brandon asks.

"Sorry." She shakes her head. "I got used. Same as you, really. Ellen lied to me, led me around like there was a collar on me. 'Report on what your friends are doing. Tell me if you find Jon. Tell me where he is.' She knew everything that was going on... I don't know when. By the time we..." She blushes faintly. "She had me text her about him all night. I told her when he left. Which is right after Victor left, too. She told her client, and they didn't know who Jon—or Connor—was, really, so they grabbed both of them. Because of me."

She looks sad for a moment, then angry. Not at Ellen though, Ollie thinks, but at herself.

"She was your boss," Ollie says. "She manipulated you."

"I know," Nicole says, her hands clasping into a tight knot. "I hate that."

"So let's get her back," Ian says. "Let's fuck her up."

"How?" Brandon asks.

"This is what Heart-Eyes was looking for, too, right?" Ollie asks, an idea starting to percolate.

"Yeah," Ian says. "But I don't want to turn it in for ten million and get Victor killed. I hate him right now, but...you know."

"Yeah," Brandon says, taking Ian's hand.

"Maybe he's working with Ellen," Nicole says. "You said there was some woman on the phone, right? We assumed it was Battle, but it could be someone else."

Ian nods. "Possible, but then why kidnap Victor for ransom when they already promised us a lot of money? And that definitely wasn't Heart-Eyes on the phone just now."

Everyone is silent as they try to turn everything over in their mind. Nicole looks especially pissed off. Ollie knows how much she hates being used, and it sounds like Ellen used her in a lot of ways. Would be nice to get back at her, too, somehow, while also rescuing Victor and finally closing the case.

"I have an idea," Ollie says, smiling.

"Is this going to be dangerous?" Nicole asks.

Ollie grins. "Working a case takes risks, right?"

Ian holds their phone out on speaker and dials the number labeled *Art* in his phone.

"Hello, beautiful," says a voice after one ring. "You find what we asked you to?" *Beautiful?* Ian said he'd been flirty, but Ollie didn't realize how direct.

"You're on speaker," Ian says. "We're all here."

"Ah, well, hello. Is Connor there?"

Ollie nods at Ian; that confirms that he didn't take Connor, isn't working with Ellen. They can go on to part two.

"No," Ian says. "We have the drive, but someone else wants it, and they've taken Connor and our friend Victor hostage."

"Mmmm, so you want me to get them back?"

"Victor is innocent," Ian says. They smile slightly at the phone, and Ollie doesn't know if they're thinking about Victor or unconsciously flirting back with Heart-Eyes. "So yes, we'd appreciate you rescuing him."

"And Connor," Brandon says, looking a little ashamed as he says it.

"Ah, that Connor's lover boy?" Heart-Eyes asks. "Still into him, knowing everything you do?"

"I don't know," Brandon says. "But he shouldn't die."

There's a pause. "I understand that. Love is a confusing thing, ain't it?"

Nicole frowns. Ollie knows why—Heart-Eyes sounds almost likable.

"I guess," Brandon says.

"So can you rescue them?" Ian asks.

"Let me see what the boss lady thinks about it," Heart-Eyes says. "You know I could just break into that fancy house you're all in and take the drive from you."

"Not as fast as I can crush it," Ollie says. He expected that.

Heart-Eyes laughs. "Oh, you're friends with a Tough Guy as well as a Lover Boy, huh, beautiful? I like them."

"Can you stop flirting?" Nicole asks. "Check with your boss—Judith Battle, I assume—and tell her we think the folks who have our friend are clients of Ellen Kang's. She'll know the name."

"And a Clever One." It sounds like he's smiling. "All right, hold on a minute."

"We're all clever," Ian says. "Go talk to Judy."

Heart-Eyes snorts. "I won't tell her you called her that."

The line goes dead. Everyone looks up at each other.

"We really did that," Ollie says, pointing at the phone. He feels a huge grin on his face. No one else has one though. "Come on, that was good stuff."

"Only if it works," Nicole says. "And then we still need to make the rest of the plan work."

Everyone is silent, and Ollie can tell they're all still hurt from their blowout. Ian is slumped, looking at the floor, Nicole has her arms wrapped around herself like she's cold, and Brandon's eyes are still red and watery. But so what? Ollie was hurt, too. But he knows these are his best friends and everyone is sorry, and they can get past it. They need to.

"Come on," Ollie says. "Look what we can do working together!"

Everyone is silent. Nicole rolls her eyes. But the mood shifts. Ollie can feel it. Ian looks up, Nicole drops her arms, and Brandon smiles a little. They're going to be fine. Ollie wants to say even more, but Ian's phone rings and they tap it.

"Judy"—Heart-Eyes pauses to chuckle—"says it's a deal. Your friend for the drive. I'll handle the rescue personally. She's guessing it's McClintock, which means good weapons and good marksmen, but terrible up close."

Nicole nods. "They're one of Ellen's clients—an arms manufacturer. With that drive, they'd control the weapons black market."

"But they won't," Heart-Eyes says. "Because you'll give the drive to me, and I'll save your friend. And Connor. Though you can let him know his position with us has been eliminated. And considering what he did to get it..."

"He'll go to prison." Brandon nods. "Or spend his life on the run. He deserves that."

"Please don't tell me you're going with him," Ian says.

"No." Brandon's voice is too loud, like he's forcing the word out.

"So where are you supposed to deliver the drive?" Heart-Eyes asks.

"An abandoned gym," Ollie says. "We're going to go, too. We'll be a distraction so you can rescue everyone."

"I know you think that's smart, Tough Guy, but if I'm worrying about all of you—especially you, beautiful—then it'll be harder to take out the McClintock soldiers. Better if you hang back."

"No," Nicole says. Being a distraction is part of the plan. "We want to see it happen so we know this isn't all some big setup to get out of paying us. And to be clear, we've seen the auction—we know how high you're willing to go."

Heart-Eyes laughs. "Clever, clever. But civvies in the area is dangerous. For everyone, including me."

"If we're willing to risk it, you should be," Nicole says.

"So we'll be there," Ollie says. "You save our friend, we give you the drive. Then we never have to see you again."

"Never say never," Heart-Eyes says. Ian smirks. "Give me an hour to get there and get ready. Then you four do your thing, and I'll handle the rest. Duck when the bullets start flying."

Ollie can feel his heart speed up at that phrase. They're really doing this.

"See you then," Ian says, their voice maybe a little flirty. Ollie can't tell. Does Ian really like this guy, or are they trying to be a nonbinaire fatale?

Nicole reaches out and taps the phone off, one eyebrow raised at Ian. "Are we all ready for this?" she asks, turning to look at each of them in turn. Brandon looks the most scared, his eyes still red from crying. Ian looks a little nervous and a little surprised, too, like they didn't think it would work. Nicole's mouth is a line of determination, though she doesn't look thrilled about it.

"Come on," Ollie says. "I know this is dangerous, but it's an adventure, right?"

"Let's hope the plan works," Nicole says. She waves them away, lifting up her own phone but putting it on speaker. She hits Dial, and someone picks up after a moment.

"Nicole? Everything all right? Or were you calling to see if you could come over?"

Nicole frowns as Ollie and the others hold in laughter.

She glares at all of them, then turns back to the phone. "Someone kidnapped my friends and wants this drive thing that Jon left here. What should I do?" She's trying her best to sound scared, but anyone who really knows her can tell what an act this is. Ian snickers softly.

There's a pause. "Jon left the drive there?"

"Yes, but if I don't give it to them, they'll kill my friend. They said to meet them at this abandoned gym in Williamsburg. I'm afraid if I go alone, they'll kill me."

"Okay, okay," Ellen says, half sighing. "I'll come with you. I represent a lot of people in their world. No one will kill me. And by extension, you."

"I— Well, if you're sure," Nicole says, still overacting, but now waifish and appreciative. "We should meet there. I need to go soon." She gives the address and even throws in a sob before thanking Ellen and hanging up.

"We'll work on the acting," Ian says flatly.

"Hey, I was pretty good for the circumstances," Nicole says. The word *circumstances* hangs in the air, heavy with meaning and fear. Ollie shivers. "We should get going. And if this doesn't work and we all die, I'm just glad I did it with you freaks."

She looks for a moment a little like she might cry, and Ollie rushes to hug her. He knows he should be scared, too, but he's not. He's excited to make everything happen, excited to rescue Victor, save the drive, solve the case. It really would make a great podcast, if his friends didn't mind having their lives splashed all over the internet—which they almost definitely would. Ian and Brandon come in and join them in the hug, too.

"You know, when we survive this," Ollie says, "we really should start a detective agency."

Everyone immediately drops their arms and steps back, leaving Ollie alone in the middle of the room.

"Come on," Ian says. "Let's go get shot at."

31.
Nicole

THEY DECIDE TO LYFT TO the hostage showdown. The G isn't running, so it would require taking two trains, and the transfer is always, like, twenty minutes, so Nicole uses her account to call them a ride, which arrives in the highly absurd form of a baby-blue Kia Soul.

"Remember that hamster commercial from when we were kids?" Brandon asks as it pulls up.

Nicole doesn't respond. He's going through something, so it's time to cut him some slack. In the car, the driver is blissfully silent, aside from asking her name. No one says anything, maybe afraid like Nicole that the driver might hear something about their plan and turn them in. Although, at this point, it feels like everyone knows—they called a lot of people.

So now they all sit in silence, with just their thoughts. Which in Nicole's case are mostly about what an idiot she is. For trusting Ellen, for fucking Ellen, for wanting to be like Ellen. Has she lost so much of herself that she wanted to be a corrupt lawyer for criminals? She knows so much of it was burnout in law school, learning all the tricks people had for avoiding consequences as if they were virtues of the system that had worn her down in ways she hadn't expected. So she'd come up with an easier dream than changing the world—making a small little world, just for her and her friends, someplace cozy and safe. But then that had seemed far away, almost impossible, a deadly mountain trail she might not survive. And she just became a cog in a machine she'd once said she wanted to take down. And then she wanted to be a better cog, a cog like Ellen.

She takes a deep breath, sitting in the back seat, head against the window as the city rolls by in slashes of bright colors and black. Brandon hears her and reaches out and takes her hand and squeezes. She envies him. Brandon may charge forward into terrible ideas, but he's never lost himself. And in the end, she even ended up making a Brandon-like mistake of screwing the boss. She's just as silly as he is. She needs to make better choices. She needs to remember she has choices.

They stop first at an office-supply store, one of those twenty-four-hour ones. Ollie runs in for what they need, then hands them out to everyone before Ian calls the second Lyft, which ends up being small and smelling heavily of bad cologne. But they all cram into it and take it to their final destination. It's by the river, close to the Navy Yard, some ugly high-rise they put up a while back, all gray metal and large windows. The gym is on the second floor, the huge windows covered in torn brown paper. A faint light is inside it. Around them, most buildings are dark. This isn't the fun part of Williamsburg.

"You sure?" the driver asks.

"Yeah," Nicole says, getting out. The air hits her, cold and smelling like the fish and trash of the river. But she likes how cold it is. Makes the edges of her body feel like knives. And that's what she has to be now. She has to cut through a lot of shit to pull this off. She nods at Ian, who pulls out their phone and sends two texts.

She hopes this works.

They walk up to the front door, but there's a doorman, and she's not sure how to get past him, so she walks around the building, the others following her silently, until she finds a back stairwell, door propped open with a free weight.

"They left the door open for us," Ollie says. "That was nice."

"Well, they want this to go smoothly," Nicole says.

Ollie laughs. "They don't know who they're dealing with."

Nicole rolls her eyes but smiles as she walks up the stairs. Yes, this is an insane plan that Ollie came up with, but it could really work and do the most good all at once. She hopes. They all turn on their phone flashlights as they walk farther into the darkness.

The stairwell opens on the gym locker room, her phone light shining on white tiles, their footsteps echoing off them. They're not trying to be stealthy, but if they were, they'd suck at it.

"There," Ian says, pointing at a shower stall and shining their light on it. "I think there."

Nicole looks at it, unsure what they mean until it hits her. "Please tell me you're not pointing out the shower you had a threesome in right now."

Ian shrugs. "Nice to remember something fun as we walk toward our deaths."

She doesn't respond. The locker-room door opens on a lobby: a built-in reception desk they couldn't cart away, the elevator bank. Here it's wooden floors and a vague smell of industrial air purifier and mold.

"Hello?" Nicole calls out.

"Welcome," says a voice from the darkness. Nicole swallows as her friends line up next to her. She looks down the line at each of them: Ollie eyes-wide excited; Ian glancing around, taking everything in; and Brandon biting his lip, nervous. They're all nervous, she realizes, even her. They shouldn't be here, shouldn't be doing this, should never have gotten wrapped up in it, but here they are. Brandon is closest to her, and she takes his hand and squeezes, and he squeezes back, taking Ian's hand, and they take Ollie's, like they're about to skip down a yellow brick road to their violent deaths. But at least they're together.

Nicole drops Brandon's hand, takes a deep breath, and marches forward, shining her light out. They walk into what must have been the main equipment room at one point. Now it's mostly empty, aside from the dead body in the middle of the floor. The mold smell vanishes under the scent of blood. She hears Brandon gasp, and even she pauses slightly. Around the body are five figures. One light is on over them, so she can see most of their faces clearly: Connor tied to a chair and gagged, his hand a deep gash of red. Victor tied to another chair, uninjured, thankfully. He meets her eye and looks hopeful for a moment, then quickly finds Ian and looks something else—sad, maybe.

In front of them are two plain-looking men, one with a fancy gun, the other with a bat. And between them is Ellen. She's in a ruby-red suit with a black cowl-neck top.

"It occurred to me after we spoke," Ellen says, a small smile on her lips. "The timing. I texted these gentlemen, and they said they'd called your friend almost half an hour before you called me. You weren't calling in a panic. You had taken time for something."

She tilts her head and tucks a stray hair behind her ear. "And I remembered you—I remembered *being* you. Young, smart, ambitious, and overlooked. Girls like us, we make plans. And that's what you've done, isn't it? You figured out that the kidnappers were my clients. What was it, something I said?"

Well, fuck. "I saw the auction site on your phone and on his." She nods at Connor. "Wasn't too hard to figure out you knew more than you were telling me. So I just needed to reason out why."

"Nicole—" Ollie starts, but she puts her hand up to stop him from talking. This isn't part of the plan, but the plan will still work.

"I knew I shouldn't have checked it while you were there." Ellen shakes her head. "But I couldn't resist. Have you seen how much money it is? And my clients here are happy to pay a finder's fee of half their maximum bid, sign a ten-year contract... Do you know what kind of bonus I'd get? And my hands stay clean." She shrugs. "Or would have."

"You're not someone who strikes me as good at staying clean," Nicole says. "I've seen your apartment."

Ellen purses her lips, looking a little annoyed. "If you just hand it over, we'll let your friend go, and I'll make sure you get a promotion—a year ahead of schedule."

Nicole pauses. That's tempting. Very tempting. She would finally be clawing her way to the top. Queen rat. She wouldn't have to be like Ellen. She could go back to her dreams of being a TV lawyer with a soft life, or maybe even further back, to what she wanted to be originally: someone doing good in the world. She knows the firm has a pro bono department. That might be a good start.

"Send the email saying I should get the promotion now, and let Victor go," Nicole says. "Then we'll give you the drive."

"Nicole!" Ollie says, but she silences him with a hand again. She can feel Brandon and Ian shifting nervously.

"Smart. First show me you have it."

Nicole takes a drive out of her pocket and holds it up. "We're each carrying a few of them. Only we know which one you want, and if you start firing, there's a good chance we can destroy it before you take it from us."

Ellen smiles widely. "Oh, you're *very* good."

Nicole shrugs. Ollie came up with a lot of the plan, but this touch was hers.

"All right," Ellen says, taking out her phone and dictating as she types. "Barbara"—one of the senior partners—"I've spent the day working with Nicole Davis, and she has a mind like a steel trap. I think we should fast-track her. There's a lot of potential there, and I don't want to lose her."

Nicole smiles. "Nice. Now Victor."

Ellen tilts her head, considering. "You don't want Jon, too?"

Nicole looks back at Brandon, whose eyes are red and watering again.

"Is he dead?" Brandon asks softly.

Ellen smirks. "No. Just very badly beaten."

Brandon stares back at Nicole, and she knows he can't make a decision.

"After we give you the drive, we'll take him," Nicole says. "Though I'm not so sure what we'll do with him yet," she adds, glaring at Connor, who slowly lifts his head.

"I'd start with an ER," Ellen says, then waves her hand at Victor. The man with the bat unties him as the man with the gun keeps it pointed at him. Victor stands, rubbing his wrists where they were tied, and walks slowly across the room. His eyes meet Nicole's once, looking confused, but then he stares at Ian, moving to stand between them and Ellen, like a shield.

"There," Ellen says. "I'm very reasonable. So now the drive please."

Nicole nods, fishing out a handful of drives from her pockets. So does everyone else. They each have a dozen drives, all identical, now piled in their hands. Ellen taps her foot.

"Uh…" Ian says. "Anyone remember which of us has it?"

Nicole's eyes go wide, and she grimaces.

"Fuck," Ian says.

"Guys…" Brandon says, voice tearful.

"Really?" Ellen asks. "You didn't mark it?"

"We have this," Ollie tells her.

Nicole holds up a finger and goes over to the others. They gather in a little group, pointing at the drives. "It has a blue dot on it," Nicole says loudly.

Which is when the shooting starts.

32.
Ian

THEY DUCK, THE EMPTY DRIVES flying up and around like confetti. Ian pulls at Victor's waistband, too, yanking him to the ground as the window behind the man with the bat splinters from the bullets, glass flying everywhere.

"What the fuck is happening?" Victor asks them, his voice high with panic.

"Stay down," Ian says as Heart-Eyes suddenly comes in feet-first through the shattered window, swinging on a rope. The brown paper tears aside for him like for a football team at homecoming, and he lands his feet squarely in the chest of the guy with the baseball bat. He slams him to the ground with a heavy thud and grins, pointing a gun at the last thug.

What's happening is the plan. The touch of drama was Ian's idea. The fake confusion, all that. Ollie was the one with the grand plan, of getting everyone together and causing this chaos. Nicole came up with the multiple-drives idea to keep them safe. But Ian knew how to make it a spectacle enough to get everyone off guard.

And "blue dot"—Brandon's idea, like a "special tattoo," he said—was the code word for Heart-Eyes.

Ellen has ducked to the ground like the rest of them, but she's focused on Nicole, glaring with a mixture of annoyance and... pride? She seems fucked-up, Ian decides.

"So I guess I could shoot you," Heart-Eyes says to the guy with the gun. "Or you could shoot me. Think you're faster?"

"Who the fuck are you?" the thug asks.

"The original buyer of the drive," Heart-Eyes says. "Or at least a representative of them."

"You called KBA?" Ellen shouts at Nicole, incredulous. "I thought you were smart! These people are dangerous."

"Oh relax," Heart-Eyes says to her, eyes still on the thug. "I have a deal with them, and I wouldn't betray anyone as good-looking at Ian over there." He briefly turns to wink at Ian.

Ian looks away, blushing, and meets eyes with Victor, who is wide-eyed.

"You didn't," he hisses.

"No," Ian hisses back. "Not that it's your business. He's just flirty."

"Only with you, beautiful," Heart-Eyes says. "And Victor, is it? I'm saving your friend here, so be nice."

"My ex," Victor says.

"Ah," Heart-Eyes says. "I see it."

"Can we not?" Ian shouts. Where's the final piece of this? They know they texted him. They glance back at the door but just see their friends all huddled and hiding—Brandon is trying to scoot behind an empty weight rack that casts thick lines over him like bars; Nicole is on her belly, face-to-face with Ellen; and Ollie has managed to get himself around the corner.

"Just shoot him!" Ellen shouts at the thug.

The thug fires. For a moment Ian's throat constricts as they see the flare from the gun and think of Heart-Eyes getting shot. If he's down, this plan might not work.

But Heart-Eyes dances out of the way, more elegant than a man of his size has a right to be. He grabs his side, where there's a bloodred slash, but he stays standing, an almost-feral smile on his face. He raises his own gun to fire back, and Ian closes their eyes.

And then hears footsteps behind them. They open their eyes to see everyone staring behind them, at the door, where a handful of U.S. marshals are running in, led by Victor's partner, Willis. They all have guns, and they're all pointed at Heart-Eyes and the thug.

"U.S. marshals," Willis announces to the room. "The cavalry is here." Willis pulls Victor up off the ground and hands him a gun. Ian doesn't get up though. Now it's just a room filled with people pointing guns at each other. That doesn't seem especially safe. Around them, all their friends stay down, too. Willis turns back to the room. "Why doesn't everyone put the guns down and peacefully surrender so we can work this out without any additional violence?"

"Who called them?" Ellen asks, voice wavering a little.

"Kidnapping a marshal is a big deal," Nicole says.

Ellen narrows her eyes. "A marshal? Really? Those aren't friends in costumes or something?"

"No," Willis says simply, holding out a badge with his free hand.

Ellen's face shifts. "Well, thank goodness," she says, crawling over to Nicole. "Such smart thinking."

Nicole snorts.

"Beautiful," Heart-Eyes calls, eyes on the marshals, "is the drive even here?"

"No," Ian calls back. Then, feeling weirdly guilty: "Sorry." Why are they apologizing? That man is a literal killer.

Heart-Eyes turns and grins at Ian and winks again. He has one scratch on his cheek from the shattered glass he flew through, but it just adds to how hot he looks, a little sweaty, but standing calmly as though none of this is bothering him. "Ah, don't worry about it. You win some, you lose some."

Ian swallows, much calmer about this than they expected they would be. The plan was that the marshals take everyone in now, but instead everyone seems frozen.

"Seems we're caught in an odd situation," Heart-Eyes says, looking around the room. It's another standoff, Ian realizes. They hope there won't be more shooting. "And with little opportunity to benefit in the way my employer hoped. So I hope you'll all excuse me." He nods at Willis and the thug, then smiles at Ian, and—again, faster than he has any right to be—spins and leaps out the window. The thug fires after him. One of the marshals responds by firing at the thug, who drops like the contents of a wet paper bag.

The room suddenly feels quiet. There's a haze from the guns, and the smell of sweat and industrial cleaner mingles with the sulfuric smell of gunpowder. Cold wind rushes into the room through the broken window, making Ian shiver.

Then they hear the sound of footsteps outside the building, running away. Victor dashes to the window and looks out, gun ready, but turns back and shakes his head.

"Well," Willis says, "this is quite a mess." He directs the other marshals to start taking photos, to bandage Connor's hand and call for an ambulance.

Nicole stands, and Ian and the others follow her lead.

"Thanks for calling," Willis says, shaking Ian's hand. "We'll need a statement."

Ian glances at Victor, who is staring at them with an expression Ian doesn't recognize. Victor's eyes water, and he looks away. Ian looks back at Willis. "Can we do that later? This was, y'know, a lot."

Willis laughs. "Sure." He turns to the rest of them. "All five of you, we can get your statements later."

Five? He thinks Ellen is with them, Ian realizes.

"Actually—" Ian starts.

"Thanks," Nicole interrupts. "I think we all need to get some sleep."

"Yeah," Ellen says, eyes wide, looking at all of them. "Sleep."

A few of the marshals have a stretcher that they load Connor onto, bandaging his hand as they move him out of the room. Ian, his friends, and Ellen follow them, leaving Victor and the others behind.

"Why?" Ellen whispers to Nicole.

Ian gets close; they want to know, too. They desperately hope this isn't her falling in love now. They see Ollie sidling up on the other side, leaning in to listen with no subtlety.

"Blackmail," Nicole says with a shrug, turning to look at Ollie and Ian as if asking for their okay. Ian nods, and so does Ollie, and she turns back to Ellen. "Plus, that email you sent wouldn't go down great if you were arrested right after sending it. So you can keep your job. But you're making mine a lot easier."

"You're really good," Ellen says appreciatively. "I'm going to mentor you."

"Maybe," Nicole says. "But I've been thinking about pro bono work, too."

Ian snorts a laugh as they wait for the elevator. Brandon gets in with the EMTs and Connor, filling it up, and the others have to wait for the next one.

"Case closed," Ollie says, sounding happy. "It was fun, right?"

No one answers. A bit of ceiling, maybe hit by a stray bullet, crumbles and falls next to them like snowflakes. No one flinches.

"Ian, wait," comes Victor's voice behind them. Ian turns and walks down the hall, meeting Victor halfway. "Thank you," Victor says softly, reaching out for Ian's hand. Ian lets him take it. "Especially after what I said to you tonight. That wasn't kind. You don't make me feel angry, you—"

"I know," Ian says. "I get it. I feel it, too."

"Maybe I was wrong. I ran away from it, but..." Victor leans in for a kiss, and Ian lets themself be kissed, wondering what they'll feel.

Sad. That's how they feel. The fire dies, and they remember all the good with Victor and all the bad, and then it washes away with the tide. They pull away. "Bye, Victor."

"Wait, should we...? I want to see you."

"I'm not going to let you do to Raphael what you did to me," Ian says. "You don't need two angry exes, Victor. You're not that guy."

The elevator dings behind them, and they turn and walk into the elevator with Nicole, Ellen, and Ollie.

"That was pretty awesome, huh?" Ollie says.

"I'm just glad we made it out alive," Nicole says.

"I have blood on my suit," Ellen says, sounding tired.

"Maybe that'll inspire you to finally do your dry cleaning," Nicole says.

Ellen snorts. "Okay, none of this in the office though."

"We'll see," Nicole says.

"We really should start a detective agency," Ollie says.

"Please stop with that," Ian says. "It's genuinely the worst idea I've ever heard."

33.
Brandon

IN THE ELEVATOR, BRANDON STARES at Jon. Connor. Whatever. He's pale and staring at his hand. The bandages the marshals wrapped around it are turning pink.

"I really liked you," Brandon says. Oh fuck, he can feel himself starting to cry.

Connor looks up at him. "I'm bleeding."

"I thought we had a connection."

"We did." He shrugs, his face a sleepy smile. "I'm good at that. Making connections. Half the job."

"So it was all fake?" Brandon wipes his nose with the back of his wrist. He feels like a child.

"Sort of. To seduce someone, you need to be honest about some stuff, make some of the connection real. You have to give a little of yourself to feel it." Connor laughs a little. "I am so lightheaded."

"So you did feel it?"

"Sure. As much as I ever do."

"You 'ever do'?" The elevator dings, and the marshals, who have been pointedly avoiding eye contact with Brandon and Connor, begin moving him out into the hall. Brandon follows. "What do you mean, as you 'ever do'?"

"I like seducing hot guys. It's half the fun of being a spy."

"Fun?"

"Yeah. It's all just for fun, right?"

Brandon stops on the sidewalk, but the marshals keep carrying Connor away. The night air tastes like fall leaves, and the wind is rustling through Brandon's hair and making the tears on his cheeks feel cold. He wipes them away and takes a deep breath. Then he smiles.

He called Brandon *hot*.

34.

Ollie

"SO THEN HE JUMPED OUT the window and landed on the street and ran off!" Ollie tells Safiya as they sit in the dog park, the puppies frolicking around them. "It was so fucking cool."

Malkia brings a tennis ball over, and Ollie takes it from her and throws it again, then turns to Safiya. She doesn't look as impressed as he thought she would by what happened after she left last night. Her mouth is open a little, but her eyes look sort of frightened.

"You had me at a party where you were interrogating a guy who got someone else killed?"

"Uh." Ollie scratches his chin. That doesn't sound great. "Well, it wasn't an interrogation exactly..."

Safiya closes her mouth and smiles. She looks sad. Ollie knows this look. "Ollie, I like you, but that's insane. Everything you just told me is insane. And you involved me in all this dangerous stuff and didn't even tell me!"

"I'm sorry, I just wanted to see more of you."

She stands up from the picnic table they're at and brushes her jeans off. "That's sweet. But I don't need that kind of drama in my life." She reaches out, and Ollie thinks she's going to take his cheek, give him one last kiss, but instead she pets Pete, who is sitting on the bench next to Ollie. "I'll miss you," she says. Probably to Pete. Then she shrugs and starts walking away.

Ollie lies back and sighs. She's not wrong, he supposes. He can't blame her. But he also just feels so excited after everything they did. They saved the day! He's a hero, right? But maybe that life isn't for everybody.

He pulls a zip drive out of his pocket. None of them were sure what to do with it exactly. Hand it over to the marshals, who would give it to the CIA or someone, who would probably use it to take over the Velvet Alley and use it for U.S. interests? He wants to talk to Victor about it. Find someone they can really trust to take the place down. But for now, it lives with Ollie. They told everyone else it was destroyed. Maybe one day it will be. Easy enough to throw in a sewer. He puts it back in his pocket as his phone dings.

SAFIYA

I just dodged the biggest bullet

Oh sorry, this was for someone else

Ollie frowns and dials his mother.

"Ollie! It's my son, gals! He's starting a podcast. We'll all have to listen to it. Which means you have to get better hearing aids, Sally. I mean it! Just a second, Ollie, let me go outside." Ollie hears the laughter in the background. "Now, what's up? Did you find anything new in the case?"

"Actually...yeah," Ollie says, then tosses the tennis ball back and forth with the puppies as he tells his mother everything. She takes it a lot better than Safiya, "oooing" and "aaaaahing" in all the right places and gasping at the ending.

"I can't believe Nicole did that!" she says.

"Yeah," Ollie says.

"And Ian turned Victor down?"

"I guess," Ollie says.

"That's all so exciting. I'm so proud of you, honey."

"Thanks, Mom."

"It's going to make a great podcast."

"Actually, I was thinking, instead of a podcast, maybe I should start a detective agency."

There's a pause as his mother considers it.

"That's a great idea!" she says with glee in her voice.

"Really?"

"Yes, I'll help! Oh, and then *I* can do the podcast. About your cases. You can be my cohost, and we'll talk about all the exciting things you did. Won't that be so much fun? Oh, I'm *so* proud of you, Ollie."

"Thanks, Mom," Ollie says, relieved that someone thinks it's a good idea. "I've been thinking about what I need to do. I'll need a website, and then I'll need to put some ads out, develop a clientele..." He lists everything he needs to do as the dogs circle around him.

35.

Nicole

NICOLE IS GETTING COFFEE FOR her and Eli. Eli is the head of the pro bono department, and with Ellen's help, Nicole has been reporting to him for the week, just to see if she likes it—though Ellen says she won't. But Nicole thinks maybe she could. It's a lot of work—maybe more than she had before—but it reminds her of a version of herself she used to be. A version she maybe liked a lot more. They're working on lawsuits against an oil company for illegal dumping and a discrimination suit against a modeling agency and a brutality suit against the NYPD and fourteen other cases. Nicole doesn't know how Eli handles it all. He looks so tired all the time, she was happy to grab him a coffee, too.

"Hi there," Sam says as Nicole gets to the counter. "I like the suit."

"Thanks," Nicole says. It's a good suit. Royal purple. She's only ever worn it for graduation from law school and one interview with a firm, where the interviewer told her she clearly had a lot of "personality." But she doesn't mind that now. She has Ellen in a corner—her corner—so she can get away with being a little more eccentric at work. And she wanted to look good today.

"Usual?" Sam asks.

"Yes, and a tall black with three shots of espresso. New boss looks tired."

Sam laughs. "Well, hopefully you can keep them on their toes. Was that stuff you texted me about helpful?"

"Yeah," Nicole says as Sam starts making the coffees. "It really helped a lot. Sorry I didn't respond; there was a lot of work."

"I figured."

"But I definitely owe you a thank-you."

"Yeah?" Sam asks, glancing up with a smile.

"Maybe dinner?" Nicole asks. "If you want, I mean."

Sam leans forward and hands her one of the coffees. "That sounds nice. I'm free Friday."

Nicole takes out her phone and looks at her schedule. "This weekend is bad. I have to review a bunch of new briefs."

"Next weekend?"

"Maybe..." Nicole says, looking at the calendar. "It depends if this judge takes our motion; otherwise that's going to be an insane cramming weekend."

Sam hands her another coffee and smiles wider. "Well, you have my number. Text me when you're free."

Nicole puts her phone away and looks up at Sam. "I will. I'll definitely text you." She takes the coffees and walks back to work, smiling. She has a date! As soon as there's time.

36.
Ian

VICTOR'S CAR GLEAMS IN THE dim light of the streetlamps on the block. Around them, the city is dark, with buttery-yellow light in a few windows in the small buildings. There's the sound of old jazz from a few flights up. Victor really should find a garage for his car, Ian thinks. It's such a tempting target.

"I wasn't sure I'd hear from you," says a voice behind them.

Ian turns and smiles. "Well, I'm known for making bad decisions."

"Oh yeah, is that what I am?" Heart-Eyes—no, Art; Ian can't do this thinking of him as Heart-Eyes—steps closer.

When Ian texted him to meet him at this corner, they wondered if they'd regret it once they saw him. But not yet.

"This is my ex's car," Ian says, dodging the question. Of course he's a bad idea—he's a murderer. "He cheated on me, so I used to key it now and then."

Art laughs. "I like that." He stares at Ian. "Wait, is texting me a better or worse decision than keying your ex's car?"

"Well, you are a trained killer who has reason to be angry at me," Ian says, running a finger along the car as they walk toward Art.

"What would I be angry about?" He looks genuinely confused. "That little trick you pulled? Eh." He shrugs. "I've been on the bad end of a lot worse."

"Really? And you're fine with it? No hit out on me?"

"It was a cheap operation for us. One dinner with an easily compromised narcissist who wanted to be back in the field. A few empty promises. There was the cleanup with that one guy I accidentally killed, but that wasn't so bad. We decided to call it a minor loss. No hard feelings. We're not really the revenge types."

Ian swallows at the mention of the guy Art apparently murdered.

"So you're not going to tie me up and make me talk?" Ian asks.

Art smiles, stepping close. "Do you want me to?"

Ian looks up at him. Aside from the tattoo, he is really very good-looking. This is a better bad decision. Probably. Or worse. But different, at least.

"Honestly," Ian says, "what I really want is someone to curl up in bed with so we can get angry at YouTube videos together."

"Did you know their algorithm specifically tries to push tradwife shit on girls who are interested in sports?" He almost snarls it. It's very hot. "They all ought to be shot."

Ian grins. Art grins back and then leans in, pulling Ian close and kissing them. His mouth tastes like a new kind of fire—the gunpowder kind. Ian kisses him back.

A better bad decision. Or at least a different one.

37.

Brandon

A few months later

BRANDON ISN'T QUITE SURE HOW he got roped into this. Sure, he still works the night shift, so his days are free, but Ian could have moved their hours around. And it's really unfair to leave Brandon unpacking Ollie's new office alone so Ollie can keep his dog-walking job. You can't be a dog walker and a detective at the same time, right? But apparently Ollie is trying it. He's rented this little apartment at the bottom of a brownstone. And Brandon, apparently, is his secretary, because he's minding the office—for no pay—while Ollie is out walking the dogs.

It's a ridiculous idea; he shouldn't be encouraging Ollie, much less working for him for free—though maybe sitting at a desk and playing on his phone isn't work exactly.

BRANDON

Remind me again why I agreed to do this?

NICOLE

Because you're a pushover

IAN

Are you crying again?

NICOLE

No

IAN

Then why are you on your phone?

NICOLE

I genuinely had to pee

OLLIE

You're doing it because you love me!

Brandon minding my office I mean, not Nicole peeing

IAN

We assumed

OLLIE

I mean maybe you don't want a UTI because you know I'd hate that for you

NICOLE

Can we stop talking about my bladder?

BRANDON

What else should we talk about?

NICOLE

Your ex was on the news. Terrorism charges.

BRANDON

Ugh, no I don't want to talk about Jon

IAN

Connor

BRANDON

Whatever

We can talk about why Ian has been getting home late recently

IAN

A girl should be allowed some secrets

OLLIE

Ooooh, a new boyfriend?

IAN

No

Shut up

NICOLE

Oh no, you really like him

IAN

I demand another topic change!

OLLIE

We should plan our next game night

BRANDON

Oh yes and Ian can bring their new boyfriend

IAN

Absolutely not

But I'm okay with game night

As long as it's just us

Let's keep the chaos low

NICOLE

You think just us will keep the chaos low?

Brandon laughs. There's a knock on the door. Brandon puts the phone down, staring at the door, which doesn't open.

"Um, yes?" he asks.

"Is this the DW Agency?"

"Yes." It was a terrible name, but Ollie thought it was funny—Dog Walker. "You can come in."

Brandon leans back, trying to look professional. It would be wild if Ollie, unlicensed investigator—which it turns out is legal, somehow, according to Ollie's mom—actually got a client.

"I need some help," the voice says as the door opens.

And then a beautiful man walks in.

THANK YOUS!!!!

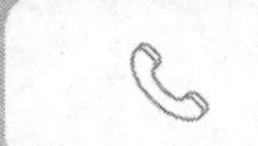  

Jenna (brilliant editor, best memes, better edits, book would suck without her)

Joy (agent, bestie for decades, genius, defender, everything)

Abby (marketer/publicist/everything, not fair how good she is at all of it)

Erin (cover designer, amazing, EUROVISION)

Eleanor (cover artist, so talented, drew so many dogs for me)

Laura (internal design, probably hates me for these insane acknowledgments but everything looks so so good)

Mandy (visionary, makes me laugh every time we talk)

THANK YOUS!!!!

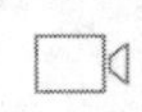

Manu (sweetest, smartest copyedits—seldom do I smile doing copyedits but I did here)

Jessica (the woman behind the curtain, regularly saves Jenna's life—and mine!)

Nia (Jenna's second-in-command, so smart)

Sara (proofreader, brilliant, caught all my stupid mistakes)

Ash (cover production, got the cover colors spot-on, so talented)

Anna (the big boss of the poisoned pen, the leader, the genius, the one we all march behind)

Dominique (QUEEN)

Chris (for being Chris)

About the Author

Lev Rosen writes books for people of all ages, including the Evander Mills series, which began with the Macavity Award–winning *Lavender House* (Anthony finalist, Lambda finalist, Best Book of the Year from Buzzfeed, *Library Journal*, Amazon, Bookpage, and others) and continues with *The Bell in the Fog*, (*Publishers Weekly* Editor's Choice, Best Book of the Year from Amazon, CrimeReads, and Autostraddle), *Rough Pages* (Lambda, Joseph Hansen, and Audie Award Finalist, Autostraddle Best of the Year), and *Mirage City*. His recent YA novels include *You've Goth My Heart*, *Emmett* (Best Book of the Year from *Kirkus Reviews* and Amazon), *Lion's Legacy* (Best Book of the Year from *Booklist* and the New York Public Library), and *Camp* (a *Kirkus Reviews* Best Book of the Century, Best Book of the Year from Forbes, *Elle*, and the *Today* show and others).